SLEEPER
13

Rob Sinclair specialised in forensic fraud investigations at a global accounting firm for thirteen years. He began writing in 2009 following a promise to his wife, an avid reader, that he could pen an 'unputdownable' thriller. Since then, Rob has sold over half a million copies of his critically acclaimed thrillers in both the Enemy and James Ryker series. His work has received widespread critical acclaim, with many reviewers and readers likening his work to authors at the very top of the genre, including Lee Child and Vince Flynn.

Originally from the North East of England, Rob has lived and worked in a number of fast-paced cities, including New York, and is now settled in the West Midlands with his wife and young sons.

Also by Rob Sinclair

THE ENEMY SERIES
Dance with the Enemy
Rise of the Enemy
Hunt for the Enemy

THE JAMES RYKER SERIES
The Red Cobra
The Black Hornet
The Silver Wolf

OTHER BOOKS
Dark Fragments

SLEEPER 13

ROB SINCLAIR

ORION

First published in Great Britain in 2018 by Orion Books,
an imprint of The Orion Publishing Group Ltd
Carmelite House, 50 Victoria Embankment,
London EC4Y 0DZ

An Hachette UK company

3 5 7 9 10 8 6 4

A CIP catalogue record for this book is
available from the British Library.

ISBN (Trade Paperback) 978 1 4091 7592 6

Typeset by Born Group

Printed and bound in Great Britain by Clays Ltd, St Ives plc

www.orionbooks.co.uk

For everyone who had faith in me.

ONE

2018 – Paris, France

Faces had always stayed with him. He could walk past a thousand people in a busy market square and pick out a familiar face in an instant, even people he hadn't seen in years.

From the threadbare sofa in that wreck of a Paris apartment, Aydin watched the still images of men's faces flash up one by one on the flickering TV screen. The documentary was supposed to be about the youths of jihad; the young guys from Western Europe who travelled to the Middle East to fight for their religion. But so far all he'd seen were thugs who'd taken it upon themselves to pick up guns and bombs to live out some violent fantasy. Was it boredom that made them do it?

All he knew was that these men weren't the real problem for the West. Nor was it the weak-minded individuals who were so easily swayed into strapping plastic explosives to their chests. So far the real faces of Terror hadn't featured in the programme at all. The millions of people watching had no idea who those people were. But Aydin knew. Because they were the ones who created him, and the others like him – the ones who told him what to do.

A much more familiar face flashed on the screen. His name and 'title' appeared beneath the grainy photograph of his face, but the words did nothing to describe the full extent

1

of the man's remit. 'Aziz al-Addad, Head of Youth Training'. To Aydin and his brothers the man was simply *the Teacher*.

Aydin couldn't hear the TV any more for the sudden onrush of memories the man's grinning face induced in him – his barked orders, spitting venom. Aydin could hear the Teacher telling him what he had to do, his eyes bulging. His was the only way Aydin knew.

Shaking, Aydin turned off the TV.

Minutes later he was outside roaming the streets. In the district of Clichy-Sous-Bois he was just a few miles from Paris's most treasured landmarks, yet in that shithole of a neighbourhood he felt several worlds away. To Aydin, the whole district was a mess of clashing cultures. Paris was the world's capital of romance, but he couldn't see any of that – decay and misery were too prevalent, and violence both the cause and answer to most problems.

He kept his head down as he walked past a gang of black youths. Did they appreciate that they were no longer the centre of the white man's ire in the city? People like Aydin had taken that mantle.

Round the next corner he reached the same car he'd walked past dozens of times on similar nights: a battered Citroën older than he was. The street was quiet. He slipped a length of wire down the side of the Citroën's rusted window frame and released the lock. Within seconds he was sitting in the driver's seat, his head swimming.

He'd hot-wired the car several times in the last few months, repeating the same ritualistic series of actions; sat there with the engine turning over loudly, thinking about driving off into the night. But he never had. Each time he simply shut the engine down, stuffed the wires back into place and pushed the lock back down on the door before leaving the car where it was.

He wondered who the car belonged to. Did they have any idea it had been broken into? The car was always in the same spot, a thick layer of dust covering its corroded shell. It was clear it hadn't been moved for some time. Maybe its owner had died, or moved house and left the crappy tin can behind.

Aydin was snapped from his thoughts when he saw two men further down the street, coming his way. In the darkness, he couldn't make out their features, though both had their heads covered with hoods. As they approached, Aydin felt his heart rate quicken. It wasn't fear or apprehension, simply his body ready and primed for the possible threat. He pushed the gear stick into first and released the handbrake, grasping his hands tightly round the steering wheel. As the men walked beneath a streetlight their faces were caught in a flash of orange light and Aydin avoided their gazes. Did they know who they were looking at? His mind was busy trying to determine whether to thump his foot down on the accelerator and hurtle off, when the men carried on past before fading into the darkness.

After a few seconds Aydin heaved a sigh, wrenched the handbrake, killed the engine and stepped out into the night.

Twenty-four hours later Aydin was walking the same dark street. A long and tiring day of planning had left him weary both in body and mind, and the walk through the fresh Parisian night hadn't yet rejuvenated him. Not least because he knew this night would end – just like all the others – in disappointment.

No. This night was worse. As he approached the spot, he realised the Citroën wasn't there. He spun round, looking up and down the street. No sign of it anywhere. Just an empty space, a dark outline of tarmac around where the car had been sitting untouched for so long.

A thief? After all, the car had been unlocked for some time. Or had the owner finally reunited with the heap of junk?

Aydin's heart sank, as though his one solace – that dream of another life – had been torn from him.

Confused, he couldn't face going back to the safe house so soon. Instead he sat on a wall in the dark, took out his phone and dialled the number from memory.

'Hello?' The woman's soft voice filled his ear, her English accent smooth in the dark. He shut his eyes and kept the patchy image of her smiling face in his mind as long as he could before it cracked and faded away.

'Hello?' she said again. 'Who is this?'

He hung up. He didn't want to spook her, just to hear her voice.

When Aydin opened the apartment's front door almost an hour later he heard the noise of the TV, and saw the lights were on. He'd hoped Khaled would be in bed, but he was sitting upright on the sofa, a sickly grin on his face.

'Hey, Talatashar, come and see this.'

Talatashar: the number thirteen in Arabic. By birth he was Aydin, but among his people he was referred to only by number.

He slumped down beside Khaled, his attention turning to the BBC World news report playing on the TV: helicopter footage of the destruction caused by a suicide bomb attack at a market in Aleppo. Over twenty people were already known to have died, the report claimed.

'Good work, eh?' Khaled said, still smiling.

Aydin said nothing. Khaled was in his thirties – an administrator, and Aydin's link to those who gave the orders. They weren't friends; their relationship was one of necessity. Aydin's ill feelings towards the man were nothing to do with their relative positions in the hierarchy, he simply hated everything about him.

4

The stench of sweat and tobacco stuck in Aydin's nose as Khaled rambled excitedly about 'infidels' and 'our holy war'. Khaled's was a face Aydin would do well to forget: that large scar stretching from his right eye to his left ear; those yellowed, misshapen teeth.

'And so it begins,' Khaled proclaimed. He often spoke as if he knew what was really going on, the real story. His smile grew. 'This is just the start.'

Khaled seemed to take issue with Aydin's silence and his smirk dropped away – irked, as he often was, by Aydin's apparent lack of enthusiasm.

'Allah looks upon all martyrs with the same regard, Talatashar,' he said. 'There's nothing special about you.'

It was true, Aydin knew. He didn't see himself as special – none of them were.

Aydin fixed his gaze on the TV as the reporter continued. One of the known victims of the blast was a British citizen: a woman in her twenties, working in Aleppo with an inter-national humanitarian charity. He didn't recognise her name, but then came her picture, a small square nestled in the top corner of the screen. She was a similar age to him, her eyes squinting from the sun, a bright red lanyard dangling around her neck.

He froze.

It felt like he couldn't move at all. For a moment he wondered if his heart had stopped beating.

After a few agonising seconds, he slowly exhaled, his eyes still fixed on the face of the young woman. Her *eyes*. The rest of her face could have been covered but he would still know those eyes. Faces had always stayed with him. He'd not seen hers since he was a child – since the night he was taken from his bed – but he had absolutely no doubt that the dead charity worker was Nilay. His twin sister.

5

TWO

Aydin was shaking again, caused by something else entirely this time. He was losing control.

'There'll be no place in paradise for that bitch, or any of the others,' Khaled said.

Aydin closed his eyes tight, trying to shut out Khaled's voice.

Soon everything was drowned out by the onset of rage, the throbbing of blood in his ears. As he struggled to control it, he saw his mother and twin sister Nilay in flashes.

By the time Khaled slapped Aydin's head to snap him out of the trance, it was too late. Aydin released a deep, guttural yell and threw his elbow out in an arc, catching Khaled in the left eye and causing his head to jerk back. He shot up from the sofa and glared down, snarling, panting. He tried to hold back, to control the beast, to not let it conquer him – but it wasn't working.

'Sometimes I wish you'd just shut that ugly fucking mouth of yours for more than five seconds,' Aydin said, fists clenched at his sides. He took a deep breath and stepped back, in two minds as to whether the situation could be diffused from there, or if it had already gone too far.

'What the fuck is your problem anyway?' Khaled spat, holding a hand up to his bruised face. 'You care so much about some little Western whore?'

Aydin's eyes remained on him. He could see Khaled was fuming, even as he glanced to the coffee table where the blunt knife he'd earlier used to peel an apple lay next to the twisted skin and discarded core.

For a moment they were both looking at the knife. Part of him willed Khaled to make the move.

Aydin lunged first, but Khaled was closer. He grabbed the blade and was up on his feet in a flash. He was a good four or five inches taller than Aydin, and a few inches thicker too. Much of the extra mass was muscle, and Aydin guessed most people would steer well clear of him under challenge.

But Aydin wasn't most people.

He was on Khaled before the administrator could swing the blade round in an arc towards Aydin's side, and he blocked easily and countered with a jab that split Khaled's lip. Khaled came forward a second time, but Aydin blocked with force again, feeling a jarring in his lower arm from the impact of the blow, as if he'd smacked it against a lump of steel. But it didn't stop him. Khaled was big and strong, but he wasn't like Aydin.

They had made damn sure of that.

Again Khaled attacked, with everything he had left – fist and knife and feet, over and over. Aydin moved in a steady rhythm to thwart his every move, an autopilot he'd developed from childhood but had never had to utilise for real until now. Before long, a look of defeat crept across his opponent's face.

Then a straight fist flew towards him – a final, futile attempt. Aydin shimmied to the left, caught the arm and swivelled. Bringing his other arm around Khaled's neck, Aydin sent him spinning over his knee and crashing to the ground. He grabbed Khaled's knife hand, twisted it around and pushed the wrist back until it cracked. Khaled screamed in pain and dropped the blade. Aydin twisted the arm further and smacked just below the shoulder, hearing the pop as the arm dislocated.

He picked up the knife and stood over Khaled, who panted and wheezed.

'I was right to keep my eye on you,' Khaled spluttered through pained breaths. 'I knew you were too weak to see this through.'

Aydin said nothing.

Khaled turned over and crawled away. Aydin watched him struggle, but another snapshot of his sister's face burned suddenly in his eyes and he had to press his palms to his temples.

Would she have wanted him to finish this?

He snapped out of it to discover Khaled reaching up for the laptop, which sat atop the battered Formica dining table across the room. The injured administrator mashed the keyboard with a broken hand, and a second later a long tone signalled the software's attempt to connect the call.

Aydin couldn't let that happen.

He darted forward, lurched at Khaled. He lifted his foot and hurled it under Khaled's chin. His head whipped back at such an angle Aydin wondered if he'd broken his neck. His head bounced forward again, his face smacked sickly against the lino floor. Aydin plunged the knife into the side of Khaled's neck and yanked it out the front, tearing a gaping hole in the flesh from which the man's blood sprayed out.

Spinning round, Aydin reached out to kill the call on the laptop . . . but the dial tone had already stopped.

He hoped – *prayed* – that the call hadn't gone through, that it had simply timed out. Then he saw the all too familiar browser window open up. Just a plain black screen, the same as always. He knew on the other end of the line his face would be clearly visible.

His face, dripping with Khaled's blood.

Breathing hissed through the laptop's speakers; slow, deliberate and calm breaths. Aydin stared at the blank screen, unable to move, as though it was a black hole sucking every ounce of energy from him.

'Why?' was all he could think to say. No answer. 'Why her!' His voice was hoarse as the well of emotion overflowed. Anger, sorrow, regret – he wasn't sure which was in control.

Still no answer.

A short bleep sounded and the call disconnected, the black screen replaced by generic Microsoft wallpaper. Aydin knew exactly what that meant.

Hurriedly he grabbed the only possessions he needed – the stash of money in a hole in the wall behind the bathroom cabinet, the pistol and his pocket multi-tool. He left the several fake passports behind. Despite their undoubted quality, he couldn't use them now.

Outside, he walked quickly down the street and took out his phone. He stopped to turn it on and thought about calling her again. After a few moments he stuck the phone back in his pocket and continued walking.

He headed on past the spot where the Citroën used to be, ignoring the nagging in his mind – why hadn't he just gone when he'd had the chance?

For once he was at least glad he lived in such a desperate neighbourhood, and it wasn't long before he found an old Fiat in a similar state to the recently departed Citroën.

After checking the dark street was clear, he took out the multi-tool and used the flathead screwdriver and a bit of muscle to pop the lock and the door open. Less than a minute later he had the engine running. For a few moments he just sat there as the engine grumbled in his ear.

This time he really didn't have any choice.

With a look over his shoulder, he pulled out into the night, no clear destination in mind. Only one thing was clear: he was on his own.

THREE

Aleppo, Syria

Rachel Cox stared out of the window of the seventh-floor apartment, gazing across the twinkling nightscape of the city. In the near distance she could make out what remained of the Al-Madina Souq, treasured buildings that had once formed part of the original ancient city that had seen continuous habitation for over eight millennia. Yet look what had become of it. Even at night the thin orange illumination was enough to highlight the destruction of the still raging civil war. On top of the monumental human loss, many treasured buildings were now nothing more than piles of sandy rubble. Cox would never cease to feel sadness to see a city she had grown to know so well look so vulnerable and decrepit and seemingly beyond repair – and not just its buildings, but its inhabitants too.

The sound of her vibrating phone stole Cox's attention from the window and the misery outside it. She moved over to the scratched and stained wooden side table and picked up the phone. A text message:

White line, five minutes.

Cox put the phone back down and went over to the crumpled sofa covered in a faded sheet, where her high-spec laptop sat. The city may be in ruins, but Cox wasn't without budget, and if you had the resources you could still get all the mod cons in Aleppo one way or another – electronics, mobile phone signal and even Wi-Fi. Up in the safe house, operated by the UK's Secret Intelligence Service, Cox had all that and more.

She flipped open the lid on the laptop and went through the familiar routine to initiate the white line – a voiceover IP line that was encrypted through a secure real-time transport protocol, or SRTP for short. It meant that both of the devices on either end of the conversation were encrypted, as was the line itself. The system wasn't foolproof, nothing involving the Internet was, but it was as secure a communication channel as SIS had for transnational conversations with active agents.

Of course, the multi-layered security on the line was to prevent sophisticated computer hackers from listening in, but did nothing to deter more classical eavesdropping techniques, which was why the otherwise plain-looking safe house was professionally soundproofed, and why Cox swept the place every day for listening devices, just to be on the safe side.

'Rachel Cox on the line,' she said when the call connected after a few seconds.

'Cox, it's Flannigan and Roger Miles here,' came the crackly voice of her immediate boss after a short delay – the less than perfect sound quality a result both of the geographical distance and the heavy security measures.

Cox did her best not to let out a groan. Henry Flannigan, the man she reported to, was a level four supervisor back at Vauxhall Cross in London – SIS headquarters. She'd worked for Flannigan for several years and the two of them had plenty of professional baggage between them. Their shared head-strong nature meant they regularly clashed, but overall she thought he was an okay guy, as long as she did as he asked (and if his arrogance and general superior attitude could be excused). Roger Miles was a level six director, the highest rank before numbers stopped and plain old extravagant titles took over, just a few small pay grades from the SIS Chief himself, right at the top of the food chain. Cox didn't know too much about him on a personal level, just that when he got involved in matters it generally meant there was a problem. Often it felt like the problem was *her*.

'Evening,' Cox said. 'You're both still in the office?'

She looked at her watch. It was gone eleven p.m. in Aleppo, so after nine back in London.

'Your request was urgent so we dealt with it urgently,' Flannigan answered.

Cox felt herself tense up. She could almost tell by the way he said it what the answer was going to be.

'Miss Cox—'

'It's still Mrs, actually,' Cox said, cutting off Miles without thinking, that 'single' title sending a flurry of unwelcome thoughts through her mind. 'Just call me Rachel. Or Cox. Whatever.'

'*Rachel*, I've looked through all of the information you provided, and I've discussed this at length with Henry too, and I'm afraid the conclusion I've come to is that I have to turn down your request for Trapeze assistance at this time.'

Now Cox did let out her groan. 'But sir, the evidence I—'

'Well that's the problem, Cox,' Flannigan interrupted. 'There really isn't much by way of evidence. Assigning the resources of the Trapeze team is a serious and expensive step to take—'

'Which is why it needs level six approval,' Miles butted in.

'. . . And it's just not clear that there would be any benefit to your work in doing so at this stage. In fact, it might jeopardise events down the line if we've extended our reach without good justification.'

Cox gritted her teeth as she bit back her retort. The way she saw it the term *good justification* was basically a movable feast that could be placed wherever those at the top end of the hierarchy wanted it. For months her work had seen her edging closer and closer to the identities and the truth of a group of extremists that she'd colloquially labelled *the Thirteen*.

After 9/11, Cox was placed on a special investigation to track the activity of family groups of known terrorists. Every year, thousands of children were brought up in extremist jihadi households across the Middle East – it was her job to track those kids to adulthood, and do her best to prevent them from becoming the next wave of terrorists to threaten the region, and ultimately the West. What had begun as a mind-numbing exercise in basic local surveillance had transformed into something Cox felt held far-reaching significance. It was in Iraq that she'd first come across tales of a group of young boys being trained in a secret and secluded institution, and her work since had led her to believe that those tales – as tall as they often were – held real truth.

Her boss at SIS had agreed, and had sanctioned a formal investigation with Cox's remit to identify and track down the Thirteen and the facility they were being trained at. Although she firmly believed the notorious Aziz al-Addad was likely one of the key players behind the group, she'd not yet come close to completing her mission. For weeks now it felt as if she'd been hitting brick wall after brick wall. In fact, several months ago, even the few small leads she had dried up over-night. Despite her best efforts, she no longer had any active intelligence on where any of the Thirteen were, as though they didn't even exist any more. To Cox that meant one thing: bad news. The graduates of destruction were likely now out in the world awaiting activation. Yet the lack of tangible evidence she had on who the Thirteen were, and where they were, meant the bigwigs at SIS were fast losing interest – and patience – in the investigation.

Cox, on the other hand, remained unmoved in her belief that the Thirteen formed not just a potent potential weapon, but also an immediate threat to the UK and indeed the whole of Western Europe. So far she was having a hard time convincing Flannigan of that.

'I think you're wrong,' Cox said. 'And I think the longer you delay giving me proper assistance for this investigation the greater the risk to us all.'

Getting access to the Trapeze team – a highly sophisticated surveillance unit operated out of the UK government's GCHQ – would finally give her the resources she needed to help track down the Thirteen and enable the authorities to stop them. Roger Miles had already turned down Cox's previous request some three months ago, and given Flannigan's attitude towards her of late she was beginning to question the level of influence he had over the decision, too. Was he deliberately trying to scupper her work behind her back? But why would he do that?

'Can you imagine the public reaction if the Thirteen initiate an attack that could have been prevented?' Cox added.

'*Public* reaction?' Flannigan said. 'Sorry, but is that a threat?'

'What do you think? I'm not in this for public recognition, you must know that about me by now. But I *have* to stop this group before it's too late.'

'You don't even know the Thirteen exist!' Flannigan blasted. 'For all we've seen it's just your wild, personal theory.'

'That's ridiculous. Of course they exist, they—'

'*Existed,* perhaps. We know very well the recruitment techniques of these jihadi outfits, including those run by the so-called Teacher. And yes, I'm certain there are many young boys who were kidnapped or otherwise forced into training under that vile man. But to suggest there's some group of thirteen kids who sit above all that, and are about to bring the world to its knees, is just . . . baseless.'

'According to you.'

'According to fucking everyone except you actually!'

'Okay, Henry, let's keep this level,' Miles said. 'Rachel, I know you've put a lot of time and sacrifice into this, but the problem is I'm seeing little tangible progress—'

'That's because you're having me operate with my hands tied behind my back!'

'Enough! Let me be very clear with you. For a while now I've tried to see this operation from your point of view, and I've given you the benefit of the doubt plenty. But it really is getting to the point now where I have to decide whether continuing this work remains in the public interest.'

'You have to trust me.'

'I do. Which is why I'm giving you another two weeks. But if you don't have any new evidence before then – and I mean real, solid, tangible evidence that we can act upon – then I'm shutting this operation down.'

Silence fell for a few seconds and Cox wondered whether they were expecting her to respond. She didn't. What could she say?

'Do you understand?' Flannigan asked.

'Of course,' Cox said.

'Okay, good,' Miles said. 'Then I think we're done for now.'

'Looks like it, doesn't it?' Cox said, before reaching out and ending the call.

She was fuming. Sod them both. If they wouldn't help her she'd just have to do things her own way. It wouldn't be the first time she'd broken protocol to prove she was right. The last time she'd been able to dismantle a small cell planning a car bomb attack at the British embassy in Cairo. For her efforts she'd been given a formal reprimand, *and* had her promotion to level four rejected. Yet she firmly believed her actions then were justified, as they were now.

Cox shut the laptop lid and picked the phone back up. She saw there were two missed calls from Subhi, a local asset of hers who officially worked for the Military Intelligence Directorate of Syria, though for the last eighteen months had been passing intel to her – payback after she'd helped his mother and grandma escape the war-torn country to Egypt.

He'd left no message – neither text nor voicemail. She was still thinking what to do, how to respond to him, when another call came through.

'Hi,' she said, expecting a coded response in return, perhaps a request for them to meet somewhere to discuss whatever he'd so urgently been calling about.

'Rachel, have you seen the news?'

Cox frowned. 'The bomb attack?' she said. She'd heard it on the news but hadn't paid much attention. Such an attack, although horrific, was becoming par for the course in the beleaguered city. In fact rarely did a day go by without an atrocity of some sort, committed by any one of the many sides in the war. A few hours ago, towards the end of the working day, a lone man had walked through a crowded open-air food market in the centre of the city and blown himself and over twenty other people into pieces.

'Check the news,' Subhi said. 'Then call me back.'

'Wait,' Cox said, hoping to stop him before he ended the call. He sounded harried, and she could sense his anxiousness. 'Are you still there?'

'Yes.'

'Just tell me.'

Subhi let out a deep sigh. 'She was there, Rachel. In the market when the bomb went off. I'm sorry, but she's dead.'

Subhi didn't need to say anything more than that. Cox slumped. She knew exactly whom he meant, and what it meant for her investigation.

16

FOUR

Paris, France

Aydin's first focus as he drove off in the Fiat was simply to leave Paris as quickly as he could, and get some breathing space. He initially headed south, away from where he really wanted to be. He had a phone in his pocket that his people would surely try to trace. He couldn't keep it on him for long, but he had to at least hope that a simple subterfuge would hold the chasing pack off for a short while.

He drove on for two hours in the clunking Fiat before he stopped at the side of the four-lane highway. He stepped from the car. There were no other vehicles in sight, everything quiet and serene compared to the inner city, and an uncomfortable contrast to the turmoil in his mind and to the chaos that would surely follow him from there.

He dropped the phone to the ground and stomped on it until it was clear the device was smashed beyond reasonable repair. Not dismantled fully, but then he didn't want it to be. He wanted its pieces to be found. He picked the remnants of the phone back up and flung them into the overgrown verge. No point in making things easy for them.

He didn't know why but for the next few seconds he just stared off into the dark distance, unable to pull himself away. He thought about Paris. The apartment. Khaled's bloodied and lifeless body. He wondered how long it would take the police to find out about the murder. Was it murder? Two hours into his drive there hadn't been a single siren or flashing light in sight. Did that mean the police weren't yet after him?

Or, before they hunted him down, would his own people get to the apartment first and remove the body, cover it all up as if neither he nor Khaled ever existed?

Aydin wasn't sure which outcome was better or worse.

He wrenched himself from his thoughts and got back into the car. With the bait set, he looped back around Paris, heading north but giving the city a wide berth. It was gone two a.m. by the time he ditched the car in a lay-by four miles from the port of Calais. The thick cloud above stifled the moon's illumination, and once he was away from the orange glow of the streetlights the surrounding land was pitch black.

That's where he headed, into the darkness. It sucked him in and he wondered if he'd ever escape it. He traipsed across soggy fields of overgrown grass, using the distant lights from the line of the road a hundred yards to his right to guide him further in.

Even in the darkness the place felt eerily familiar, and before long he saw the first signs of life. Torchlights. Phone screens. Flickering flames and the wispy smoke of campfires. The hunched forms of sorry people huddled together with nowhere better to go and nothing better to do.

Above the sweet smell of the grassy fields, and the salt from the nearby sea, was the stench of smoke and chargrilled food and festering human waste. All around the people in front of him, past where the eye could see, were a mishmash of tents and plastic tarpaulins stretched over wooden supports, torn metal sheets propped up on poles. Like a holiday campsite gone wrong.

He was in the area known commonly as the Jungle, though the reality didn't fit that word at all. There was no dense vegetation, no thriving eco-communities of wondrous beasts. Shitpit was closer to the truth.

A few years ago the Jungle lined the area immediately outside the ferry terminal and Eurotunnel station in Calais. Refugees from Syria and Libya and elsewhere had flocked there hoping for a free ride to the UK. Many had made it to the promised land in those initial waves, but those days were long gone. The much smaller camp was a few miles further back now, but then, the Jungle remained an ever-evolving beast. The French authorities did their best to destroy the hastily erected shantytown at every opportunity, but as quickly as the bulldozers flattened, the people simply set up shop somewhere down the road. They were beyond desperate and simply had nowhere else to go.

But while the location of the masses of people and their hand-built shelters was forever changing, the place and its people remained familiar to Aydin. He'd seen areas like the Jungle countless times all over Europe and beyond.

He knew exactly what he was looking for.

He had his hood pulled up and kept his head down as he squelched through the thick mud underfoot. There'd been no rain that night but the grassy fields that had been taken over by the camp remained churned. As expected, he didn't get a single glance from the first several groups of people he passed. They felt safer not interacting with the outside world, just sticking in their groups and their imaginary safe bubbles. That wasn't a problem. It told Aydin they weren't the ones he was looking for, that they couldn't help him.

Then he spotted someone who could. The man, standing under the beam of a flashlight, dangling from what looked like a wooden sentry post, was tall and beefy with a shaven head and a thick nose that was squashed to his face. The angle of the light made his deep-set eyes seem like two pools of black. His arms were folded over his chest as he barked at his friend next to him. The friend was a near carbon copy except he was shorter and slightly thinner, and the way he held his body showed he wasn't the one in charge. The two men weren't anything like the others in the camp. Not just in the way they looked, their lighter skin, round faces, high cheekbones, either – typical Slavic features. The biggest difference of all was the lack of desperation and fear. Instead, Aydin saw greed and malice.

The big man looked his way and Aydin quickly darted off to the right, sheltering behind a falling-down wooden hut. The man didn't see him and turned back to his friend. Aydin was in the shadows, while the man's face remained well lit by the light above him. Aydin watched the two men for a short while, straining so he could hear their gruff conversation. In the quiet of the night he heard their words clearly, but he couldn't understand them, their language not one that he spoke or was even familiar with.

Born in England, Aydin still spoke that language with a native, southern accent. His father was from Turkey and had taught him Turkish at home. Through his training at the Farm he'd become proficient in a half-dozen other tongues; Arabic, Persian, Kurdish, Russian, French, German. But these men were speaking something else, a language with a whole host of unfamiliar guttural sounds. Together with their looks, he could only guess they were from Eastern Europe, or perhaps the Balkans, but that could still be one of tens of countries he wasn't particularly acquainted with.

What he did know was *who* the men were: gangsters or low-level mafia who'd travelled west and found a home in France for the simple reason of exploiting vulnerable refugees for financial gain.

Aydin quickly put his ill feelings for the scumbags to the side. As much as he detested men like them, he had to see them for what they were: his ticket out of France.

Two weary-looking and scruffily dressed young men walked up to the brutes. There was a quick exchange of words and the big man pointed away into the distance. The two refugees skulked off in that direction. The big man checked his watch once. Then again a minute later. Aydin sensed what was brewing.

Focused on the two men, he was surprised by a young woman emerging from the shadows of the wooden hut he was standing by. She jumped in shock and cupped her mouth with her hand when she saw Aydin standing right there, outside her makeshift home. He lifted a finger to his lips and together with his pleading look managed to avert a shout or scream from her, but the look of panic in her eyes remained.

'What are you doing?' she whispered in Arabic, perhaps sensing the need to not raise the alarm. Her accent suggested she was from Syria, as many of the refugees undoubtedly were.

Aydin indicated the two men with his head. The woman understood. He quickly figured she wasn't a new arrival at the Jungle; her home was too sturdy – comparatively speaking – and the look she gave told him she not only knew the two men, but disliked them just as much as he already did.

'If they catch you spying—'

He cut her off by holding his hand up.

'Don't worry about me,' he said. 'You just carry on. I'll be gone by the time you get back and you'll never see me again.'

She looked uncertain about that, though he wasn't sure about which part exactly. After a couple of seconds she moved away, edgily. He turned his head and watched her walking over to one of the groups of people by a fire that was on its last legs, with more smoke than flames. She didn't look over at him at all – either she was doing her bit to not alert the brutes, or she'd simply already put him out of her mind now that she was back in the safety of her group.

When Aydin turned back he saw the two gangsters were walking away. After waiting a few seconds he followed, hugging the shadows like he was simply part of the darkness. They were soon out of the main Jungle, past the living spaces, just grass and mud as they headed across undulating fields, moving closer to the main road once again.

As Aydin came over the top of a small hill, he peered down into the darkness below. Further away the area was clearly lit up by the lights of the road, but for now the men had disappeared into a crevice between the tarmac and where Aydin was standing and he couldn't see them at all. He kept moving forward, heading into the blackness behind them, moving cautiously as if he might stumble upon them at any second. Then the clouds above parted, spitting out faint moonlight. Enough for him to understand what he was staring at.

He stopped. He counted twenty-one heads, mostly men, sat or hunched in a group on the soggy ground in front of him. He saw the two gangsters, on their feet, going around the group, one by one, taking the bundles of cash, flitting through the notes and stuffing them into their jackets. He wondered what the price was tonight. A few hundred euros perhaps. Maybe as much as a couple of thousand. He had nearly ten thousand in his backpack. Not that he was planning on paying these two.

Instead, he crouched down and continued spying the group, looking for a suitable candidate. He spotted two. Young men, sitting at either end of the group, far enough away from the others to show they had no one. They weren't talking, weren't looking at anyone else at all. They were loners. Nobody gave a shit about them.

Now all he needed was the opportunity.

He waited for several minutes. The shorter of the gangsters headed off towards the road, probably to wait for the lorry that would take these people to the cherished lands of England. After another ten minutes passed, one of the refugees got to his feet, spoke a few words to the tall gangster, and headed in Aydin's direction.

Aydin remained absolutely still as the man came to within five yards of where he was crouching. The man was peering into the darkness all around but there was no indication at all that he knew Aydin was there. He unzipped his trousers and urinated on the ground. He was so perfectly positioned, but Aydin couldn't take his place. He was certain the woman the man had been sitting next to was his friend, possibly his wife.

Nonetheless Aydin felt his tension rising. He wanted to be out of France by morning. No, he *had* to be. He needed to be part of that group, and as the man walked away Aydin realised he may have just lost his only opportunity.

Just then, though, as the man reached the group, one of the candidates Aydin had his eye on got to his feet. The tall gangster shouted angrily, but didn't try to stop him moving away to relieve himself. The man headed off to the left and Aydin snaked round, following his movement until they were just a few yards apart. Aydin glanced around while the man did his business. They were out of sight from the group. He uttered a small prayer of thanks for his good fortune, and another to ask Allah to take care of the man. He wasn't Aydin's enemy. The man finished and went to zip up his fly. He didn't sense Aydin at all as he sprang forward.

Aydin used the heel of his hand to smack down onto the base of the man's neck – a pressure point of nerves that he knew would cause chaos through his central nervous system. His legs went from under him and Aydin caught his falling body and helped him down to the earth, laying him gently on his side. But his assistance was little to do with him caring for the man's wellbeing; he simply couldn't afford to make a sound.

He looked down at the man. He was a similar height and build to Aydin, and about his age. A little more facial hair, and a straighter, pointier nose perhaps, but it was the middle of the night and Aydin was sure those two gangsters thought every young man who looked even remotely like he was from the Arabian peninsula was indistinguishable.

The man's trousers were dark, like Aydin's, and he was wearing a hooded top. His, though, was much lighter-coloured than Aydin's black one. He quickly stripped his own hoody off and put on the man's. It fitted just fine.

The man was unconscious, but Aydin didn't know for how long. He could easily kill him, to reduce his risks of detection, but he didn't want to be that person. Yet he had to be certain that the man stayed on the ground. So he lifted his foot and drove his heel into the side of the guy's head. Enough to punish his brain for a few minutes at least, but hopefully not enough to leave him with any lasting damage.

In the distance Aydin heard the hiss of powerful airbrakes. He quickly moved away and over at the roadside he saw the bright beams of light from an articulated lorry. Moments later the second gangster returned and started corralling the group of escapees into shape. Aydin reached the group just in time, fading into the masses, becoming just another anonymous shape in the eyes of the two men in charge.

They did a quick count of heads, not blinking an eye that Aydin was now standing there among the others, rather than the man he'd just left in the mud. But Aydin did feel eyes on him. He glanced to his right and caught the suspicious gaze of an ageing man with a thick wiry beard that must have been nearly white given the way the thin light reflected off it. Aydin held the old man's stare and his eyes squinted further. Aydin got ready for a challenge. Would the man confront him? Or just go straight ahead and call him out to the gangsters?

Neither. A few seconds later he just looked away without saying anything at all.

The next moment the goons were marching the group towards the waiting lorry. Without further hitches, in a few hours Aydin would be back in his country of birth. England.

FIVE

Dover, England

Aydin spent most of the journey with his eyes closed, though he wasn't sleeping. Partly he just didn't want to interact with the group of immigrants that were with him. He wasn't one of them, not really. The main reason for his unrest, though, was because he was thinking about Nilay and his mother. Thinking of his father too, in fact. Thinking about everything that had happened in his life, imagining the *others* and what they'd do to punish him now that he'd killed one of his own and broken away.

However unsettling and gruesome those thoughts were, he didn't regret slitting Khaled's throat, only that he'd done it without properly thinking through his next steps.

Regardless, he was certain that London had to be his first destination. Nilay's death had catapulted him onto this course of destruction and he needed to find out what had happened to her and why.

There was little chatter among the group as they sat in the back of the lorry among boxes and pallets. Most of the men and women either slept or stared aimlessly into space for the journey. The trailer was dark and the air was thick with sweat and fear. The only light they had came from two finger-sized torches that a couple of the men had with them.

The few people that Aydin saw with mobile phones back in Calais were ordered to turn them off before the lorry departed and they'd so far kept to that instruction.

Aydin listened to the sounds from outside, trying to decipher where they were on the journey. After the bobbing and swaying of the ferry ride, where one of the women violently vomited into one of the two buckets they'd been provided with for emergency toilet needs, came the most nerve-wracking part. UK Border Force.

With the ferry ride over, car and lorry engines fired up and Aydin could hear other vehicles moving past as they sat waiting, the look of anxiety on the faces of the people around him growing. It took close to half an hour before the lorry engine erupted into life and Aydin was already wondering whether there might be a problem. Finally they began to move, but he could tell from the vibrations and the sounds that the lorry was only crawling, and before long the engine shut down once more.

Aydin heard the driver's door open and moments later muffled voices outside, just a yard or two from where he was sitting, though the sounds felt distant and removed.

He planned in his mind how he would get away if the boxes in front were peeled away and he was left staring into the faces of the UK Border Force. He had the gun in his trousers, his training and his wits, but that still might not be enough.

The look of worry on the faces of the other passengers grew further as they waited. Then the driver's door opened and closed again, the engine growled to life, and the wheels began to turn. Moments later the lorry was speeding up and the heave of relief from the people around Aydin was almost overwhelming.

It wasn't long before chatter grew among the group. Smiles broke out. The men and women probably felt like they'd finally made it, as though their trip through hell was finally over. This was it, a new life. Aydin wouldn't break it to them that the chances were their ordeals had only just begun. Who or what awaited them when the lorry reached its destination and those boxes were pulled away, he really didn't know, but he was sure it wasn't paradise.

They drove for nearly an hour before the lorry once again stopped. The driver's door opened. Aydin heard more voices. Then noises as the fabric sides of the lorry were drawn back. Light rays surged into the interior and Aydin had to shut his eyes for a few seconds. When he opened them he saw the other men and women squinting, holding hands up to their faces. There was a wall of white light next to them, so bright Aydin couldn't make out anything of what lay beyond. It reminded him of alien invasion movies he watched with his family as a boy in London. The moment where the spaceship landed and the doors opened and for a minute all that could be seen was light and smoke, before the alien life forms finally appeared.

There were no alien life forms here, though. What Aydin saw coming through the wall of light was much more sinister. White faces, with heavy, furrowed features. If not the actual brothers of the two gangsters in Calais, then certainly close relatives. There were four of them. They shouted at the group in English, though their accents were thick with rolled consonants. None of them appeared to be armed but they immediately instilled fear in the group, hauling people up, pushing and pulling and shoving.

The travellers cowered and did as they were told, filing out of the lorry one after another. Aydin played along, muttering pleadings to the men in Arabic. One of them shoved him in the back and he fell forward, over the edge of the lorry and to the tarmac below. He tried to roll into the fall, but was unable to stop his hip and elbow smacking onto the surface painfully. Before he could recover, another heavily muscled man lifted him back to his feet. He worried for a second that the man would feel the gun. Or maybe that the weapon had already come loose in the fall. What would the men's reaction be if they realised Aydin was armed?

He took in the scene around him. The first thing he noticed was the green. Many years had passed since Aydin was last in England and he'd forgotten just how green it was. The grass, the hedgerows, the trees. They were surrounded by dense emerald colour. And the smell. A fragrant yet earthy scent that tickled his nose – a smell achingly familiar but one that he hadn't ever thought about until then.

Aydin saw the lorry was parked on a pothole-covered lane, among farmers' fields. Across the road were two battered and rusting white vans. Fords, he thought. He was shoved back into line, towards the vans where other grunts in jeans and leather jackets were hastily stashing the new arrivals. Just as Aydin expected, these poor people hadn't just paid for their freedom at all. They'd been conned, and their nightmares had only just begun.

Aydin wouldn't be part of whatever misery and slavery lay ahead for the others, and no matter how sorry he felt for them, he couldn't and wouldn't try to save all twenty of the people he'd travelled with. But he had to save himself.

He let the grunts move him towards the first of the vans as he scoped out the threats around him. He saw there was already a man in the driver's seat of the van he was heading to. The side door was open. Three sorry faces peered out of the dark interior. Several other immigrants were waiting in line in front of him, soon to join them. He took another shove to the back.

Then leapt into action.

Aydin crouched and swivelled, using his instincts to tell him where the man who'd just shoved him was standing. His sweeping leg took away one of the man's, sending the guy off balance. Aydin crashed his forearm down onto the man's chest, aiding his trip to the blacktop below. He landed on the ground with a thump, and Aydin knew in that moment that for all his tough-guy bravado and muscle, he didn't even have basic hand-to-hand combat training. Prone on the ground, he should have immediately brought his arms up to defend his head, neck. He didn't. Aydin crashed his foot down onto the man's windpipe. Unlike in Calais, he had no care of the extent of damage the blow would cause. There was a crunching sound and the man's eyes bulged, but Aydin didn't keep his sight on him for even a second longer to inspect the full damage – he needed to keep moving.

He darted for the man at the open side door of the van, who was shepherding travellers into the back. Aydin glanced left and right as he moved. The guy in front was quick to react and peeled from his position, an angry snarl on his face as he headed for Aydin. There were shouts and calls all around. Aydin half expected gunfire to ring out any second. In fact, he found himself reaching behind for his own weapon as he watched the hand of the man in front disappear behind his back. Yet it wasn't a gun that he pulled, but a hunting knife. A six-inch serrated blade that Aydin knew could cause all sorts of damage to the soft tissue of a human body. As he was about to demonstrate.

Aydin left his gun where it was. There was no need for it yet. He didn't have endless supplies of ammunition so the weapon was a last resort only.

The man shoved the blade towards Aydin, who shimmied sideways. Still moving forward, he grabbed the man's forearm and twisted. He came up behind the man, still pulling on his arm, his hand close to the man's wrist. When the pressure of the twist became too much, the man released the knife. Aydin let go of the wrist, grabbed the knife handle and plunged the blade into the man's stomach. He let out a gurgling groan as Aydin withdrew the knife. Blood now covered his hand. He kicked the man away and he fell into a heap on the ground.

All around Aydin saw the other men coming forward for him. They were angry, and intent on doing him harm, but despite his inferior size there was already a wariness in their eyes, even after just a few seconds of fighting.

Aydin, panting from the rapid exertion of taking down the two big lumps, turned and slid shut the side door of the van, then stepped forward and flung open the driver's door. The driver had figured out what was happening. He went for his knife, on the passenger seat. Aydin's eyes locked with his. The driver lifted the knife, but in the confined space he was simply out-positioned. Before the guy could find an angle for a successful attack, Aydin simply grabbed him and roared as he hauled him out of the cab to the ground.

Aydin, his head on fire, was tempted to turn and take on everyone else coming his way. Pull the gun and blast them all down. The release of adrenaline he was experiencing made him feel powerful, almost invincible. Just how they trained him to be under pressure and in the fight.

But he stopped himself. Fighting, beating and punishing those goons wasn't what he'd come to England for, however much they deserved it, and however good it would make him feel.

He realised it was time to draw his gun, though. As he did so, the sudden sight of the shiny black metal caused everyone honing in on him to reconsider their intentions. He let off a warning shot that cracked into the tarmac just a few inches from the toes of one of the men. He turned and fired off one more shot that caused the front tyre of the second van to explode. He wasn't in the mood for a car chase.

Not wanting to waste any more bullets than he needed to, he slung his backpack inside then jumped into the driver's seat and slammed the door shut just as one of the men rushed forward. Aydin pushed down the lock and the man charged into the door, shoulder first. He tried the handle then began angrily pounding on the glass as Aydin searched for the keys. They were in the ignition still. He turned the key and the engine grumbled to life. Another man was at the front of the van. He held his arms out and put his hands onto the bonnet as he glared defiantly at Aydin.

Their continued machoism surprised him. They'd seen the gun, they'd seen how Aydin fought, but they weren't giving up. It didn't worry him, but it did make him wonder just who they were, who they worked for.

He crunched the gearstick into reverse, released the hand-brake and thumped on the accelerator. The van lurched back and crashed into the front of the second vehicle. He quickly shoved the gearstick into first. The man at the front remained, as though standing there might stop the getaway. Aydin pushed on the accelerator, just gently at first, giving the man one last chance to see sense.

He didn't. And when a booming gunshot rang out a second later, Aydin was left with no choice. The driver's side window exploded into thousands of tiny pieces of glass which filled the cabin around him. He ducked instinctively even though he knew the move was too late. There was no indication of where the bullet landed, but Aydin wasn't hit.

He couldn't hang around to figure out where the shot came from. He thumped his foot onto the accelerator and the van jerked forward. The man at the front, finally realising his mistake, tried to dive to the side at the last moment. He didn't quite manage it, and there was a loud thud and the van jumped up as it raced over his body. Whether it was just his legs Aydin had crushed or worse he didn't know, and he didn't care.

The only thing that mattered was that he was tearing away, and as he looked into the side mirror and saw the men and their vehicles fading into the distance, he knew he was in the clear.

SIX

Berlin, Germany

Ismail Obbadi sat alone on a park bench, surrounded by an endless sprawl of discoloured communist-era apartment blocks. As the early morning commuter traffic bustled around him in the crowded district of Lichtenberg, Obbadi was almost entirely ignored by passers-by – just another anonymous face in another decrepit cesspit.

As strange as it might seem to many, it was a pleasing change of scenery and circumstance for Obbadi, given his more public image of late. Obbadi had dressed down for the occasion too, sporting battered old shoes, a pair of jeans and black cotton jumper rather than his more usual and more formal designer gear. His hair was unkempt and covered by a blue baseball cap and he hadn't shaved for nearly forty-eight hours. His appearance was far from his immaculate norm, yet he didn't feel at all scruffy – he felt powerful, knowing he could so easily assume different personas, and blend in to different surroundings so seamlessly.

He felt his phone vibrating in his pocket. He lifted it out and stared at the screen. It was a Skype call. He recognised the caller ID. It was far from ideal to have to speak like this, but under the circumstances he wanted to hear what his brother had to say.

'Yes?' Obbadi said, answering the call.

'He got out, in the middle of the night we think. But we'll catch up with him.'

'How did you let him get away? You told me you were tracking?'

'I said it felt wrong that he'd been so careless. I warned you it was a trick.'

'You did. And I insisted you made sure. But you still shouldn't have been that far behind.'

'I'm sorry. What do you want me to do?'

'Go back to your position. I'll get your brothers to pick up the trail.'

Obbadi ended the call before either of them said too much. Seconds later, still grinding his teeth as he thought about the previous night's events, he spotted the young man – short and squat – heading his way. His face was covered in a thick black beard and he wore a taqiyah skullcap. It pleased Obbadi to see the man's traditional and more conservative attire, though with his brown jacket unzipped Obbadi could see his gut was much flabbier than when they'd last seen each other. Perhaps he'd become too used to a life of relative freedom in Western Europe. Or was it just that he wasn't responsible enough to have kept himself in shape now that the elders weren't there to look after him day in, day out?

'It's good to see you, brother,' the man said as he sat down next to Obbadi, a relaxed smile on his face.

'You too, *Sab'ah.*' Number seven.

'I'm sure my home here isn't as grand as yours,' Sab'ah said, indicating the grim housing blocks in front of them.

'Brother, we may live in different places now, but there is only one place that either of us will ever know as home.'

'True. I still think of the Farm every day. Do you?'

'That place changed our lives, yet I'd be lying if I said it was somewhere I'd ever want to return to.'

Sab'ah laughed. 'I think I know what you mean. Did you know I was actually born in this city? Germany is my home country. I lived in Berlin for six years. Until . . .' Sab'ah bowed his head. 'Until my mama died.'

Obbadi didn't offer any response to that, though he was far from pleased with the clear sorrow that he sensed in his brother as he recalled his former life. That was behaviour that certainly would never have been tolerated at the Farm. The West was so quick to destroy the weak, though Obbadi was surprised to include Sab'ah, usually so headstrong, in that bracket. He'd have to think carefully about whether to report this to their Father. Perhaps he should just give Sab'ah the benefit of the doubt this one time. If he completed the tasks Obbadi had come here for, it would surely prove his brother remained capable and ready.

Sab'ah's face turned sour. 'I heard about Talatashar.'

Obbadi clenched his fists in anger. He was still reeling about what had happened in Paris. 'Heard what, exactly?'

'That he's gone. He left us.'

'Nobody leaves,' Obbadi said, feeling anger sticking in his throat. 'We'll find him, and he'll suffer for what he's done.'

'He deserves nothing more than what's coming. I'll help in any way I can. I'll kill him myself if I have to. You just need to say.' Sab'ah's eyes narrowed. 'Is that why you're here early?'

'No, it's not. I don't want anyone else moving from position now. Talatashar isn't in Germany. If he does come here, then I will seek your help. But right now, we stick to our plan.'

'Understood,' Sab'ah said with a determined and resolute look on his face. 'How long will you be here?' he asked. 'I'm sure you wouldn't want to stay with me, perhaps a hotel? There would be many to suit your taste here.'

'I'm not staying. I'll be flying out of Germany before tomorrow. Is everything ready?'

'Of course. The van is round the corner. Are we going now?'

Obbadi looked at his watch. 'Very soon. But first, I have something else to discuss with you.'

Obbadi saw the questioning look in his brother's eyes. He reached into his jacket pocket. It came out clutching a rolled piece of paper wrapped around a small cylindrical object. He passed it to Sab'ah. Looking confused, Sab'ah unwrapped the paper – a black-and-white photograph – to reveal a small vial.

'Do you know who that is?' Obbadi asked.

'Yes, but—'

'Not buts. No questions. Do you know who he is?'

'I do.'

'Can you get to him?'

'I'll find a way.'

'And you know what *that* is?'

'I think so.'

'Always wear gloves. My advice is to put the liquid into a sprayer. Get it into his face – his mouth, his nose. Once it's in his circulation he'll be dead within minutes.'

'But I don't understand. Why this? Why now?'

Obbadi looked at Sab'ah, but said absolutely nothing. Eventually Sab'ah got the message – no questions – and just looked down to his lap. He folded the photograph back around the vial and stuffed both inside his jacket pocket.

'You should come and see where I live,' Sab'ah said. 'We've fresh food, you must be hungry. We can show you our work, make sure everything is to your satisfaction.'

'That won't be necessary. And there isn't time. Just make sure this happens before the week is over. Can you do that?'

'I'll do anything for you. For the others.'

'I know you will. Okay, then let's get going.'

Obbadi got to his feet and Sab'ah followed suit. Obbadi reached out and put his arms around his brother, slapping his back and squeezing him tightly.

'Are you ready for this?' Obbadi said.

'You shouldn't have to ask.'

'Of course,' Obbadi said. He half-turned, making to go away, but then stopped.

'Oh, and brother?'

'Yes?'

'If I ever hear you talking about your childhood like that again, then I'll kill you myself.'

The colour washed from Sab'ah's face. 'I understand,' he said.

'Good. Then let's get this done.'

SEVEN

Obbadi sat in the passenger seat, looking out of his window as Sab'ah drove the van through central Berlin, heading west from Lichtenberg. They were soon passing the Brandenburg gates, then out of the window Obbadi caught a glimpse of the looming Reichstag with its lofty domed roof, moments before they headed onto the wide highway that bisected the dense green of the sprawling Tiergarten. Obbadi realised he was smiling to himself as they passed the famous sights. He'd been to Berlin many times before. He found the history of the city intoxicating, and could dwell in his mind for hours imagining what it must have been like to live there – anywhere in Europe really – through the Nazi regime, World War II and the Holocaust.

It was certainly ironic, almost fitting, that it was in Berlin of all places that Obbadi now found himself on this mission.

'Are you sure this will work?' Sab'ah said. 'You don't want to take the weapons in there with us?'

'Of course it will work.'

They had two Glock handguns in the back of the van, a G36 assault rifle, plus all of the other equipment they needed. But they'd go into the meeting empty-handed. It was the best way.

'And what if they decide to just kill us the moment we walk in?' Sab'ah asked, still not sounding convinced at the plan.

'Do you really think they could?'

Obbadi focused hard on his brother's features as he waited for an answer, looking for any tell, any sign of weakness. He saw none. That was good.

They'd soon made it out of Tiergarten and after several minutes of driving past the grand upscale buildings of West Berlin, apartment blocks with wrought iron balconies and stone-arched entranceways, they were heading into the industrial periphery of the city. They drove past various forms of office and warehouse, new and old, brick and stone and corrugated metal.

'This is the one,' Obbadi eventually said, stooping low so he could look up at the huge red brick structure that rose up from weed-filled grounds behind a rusted chain-link fence. 'Go in there.'

Sab'ah nodded and pulled the van off the deserted road and through what was likely once a car park but was now a pothole-ridden expanse of four-foot-high plant life. The greenery crunched under the wheels of the van. Obbadi spotted the two parked vehicles in a small clearing by a side entrance to the building. One of the vehicles was a luxury black BMW X5, the other a black Mercedes van – similar to the one they were in, but in much better condition. There were two men standing by the vehicles. Both white-skinned and burly, shaved heads, wearing jeans and leather jackets. Both were armed with assault rifles.

'Park next to the van,' Obbadi said.

Sab'ah did so and moments later they were both stepping from their vehicle. Obbadi caught the eyes of the men; the shorter, older one seemed to be the one in charge, by the way he stepped forward.

'No weapons,' he said with obvious distaste for the new arrivals, speaking in his native German, a language Obbadi spoke fluently.

Obbadi raised his arms in the air. 'We're not that stupid,' Obbadi said, calm, accommodating, friendly. 'But you can check us if you want to.'

The man looked slightly put off by Obbadi's coolness, though the hostility in his expression remained clear. These men were not natural allies of Obbadi's. They certainly didn't believe in the cause. In fact they were most likely vehemently opposed to it. But this was a business transaction.

The short man nodded to his friend who came forward and quickly patted down both Obbadi and Sab'ah. He didn't do a very good job. He nodded back to his boss.

'They're inside.'

Obbadi smiled then walked towards the large double doors, Sab'ah striding along with him.

'What about the equipment?' Sab'ah said.

'Not yet, my friend. Just follow my lead.'

They entered the building, an old textile factory built in the 1930s, and found themselves in a gigantic open space with bashed-up wooden floors, paint-peeling metal struts and boarded-up windows that let through only slivers of light. Even though it was dark and gloomy, the air musty with a heavy stench of wood oil, it was clear there was no one there.

'Next floor up then,' Obbadi said, spying the metal spiral staircase in the near corner of the room.

'Are you sure about this?'

'Sab'ah, if you haven't got anything useful to say, then can I suggest you say nothing at all.'

Obbadi set off for the stairs and started up them without another word between him and his brother. The staircase swayed and rattled with each step he took. Obbadi soon found himself emerging into a near-identical space to the one they'd just come from. Nearly identical, except for two big differences. First was that several of the boards covering the windows had been removed, meaning the space was light and airy. Secondly the space wasn't empty. There were four men, crowded around a makeshift table, in the centre of the floor.

Obbadi beamed a genuine smile – at least it looked genuine enough.

'Herr Streicher,' Obbadi said, outstretching his hand as he moved towards the disgusting fat blob of a man who stood, arms folded, at the head of the others.

Streicher, large round blue eyes that matched his overall rounded appearance, glared suspiciously, then uncurled his arms and gave Obbadi's hand a crushing shake. Despite his obvious confidence and self-satisfaction, Streicher's azure eyes were strangely dull, his rosy-red cheeks and sagging chin further adding to his dishevelled appearance. He was wearing casual clothes, a tight white shirt that was buttoned up to the neck, but Obbadi could still see the black of tattoo ink poking out of the top. Probably an SS insignia or a swastika, such was the lack of originality of men like this. In fact, Obbadi could see the other three men had similar swirls of ink creeping up their necks and one very clearly had a small SS symbol tattooed on his left temple. Another had teardrops inked under one eye. Obbadi resisted the urge to roll his eyes at these sad specimens.

'You're travelling light for a man who's supposed to have fifty barrels of Uragan D2 for me,' Obbadi said as he looked beyond Streicher to the table where he could see just two large metal canisters. *Uragan D2* was written in big red letters on a white label across each of the containers, right next to various warning signs as to the contents' potency.

Streicher shrugged. 'And you're travelling very light for a man who's bringing me two million dollars,' he said, his guttural voice croaky. He folded his arms again and Obbadi saw his minions tense up. Each of them had weapons in their hands, though they were holding them casually.

'The wonders of modern technology,' Obbadi said. 'Your money is a click away. As agreed.'

'And your Uragan D2 is a few metres away,' Streicher said, which Obbadi took to mean it was in the van downstairs. Streicher glanced at the table, then back to Obbadi. 'This is just a sample. You want the rest, I need the money first.'

'I guess that's fair. But we need to test the material before we can pay you. I'm not handing over two millions dollars only to find you've given us slug pellets.'

'Is that some sort of joke?' Streicher said. 'How the fuck are you going to test the material here?'

'Why would it be a joke? We have the equipment, in the van. It'll be perfectly safe.'

Obbadi turned to Sab'ah, about to give him the instruction to head back to the van, but Streicher soon stopped that.

'No,' he said, his voice raised enough to grab the attention of everyone in the room. 'You pay, otherwise you and your rag-head friend will leave this building in pieces. And you can be sure we'll take as many of those pieces while you're still breathing as we can.'

Obbadi stared at the man for a few moments. The animosity seeping through the big man's every pore was unmistakable. Quite simply, Obbadi felt exactly the same way about each of the revolting excuses for men in front of him. It was one of the reasons Streicher and his crew were the perfect source. Who would ever believe that these neo-Nazi thugs would be suppliers to the likes of Obbadi? Yet this was strictly a one-time-only transaction. Obbadi had hoped there might be a way to not pay. Perhaps it was easier to get the deal sorted quickly.

He reached into his jeans pocket. Two of Streicher's men hauled up their weapons. Obbadi, not hiding his annoyance, pulled his empty hands into the air.

'I'm reaching for my phone, you morons,' he said. 'You want your money, I need my phone to wire it.'

Streicher thought for a moment then nodded. His men left the guns pointed at Obbadi but relaxed in their stances. Obbadi took the phone out and with his eyes flitting between the gun barrels and Streicher and his phone screen he went through the process of transferring the money.

'Two million dollars, sitting in a Grand Cayman bank account, just for you,' Obbadi said, showing the screen to Streicher briefly before stuffing the phone back into his pocket. 'I expect your accountant will call any second to confirm.'

Sure enough moments later there was a shrill ringing and Streicher picked his phone up from the table. He didn't say a word. Just listened with the phone pressed up against his ear, before putting the device back down again.

'You're happy?' Obbadi asked.

'I've been worse.'

Obbadi turned to Sab'ah. 'Go and fetch the equipment.'

Sab'ah nodded then scurried off, and Obbadi listened as his brother headed down the stairs and across the wood floor below to the outside. He kept his eyes on Streicher, who held his gaze.

'Quite something to be working with a man like you,' Streicher said.

'Capitalism knows no bounds,' Obbadi said. 'I'm only surprised that it's in Germany that we had to come for this. I'd have thought given history that this would be the hardest place on earth to find the infamous Zyklon B.'

Streicher twitched at the name. Obbadi wondered whether the Nazi Holocaust was a source of pride for men like these, or of embarrassment and shame.

The world over people knew of the notoriety of Zyklon B, the brand name of the cyanide pellets used to kill millions of Jews in the concentration camps in Poland during World War

II. What few realised was that the substance had originally been developed as a pesticide, and hydrogen cyanide was still produced for industrial use all over the world in various forms, under various different brand names. Finding it packaged in pellet form was difficult, and finding a supply that wouldn't get radars bleeping was even harder. Hence the lofty price tag. But two million dollars was well worth it, as far as Obbadi was concerned.

Obbadi heard the doors of the van open outside, then moments later they were slammed shut again.

This was it.

He saw Streicher's eyes twitch. Did he know? It really didn't matter now.

There was a double-tap of suppressed gunfire outside as Sab'ah took out the two sentries. Streicher was surprisingly quick to realise something wasn't right. But not quick enough.

Obbadi lifted his arm and raced for the nearest of the guards. The hidden blade shot out from under his sleeve and Obbadi stepped behind the man for cover and drove the knife into the man's neck. The other two men began firing their weapons but they had no clear shot of Obbadi, and he reached forward and grabbed hold of the rifle the man was still clutching and with four quick pulls he fired off enough shots to put the other two men on the ground. Down, but not out. He needed them alive.

He drew the knife from the man's neck and pulled the rifle off his shoulder and let him slump to the ground. Obbadi twisted the rifle to Streicher, who'd had just enough time to grab his concealed weapon and aim it at Obbadi's head. But it was a stalemate and neither man fired.

'You forgot about the man behind you, though,' Obbadi said, looking beyond Streicher to the head of the stairs where Sab'ah was standing with the G36.

Streicher whipped his head round and Obbadi lunged forward and swiped the butt of the assault rifle across the back of the big man's head. He keeled over.

Ten minutes later, Streicher and his two still alive accomplices were roped together in the back of Sab'ah's van.

'You have no idea what you've done,' Streicher said, still defiant. He spat out a mouthful of blood. 'You, your whole family. I'll find them, I'll skin you all alive.'

Obbadi, who was standing by the open back doors of the van, busy pulling on large industrial rubber gloves, stopped and pondered that for a second.

'I'm wondering,' Obbadi said. 'Is it just bravado when you say things like that, or do you really think you're capable of such an act?'

Streicher fumed, but said nothing.

'I ask because it's an easy thing to say.' Obbadi reached for the hunting knife that he'd pilfered from one of Streicher's men and held the blade out towards Streicher. 'But actually cutting into someone, then taking the skin and peeling it from their body as they writhe and scream . . . that's not such an easy thing to do. What do you think, Sab'ah?'

'No, not for me, brother,' Sab'ah said, head down.

Obbadi shook his head and pursed his lips. 'See? And he *knows* what it's like. He's seen me do it.'

Streicher was now looking less confident than he had done moments before. Obbadi smiled.

'Brother, it's time. We really do need to do the test before we can conclude this deal.'

'Right away.'

Both Sab'ah and Obbadi grabbed the heavy-duty gas masks and pulled them over their heads. Streicher's face still had a certain amount of resolve remaining but the intermittent flickers of fear were becoming more frequent and lasting longer.

'Okay, we're ready,' Sab'ah said, plonking down one of the canisters from the warehouse onto the floor of the van, right by Streicher's feet.

Obbadi and Sab'ah climbed into the back of the van and pulled shut the doors. Obbadi took the knife and held it up in the air, the blade pointing down to the floor.

'I've long wanted to see exactly how this works,' he said, grinning in anticipation as he locked eyes with Streicher. 'I hope I won't be disappointed.'

He plunged the knife down into the lid of the metal drum and then sawed around the rim to remove a crude circle of metal. Behind the plastic that covered his face his eyes opened wide as he stared down at the off-white pellets inside that looked completely innocuous. He wondered what would happen next. Would they fizz or froth or let off smoke as they reacted with the air and spat out their poison? Or would they just sit there looking inert despite their deadly nature?

After thirty seconds Obbadi, his eyes flicking from the pellets over to the three shackled men, realised it was the latter. There was no indication whatsoever that those little white pellets were filling the van with hydrogen cyanide gas, yet he could tell from the faces of the three men that the poison was already taking control.

Obbadi watched with rabid interest. As the gas reached the men's lungs they choked and gagged, the panic in their eyes growing by the second. The men moaned, then screamed as the cyanide rapidly worked through their bodies, blocking oxygen from muscles and organs. Soon they were convulsing. Frothy white and red spittle dripped from Streicher's mouth. A line of blood dribbled out from the ear of one of his men. The other, the more alert of the three, was screaming louder and louder. With his body shaking and spasming he slammed his head against the side of the van like a crazed beast, the vehicle shaking on its suspension. Obbadi winced with each strike and after several self-inflicted blows the blotch of red on the side of the van grew. Obbadi let out an amused laugh and looked away from the maniac over to Sab'ah. His face was hard and emotionless. He gave a slight nod to Obbadi.

'I think it works,' Obbadi said.

Sab'ah said nothing. Obbadi looked back at the men. Streicher's head was bowed, but his body still twitched violently. The lack of oxygen to his brain had rendered him unconscious but his muscles were cramping severely making his whole body shake. Could he still feel the pain? Obbadi hoped so.

It was several minutes more before the three men were still. By that point their skin was an unnatural pink colour and was covered in bright red and in some places greenish spots.

Obbadi moved over and lifted up Streicher's head. Blood dripped from both of his eyes. There was no doubt he was dead. Obbadi let go and the head flopped down.

'It's done,' he said, his face deadpan as he turned to Sab'ah.

Obbadi reached out and opened the van doors and stepped outside. He removed the mask and took in a lungful of fresh air. Sab'ah joined him.

'You're satisfied?' Sab'ah asked.

'More than satisfied,' Obbadi said. He looked over to the black Mercedes van. 'I'll take the rest of the barrels now.'

Sab'ah looked unsure about that. 'How will you get out of the country?'

Obbadi scowled at his brother. 'You let me worry about that. Put all the bodies in your van. All of the equipment too. Then burn it. Make sure there's nothing left.'

'I'll do it right away.'

Obbadi reached over and put his hand on Sab'ah's shoulder, then pulled his brother over and hugged him tightly.

'We're almost there,' Obbadi said.

'I only wish you could have stayed longer.'

'Next time, I promise.'

Obbadi let go and took a half-step away.

'*Ma'a salama*,' Sab'ah said.

Obbadi turned and smiled. 'And may peace be upon you too, my brother.'

EIGHT

Aydin glanced up at the buildings as they walked along the streets of Kandahar. It was colder than he'd expected. He had thought the country was just a huge sandy desert and would be baking hot, but despite the blue sky above he was shivering in his jeans and woollen jumper.

They'd only arrived in the city two hours ago. Already Aydin hated it. Everything was just so . . . unfamiliar. So different to home. Not just in appearance, but in the way it felt, the mottled textures of the stone buildings, the cracked pavement. A heavy, musky smell permeated everything – what was that? Aydin had no idea, but it was so very different to London.

They'd checked in to a hotel that wasn't like any other hotel Aydin had ever seen before. It was just grim. Though he didn't think they'd be staying there long.

'Do you remember what I told you?' his father asked, in his native Turkish. At nine years old it was a language Aydin understood perfectly, at least in his father's accent, yet he didn't feel comfortable speaking it himself. He didn't like it. Perhaps there was a part of him that wanted to rebel against his heritage, though there was no clear reason he could pinpoint as to why. The only answer was because the language was one more thing that marked him out as being different back home. His friends

teased him about his dark skin, his eyes, his face, the way he talked. They teased him for being Turkish, they called him a chicken and made stupid clucking noises.

All he'd ever wanted was to be normal, like everyone else.

'Did you hear me? I asked if you remember what I told you?'

'Which part?' Aydin asked him in English.

His father glared at him though didn't comment on his choice of tongue.

'You're special, Aydin. So, so special. In this place they'll teach you everything you'll ever need to know. Make me proud, son.'

'But you're staying with me here, aren't you?' Aydin asked, the nervousness in his voice clear.

'It's not here, in Kandahar, that you're staying. But this is where I have to leave you. There'll be others like you where you're going. Other boys. Think of it like a school.'

'But I like my school in London,' Aydin said, which wasn't exactly true, but it was much more familiar than this place at least. 'And I have my friends. Mumya, Nilay. I don't understand—'

His father reached down and put a finger to his lips.

'You'll understand in time. I promise. You trust me, don't you?'

'Yes,' Aydin said, though he wasn't sure he fully understood the concept of trust. This was his father, and Aydin believed anything the man told him. Was that trust?

They reached the end of the street and turned left onto another gloomy yellow, dusty street. Up ahead was a Jeep, parked up on the kerb, its white paintwork spattered with yellow and orange dust and muck.

Aydin's father tried to let go of his hand but the boy squeezed it tightly – he was scared. His father wrenched his hand away then moved forward to the Jeep.

'Wait there,' he said and Aydin stopped.

A cold wind blew across the street and the hairs on the back of Aydin's neck pricked up in defence as his shivering worsened.

51

*His whole body was shaking. Two men stepped from the Jeep.
One, the driver, stayed by the car. The other began a conversation with Aydin's father. The man was tall, he wore a skullcap
on his head and his pockmarked face was largely covered with
a thick black beard. Aydin didn't think the man was frowning
as such, but the look on his face was hard and mean, the skin
between his eyes pinched and lined. He gazed over to Aydin and
his eyes twitched. No hint of a smile.*

*After a few moments Aydin's father turned round and looked
at his son. There was a strange glaze in his eyes. He seemed . . .
weak. That wasn't how Aydin had ever seen his father before. The
man was Aydin's rock, his superhero. He waved Aydin forward
and the boy cautiously moved towards them. His father put his
hand around his son's shoulder and for a moment Aydin felt the
strength and security that his father's presence always gave him.*

Until he looked up into the other man's eyes.

*'Aydin, this man will take you from here. His name is Aziz.
But you should call him the Teacher.'*

*'Come on, Aydin,' the Teacher said. 'It's time for you to come
and meet the other boys.'*

*He held his hand out. Aydin didn't want to take it. He was
a strong boy, his father had always told him that. But his eyes
were filling with tears. He tried to fight them off, hoping they'd
sink back inside, but they didn't.*

'Please, Baba, please come with me.'

'I can't. Not now. The Teacher will look after you. I promise.'

'Come, Aydin,' the big man said, grabbing his hand.

'No, please! I don't want to go!'

*Aydin's father opened his mouth but didn't say a word. The
Teacher opened the back door of the Jeep, put his hands under
Aydin's armpits and lifted him up onto the seat. He shoved him
along then jumped in the back with him. Inside, the air was
thick with the stench of sweat and tobacco.*

'Baba!' Aydin shouted again.

He was sure he could see his father crying, and although he was doing a better job of fighting it than his son was, Aydin thought it was his father's unease that was making him so much more terrified.

Why was he just standing there? Why wasn't he helping him?

'Make me proud, son,' his father said again, before the Teacher wound up the window and the driver pulled the Jeep out onto the road.

Aydin turned his head to watch the figure of his father disappear into the distance behind.

'It's time to stop crying,' the Teacher said, his tone level, though Aydin still sensed menace behind his every word. 'Your father wants you to be strong. You don't want to disappoint him, do you?'

'No,' Aydin said.

'Good. Now put this on.' He handed Aydin a brown cloth sack.

'On what?'

'On your head.'

'But—'

'Just do it.'

Aydin hesitated. He wasn't sure why, other than he was frozen with both confusion and terror.

'Let me make this clear for you, Aydin,' the Teacher said, his eyes narrowing and his teeth gnashing together like an angry dog. 'There's only one rule for you from now on.' He grabbed the sack and pulled it over Aydin's head, the force causing his neck to twist painfully. 'You do as I tell you. Understand?'

Aydin said nothing, and seconds later the Teacher slapped or thumped him across the face, causing his head to smack against the window.

'I said do you understand!'

'Yes,' Aydin said, his voice pathetic.

'Good. Now be quiet. We've a long journey ahead.'

NINE

Sevenoaks, England

With thoughts of his father and that first encounter with Aziz al-Addad playing over and over in his mind, Aydin drove on for several miles before he figured out where he was. He was no expert on UK geography, but he knew given how long they'd been in the lorry before it stopped that he was still some way south of London. When he saw the sign for the M25, he knew he was heading in the right direction. He still had quite a trek to his next destination, but the longer he stayed in the van, the bigger the risk he was taking. Before he reached the motorway, on the outskirts of the leafy town of Sevenoaks, he pulled the van to the side of the road, stepped from it and walked away.

He didn't know how many illegal immigrants were in the back of the van, or what they'd do next. Perhaps they'd be thankful for Aydin getting them away from the exploitative mobsters. Or maybe he'd inadvertently split those poor people from their friends and family. Either way they weren't his problem any more, and he felt little guilt for leaving them there. The way he saw it, Sevenoaks was a hell of a lot better than a Syrian war zone.

After a short walk Aydin found himself in the town's main shopping area with narrow streets crammed with handsome red brick and Tudor-style buildings with lashings of white render and black wood. There was much about Western civilisation that confused, and made him angry, but walking through the peaceful town, seeing people relaxed and going about their daily business quietly, was almost surreal to him. It left him feeling bemused and oddly embarrassed.

Pushing the conflicting thoughts in his mind aside, he exchanged five hundred euros for pounds in a post office, then without stopping for rest he set about figuring out his travel route.

It turned out the town had good travel connections, and its station was a direct link to central London. By midday he'd travelled right through the capital city on a combination of train and Tube and he was walking through the dilapidated streets of Tottenham, past boarded-up shops and crumbling townhouses. Quite a contrast to Sevenoaks, though oddly it was more familiar and more suited to his mood.

He thought he'd remember the area, the streets at least, but nothing felt or looked or smelled the same as how he remembered it. Had the world moved on that much in the sixteen years since he'd left this place, or had his memories simply morphed and faded?

The streets he walked down, although typically English, typically London, reminded him somehow of the place he'd left behind in France. In Tottenham the area was both poor and culturally diverse, clearly evidenced by the vast array of shops and different cuisines of cafes and restaurants – both open and closed down – and also the appearance of the pedestrians milling about the place. Even though many people on the streets looked at him suspiciously, he knew that was the way these people looked at the world. There was such a variety of colours of skin and shapes of faces, of language and clothing, that in London Aydin knew he was just another face, nothing unusual or distinctive about him at all.

Yet he still sensed watchful eyes on him. He had to be prepared for the worst.

First things first, though. He'd not eaten in hours, so he took the chance to stop at a cafe run by a family of Turks. The inside of the place had a sweet cumin-tinged scent. It was a pleasant and familiar smell, yet it grated with Aydin because it somehow reminded him of his father. Before eating he used the toilet and did his best to clean the grime off his face and the blood from his hands and clothes. He had enough cash to buy new clothes but he wouldn't do that yet, not until absolutely necessary. He didn't know how long he'd be running and needed to conserve resources as long as he could.

By the time he left the cafe the thumping of his heart in his chest was growing faster, the whoosh of blood in his ears getting louder. Nervousness was a state rarely experienced in his adult life, not after what he'd been put through, yet the simple first task ahead had him both anxious and terrified.

He turned off a small shopping street and as he looked down the residential road ahead, a rush of memories hit him and he wobbled, his legs feeling like they might cave in. Off to his left was the sparse recreation ground. A plain strip of grass with one corner taken over by a small children's playground. Swings, slide, seesaw. He heard the sounds of memories in his head. Giggling, shouting, crying. The oomphs as footballs were booted about the place. The clicking of oiled chains whizzing round the cogs of pedal bikes. Sounds of children being children. They were almost exclusively happy memories, yet they were irrevocably tarnished.

In contrast to the grimy buildings surrounding the play area, all the equipment looked new. Not how he remembered it at all, yet the strength of the memories of being there – the happiness of them – was still real and vivid as he stared.

Across the road sat the four-storey red brick row of apartments: a step up from the 1960s concrete monolith towers that dominated much of the London skyline, but no doubt still some of the cheapest accommodation available in the vast city. He was only three years old when he and his family had first moved there, and the apartment had seemed new, luxurious even. Looking at it now he felt immense sadness that the whole street had been left to slide downward so severely. Many of the windows were boarded up. Front yards were filled with rubbish and unusable cars and discarded broken and soiled and mouldy furniture. Unreadable graffiti covered front walls.

He walked right past 12c and kept on going. Net curtains filled the windows so he couldn't see inside, but he noticed a light on in the front room. He headed further down the street and then turned into the recreation ground through an open gate.

He doubled back and walked across the grass. He found a bench, close to the children's play area, and sat and looked back to the road. Beside and behind him toddlers were screeching happily while mothers with their laden strollers chattered. The sounds of innocence and joy were quite alien to him and after a short while it made him feel uneasy.

Two young ladies pushing prams walked past in front of him and they both glared as though they could sense his awkwardness, only making him feel further out of place.

He didn't move – he just sat there, lost in his own world, staring across the grass to the door of 12c. Finally, the door edged open. When the doddery figure appeared in the doorway it was as if his heart had lost its rhythm. He could barely breathe as the woman emerged, a headscarf covering her hair and neck, but face perfectly clear. Even at that distance he knew it was his mother.

He was part ashamed and part saddened to see her like that. To see that she still lived in that place. That neither he, nor his sister nor his father had helped her to prosper.

Gritting his teeth, angered with all three of them, even his dead sister, he watched as his ragged mother closed the door then hobbled along, back hunched, head down, to the stairwell. Out on the street she moved off to the right. Aydin watched her until she was out of sight. Then he got up from the bench, and headed for his childhood home.

TEN

Aleppo, Syria

A strong gust of wind smacked Rachel Cox in the face, battering her with tiny specks of sand that made her cheeks sting. She battled against the wind as she walked along the alley, the tall stone buildings on either side of her concentrating the force of the air flowing through. The height of the buildings meant there was no sunlight in the alley, and Cox felt the skin on her neck and her arms goose-pimple, sending a shiver right through her.

She picked up her pace and seconds later took the left turn onto a wider street lined by bombarded apartment blocks. She'd known the city, the area, before the civil war. Not long ago the street she was walking down had well-maintained, wide pavements, ornate streetlights, trendy shops and cafes. Now there was no distinguishing the pavement from the road at all; it was just one continuous mess of rubble and stone and broken slabs as far as the eye could see. As for the buildings . . . it was a mystery how they were still standing. Yet somehow many remained inhabited.

Cox took another turn and the contrast couldn't have been greater. Although the signs of violence and war were still clear – bullet holes in walls, buildings missing large chunks of their structure, and that persistent smell of burning fuel from fires and bombs – there was life here. People on foot and on mopeds and in cars moved about on their daily business. There were plain-looking shops and stalls and cafes. Not exactly the old Aleppo, but a semblance of community and of desperate people trying to make the best of a terrible situation.

The breeze, away from the wind tunnel, was gentler, the sun was shining and Cox enjoyed the warmth it provided as she walked. She soon arrived at a small coffee shop on the corner of what used to be a bustling crossroads. There was only one other patron outside and she found a table as far away from him as she could. She wiped the sandy dust off one of the two chairs there and sat down. She checked her watch. Two minutes early.

Less than a minute later she spotted Subhi striding along the street towards her. In his late twenties, Subhi was tall with olive skin, thick stubble, flowing dark hair. To Cox he looked more Italian than Syrian and she could tell he knew he was handsome by the way he strutted and the smart clothes he dressed in, topped off with shining aviator sunglasses. Handsome, but not Cox's type, despite a previous attempt by him to take their acquaintance to another level. She'd seen first-hand in others how workplace relationships in the field of intelligence were nothing short of massive volcanoes waiting to erupt and destroy everything in their path with their white-hot excrement.

She hadn't explained the situation to Subhi quite like that. The fact was, she was happy to string him along if it furthered her position.

Subhi took the seat next to her and, arms and legs spread, slouched back in his chair nonchalantly to look out onto the world, like an A-list film star might.

'Have you ordered?' Subhi said in English. Cox could speak both Arabic and Persian fluently, but she regularly spoke

English when out and about. Despite her conservative attire – relatively speaking – and her wearing a headscarf, there was nothing she could do to hide her pale features and the line of freckles across her nose that marked her out as a Westerner. That was fine, though. Her cover in Syria was as an Irish news reporter and with the lanyard around her neck identifying her as such, there was nothing untoward about her being there or her sitting out in the sun drinking coffee and speaking English to a man who may or may not be a local.

'Yeah, I ordered. Just coffee for me,' Cox said.

'The fattoush here is excellent.'

'I know. You tell me that every time.'

'One day you might cave in and eat with me.'

Cox said nothing to that and was angered by his need to talk so causally, under the circumstances. She was more concerned with the death of her informant – a friend too – than entertaining his lame attempt at flirting. He hadn't known Nilay personally, but he knew of her, because Cox had asked him to keep an eye and an ear out, and to pass any intel back if it looked like she was in trouble. Fat lot of good that had done, in the end.

Still, Subhi remained a key asset for Cox in the city. She'd been in Aleppo for months, her trail of the Thirteen bringing her there just as it had Nilay. For more than two years Cox had been working on uncovering the various training camps used by ISIS and their affiliates across the Arabian Peninsula, where young boys from various walks of life were taken to be trained as jihadis. Cannon fodder, more usually. But then, just over twelve months ago, her work had taken a worrying turn. While working in Iraq, travelling to villages and towns that had been ravaged by war and seemingly never-ending conflict, she'd come across a family who'd lost their only son to Islamist militants some fifteen years previously, at a time when the Americans were busy strong-arming their way around the country.

The ageing and beleaguered mother claimed her son had been kidnapped aged eleven and taken to a secret training camp in neighbouring Iran. She had no real tangible evidence of who had taken him, or why, or even where exactly he'd gone to, but some years later she'd received a letter, in his handwriting.

The single piece of yellowed paper, frayed and blotchy from the number of times it had been read and the number of tears spilled on it, told a horror story through a young boy's eyes of a training camp like none Cox had heard of before. A group of fifteen boys imprisoned in the most harsh and extreme environment. Not just being force-fed violent religious doctrine, and trained to fight with guns and knives and bombs like so many others, but they were being very strategically educated in all manners of science and engineering too. Cox had sensed even back then the potential significance of what she'd uncovered. A bunch of super-smart and highly trained warriors.

The mother of the boy had no idea how the son had managed to smuggle a letter out of the facility where they were kept, but a few months later she'd had an even more agonising delivery. His severed hands, and a picture of his dismembered and decapitated corpse. Punishment for him having broken the rules by communicating with the outside world.

Since that visit, Cox had made it her mission to uncover the truth behind the site. She'd travelled through Iraq, Iran, Afghanistan in search of answers. She'd found some. Other stories of boys being taken, stories of a place known as the Farm. She'd never doubted its notoriety, people talked about it in hushed tones far and wide, but it had taken her a long time to convince her bosses that the place really existed, and that the boys who'd trained there were likely to pose a significant threat when they were unleashed on the world.

Cox firmly believed that remained the case. Her intelligence had led to her identifying more than half of the boys that were believed to have made up the thirteen who'd trained at and survived the facility, though she had no active intelligence on where they now were.

The trail, though, had brought her to Syria, where she'd met Nilay. Her brother was possibly one of those thirteen boys. At least he *had* been a boy. Now he was a man, and very possibly a potent weapon for the terrorist organisation.

The waiter came over with Cox's espresso and she snapped out of her thoughts. Subhi ordered himself a coffee too.

'What have you found?' she asked when the man disappeared inside.

'It's definitely her. I was at the morgue this morning.'

Cox put a hand to her head but quickly pulled herself together. She couldn't deny that she was feeling emotional about the young woman's death, but she had to think about the situation objectively. This was her operation, she had to keep going.

'They're still trying to trace someone to formally identify her,' Subhi said.

'What do you think?'

'You mean the bomb?'

'It can't be a coincidence that she was there.'

Subhi just shrugged.

'Did she have anything with her?' Cox asked.

Subhi's eyes narrowed. 'Just a phone and her purse.'

'You saw those?'

'Yes. The phone is destroyed. It's just a lump of melted plastic and metal. The purse was badly burned too. Some pieces of credit cards, notes, but nothing else.'

Cox looked away and across the street, her mind thinking through Subhi's words. Did she really trust his answer?

'Were you expecting her to be carrying something else?' Subhi said as the waiter came back out with his coffee.

'No,' she said when the man was once again out of earshot. 'But I do need to get into her apartment. Have the police searched it yet?'

'Yes. They had to, to look for evidence of who she was and who to contact about her death.'

'Have you been there too?'

'Yes.'

'And?'

'And nothing. It's just an apartment that looks like a young woman lived there. I know she was helping you, but the truth is she's just a charity worker.'

Though the way Subhi said it made it sound as though he wasn't quite sure about that, that he realised there was much more to Nilay than her job, which had been little more than a convenient front.

'Did the police recover anything?' Cox asked.

'Not that I know of.'

He gave her that look again.

'Are the police still there?' she asked.

'No. There's no need for them to be. She's not a suspect in anything and it's not a crime scene.'

'Okay. Then I'm going there now.'

'Now?'

'I don't have time to sit around getting a sun tan.'

'But it might suit you.'

Cox wasn't quite sure how to take that, and the awkward look on Subhi's face suggested he knew his quip hadn't worked.

'I'll come with you,' he said. 'In case you hit any problems with the locals.'

By locals she knew he meant either police or possibly even a roaming militia.

'I know how to deal with the locals,' she said.

'I'm sure you do, but I'm coming anyway.'

She wanted to say no. There was a very good reason why she didn't want him rummaging around Nilay's apartment with her, but she also didn't want to make him overly suspicious by saying no.

'Fine,' she said.

Subhi smiled and threw some coins on the table for the coffees as they left.

ELEVEN

It took them thirty minutes to navigate through the largely destroyed city streets to where Nilay Torkal had lived for the last three months. Nilay was a university graduate from London – twenty-three years old – who'd come to Aleppo working for a not-for-profit called Believe. And her work with that charity really was genuine, it was no bullshit cover story. Having attended the London School of Economics, Nilay had given up the chance of a glittering graduate position back in England to help those less fortunate than her. She had quite the hidden agenda for doing so, but she wasn't a paid intelligence agent like Cox. Nilay Torkal's ulterior motivation for heading to Aleppo had been much more personal than that.

When they reached the heavily weathered wooden door to the apartment building, Subhi stepped forward in front.

'Let me go first,' he said. 'Just in case.'

Cox said nothing. She wasn't sure if he was just playing a power trip on her, given his relative position with the locals, or if he was genuinely being chivalrous by wanting to put himself in the firing line for her should there be an unlikely threat inside.

Subhi turned the handle and pushed the door open, its rusted hinges squeaking and the frame creaking as he did so.

'Good security,' Cox said, to no response.

They walked up the dark and dusty stone staircase to the second floor where there were doors to four apartments. Cox had been there several times before, and her eyes were already on Nilay's front door as she came up the last few stairs.

'Is that how you left it?' Cox said, spotting that the door was ajar.

'No. It's not,' Subhi said, reaching behind him and drawing a Beretta pistol from the waistband of his khaki trousers. Cox wasn't carrying today. She had a gun and some magazines that had been provided when she'd first arrived at the current safe house, but she'd not yet had to use the weapon, or even felt the need to carry it around regularly. The day that happened was the day something had gone badly wrong with her undercover mission, as far as she was concerned.

Badly wrong? she thought. *Well what the hell do you call the murder of one of your lead informants?*

She caught her breath for a second. Subhi turned round. She gave him a plain look and he turned back to the apartment and used the tip of the Beretta's barrel to inch the door further open.

Nilay's apartment was what in modern terms was called a studio. A simple open-plan space with a small en suite off it. Cox would more readily have called it a large cupboard. The home was modest to say the least, the furniture cheap and functional.

'Shit,' Cox said, when she saw the state of the place inside.

It was clear even from the glimpse she had standing in the doorway that the apartment had been ransacked.

'I'm guessing that's not the police's handiwork,' she said.

Subhi didn't answer. Just moved further into the apartment, whipping his gun this way and that until he seemed satisfied that no one was hiding in there ready to take potshots at them.

When it was obvious the coast was clear, Cox moved in and shut the door behind her.

'Any ideas?' Subhi asked.

'As to who or to why?' Cox said.

'Both.'

'Yes.'

'Are you going to tell me?'

'No.'

'You really trust me that little?'

Cox didn't answer that. 'Why don't you go speak to the neighbours. They may have seen someone. It may even have been your own people who did this.'

'I think what you're trying to say is, *Subhi, please leave me alone so I can retrieve what I hope the ransackers didn't find.*'

'You know me too well.'

Subhi didn't move. Just stood there, gun in hand, looking at her. After a few seconds passed an eeriness crept through her. She glanced down and noticed his knuckles were white from holding the Beretta's grip so tightly. What was going through his mind?

Perhaps today really was the day she should have brought the damn gun.

'Please?' she said, her mind now swimming with different possibilities – mostly horrible – about how the situation could go south. She'd always felt she could trust Subhi, but really, few people living in such constant danger like he was were incorruptible. If the right people put the right pressure on him . . .

'Okay,' Subhi said. 'Seeing as you asked so nicely.'

Cox stepped to the side as Subhi moved past her. He pulled the apartment door to on his way out. Cox left it like that and headed straight for the en suite. She turned on the light and locked the door behind her. She looked at herself in the

68

mirror for just a moment, not really liking the reflection she saw. And it wasn't just because of the green contact lenses that hid her natural blue. There was so much about the woman she saw that wasn't *her*, that she didn't like. All the lying . . . however good-intentioned, after a while there was simply no way to stop it taking its toll.

Cox moved across to the shower cubicle, opened the door and got down onto her hands and knees. She rolled up the sleeve of her blouse on her right arm then pulled off the plastic cover for the shower waste. Next she picked out the inner container that looked like a small cup and acted as a trap for hair and other debris. It was full of gunk and residue and the unpleasant stench of the slime stuck in her nose. She pushed the sensation aside and stuck her hand down the drain, feeling around inside. She found the clean circular hole for the waste pipe and moved further to the left. The skin on the top of her hand scratched against the rough surface of the holed-out section and she winced in pain. She wormed her arm further in, past the elbow, as far as she could reach. Her fingers were extended out, grasping.

There was nothing there . . .

But surely whoever had trashed the apartment wouldn't have looked here?

Unless . . . they already knew what they were looking for?

Had Nilay told someone?

Cox thought again about Subhi. She held so many secrets from him. What about him with her?

She heard the front door creaking open. Footsteps. She realised her heart was drumming in her chest. She shut her eyes and pushed her arm further in, ignoring the pain in her upper arm.

She got it! She grabbed hold of the plastic and pulled.

There was a tap on the door.

'Hey, Rachel. Everything okay in there?'

'Fine,' she said, her voice sounding strained as she pulled her arm and hand free from the drain.

She stared at the plastic bag in her grasp. At the papers inside. The thumb drive. She looked at her arm. There were red marks and scratches all the way up it. The skin on the top of her hand was torn, there was a line of bright red blood about an inch long where the rough edges had gouged a section of skin. She cursed quietly, then replaced the shower parts. She flushed the toilet then went to the sink and washed her arm clean, removing the blood and hoping the bleeding would stop. She washed the grime off the bag then dried both that and her arm. She pushed the plastic bag into her handbag, then rolled down the sleeve of her blouse, leaving the cuff button undone so the fabric hung over her hand, covering the worst of the scratches.

Another knock on the door.

'Seriously, are you okay in there?'

She moved over and unlocked then opened the door. Subhi was there, leaning against the frame.

'Too much hummus last night I think. It's gone right through me.'

She could tell Subhi didn't buy it, but he didn't say anything. She noticed he'd put his gun away. That had to be a good sign at least.

'You find anything?' she asked.

'No one in,' he said. 'So come on, what are we doing here?'

'Looking for why Nilay was killed.'

'To do that you might need to tell me what the deal was between you two.'

'Let's cross that bridge when we get to it. Do you want to help me search this place or not?'

Subhi raised his eyebrows, then peeled away from the door. 'You're the boss,' he said. She didn't appreciate the tone, but wasn't going to rise to it. Not now. She had what she needed in her bag. She just wanted to get away and get it safe as quickly as she could.

Cox moved through the open space, picking up clothes and broken ornaments and furniture. Subhi did the same, though she felt his eyes on her the whole time.

'There's a chance she really was just an innocent victim of that blast,' he said.

'I know. Doesn't feel like that though, does it?'

He just shrugged at that.

After less than five minutes Cox decided she'd had enough. There was absolutely nothing left in the apartment of any worth. She wondered again exactly what the police and the ransackers had already taken.

'Did you say the police found a computer? An iPad, anything like that?'

'I don't know,' Subhi said. 'But if there was anything here like that, they'll have it.'

'And can you get it for me?'

Subhi pursed his lips.

'You can say no if it's too hard. But it would be really helpful for me.'

'Let me see what I can do. So we're done here?'

'Unless you've got any brainwaves.'

Two minutes later they were walking out of the building into the bright midday sunshine. They'd made it all of five yards from the building before Subhi put his hand onto Cox's shoulder to stop her. She turned to face him. He looked pensive, as though there was something on his mind that he wanted to say but knew it wasn't the best idea.

She guessed what that might be, and she knew he was justified in thinking that way. Their relationship was entirely one way. He helped her, again and again, and he never asked for anything in return. Yet even now, stuck in the middle of this huge mess, she still held back so much from him. She knew that couldn't work out forever, even though he *did* owe her, after what she'd done for his family. She was increasingly realising though that he was thinking his debt was now repaid, and really she had to expect that to be the case sooner or later.

'How long have we known each other?' Subhi said.

'Months.'

He let out a long exhale.

'I feel like you're about to propose to me or something,' Cox said, giving him a wide smile that was a stark contrast to how she was feeling inside.

'You must know I've always—'

There was a dull thwack and Subhi froze mid-sentence, and Cox jerked as she felt a spray of liquid on her cheek. She saw the small hole punched into Subhi's face, just under his left eye. A split second later there was a distant crack that echoed across the city's battered buildings, like the sound of a whip.

Subhi's lifeless body plummeted.

TWELVE

Cox was running before her brain had even fully processed what she'd witnessed. There was another thwack as a bullet smacked into the road next to her, followed a split second later by the same crack in the distance. Cox kept on sprinting across the street, towards cover of parked cars and the buildings opposite, clutching her handbag as she ran, her rational brain finally catching up with her instincts.

A sniper. North of where they'd come out of the building. Cox's brain whirred as she tried to recall her training all those years ago. How the distance could be calculated by the delayed sound of the muzzle blast. She couldn't remember. She was too panicked. She knew, at least, that with her hugging the edge of the building on the other side of the road that she was in cover from the shooter.

Unless there were more of them.

She quickly glanced back across the road to where Subhi's body lay in a crumpled heap. The small hole in his face oozed dark blood and his wide-open glassy eyes were staring right back at her. She realised her hands and legs were trembling.

She snapped herself into focus. There was no time for frailty. This was her job. She could deal with this. She jogged away down the road, then after a few strides slowed into a quick march. She didn't want to draw attention to herself. She had no clue who had just pulled the trigger to take out Subhi. Had he even been the target, or was it her?

Either way she had to assume she wasn't safe. Yesterday there'd been a faint question in her mind that maybe Nilay really was just an unlucky civilian caught up in a random suicide blast. Cox saw absolutely no chance of that now. In fact, she was already thinking the worst; that it was *her* cover that had somehow been blown. That she had caused the deaths of both Nilay and Subhi.

There was no going back from that. Everyone she saw now was a potential threat. She reached into her bag and pulled out her phone as her eyes darted left and right in front of her. Her chest heaving with deep breaths – adrenaline more than anything – she ducked into the arched entrance of a derelict office building and typed out a text message.

Holiday needed.

A simple SOS code. She entered the eleven-digit number that would send the message to a switchboard at Vauxhall Cross, who would route the request to both Flannigan and whichever extraction team was closest to her.

She held her finger over the send button.

No, she couldn't do that. Not so soon. She couldn't just run away from the situation without any knowledge of what had gone wrong and who was after her. First things first, though; she had to get to the safe house.

'Pull yourself together,' she told herself angrily.

Feeling a bubbling anger she deleted the message then put the phone away and looked over the street. No one else was in sight. Cox peeled away from the building and walked with purpose, retracing her steps from earlier. In front of her a man and a woman turned onto the street, heading in Cox's direction. The man, with a salt-and-pepper beard, looked to be in his forties and wore an ankle-length thawb. The woman, in a long deep blue dress, with a plain hijab around her head and neck, was a similar age. There was nothing at all unusual or alerting about them. They just looked like an everyday couple. No sign of menace or malice. Yet Cox knew how deceiving looks could be, and she was on edge.

The man locked eyes with Cox when they were ten yards away. His eyes narrowed. Cox looked away, thought about crossing the road, but then over the other side she spotted two casually dressed men walking purposefully – locals, in their twenties. Inwardly she cursed herself for not bringing the gun with her. Or even for trying to retrieve Subhi's. He certainly didn't need it now.

Perhaps she should just double back and get it?

When Cox was two yards from the couple the man reached behind him. Cox braced herself. Yes, she was scared, however strong she wanted to be, out in this war zone alone, there was absolutely no denying that, but it was largely because she didn't know what was happening. She was certainly ready to fight back if she had to, though. At such close quarters she knew she was easily capable of disarming this man if he had a knife or a gun.

A suicide bomb? Well, that would be a different story but why would anyone send a suicide bombing couple after just her?

Cox's phone buzzed in her hand and at the sound the man shifted slightly in his step and his wife took a sharp inhale of breath.

The man's hand came back into view. Empty.

The couple walked on past. Without feeling any relief, Cox kept going too. She looked back after a few seconds but the twosome were still casually walking away. The men on the other side of the road were gone too – they must have turned down a side street.

'For God's sake,' Cox muttered under her breath.

Since when had she been such a bag of nerves anyway? She looked down at her phone. The text message was from an unnamed number but Cox recognised it as coming from Flannigan.

Update for you. Can you white line?

Cox sighed and did her best to push away the negative thoughts crashing through her mind. She needed the laptop to use a white line because part of the encryption was in the laptop itself. Her phone, a standard prepaid handset she'd bought just two days ago – she changed them weekly – had no such encryption software, though the Internet line would still be secure.

The safe house was only twenty minutes' walk from where she was, but she couldn't just head directly there any more. Someone was after her, and there was a good chance they had a tail on her – not that she'd spotted anyone so far. As much as she didn't like the idea of being out in the open any longer than necessary she would take a circuitous route through the city to the safe house, sticking to populated areas as much as she could, but also snaking through the twisting old city streets and alleys where safe to do so to try to lose anyone who was following in the shadows.

She could wait to speak to Flannigan until she was back at the safe house, but that could be two hours away. Despite the deadly situation she was caught up in, she wanted that update now. Had Flannigan had a change of heart about Trapeze?

I can blue line. Now?

She sent the message then took a right turn, phone still held out waiting for a response. She headed back along the street where she'd so recently had coffee with Subhi. She felt a lump in her throat at the thought. Had anyone even found

76

his body yet? What would the police's reaction be? Would Cox be sought as a witness or a suspect?

She imagined the reaction of Subhi's mother and grandma in Egypt – the only family he had left. Would they ever even find out about the fate of their boy?

Cox shook the thoughts away. She took another turn and spied a Lebanese cafe further along the road whose outside area consisted of a blue plastic tarpaulin erected over wooden poles. The shop front had no windows, just boards and an open doorway. Cox had been before. As with every place she frequented, she'd long ago scoped out entrances and exits. She knew there was an unlocked back door that led onto an alley behind, just yards away from another busy cross street. Unless there was a whole assault team after her, the cafe was a place she felt comfortable stopping at for a few minutes to speak to Flannigan, but just as importantly to watch the street outside for signs of anyone following her.

Cox headed inside, smiled and greeted the sole worker and took a seat in the far back corner where she had a decent view up the street she'd come from.

The inside of the cafe reminded Cox of scenes from a post-apocalyptic movie. It was clear the cafe had once been a trendy establishment with its long glass-fronted cake counter, the grand coffee machines behind it, the ornate wood-panelled walls and light fittings. But it quite literally looked like a bomb had dropped inside. There were cracks in the glass counter, in mirrors on the walls. Only one of the five hanging light fixtures was working. The seat-backs and cushions on benches were ripped and torn. A few tables had no chairs at all by them. The tiled floor had whole sections missing, filled with dirt. And, like much of the city, that thick dust from the relentless bombardment, a combination of sand and grit and pulverised stone, was everywhere.

Cox felt her stomach growl. She humphed. How much she'd love to sit back and enjoy one of the proprietor's renowned baklavas. She could smell the sweet, honeyed desserts from where she was sitting. She ordered only a coffee. Her phone buzzed again.

Needs to be white. Please advise.

Cox tutted and sent a quick response. Will let you know.

She put the phone on the table and peered outside. People were moving about their business and for a couple of minutes no one caught Cox's eye. The waiter brought her the coffee and she took a sip of the treacly liquid. Outside, the street was quieter. Just the natural ebb and flow of people?

No. This was something else. Where moments before people had milled and roamed back and forth, all of a sudden there wasn't a soul in sight out there. Cox looked up to the waiter. He was standing by the counter, drying a coffee cup with a tea towel, but his eyes were on the exit. From his position he had a view further up the street than Cox did. He knew what was coming. He glanced over to Cox. No give on his face except for the nervousness in his eyes.

Cox jumped up from the table, grabbed her phone and her handbag and darted for the back entrance. The waiter shouted out to her. '*Stop!*' Cox didn't. Out on the street she heard shouting too, though she didn't bother to turn round to look who was shouting or why. Instead, she just raced through the corridor at the back of the cafe, past the storeroom and toilets and flung open the door at the back . . .

She bundled straight into the man standing there. He was tall and lean with dark skin and darker eyes. Black hair and stubbly beard. He was shocked by Cox's rapid exit. Perhaps that was the only thing that saved her. It only took her a second to realise he had a gun in his hand. She grabbed hold

78

of his wrist to stop him turning the weapon towards her, but she could tell straight away she didn't have the strength to hold him off.

He thumped his free hand into her kidney and Cox grimaced in pain. The man arced his head forward to butt her, but Cox craned her neck to the side, resulting in only a glancing blow that split the skin above her eye.

She was more concerned about that gun, though. She'd only be able to hold on for a few more seconds before the weapon was in firing line.

Cox took a slight side-step then lifted her heel and drove it down against the side of the man's knee. The leg buckled, causing the man to stumble and Cox pulled back her arm and crashed her elbow into his jaw.

Those two blows alone were probably good enough to give her space to make a run for it, but Cox wanted to make damn sure. With him already falling, Cox grabbed his head and pulled down, hauling her knee up at the same time. There was a sickly crunch as bone connected with cartilage and the man flopped to the ground. The gun clattered away. Cox had her eye on it, but then heard shouting from beyond the still-open back door.

Then more gunfire.

She dove for the ground, her arms and knees scraping across the slabs. She grabbed the gun, turned and fired three shots back to the door. Simple warning shots because she had no target. Without waiting for a response, she jumped to her feet and sprinted the few yards to the end of the alley, then turned onto the main road. She was glad to see pedestrians there, but knew she was far from in the clear. She heard shouting behind her again, but didn't dare look to see how many people were chasing or how far behind they were – she simply focused on what was ahead as she hurtled along.

Twenty yards in front a small moped with a delivery box was parked next to a makeshift grocery stall. Cox could see the young driver, helmet on his head, on his feet talking to the stall owner.

Cox lifted the gun.

'*Give me the keys!*' she shouted in Arabic.

Both men, together with just about every other person in sight, suddenly stopped what they were doing and turned and stared.

'*The keys!*' Cox screamed.

A gunshot boomed behind her. People screamed. Cox ducked, but didn't stop running. She saw the moped driver crumple to the ground. The key fell from his hand. Another gunshot. Cox was sure she felt the bullet whizz past her ear. She half-turned and fired four shots of her own, again no target in sight, simply trying to put off her attackers. It did the trick.

She bent down to scoop up the key and jumped onto the moped. Bizarrely, what stuck in her head in that moment wasn't the thought of the chasing pack, but her annoyance that the stall owner, cowering behind his vegetables, was cursing her and asking Allah to punish her, like she was the one in the wrong.

Cox turned the key and pulled the throttle and the squeaky machine pulled away. Beyond the stall she quickly turned into an alley to give herself breathing space from the shooters behind. She pulled the throttle harder, the front wheel almost coming off the ground. It certainly would have done if the engine had a bit more grunt.

Only then did she risk a look behind her. The entrance to the alley, already twenty yards away, was clear. She turned her focus back to the front. All clear there too. She took a series of quick turns, heading into the labyrinth of the old town. Streets she knew as well as anyone.

After five minutes, sure there was no one in front or behind, she ditched the moped out of sight behind some industrial bins, then, after wiping the blood from her face with her hijab, quickly walked onto a busy market street, less than half a mile from the safe house.

Losing herself in the crowds, she took out her phone and re-typed her earlier message.

Holiday needed.

This time she hit the send button without hesitation. Less than thirty seconds later the phone buzzed and she looked down at the response.

Three hours. Stay safe.

She could only hope and pray for the chance to hold out that long.

THIRTEEN

The fifteen boys were sitting on the bare concrete floor in three neat rows of five. The imam, brown thawb and flowing camel-hair bisht, was sitting on the edge of the desk in front of them in the mostly bare room. There was little furniture; it was nothing like what Aydin had become used to in classrooms back in London. Not all the rooms at the Farm were like this one. Each was functional. Designed for a specific purpose. The purpose of this room was to learn about the Quran. Paraphernalia and propaganda and quotes from the sacred text lined the walls, though all of the boys had their eyes firmly fixed on the imam as he talked.

All of the boys except Aydin, who busily flicked through the thick book in his hands, a frown on this face.

'. . . And slay them wherever ye find them,' the imam continued, 'and drive them out of the places whence they drove you out, for persecution is worse than slaughter . . . and fight them until fitnah is no more, and religion is for Allah . . .'

Aydin, eyes still glued to the text in front of him, his frown deepening, raised his hand in the air. It took him a few seconds to realise the whole room had gone deathly silent. When he looked up he saw all the other boys were staring at him. Some of their faces were accusing, others looked more astonished. Aydin

82

locked eyes with the imam, who looked annoyed at having been disturbed, but he simply raised his eyebrows and said, 'Yes, boy?'

'But isn't the context of the passage, of all the Sword verses, that the Muslims were under attack? That this was a defensive war and they were being told to fight the aggressors. This was an instruction at a specific point in time. Not just an everlasting statement to every Muslim to kill in the name of Allah.'

The imam said nothing to that, just stared at Aydin for a few seconds and the boy felt himself begin to shrink. He'd asked the question not as a challenge of the imam, but out of genuine curiosity. The truth was he was enthralled by the texts, not just the Quran, but all of the other books that taught them about the history of their people and the religion. His question was borne of real intrigue and the desire to understand, though he sensed it was not welcome.

Yet before his brain could stop him, he opened his mouth again.

'The way I saw it, was that if a leader today told his soldiers to bombard the Syrians in Damascus, it wouldn't mean that the soldiers would have to bombard every Syrian for eternity, would it? Isn't what we're reading here just a specific instruction at one point in time, in one place, to one group of people?'

'Dear boy,' the imam said, his tone at odds with his words, 'I fear it is you who may be taking this out of context. Yes, this one passage was written in relation to a particular cause. But there are many, many more, and the cause is one that is abundantly relevant today.'

'Which cause?'

'The persecution of our people. We are in a defensive war now, just as our people were then, and these same instructions absolutely apply just as much.'

Aydin wasn't entirely appeased by that, but he could tell both from the reaction of the imam and the groans and shifts of his brothers that there was no sense in pushing the point further.

'Let me ask you this,' the imam said. 'Do you think it acceptable that the non-believers can drop their bombs, shoot us with

83

their guns, divide and destroy our countries and our cities and families, and injure and kill our women and children?'

'Of course not, but—'

'Then you must see these passages for what they are. These are instructions for what we must *do. Do you understand?'*

Aydin paused for a second. 'Yes,' he said, unconvincingly.

Moments later there was a crash as the door behind the boys opened. Aydin and half a dozen of the other boys whipped their heads round to see the stocky form of the Teacher entering the room. As usual he had an angry snarl on his face that made all of the boys straighten up and hold their breaths.

The Teacher strode up to the imam.

'Okay, boys, I think that's enough for today,' the imam said before turning to the Teacher.

The Teacher bent down and whispered something into the imam's ear. The imam simply nodded a few times. Then when the Teacher had finished, the imam whispered back. He looked over to Aydin as he did so, then after a few seconds the Teacher too craned his neck so he was staring, coldly, at the young boy.

Aydin realised he was trembling.

'Please, back to your rooms now,' the imam said, and each of the boys got to their feet. 'Except for you,' he added, still staring over at Aydin.

Aydin gulped as the other boys traipsed out, some of them giving him sorry looks, one or two looking amused at his plight. When the last of the boys left, the room went silent. Aydin tried his best not to look the Teacher in the eye, though he felt the big man's hard glare burning into his mind.

No one said a word. After a few moments the Teacher loomed forward towards Aydin, baring his teeth like a wild dog. The young boy squeezed his eyes shut as tightly as he could, the only defence he could muster to save him from the monster.

FOURTEEN

London, England

Aydin wished he could fill his head with more positive memories, but as he walked out of the recreation ground and back along the road towards flat 12c it was those thoughts of the Farm and what he'd been through there, at his father's making, that echoed in his mind.

The multi-tool was already in his hand as he walked up the stairs and along the exposed corridor to the front door of 12c. He reached the heavily weathered, yellow door. It looked like it'd been that sickly colour for years, though last time he'd been there it was cherry red. The doors to all of the flats had similarly garish colours, a strange attempt to make the dwellings appear nicer, and perhaps the occupants happier than they really were.

First taking a quick glance along the corridor to check he was alone, Aydin used the torsion wrench on the multi-tool, and a hair clip he'd found on the street minutes earlier, to quickly release the simple barrel lock. He pushed open the door. For a brief second he wondered whether there was an alarm, but why would anyone around there bother? He was sure few people had anything worth stealing. The burglars all likely travelled the short distance to nearby more affluent suburbs for their nightly jaunts.

He shut the door behind him and took in the musty smell of the place. It wasn't a particularly pleasant smell, and he wasn't sure exactly where it came from. A combination of bleach and air freshener and damp, but also undeniably it was a smell that he associated with home. The sensation as the odour triggered deeply buried memories knocked his focus and for a few seconds it was like he'd been transported back in time. He could hear their voices. His little sister, squealing in delight as she charged around. His mother, her authoritative yet endlessly loving tone. He heard himself too, heard the innocence and wonder in his words, his endless questions about life and everything in it, mostly mundane, but occasionally profound. He heard the sound of the TV, could recall sitting in front of the screen; always too close, his mum would yell at him. He'd watch cartoons and other shows for hours, in stitches the whole time. *Tom and Jerry. Mr Bean.*

Then came the voice of his father. For many years so loving, Aydin remembered how it all changed so quickly. How his father came home one day and told his wife to stop wearing make-up, told her what she could and couldn't wear, that she wasn't allowed to see her friends any more without him. He told her God demanded it.

Remembering that brief time before he was taken from his mother was enough to wrench the more pleasant memories from Aydin's grasp.

He moved through the gloomy space. There were only four doors off the hallway. The first was what used to be his bedroom. He peered inside through the open door. He wasn't surprised to see it was completely different to how he remembered. There was no sign that it used to be a bedroom at all, the room now filled with almost senseless clutter. He'd thought perhaps Nilay had still been living there, but clearly that wasn't the case.

He walked further along, passing the bathroom which he noticed had been refurbished since he was last there, though it looked tired and scruffy still, no doubt because it was cheaply fitted with even cheaper fittings. Next he passed his parents' bedroom. It was neat and tidy in there and the smell of his mother filled his head, initiating a burning – a yearning perhaps – in his heart.

He spotted two picture frames by one side of the double bed. One was of Nilay as a teenager. She looked beautiful, her dark eyes dazzling, her black hair glistening, the softness of her unblemished skin evident even on photographic paper. The other picture was of Aydin and his mother, smiling faces, on one of their rare trips abroad, to visit family in Turkey. That trip, the first time he'd left the UK, remained one of the most wondrous experiences of his life.

Trying to hold on to the fond reminiscence, he moved to the end of the hall where the last doorway led onto the cramped everyday living space; kitchen, lounge, diner. Three spaces that together weren't much more than fifteen feet long, and narrower than that. It had never seemed small when he was little, though, and actually was way better than what he'd become used to after he was taken. Looking at it all these years later it seemed uncomfortably pokey, and he could sense just how poverty-stricken his mother remained, to have been stuck in such a rotting place for so long.

Despite the meagre size of the home and her obvious lack of wealth, the living space was lovingly decorated and crammed with traditional Turkish, Middle-Eastern and Persian art and ornaments, together with photos and knick-knacks that told the stories of the family, their history, and of their home country.

Again Aydin noticed not a single picture of his father anywhere in sight. There were one or two photos of Aydin, but most were of Nilay, the undoubted jewel in the family.

And rightly so. He moved over and picked up one of the pictures of her. A candid photo, taken in profile, set against a yellow sandy background. Wearing a silky hijab, a pair of large-framed sunglasses covering her eyes, her mouth was open in a broad smile, though it wasn't clear who or what she was smiling at.

He noticed a white van in the background, emblazoned with a company logo. His first instinct was that the picture was of her in Syria, where she was killed, working for the charity Believe. But when he looked more closely he saw the logo was actually of a security company, and the website address on the van ended in '.tr'. Turkey. He frowned and turned the frame over then slid away the clasps to remove the back cover. There, in his mother's handwriting, was the date and place of the picture. Istanbul, Turkey. The date was just three months ago.

'What were you doing there?' he said out loud to his dead sister.

As if in response there was a sound from out in the hallway. Not his sister's ghost, but a key turning the lock on the front door.

FIFTEEN

His mother was home. Aydin had come all this way because he *needed* to see her. But not like this. He moved over to the fire-exit door in the kitchen that led onto a metal staircase that connected all of the flats at the back. He turned the lock and opened the door and quietly shut it behind him, then quickly retreated down to street level. He moved across the yard and round to the road, and then headed away, his mind filled with disappointment at his behaviour.

Why hadn't he just stayed and seen her? Wouldn't she want to know that he was alive, that he was okay? Most likely she believed she'd lost everything – her husband, her daughter, her son. But she hadn't.

Although his mind was distracted as he walked away, his training was still there – part of his subconscious – and it wasn't long before he spotted them, fifty yards behind him. Two men. He only got a brief glimpse before they disappeared from sight but one of them was big and wide, the other smaller, perhaps a similar build to himself. Both were dressed casually, and although their faces were somewhat obscured by their hoodies, Aydin could see from the colour of their hands that their skin was not pale, but like his.

He despised what *they* had made him into, in so many different ways, yet he realised he should also be grateful for some of the skills he had. One of which was a sixth sense as to when he was being watched and followed. He barely even needed to think about it any more. He simply noticed people. He noticed everything and everyone around him, his brain automatically filtering the world he saw and putting everything and everyone into different categories. No threat, minimal threat. Red alert. The two men behind him fell somewhere between those last two categories. He had no doubt that they were tailing him, but he didn't yet know who they were. Possibly just local gangbangers wondering who the new face on their patch was, but it was equally likely they were undercover police or intelligence agents who had somehow tracked him from Dover. Or even the traffickers who he'd earlier attacked.

The most obvious possibility, however, was that the two men had been sent by his own brethren to end his sorry existence permanently.

Aydin was determined to find out which of those options was true, but there was no need to rush the situation. He needed to retain the upper hand, fight back on his own terms and in his own time and place of choosing. That's why he didn't just lead the two men into a deserted alley and attack them there and then. Instead he went for a walk. A long walk. For three hours he took winding routes through north London streets, never veering into territory that would allow them to spring an attack. He stopped for food and drink twice. He bought some replacement clothes from a charity shop; jeans, T-shirt, a hooded jacket that together cost less than twenty pounds. There was heat on him, and before long he anticipated he'd need the new clothes, so he decided it was better to be prepared than to wait too long. The clothes he was wearing were already smeared with blood, and he was only expecting that situation to worsen in the not-so-distant future.

As early evening approached the streets and the roads became busier and busier and finally were crammed with commuters on their way home from work. The crowds made the job of the watchers all the more difficult, but Aydin knew they were still out there. When the rush hour began to die down, he decided it was time to make the first move. He wanted to find out who the men were.

He worked his way around to the nearest Tube station, Wood Green, and walked quickly through the curved corner entrance that was flanked by two large ventilation towers. He headed straight for a machine and with the loose change in his pocket bought a single trip ticket – not that he was planning on actually stepping onto a train. Instead he moved across and out of sight of the main entrance and quickly stripped off his hoody and pulled on the blue one he'd bought earlier. He swapped his white trainers for the black ones in the bag as he hopped along, then placed the new maroon cap over his head. A light transformation, though hopefully one that would buy him a few seconds at least. Without breaking stride, he slung the backpack over his shoulder again and moved over to where he could see a help desk. The young woman behind the desk gave him a disinterested smile as he approached and he put his face up to the vent in the plastic screen to speak to her.

'I was told to come back after six,' Aydin said to her. 'I dropped my phone on the track this morning. Is it possible to get it now?'

'What was your name?'

'Emre Arslan,' he said, the name popping into his head seemingly from nowhere – a trick he'd learned long ago for thinking on the spot by using the familiar. The name was an amalgam of two different Turkish footballers

'Okay, just wait a second,' the woman said before spinning round on her chair and moving out of sight.

Aydin looked around him. No sign of the two men yet. But this needed to be quick. He was glad seconds later when the woman came back and indicated over to Aydin's right. A podgy middle-aged man in a bright orange jacket was heading straight for him. He didn't look particularly accommodating.

'What did you say your name was, mate?' the man said in a thick cockney accent.

'Emre Arslan.'

'Who did you speak to earlier?'

'Sorry, I didn't get a name.'

The man huffed. 'Come over to the control room, I'll see if we can figure this out.'

Aydin's eyes flicked over to the other side of the open space; he spotted the two men out of the corner of his eye and quickly averted his gaze, looking down and away. He followed the man the short distance to the plain-looking door and sighed in relief as they stepped inside and out of sight of the concourse.

Sure enough, they were in the control room, a small, windowless box room with one side taken over by a desk that had a clutter of CCTV monitors above and around it. This was exactly where Aydin wanted to be.

'Just give me a minute,' the man said, pulling his radio off his jacket and up to his face.

'Is there a problem?' Aydin asked.

'Well I'm not sure who you spoke to. I'll see if I can find out. The problem is I've not seen a phone down there at all today.'

'Someone's already taken it?' Aydin said, in such a way that made it clear he would be blaming the staff in the station if that was the case.

'Who knows.'

He turned away from Aydin and pressed on his radio and began a conversation with whoever was on the other end.

Aydin turned to the monitors, his eyes darting over them quickly until he found the right one. There they were. The men who'd been following him for hours now. They were still on the concourse, past the turnstiles. They'd paid for tickets but they were still contemplating what to do next now that their mark was out of sight. The angle of the CCTV camera meant he couldn't see their faces clearly and Aydin flicked his eyes over the other cameras to see if there was a better shot. There wasn't.

The man turned back round again.

'What did you say your name was again? Emre?

'Emre Arslan.'

'Got it. Thought you'd said Arsenal. Glad you didn't.'

Aydin smiled in acknowledgement of the quip and the man resumed his conversation. Aydin turned back to the screens. The men were splitting up, each of them heading towards a different platform. The next second he'd lost them both. His eyes darted back and forth, trying to find them again. He focused in on a screen showing one of the staircases leading down to the platform. He spotted one of the men. Now the angle of the camera showed the man's face clearly.

Aydin froze when he realised he was staring into the eyes of his brother. Hidashar. Number eleven.

SIXTEEN

'Sorry, mate, but no one seems to know anything about this.'

Aydin was back to thinking on his feet. Should he run or try to confront his brother and whoever his accomplice was? He even contemplated whether to cry foul to the man in the control room – shout out that the man on the CCTV screen was carrying a weapon. As soon as this guy saw the face his terrorist alarm bells would surely blare. There'd be waves of police hurtling for the station within seconds.

Yes, that would put Hidashar in one hell of a sticky situation, but it wouldn't get Aydin any answers. He needed answers.

'Seriously?' Aydin said, now sounding less amenable. 'I was here this morning, this is ridiculous.'

The guy didn't take too kindly to Aydin's change of tone. His face creased up and his cheeks flushed.

'Sorry, pal, but there's no phone down there, and no one here has spoken to you about this today. Are you sure you've got the right station?'

Aydin looked again at the screen. After roaming the platform and coming away empty-handed, Hidashar was now heading back up the stairs. Aydin made up his mind.

'Of course it was here! I pass through here every day to work.'

The man just shrugged. 'I'm sorry, I don't know what else to say. Perhaps you can show me the spot where you think it was? Sometimes items that are dropped onto the tracks just get swept away you know.'

'But it was someone here who told me to come back later in the day, because it was too busy this morning. So you're saying because of that I've now lost it for good. That's a six hundred pound iPhone!'

Another shrug. 'It was you who dropped it.'

Aydin saw that Hidashar had now regrouped with his friend and the two of them were heading back towards the turnstiles. It was time to go.

'Thanks for nothing,' Aydin said with just enough bitterness, then he turned and opened the control room door and stomped out.

Looking ahead beyond the turnstiles he could just see the back of Hidashar as he turned right on the street outside. Aydin followed at a safe distance behind, never getting to within fifty yards of the two men. He would confront them, but he needed to wait for a suitable location.

When darkness fell soon after, the two men were still ahead of him, and Aydin decided it was time to put an end to the charade. But it soon became apparent that his well-laid plan turned out to be not so well-laid. The problem with darkness was that it had both advantages and disadvantages for all. It was easier for stalkers to remain unseen, yet it was also easier for prey to escape into the shadows. Which was exactly what happened. Aydin realised he simply had no idea where they'd gone.

But had he lost them by accident, or had they known all along that Aydin was there?

With no sight of them, Aydin decided it wasn't worth the risk of continuing on ahead. He had no intention of walking into a trap. Instead, he turned on his heel and retraced his steps. It hadn't escaped his attention that for the last half a mile or so they'd been worming into the dark bowels of England's capital city. He wanted to get back to the more busy streets with their overhead bulbs as quickly as he could and figure out a plan from there. He was on unfamiliar territory, and although he still felt he knew the area well – at least he knew areas *like* it – he was anxious as to what would unfold.

As he passed by a pitch-black alley he shivered. He had the eerie feeling that there were still eyes on him. An unseen presence somewhere in the shadows all around.

This was it, he realised. But he wasn't running.

When he got to the head of the next alley, behind a row of mostly derelict shops, he turned and stopped behind an industrial bin. He was within striking distance of the edge of the alley, should the men make an appearance from there. He drew his gun, and held the barrel with both hands, pointed at chest height. He'd use the weapon if he had to, though his preference, if the men did appear, was to take them down without the need to fire shots. He didn't want the police on his case, and he didn't want to kill his brother without first getting some answers.

After five minutes with no hint of life other than the sound of his own shallow breaths and the calm pumping of blood in his ears, Aydin heard footsteps from out in the street. Soft footsteps. Just one set. He primed himself. But before he got sight of the person the footsteps belonged to, another set joined the mix – again from out in the street. The second set were louder, more deliberate. Aydin's brain worked through permutations of who was out there.

Then a sound behind him. A soft *thunk*. Something banging in the breeze perhaps. He had no choice but to look. No sooner had he turned his head than a long shadow loomed

96

in the corner of his eye. He swivelled back to the street and saw the legs of a man appearing in the head of the alley. The footsteps were soft because he was wearing trainers. He was tall, and young, casually dressed. It wasn't Hidashar, nor his accomplice. Not sensing Aydin's presence at all, the young man walked right past, not faltering in his step.

There was no sound of the second set of footsteps now. All was silent.

Until the sound from behind him came again. Closer this time. Aydin spun round, but kept himself pressed up against the metal bin. In the darkness he could see virtually nothing in front of him, but he sensed the movement, as though the gloom of the alley was coming to life, and he glided to his left, ducked and hauled himself forward. He crashed into the figure there. The man held Aydin's weight and for a few seconds they were both upright, grappling.

The gun was still in Aydin's hand. He swung it around and crashed it where he knew the man's head was. The guy's strength faltered and Aydin smacked him two more times before his grasp failed. As the man fell there was a whooshing sound and Aydin felt a sharp slice across his calf. He winced in pain and stepped away as the man's body thudded onto the ground.

Then an arm came around Aydin's neck from behind, squeezing hard and pulling him off his feet. The guy was big. Aydin knew it had to be his brother. The jerking motion caused him to drop the gun and it clattered away. His heels dragged across the ground as the hold was pulled tighter. He couldn't breathe, his windpipe crushed under the pressure of his attacker's muscled arm.

Hidashar had always been freakishly strong, and Aydin scrabbled to get his feet back onto firm ground, at the same time pulling on Hidahsar's arm to try and release the pressure on his neck. He had to find his feet, otherwise he had no chance of shaking Hidashar off.

Rather than thrashing, Aydin relaxed his body, and Hidashar seemed to take that as a sign that Aydin was either complying or dying. He let up just enough and Aydin planted his feet on the ground. Not a second later he moved quickly and stepped backward, snaking his right foot behind Hidashar. Then he pushed his body weight down and lurched back, making himself fall to the ground. His left foot was up in the air, momentum sending him backward. Hidashar was certainly stronger, taller and heavier than Aydin, but there was nothing he could do about simple physics. With Aydin's weight moving down and back, it was enough to send Hidashar's mass toppling over the outstretched leg. Then Hidashar had a simple choice. Stay holding onto Aydin's neck, and risk his skull smacking onto the tarmac below, or let go and cushion his fall.

He chose the more sensible option and freed Aydin's neck. They landed in a tangled heap on the ground but Aydin was quicker to manoeuvre into the dominant position. He grabbed the gun as he moved, twisting on top of Hidashar and pinning his arms. He drew the gun up and pushed the barrel against his brother's eyeball.

Then Aydin froze.

From where they were positioned, just a couple of yards into the alley, there was a thin beam of light creeping over. One side of Hidashar's face was lit up clearly. Aydin had expected some resolve in his brother, but what he hadn't expected was to see him smiling.

A sickly feeling washed right through him.

SEVENTEEN

Aydin was sitting with his bare back against the cold stone wall. He was still out of breath from the sparring. Sparring? Brawling was a better word for what they made the boys do. His body was covered in sweat, and he was beginning to feel the onset of a chill now that he was out of the sun and his body was resting in the cool interior. Across the bare room from him, Hidashar was sitting in an almost identical position. At two weeks short of sixteen years old he was already a man mountain. It was several years ago that Aydin had first met Hidashar. Even then, the way he remembered it was Hidashar being over six feet tall and heavily muscled, while Aydin was a puny nine-year-old less than five feet tall. But perhaps that wasn't the way it really was.

Hidashar too was covered in sweat, though as well as the obvious size mismatch between them, there was one other big difference in their appearances: Aydin was covered in blood, Hidashar was not.

Aydin had a cut somewhere in his hairline, and thick blood was running down his face and dripping onto his torso. Both his knees were badly grazed, his back, too, from having been dragged across the dusty ground. His knuckles were raw, his lip split and his left eye was quickly swelling shut.

'And now you know why they made you number thirteen,' Hidashar mocked. 'Last place. The runt of the litter.'

Aydin didn't say anything in response, just fixed his one good eye on his brother. Aydin was used to Hidashar mouthing off, used to his bravado. It was, he guessed, one of the reasons why, despite his obvious physical prowess, they were only two numbers apart. Quite simply, despite his talents, Hidashar remained a hot-head, and he was almost hopelessly arrogant. At the Farm the boys had already been taught so much, both physical and mental training. Yet the elders had never tried to take away Hidashar's natural fiery temperament. If anything it was their natural traits that the elders looked to exploit the most.

Regardless, at the still tender age of not quite sixteen, Hidashar was quite simply a brute of a human being. Yet he was far from stupid. He was deviously cunning.

'You're smart, Talatashar,' Hidashar said, before letting out an amused grunt. 'Smarter than me. But you think too much. Your brain's too busy, analysing every possible move. You miss the obvious. It's why I find it so easy to beat you. It's why you're so easily fooled.'

As Aydin stared down at the smiling face of his old friend, his old foe, those words haunted him.

'Same old Talatashar,' Hidashar said.

He didn't have to explain what he meant. *You're so easily fooled.* A disturbing thought blared in Aydin's mind. They knew why he was there, in London – they'd followed him from his mother's home after all. Hours earlier he'd been so confident that he was the one in control, leading the two men on a merry-go-round at his own convenience, before turning the tables and trailing them. But now he realised they'd played him the whole time. Aydin still didn't know who the other man was, the one down on the ground in

100

the shadows. Perhaps it was Arab'ah – number four – who he knew was in London too. Most likely though it was just some grunt. But Hidashar certainly knew Aydin. He knew him as well as anyone else.

He knew this was how Aydin would react to being followed.

The sickly feeling was growing and sticking painfully in his throat. He hoped he was wrong, but there was an unshakeable feeling that he wasn't. As if realising Aydin's moment of clarity, the look of power in Hidashar's eyes grew, even though he was about to have his brains blown out.

That's what he and his brothers were, though, Aydin realised. Not individuals, but a collective. It didn't matter to Hidashar if he died, only that his orders were carried out and that the group succeeded.

Aydin's finger twitched on the trigger . . .

Then he sensed movement in the shadows. The man with the knife, making another attack.

Without hesitation Aydin lifted the gun and fired two shots. He knew he hit the target because of the sound the bullets made as they sank into flesh, and the cry of pain that escaped the man's lips. Whether or not Aydin had killed him, he didn't know, and he had a more immediate problem: Hidashar was coming back at him.

Perhaps feeling a moment of safety, with the gun away from his face, Hidashar bucked and lifted Aydin's body up, just enough to free his hands. He whipped one up to tackle the arm holding the gun. With the other he pummelled Aydin's side. Aydin tried to bring the gun back in line to fire but Hidashar's strength was more than enough to hold him off.

Aydin fired anyway, hoping that the noise, so close to Hidashar's ears, would be enough to disorientate and cause him to stutter. He was partly right. Hidashar's strength did waver, but a second later he switched tactic. He released Aydin's gun hand and used his tree-trunk legs and the muscles in his core and his arms to twist them both around as he tried to shove Aydin off him. Aydin could let go of the gun and fight the move, but he didn't. He wanted the weapon in his grasp, but it meant he could do nothing as Hidashar hauled him over onto his back and then slid away.

Hidashar leapt up and dashed into the darkness of the alley. Aydin arced his head back, looking after him, and fired off two more shots into the black. The clanking and banging of the bullets told him he'd missed.

He wanted to chase after his brother, to finish him off, but he couldn't. Instead he jumped to his feet and raced for the road. He ran as fast as he could as the nightmarish thoughts took over in his mind, but at full pace it wasn't long before his lungs were burning and his legs ached from lactate build-up. He had to slow to a jog, only adding to his aggravation. As he headed along he thought of the mistakes he'd already made since he arrived in England, not least the four shots he'd just fired in central London; but there was one mistake that he feared might haunt him for the rest of his life . . .

It took him fifteen minutes to retrace his steps back to Adlington Road. As soon as he turned onto the street he realised to his horror that those agonising thoughts weren't just hocus-pocus. Up ahead, outside the flats, were the blinking blue lights of an ambulance. Two police cars too. Together with the illumination of the streetlights it was enough to make out the scene quite clearly. Aydin could see the blue-and-white tape marking a cordon on the street, snaking upwards to the first floor of the flats. He slowed down to a casual walk, not wanting to alert the police at the scene to his presence.

As he cautiously approached he saw several onlookers gathered at the cordon, eagerly peering beyond the tape for a glimpse of the macabre. The door to his mother's home was open slightly, but not enough to get a meaningful glimpse of what was within.

Aydin's head was a mess. He stood by the cordon, not sure what he should do, what he *could* do now that he was there. He wanted to go up, even though he knew there was absolutely nothing he could do to help.

He didn't know how long he stood there. Maybe only a minute, maybe ten. He heard the chatter of the people all around, but his brain didn't really take any of it in. Then the door opened fully as a uniformed officer left the home. The policeman stepped out into the corridor and looked at the crowd below. He hung his head and gave a sorry shake before replacing his helmet and walking away. Beyond where the policeman had stood, Aydin caught a glimpse into the hallway. He saw the paramedic, dragging the gurney towards the entrance. Behind him, Aydin saw the far wall of the lounge. The bookcase, the pictures of him, his mother, Nilay. Speckled and smeared with red splashes of blood.

Aydin's legs felt weak. He was surprised he didn't collapse right there. If he'd been hit hard when he saw Nilay's death on the news, then this was something else entirely.

He was completely numb.

But he didn't want to be numb. Being numb wouldn't help him. Begrudgingly his mind took him back to *that* place again. To the Teacher. Aydin could hear his words. Telling him to use his anger, to let it drive him. People might have thought that to be highly trained like he and his brothers were you needed a calm and level head to operate. That was true to some extent, but they'd also been taught to use hatred as

103

a motivator. It was only through antipathy that they could carry out the acts they were asked to.

With focus, Aydin felt that anger growing inside as he watched the gurney being wheeled along the corridor. It didn't take long before rage was surging through his veins.

He looked over and spotted a policeman standing by the open doors to the ambulance. A female colleague was muttering in his ear, but he was looking directly at Aydin. He wasn't sure why the officer's interest was focused on him. Perhaps it was just the animal in his eyes, or did he somehow recognise Aydin from the pictures in the house from when he was just a child?

The policeman said something to his colleague then edged forward. Whatever his motive, it was time for Aydin to go. He didn't need a fight with the police tonight. He turned and, on shaky legs, walked away, not looking back at all. When he reached the end of the road he turned right and ran. Moving on a strange mixture of adrenaline and fury, he kept running until he was back in the shadowy depths of the city. Where he belonged.

Then he stopped.

That was enough running. That was no longer an option. Hidashar, the Teacher, all of the others, they were out there, and Aydin was damn certain they all wanted him dead. They would come for him. One after the other or all together, they would come again and again to kill him, as long as it took, and they would harm anyone who got in their way. Especially people who Aydin cared about. They didn't just want him dead, they wanted to punish him.

If he ran he had no chance. What he needed was to fight back.

It was time to use his hatred. It was time to become the hunter.

EIGHTEEN

Rome, Italy

Ismail Obbadi placed the coffee cup down on its saucer then sat back in the booth as he looked out across the luxurious bar, crystal chandeliers dripping from the ceiling, gold trimmings here, there and everywhere. As much as there was that he despised about the city, it felt good to be back, after his short trip to Berlin. Good to be back playing *this* role.

The Uragan canisters were now safely stored in an industrial unit on the edge of the city. They'd be safe there until needed. Obbadi smiled to himself as he reminisced about watching Streicher take his last few pain-ridden breaths. He imagined with glee what it would be like to witness that on a grand scale.

The bar around him was just starting to get busy, the hubbub growing as the place filled out and as the rich but young revellers became more intoxicated. A group of young stallions who'd been in for more than two hours were becoming increasingly rowdy, and Obbadi noticed them wolf-whistle at several young ladies walking past. Their banter was growing more and more lurid, their behaviour leery.

Obbadi watched them closely, showing little reaction on the outside despite inwardly being disgusted by their behaviour. But then many of the young women the group were harassing were just as bad, blind drunk and with their breasts falling out of their tops and their arses hanging out of their skirts. If there was ever an indicator needed of just how far Western civilisation had fallen, Obbadi believed that young men and women like these were the epitome.

Staring blankly, Obbadi noticed one of the men was eyeing him up coldly. The group of twenty-somethings were all fashionistas, with tight-fitting clothes and slicked hair, tattoos and manicured stubble. Pristine prima donnas. Too much money, too little sense and zero responsibility. Obbadi, lost in his thoughts, continued to look on and drew the attention of others from the group. Soon they were gesturing over to him, their yobbish insults wide-ranging about his appearance, his formal clothes, his choice of drink, his skin colour and his Middle-Eastern origin – well they were wrong on that one, but how to explain to these cretins that he was in fact North African?

All of their ill-thought words only added further to the growing distaste in Obbadi's mouth. Yet this was exactly why he'd come into the bar on a Friday night, when he knew it would be busy and filled with groups like these. It was a gentle reminder of exactly who Obbadi was, and who *these* people were.

He downed the rest of the coffee then stepped out of the booth. One or two of the men shuffled just a little, as though they sensed a scuffle was brewing. Obbadi straightened out his cream suit and walked towards them. The bull of the group, tall and athletic with piercing brown eyes and chis-elled features, got up from his seat, ready for the challenge.

At least he thought he was. Obbadi wasn't in the mood to show the little sod just how mistaken he was.

'You're celebrating?' Obbadi said in Italian, running a hand over his closely shaven chin as he looked over at the men. He knew his accent only further gave away that he wasn't a native to their country. He wondered how long it would be before he heard the usual buzzwords 'go back home', 'terrorist', 'Taliban', 'ISIS'.

But instead the man simply gave an unfriendly sneer, perhaps surprised at Obbadi's calm and collected question and also his confidence.

'Someone's birthday?' Obbadi asked.

Now he heard more whispered insults, guffaws. Ah, and there it was. *Terrorist scum*. Shame he'd forgotten his Muslim insult bingo card today.

'Hey, Berto!' Obbadi shouted over to the wiry young man behind the bar. 'My friends are having a party. Give them some free beer, will you.'

Obbadi turned back to the whippersnapper and gave him a warm smile that nearly knocked him off his feet.

How easily these imbeciles are manipulated.

'Thank you for coming to *my* bar,' Obbadi said. 'I hope you enjoy the rest of your night, and that you'll come again soon.'

He reached out and the man flinched as Obbadi gently patted him on the shoulder. He turned and walked towards the bar. Berto leaned over.

'You really want to give them free drinks? I heard what they said to you.'

'Why not? They may not get many more opportunities to enjoy themselves in this city.'

Berto, bemused, said nothing. Obbadi winked, then looked back to the group one more time. He gave them a friendly wave. They just sat there looking ridiculous and clueless. Obbadi walked out the back door.

He headed past the office and through the exit into the sprawling building's marble-covered atrium. He took the elevator up to the fifteenth-floor penthouse apartment. When he opened the front door he noticed the lights were already on

107

and he could hear music coming from the lounge. He took off his brown Gucci shoes and headed across the thick carpet and into the expansive space where he spotted Katja lying naked on the L-shaped sofa. Beyond her the wide floor-to-ceiling windows gave breathtaking views across the city, the Roman Forum and Coliseum in the near distance lit up beautifully as always. Another city filled with such rich history of warfare and clashing civilisations.

'I thought you were going out?' he said.

'I was waiting for you,' Katja purred, rubbing a hand over her bare skin, up towards her breasts.

'Cover yourself up.'

He grabbed the robe from the floor and flung it over her.

'*Idiota*,' Katja responded, sitting up with a sullen look on her face. 'I wanted to surprise you.'

'I'm not in the mood.' He fished in his pocket and took out the roll of notes. He began to unravel a few to give to her but in the end stopped and just flung the whole bundle. It banged off her leg and rolled to a stop on the floor. 'Why don't you go and have a good time. Maybe we'll go out tomorrow.'

'*Testa di cazzo!*' Katja shouted as she shot up from the sofa, leaving the money on the floor. She stormed up to Obbadi and banged into his shoulder as she passed. 'I don't need your money. You want a whore then go and get one.'

Even though he knew he'd provoked her, anger brewed somewhere deep in his stomach at her insulting him like that. He easily held it in, just like he had with the men downstairs. There were far bigger nuisances in Obbadi's life than angry young spoilt Italians.

While Katja grumpily banged and crashed about in the bedroom, Obbadi headed over to the open-plan kitchen and poured some chilled bottled water into a crystal tumbler. After two large swigs he took his phone out of his pocket and saw there was a message. He hadn't felt his phone vibrate when the text arrived. Ten minutes, was all it said. He'd received it eight minutes ago.

Obbadi growled under his breath and headed over to the door to the office. He unlocked it with the key strapped around his neck and headed inside, closing the door behind him. The large room was pleasantly cool with the air-conditioning on a constant twenty degrees and Obbadi sat down at the leather swivel chair behind the thick oak desk and fired up the laptop. He checked his watch. Just in time. He sat and waited. After two minutes there was nothing and he sent a text message reply.

Ready?

Moments later he heard banging doors and stomping feet outside. Katja making a stormy exit. She'd get over it. And if she didn't, who gave a flying fuck really? Obbadi got up and walked back to the door, opening it just a few inches to peep out. He looked over to where the bundle of euro notes had moments earlier lain untouched. He was amused to see the money now gone. Like all the others in this place, Katja was so predictable.

Obbadi closed the door again. While he waited he opened up the app that connected to the building's CCTV system. He was soon looking through the various feeds for the bar and found himself with a bird's-eye view of the raucous group of young men. Obbadi clenched his fists as he stared at them. It was tempting, and would be so easy, to make them all pay for their slights. Using the CCTV images of their faces he had the connections to quickly identify each and every one of them.

For a few seconds he imagined what he could do next — how he could target not just those men but their friends and families too. There was no denying that he would take great joy in showing them just how mistaken they'd been to throw their bile at him.

Just thinking about it caused adrenaline to surge through his body, but he would take it no further than violent fantasy tonight. There were many good reasons why Obbadi now found himself a very rich man, able to live a life of luxury that the majority of the billions of people on earth could only dream of. Being able to keep a level head when others would certainly have snapped was one of those reasons.

The incoming call finally came just moments later. Obbadi pressed the button on the keyboard to accept.

'Talk to me,' came the gruff voice through the speakers, no pleasantries offered or given.

'It's in hand,' Obbadi said, not wanting to show any weakness by having to justify what had already gone wrong. No point in dwelling on the past, as he'd always been told. Show your strength by how you deal with the present.

'Do you have him?'

'Not yet,' Obbadi said. 'But we will get him.'

Though the truth was that Obbadi didn't currently have a solid plan of how to make that happen.

'Your confidence is impressive, but please don't fail again. We can't let this stop our plans.'

'It won't. Paris is still operational.'

'And London?'

'This was only a small distraction. Nothing has changed.'

'Remember who he is. Remember *what* he is. He's your brother. Don't underestimate him. Finish this quickly.'

'I will. But you're wrong, he's not my brother. Not any more.'

'Just tell me when it's done. And Germany?'

'All in order,' Obbadi said. 'The goods are secured, and it works perfectly.'

He smiled again at that same thought.

'And what about the cossack?'

'Just as planned.'

He'd had word from Sab'ah several hours ago that he'd completed his task. News of the nerve-agent assassination of Roman Asrutdinov – a well-known hacker – had already made it onto the international news networks, though the idiotic reporters had no clue *why*, instead spouting all sorts of baseless theories about North Korea and Russia and spies. They simply had no idea of the malware code that Asrutdinov had helped create before his untimely – or was it timely? – death, or what it would soon be used for.

'Good. Then you know what to do next.'

The call clicked off and Obbadi, slightly reeling from the bluntness of the conversation, even though it was nothing more than he'd expected, was left staring at the laptop screen, at the obnoxious face of the man who'd minutes earlier been so ready to challenge him.

Obbadi's eyes narrowed. Yes, he could easily let this go. But that didn't mean he wanted to, or that he had to. He wouldn't take action tonight, but he also wouldn't forget.

'See you again soon, my friend.'

NINETEEN

Aleppo, Syria

Cox had her hand on the gun, inside her handbag, as she walked up the stairs to the safe house. Since ditching the moped she'd taken only thirty minutes more to reach the building. She just wanted to be inside. Lock the door and wait for the extraction team to arrive. She didn't know who it would be, or how many there would be, but she had to trust in the SIS process and that they would keep her safe from there.

She reached the apartment door and took the key from her bag. All was quiet up on the seventh-floor landing. Before she put the key to the lock she had a sudden thought. She took out her phone. Outside the door she just had enough Wi-Fi signal to connect to the Internet. She went into the app for the safe house's alarm system, then scrolled through into the data log.

The last entry was several hours ago, when she'd left the building to go and meet Subhi. Neither the magnetic contact on the front door or any of the other sensors had been triggered since then.

Cox put the phone away, unlocked then opened the door. The blips sounded as the front door contact triggered and Cox shut the door and input the six-digit code into the box on the wall to disable the alarm. She looked around the space in front of her. Everything seemed just as she'd left it.

She headed over to the laptop and flipped the lid, then navigated into the secure messaging account to check for emails. Nothing in there. She called Flannigan but got no response. Feeling her head throbbing from the crashing thoughts of what was happening, she slumped down on the sofa.

Where she went from there, she really didn't know. Her two main assets in Aleppo – or were they close enough to be considered friends? – were dead. Cox was sure she too was now a target of their killers. The only explanation she could think of was that her digging for the identities and whereabouts of the Thirteen had led to both Subhi and Nilay being murdered.

Cox growled in frustration. No. *She* wasn't responsible for their deaths. And now really wasn't the time to dwell. She had two hours to get as far ahead of the game as she could before the extraction team arrived. She first sent a message to Flannigan, saying she was ready for the white-line call. While she waited for a response she dove into the thumb drive she'd taken from Nilay's apartment.

Nilay had only recently confided in Cox about the existence of the data she'd collated. Cox had no doubt that the young woman had been killed because of the questions she was asking in Aleppo regarding the Thirteen. She had to hope there were answers to those questions on the drive.

As she scanned through she saw the documents on the thumb drive were a random mess of word files, spreadsheets and text notes. A few images – pictures of people, scans of documents. There was no filing structure or co-ordination and it was impossible to know the source of the data, who had authored it, or even in many cases the context.

One thing was quickly clear, though: Nilay had reams of data about the Thirteen that Cox had never seen. Not full details on each and every person, but way more core data than Cox herself had pulled together.

113

In their conversations Nilay had claimed her brother – when he was only nine – was abducted from their London home by their father. Neither had been seen since, though Nilay believed her brother, Aydin Torkal, had become one of the Thirteen. The trouble was, there was absolutely no credible intelligence that Cox had seen on what had become of the boy. Just stories.

Until now. Because looking through the files, there was a candid photograph of a young man. The name of the file was *Talatashar*, and she was convinced the young man she saw was the boy who'd been known as Aydin Torkal. She'd long known about the numbering system, how the boys' true identities had been forgotten and they'd been referred to not by name but by number, but this was the first solid evidence she had that linked those numbers to actual people.

The picture of Talatashar was black and white, and not the best quality, but his features were clear. He looked so . . . ordinary. Cox's theory was that the Thirteen were a group of master jihadis, trained from their early years in all manner of combat and arms and engineering skills, science and theology too. Everything needed to wage a war on the West in a new and deadly way.

Could this mild-looking man really be part of that?

Cox looked away, thinking. Then the laptop chirped. Her immediate thought was that it was Flannigan getting back to her, but she saw it was an incoming Skype call. From her mum.

Cox groaned. Yet despite the precarious situation, she soon found herself reaching out and clicking the cursor over the green button to accept the call.

'Hi, Mum.'

'Rachel! So you are still alive, then?'

'For now, yeah.'

114

Her mum sounded agitated, and really she had every right to be. Cox hadn't spoken to her for over three weeks, even though she knew her mum was an incessant worrier. She was lonely too. Just hearing her voice made Cox feel guilt, to know she was such a bad daughter.

'Where are you, honey? I've been trying to get in touch for days.'

'Still in Dubai,' she lied. 'I told you I'd be here for weeks yet.'

As far as her mum knew Cox worked for the British Government and was seconded to the Embassy in Dubai. That was close enough to the truth for a woman like Sylvia Munroe. She never asked questions about what work Cox did – working an office job for the Embassy was as clandestine as she could comprehend, bless her.

'Then when are you coming home, honey? I'm really missing you.'

'I don't know. Is everything okay? I'm really busy here, it's not a great time to chat.'

'Oh, all's fine here. I'm just on my way back to the hospital.'

Shit. Cox had forgotten all about that. The last time they spoke her mum had been for tests because of a thyroid problem. She'd never even bothered to call her to find out how that had gone.

'I'm so sorry, Mum. Are you sure you're alright? How did the last tests go?'

'Oh, don't you worry about me. Just so long as you're okay.'

Cox sighed. 'You'd tell me if something was wrong, wouldn't you?'

'Of course I would.'

Though Cox knew that wasn't really the case. Her mum hated the idea that she was a burden on anyone, Cox in particular, whom she was immensely proud of for her globe-trotting lifestyle.

'Actually the reason I was calling was something else.'

'Yeah?'

'It was a couple of weeks ago now, actually, when I first called to tell you. You'll never guess who I bumped into the other day?'

Cox grimaced. She already had an idea where this might be going. 'Who?'

'Greg. You know he's met someone new now?'

'I heard.'

'She was with him. They stopped to chat for a minute. She's not a patch on you. He doesn't know what he's missing.'

'It was me who left him, not the other way round.'

'I know. I'm just saying. She's pregnant too, I could see the bump. I'm guessing it's his, but they didn't say.'

Cox held her head in her hands. 'Okay, look, I really do need to go.'

'Oh, yeah, right.' She sounded put out.

'I'm sorry, Mum. I do want to chat, and soon, but I'm just in the middle of something.'

Just then she noticed a message ping on her mobile. Flannigan was ready to talk.

'Sorry to disturb you,' her mum said. 'You take care of yourself.'

'I will do. Love you, Mum.'

Cox clicked the red button just as her mum got a final few words in. She didn't dwell, just sent a message right back to Flannigan.

Dialling now.

Greg was going to be a dad. She was pleased for him. He was a good man. At least one of them was now happy and could go ahead living the normal life.

She tried to banish the thoughts of her estranged husband and of her mum, who might or might not be okay. Now wasn't the time for distraction. Anyway, Cox would soon be back in England. She'd see her mum soon enough.

Then, before she got the chance to initiate the call, the name of another image file on the screen caught her attention. Wahid. Number one in Arabic. She opened it up and looked at the picture of the man inside. Actually, he was just a boy in the picture – maybe fourteen, fifteen years old. For a few second she just sat there, staring.

While Talatashar looked mild and meek and . . . lost, Wahid couldn't have been more different. He had a large round face, wide jaw, thick neck muscles that suggested even in his teens that he was strong and lean. His dark hair was closely cropped. His eyes were piercing and beady, but despite a look that suggested a perpetual disgust with everything he saw, he was uniquely handsome, and he knew it. The picture . . . behind Wahid it just looked like sand and rocks. It must be from the Farm. How on earth had Nilay come across that snap?

'Shit,' Cox said to herself, realising she'd been distracted. She quickly closed the file down and dialled into the white line.

'Cox here,' she said when she heard the blip to tell her she was connected.

'I thought you said *now*,' came the prickly voice of Flannigan across the laptop's speaker. 'That was five minutes ago.'

Cox rolled her eyes. 'You said you had an update,' she said, not interested in explaining the short delay.

'I do. But first I think you'd better tell me what the hell is happening out there.'

Despite his initial irritation, his tone was actually far more measured and sympathetic than it had been the last time they spoke.

'I've think my cover's blown,' Cox said.

Silence on the other end.

'Talk to me,' Flannigan eventually said.

'Two of my informants have been killed in the space of a few hours. It's no coincidence.'

'Who?'

Cox told him. When the names passed her lips she felt that lump in her throat again and for just a split second her eyes welled. She fought it off. Crying wasn't going to help the situation. And really she was more scared than she was upset.

'I was with Subhi when it happened. It was a sniper. Someone was waiting for me.'

Flannigan said nothing to that. She wondered if – only now that everything had gone to shit – he was finally seeing just how deep she'd gone. How close she was to something big. That's certainly how it felt to her. Why else would Subhi and Nilay both have been killed like that?

'It sounds like a complete mess out there,' Flannigan said, and Cox slumped several inches. 'You need to come straight back here for a full debrief. The extraction team should be with you within two hours. The travel arrangements are already in place. They'll take you to a US airbase in the north, then on to Ankara, then you're heading civilian class to London. Bring everything you need with you. You're done over there.'

'Just like that?'

'You'd rather stick it out and see who comes for you next?'

'Of course not, but you must admit I'm on to something, given what's just happened.'

'I know. I didn't say I was closing your op down, just that you're done in Aleppo. Something else has come up.'

'Yeah?'

'I said I had an update for you. We might not have given you approval for Trapeze but that doesn't mean we've not been listening to what we can. Filtering through the noise we have what I believe is some credible intel for you.'

Cox realised she was holding her breath in anticipation.

'You still there, Cox?'

'Yeah.'

118

'There was an alert last night coming from Rome. Well, we think that was the origin anyway, but it's not clear-cut due to the way the traffic was routed. Anyway, to cut a long story shorter, we intercepted secure Internet message chatter discussing the need to capture a man referred to as Talatashar—'

'Thirteen,' Cox blurted as her brain whirred. She quickly clicked back through to the picture of Aydin Torkal. Her heart drummed in her chest as she went back to Nilay's list of documents. She remembered seeing a file with Rome in the title. She clicked on it. 'Wahid. Rome is believed to be the base for Wahid. He's their number one.'

There was a moment of silence. 'Sorry, where are you getting that from?' Flannigan said. 'That's not been in any of your reports.'

'No. It wasn't. But I'm looking at the intel right now.'

'Rachel, if you want me to work effectively with you then you're going to need to give me all relevant data you have.'

'I know that,' Cox said, trying her hardest to keep from biting back. 'It's new intel. You'll have it as soon as we're off this call.'

'Good. Anyway. We later intercepted traffic originating in France over a secure VoIP line—'

'Though not secure enough, eh?'

'Indeed. It seems whoever is looking for Talatashar honed in to a mobile phone signal coming from France, and tracked it to a location about half an hour south of Paris. But given what we've seen and heard, all they found was a discarded handset. No man.'

'Any indication *why* they're looking for him?'

'No.'

'Or where Talatashar now is?'

'Yes to that one actually. Further intercepts we've listened to refer to *Talatashar going home*. To England. Now this is actually backward to how we found the trail, but I'll give you the events in chronological order, as it's not all through this op that the data's been gathered. Early this morning a group of illegal immigrants were smuggled into Dover from Calais aboard a lorry belonging to a Scottish haulage company. The illegals were taken to a farm in Kent where one of the immigrants fought back against their Armenian traffickers, killing one in the process by crushing his windpipe with his heel. Apparently. The escapee drove off in a white Ford Transit van that was later found abandoned near Sevenoaks with five illegals cowering in the back.'

Cox shook her head in disbelief. 'He's headed to London.'

'Potentially.'

'And you think this was Talatashar?' Cox said, opening up his picture again.

'A young Arab male, yes, according to the smugglers and illegals who've been detained by the police, but we've not pinpointed any CCTV capture of him at Sevenoaks station, or in London or anywhere else to confirm his appearance or identity. Nor has there been any electronic or telephonic communication that we can match to the man himself since arriving in England. It's certainly possible this Talatashar is now in England, but if he is then he's currently dark.'

Which wasn't good at all. For months Flannigan and Miles had failed to take Cox's theories on the Thirteen seriously. Now it looked like one of them was in England's capital. It was very possible that an attack on home soil was imminent.

But then why did it also appear that his own people were hunting for him?

'That's all I have for now,' Flannigan said. 'But I need you back here to sift through this mess.'

'I think I have a picture of him.'

'Talatashar?'

'Yes.'

'Right. Well I think the best thing to do is to end this and for you to just send everything you can.'

'I'll do it now.'

'Speak later.'

There was a click as Flannigan left the call.

Cox was still sitting in the same position, hadn't got up at all, as she scoured through Nilay's files over an hour later. Her focus was finally taken from the laptop screen when she caught sight of movement on the CCTV screen off to her right. She looked over and saw the two men coming up the stairs to the seventh floor. Both were squat and bulky and were casually dressed, but there were enough tells that they were both armed. Whether they were SIS or contractors or even military, Cox didn't know, but she knew they were the extraction team. She jumped up from the chair, shut the laptop lid, bundled that, her phone, the gun she'd acquired earlier into her bag. She quickly moved into the bedroom and opened the safe, taking out the money she had, the three passports she'd brought with her and the other gun. She put those and her handbag into a small holdall just as she heard the rap on the door.

'Miss Cox. Time to go,' she heard the gruff male voice call. An American accent.

Cox slung the holdall over her shoulder. The information she'd been reading was still swimming in her head. Aydin Torkal – Nilay's brother – was Talatashar. He was now in London. Wahid, number one, was in Rome. Was he the leader?

It didn't sound like much, but these were real tangible leads to go after.

After everything she'd already been through, the last thing she wanted now was to be stuck at Vauxhall Cross for the next few days while Flannigan and Miles and whoever else gave her a grilling over how she'd lost two assets in Aleppo.

Was there another option?

She looked to the window. On the other side was a metal fire escape that led down to the back street below.

More knocks on the door: harder, angrier now. Could a knock on a door be angry?

'Miss Cox. We need to go,' came the raised voice. 'Now.'

Yes, definitely angry.

'To run or not to run,' Cox muttered to herself.

Talatashar going home. The words rang in her ear suddenly.

There was always a third option, she realised. She didn't necessarily have to go back to London on Flannigan's terms . . .

Concluding she'd play along, Cox moved out of the bedroom, up to the front door. She paused for just a second before she snaked her fingers around the handle and pushed down.

TWENTY

Cox looked over the shoulder of the driver to the speedometer. The dial was ticking over a hundred km/h. Not massively fast if they'd been on decent roads, even for the heavily weighted Land Cruiser, riding low due to the extra armouring. The 4x4 had a beast of an engine that in low gear revved freely, but one hundred kilometres an hour certainly felt fast on *these* roads.

Roads. A loose term really for the pitch-black dirt tracks they were following across sandy desert. The natural undulations of the land meant that every second or two there was a huge clunk as the hulking vehicle smacked down on its already over-worked suspension. Each time it did so a fierce jolt rushed through Cox's spine and she wondered how many pieces her vertebrae would be in by the time they finally reached the airbase.

'How much further is it?' Cox asked neither of the men in particular as the beams from the vehicle's powerful headlights raked across the hilly terrain.

The driver, who'd introduced himself as Jensen, caught Cox's eye in the rear-view mirror, but didn't say anything.

'About an hour and a half,' Hayes said from the front passenger seat.

Hayes's accent was English – Yorkshire to be precise. Cox had thought about asking where he was from, being a Yorkshire girl herself, but hadn't yet bothered. Jensen on the other hand sounded like he came from the north-eastern seaboard of the United States. Cox didn't know exactly who the men were or who they worked for, though. Not much point in asking questions she knew she wouldn't get a straight answer to. Cox guessed that was the same reason they had talked to her so little.

'You don't think you could find a motorway for us to drive on instead, do you?' Cox said, just a split second before the Land Cruiser hit a massive pothole that sent her lurching forward until her seatbelt hauled her back again.

When she'd recovered she caught Jensen's eye in the mirror again.

'I always thought it was more fun this way,' he said with a wry smile.

'But seriously,' Hayes said, 'this is the safest route.'

'Except if you have a helicopter,' Cox said. 'Budget cutbacks, eh?'

'Not much difference,' Hayes said, straight-faced. 'It's not that hard to shoot a chopper out of the sky. There's no such thing as safe travel around here. This track will take us most of the way there, but we do need to hit the main road for a few miles, there's no other way.'

The tone of Hayes's voice suggested that wasn't a good thing, and Cox's nervousness grew at the thought of what was ahead. But then, why would the threat be ahead and not behind? So far on the journey there was certainly no indication that anyone had followed them out of Aleppo. Behind them, she saw nothing beyond the churning dust, which glowed red in the vehicle's lights.

But, technically, the whole bloody country was a war-zone.

Just because there wasn't a hit squad chasing them out of Aleppo didn't mean there wouldn't be other threats to encounter.

Which was exactly what Cox's immediate thought was several minutes later when they came over the crest of a hill, the headlights catching a plume of smoke that trailed up into the air from beyond the next ridge of sand.

'It's coming from the main road,' Jensen said, looking to Hayes.

'Give it a wide berth,' Hayes said.

'I'll try. But we have to get on the road here anyway, there isn't any other choice.'

'Why not?' Cox asked.

'Because two miles dead ahead of here is the next town. And you really don't want to be driving through that place. There's a road that takes us right round it, though, just on the right side of the red line.'

'The red line?'

'The border between the definite bad guys, and the not quite the good guys,' Hayes said, 'but the ones that are normally better than the rest.'

Jensen huffed in agreement. He turned the wheel to head right, away from the smoke, and moments later Cox caught sight of the blacktop road winding through the sand. When they hit the tarmac it was like they'd found the eye of a great storm. Gone was the boom of the tyres that had been ever-present as they crunched across uneven and unstable ground, replaced with a soft roar and what felt like a velvet-cushioned ride. Jensen put his foot down and the engine growled as the Land Cruiser picked up more pace.

Initially Cox saw no other vehicles on the road, but as they snaked around, she realised they were edging closer and closer to that trail of smoke.

Cox sensed the mood in the cabin becoming more edgy as they got nearer. As they rounded the next corner, the source of the smoke was finally visible up ahead.

'What the—' Jensen said, easing up on the accelerator.

A hundred yards ahead both lanes of the road were blocked. What looked like a small cattle-truck with an open-air trailer was on its side. The smoke was coming from its crumpled bonnet. There was also an old open-topped Jeep whose front end had taken a serious prang, together with a people carrier whose rear now looked like a concertina. Several people were dotted about in front and to the side of the vehicles: an old man with shrivelled skin and drab clothes and wiry hair who looked to be the farmer. A young woman in a niqab with a baby in her arms. Two other women, less conservatively dressed, who were standing and seemed to be arguing with a second man. A third man was on his knees with his back to them all.

'Turn round and go back,' Cox said, as the Land Cruiser continued to crawl towards the scene.

'Go back where?' Jensen said. 'Aleppo?'

'Of course not. Just take us back and find another way round.'

'There isn't another way round,' Hayes said.

'Then what do you suggest?' Cox asked.

'It's just an accident. I think they're hurt,' Jensen said, leaning forward in his seat as though the extra inches would give him a much clearer picture of what he was looking at.

Cox looked again, and where the third man was kneeling she spotted the form of a person on the floor. Not a big person at all. A boy. The man was cradling him.

'We need to help them,' Jensen said.

'Then call an ambulance.'

'Around here? Hayes can stay in the car with you. I'll get out and check. If it's serious, I'm not leaving a young boy on the roadside to die.'

'No!' Cox shouted. 'Do not stop this car.'

'Sorry, Miss Cox, but I don't follow your orders. There're kids here, they're hurt.'

'Jensen, don't be a fool. Come on, Hayes, tell him.'

'We can't go back,' Hayes said. 'Keep going forward, slowly. We can squeeze through on the left.'

'You mean where the woman with her baby is standing?' Jensen said, eyebrow raised at Hayes.

'She'll move.'

'This is stupid,' Cox said, but neither of the men reacted at all to her words.

They were soon just twenty yards away. With the Land Cruiser's front beams lighting up the scene, the gaggle of people were taking notice and looking edgy. One of the women edged forward, waving her arms in the air.

'They need help,' Jensen said.

'But *we* can't help them!' Cox said.

'You don't know that.'

Jensen slowed further and then pushed on the brake and the car gently rocked to a stop. Now that they were close up, Cox could hear the shouts and cries of the people outside. They were distressed, there was no doubt about that. But even if this was a genuine accident scene, what could they do to help?

'Wait,' Hayes said, before Jensen could even think about getting out. He was no longer looking at the crash scene, but out of his window, across the sand and into the darkness. Cox followed his line of sight. She had no idea what Hayes had seen out there, and she turned her eyes back to the woman who was now right in front of the Land Cruiser. She was crying and shouting.

'She's begging for our help,' Jensen said. 'It's her son. He's bleeding out.'

He put his hand to the door.

'No!' Hayes boomed.

Cox saw a glint of light somewhere out in the black.

'Go!' both she and Hayes screamed in unison.

Jensen must have sensed their genuine urgency, because all of a sudden the Good Samaritan in him was gone and he did exactly as instructed. He put his foot down and the 4x4, engine revving, lurched forward. The woman jumped out of the way, her desperation turning to anger in a flash. Jensen headed straight for the woman and baby, the gap beyond them just large enough for the Land Cruiser to pass, but as she cowered away, another figure jumped into view from behind the people carrier. A man, dressed in black, wielding an assault rifle.

He opened fire without hesitation and the bullets raked across the reinforced bodywork of the Land Cruiser.

'Go the other way!' Hayes shouted, pointing to the smaller gap on the opposite side, where the battered farm truck was just a couple of yards from the railings at the verge of the road.

Jensen jerked the steering wheel. Cox was thrown to the side and her head smacked off the window, sending her brain spinning. Through her blurred vision she could see the shapes of people as they quickly shifted positions for the attack.

A second armed man jumped up from the other side of the carnage, immediately pulling on his trigger. The people in front were still scattering as the Land Cruiser shot forward. One of the women wasn't quick enough and there was a *thunk* as the speeding 4x4 flew past and clipped her. Cox whipped her eyes to the side to see the woman flying to the ground. She was lucky, only inches away from a likely fatal collision.

'Hold on!' Jensen warned.

The next second the front side of the Land Cruiser smashed

into the corner of the farm truck, the momentum sufficient enough to shift the mass out of the way. Even with the heavy armouring, the Land Cruiser took a battering in the process, but they were still moving.

They sped away as the bullets kept coming, then Cox again noticed that glint, more obvious this time. She turned and saw the trail of smoke . . .

'RPG!' she screamed.

But by that point there really was nothing they could do. All three of them collectively braced themselves, and the rocket hissed past and exploded just yards behind them, sending a ball of fire into the air. It was pure luck that it wasn't a direct hit, but the shockwave from the explosion was enough to lift the Land Cruiser into the air, back wheels first, and when it came crashing back down Cox was sure that the whole thing would break into pieces.

Somehow it didn't.

'Get us the fuck out of here,' Hayes said, a few seconds later, sounding as surprised as Cox was that they were all still alive and in one piece.

Jensen said nothing as he crunched into third gear and thumped the accelerator. Within seconds the crash scene was fading into the distance behind them, and all three of them began to breathe more easily.

'I'm sorry,' Jensen said, looking straight ahead at the road.

'It's okay,' Hayes said.

Cox didn't quite agree it was, and didn't say anything.

'I thought it was just an accident,' Jensen said, sounding bemused and just a little rattled. 'There was a baby there. A kid too. Women.'

Cox huffed. 'You may have been working in Syria longer than I have, Jensen, but I've a feeling I know its people better than you do.'

'You reckon?'

'I do.'

Jensen and Hayes knew the area well enough to know which rebel groups held which towns, but they clearly didn't know the people like she did. Most likely Jensen and Hayes were seasoned ex-soldiers, possibly mercenaries. Used to fighting, used to war-zones even. But Cox knew the enemy out there was different to any other she'd ever seen. An enemy who had no qualms in using any advantage they could, even if that meant not just sacrificing women and kids in the process, but using them as pawns.

'Really there's only one rule to remember out here,' Cox said.

'Yeah?' Jensen scoffed. 'And what's that?'

'There are no rules. And there's certainly no time for being a hero.' Cox saw him roll his eyes. 'Maybe next time you should just do what I bloody say. Now please, just get us to the airbase so I can leave this damn country behind.'

TWENTY-ONE

Bruges, Belgium

Leaving England turned out to be relatively simple for Aydin. Certainly more straightforward than how he'd got in. It was a plain matter of fact that it was much harder to smuggle into the UK than it was to smuggle out. Whatever people might have said to the contrary, the government and the police and the security services, and even the general public, really didn't care much if terrorists were leaving for elsewhere, as long as they didn't come back.

Employing all of his training to keep his trail clean, Aydin headed from London to the east coast where he managed to hide himself aboard a container ship heading from Felixstowe in Suffolk to Rotterdam, Holland; one of the busiest ports in the world.

Busy was good. It meant he wasn't noticed at all as he left the ship and the port under the cover of night and began a trek across the small country towards neighbouring Belgium, through a combination of plain old walking, train and bus.

The Belgian police forces and intelligence services were undoubtedly on high alert; for obvious reasons, as the country had become a breeding ground for Islamist terrorists, but on entering the country, that heightened police presence would only be of concern to Aydin if he was going through an official border crossing, like an airport, which he wasn't. Within continental Europe he could easily travel on foot or bike or by rail or road between any of the twenty-six countries party to the Schengen Agreement without the need to show a passport or identification.

Still, he had to entertain the very real possibility that he was still under watch. From Hidashar, perhaps, from others connected to their network. And really there wasn't a big list of places of where he might head to next, so he had to remain vigilant. What he wanted was to get to the head – Wahid. But he had no idea where Wahid or the majority of his other brothers were located. That was out of necessity, no point in risking one of them getting caught and spilling all about their plans, however well-trained they were to withstand interrogation.

But there was one brother who Aydin knew how to find.

Even though he'd got out of England and into Holland without hitches, he remained ultra-cautious, as he was trained to be, and he wouldn't take chances. For all he knew there could be a team of police or intelligence agents on watch close to the Belgian border, either routine, or even looking for him if he'd somehow made a mistake and left breadcrumbs for them to follow. So, before leaving Holland, he got off the bus he was travelling on five miles short of the border and once again waited for nightfall before heading on foot through fields and woodlands to reach Belgium. Only in the morning, safely inside, would he head back onto public transport.

He arrived in the small city of Bruges just before noon the following day, nearly forty-eight hours since he'd left London behind. Since he'd seen his mother being wheeled out of the family home in a body bag. He didn't know whose hand had taken her life, but he knew who was responsible. For now his mission was simple. Track down his mother's killers, his sister's too. Find them. Kill them.

To do that, though, to find out where Wahid and the others were, he needed help.

He'd never been to Bruges before, never to the country before in fact, but as he walked alongside the canal in the quaint city centre, with the sun shining above him in a clear sky, he couldn't help but be caught by its charm. The townhouses – all different shapes and sizes and colours – jutting up from the banks of the canal were well kept and many had ornate decorations to their stonework. Boats put-putted along the water peacefully, small waves lapping against the brick sides of the canal. Ahead of him, at the junction of the canal he was heading to, a church sat prominently, its Gothic spires rising into the sky proudly, above all of the other buildings surrounding it. Aydin had never seen the inside of a church, he probably never would, but he still appreciated the beauty of what he saw.

He walked down the streets not feeling any particular threat from either the people or the authorities, whose presence was seen but not felt. He wondered, if he'd been assigned to this place, would he have felt more satisfied with his role, more content with the path that had been laid out for him?

That, he guessed, was irrelevant now.

Despite the turmoil in his mind, it felt relaxed in Bruges, the people he saw were happy and . . . ignorant. That's the best word he could find, because the reality was that despite appearances, this place was no more safe than anywhere else he'd been. After all, look how easy it was for him to come and fit in. Surely it was one of the many reasons why Bruges was chosen as a location.

Looking at the street signs ahead Aydin realised he was close to his destination, but for some reason, rather than carrying on he found himself stopping and sitting on a bench to take stock for a few minutes.

He watched people idling by on foot, on bikes and on canal boats on the water in front of him. It was hard for him to describe what he thought of the people he saw. He was supposed to hate them. Every single one of them. That was how he'd been brought up on the Farm, what the imam and the others had drilled into him and all of boys every day for years. These people – these heathens – were his enemy, the reason for the misery suffered by so many of his kind across the world. He wasn't supposed to be able to look at the faces of these infidels without anger and resentment.

So why, after all these years, was it so hard for him to find those feelings now?

Back at the Farm it had all seemed so much more straightforward and clear cut to understand. Aydin and his brothers were from such very different backgrounds. That's how the elders had wanted it. They'd wanted the boys to be different from each other because each of them was needed for a different role. They were unique, and were treated as such.

Propaganda in the West often portrayed child soldiers as little more than *inghimasi* – poorly trained troops sent into battle with assault rifles and suicide vests, dispatched in droves to the front lines to die. Aydin and his brothers weren't like that. Yes, it was true that some of the boys had been snatched from orphanages or minority sects of enemies, but others like Aydin were taken from their homes by their fathers, who, like the elders, believed so deeply in the ideology the boys had been trained to uphold and protect.

Regardless of their roots, Aydin knew it was true that each of the boys represented easy prey for the elders – men who were so skilled at turning feelings of anger, exclusion and revenge into barbarity with their ultra-violent doctrine.

Which was why Aydin struggled to comprehend how he was falling apart so quickly. As he sat there on that bench in Bruges, plotting against his own, part of him wished he was back at the Farm, feeling the heavy but consistent hand of the Teacher. Perhaps what he needed most now was that strong hand to put him back onto the road that had been made for him.

No. He drove away that cowardly thought. He couldn't ever go back *there* . . .

Feeling renewed strength, he got up from the bench and walked the short distance along the canal before he turned off and moved through a narrow, twisting alley with cobblestones underneath. Tourist-centric knick-knack shops were dotted here and there, postcards crammed onto spinning display stands, T-shirts and ornaments and flags emblazoned with the black, yellow and red of the Belgian flag, or with quaint prints of the pretty buildings that lined the canals. Still, the street was quiet of pedestrians, perhaps because of the time of day or year.

After a hundred yards, Aydin reached the wide wooden doorway to an ageing townhouse. It was one of the first dwellings he'd seen that appeared less than perfect. The paint on the outside was peeling profusely, and there were large segments of render missing, exposing the stone underneath. The wooden window frames were scarred and rotten in places. There was however a relatively modern-looking intercom by the front door, with eight buttons running down the panel – one for each of the dwellings inside. Seven of the buttons had little name tags next to them, neatly filled in with blue and black pen. One didn't. That was the button Aydin pressed.

'*Oui*,' a man said after a few seconds.

Despite the crackly response, Aydin recognised the voice just fine. It was his brother, Itnashar. Number twelve.

TWENTY-TWO

'Do you still think of your family?' Aydin asked his friend as they lay on their bunks in the dark. He couldn't sleep, and he knew Itnashar was still awake from the way he was breathing.

'Yes, of course I still think of them.'

'Why do you think they left us here?'

Even after four years it was a question Aydin still asked himself constantly, though this was the first time he'd ever repeated it to another person. Why tonight, he wasn't really sure.

'Because it is God's will,' said Itnashar, though his response had no real heart to it and Aydin wasn't sure his brother really agreed with those well-drilled words. 'We were chosen for this. We are blessed.'

Aydin snorted in disgust. 'This is a prison.'

'You know what will happen if they hear you saying that.'

Yes, he did. They were just children, and so of course they naturally pushed boundaries, and they had all crossed the lines at the Farm one way or the other. And they all knew what happened when they did. People learned by their mistakes, and they were no different. Aydin had long ago learned not to challenge the elders.

'They can control what we do, but not what we think,' Aydin said, defiant.

'I'm not so sure about that.'

Aydin let out a long sigh. The room they were in was pitch black, even though the single window was uncovered. The sky outside was filled with thick cloud and with no moonlight there was nothing else out there to provide illumination.

It was just the two of them in the room. To start with, all fifteen of the boys had slept in one military-style bunker, but over the years they'd been moved about, siphoned off into groups depending on their strengths, weaknesses and the particular training they were enduring at any one point. The status quo never lasted for long, though Aydin had been sharing a room with just Itnashar for the last six months. They were close. Aydin had no idea when the next change around would come – it could be any day. He just hoped it wasn't soon. He didn't know what he'd do without his friend now.

'The answer is yes,' Itnashar said in a whisper.

Aydin didn't say anything for a few moments, but his heart beat rapidly at what now felt like an illicit conversation.

He knew Itnashar's family lived in Afghanistan, where the Farm was. At least that's where Aydin thought the Farm was. He didn't know much else about his friend's background though, or that of the other boys. They'd been living together for years, but such was the level of control the elders had over them all.

'Why did they send you here?' Aydin asked. 'What did they tell you?'

'I . . . I don't want to talk about that,' Itnashar said and Aydin deflated a little at his response. 'Come over here,' Itnashar then said and Aydin turned his head to where he knew his brother was. He saw a small ball of smothered light from under Itnashar's blanket.

'What the—'

'Shh,' Itnashar said. 'Just come over.'

137

Aydin rolled the musty blanket off him and shivered as the unheated air hit his bare skin. He put his feet down softly onto the icy stone floor and crept the few yards to Itnashar's bunk and the faint light. Itnashar pulled back the cover and shifted across to let Aydin in. They sat hunched together under the blanket and Aydin's mouth opened wide in amazement at what he saw.

'I can't bel—'

'Shh!' Itnashar said again, with more urgency this time.

'Where did you get that?' Aydin said as quietly as he could as he stared down at the green-yellow screen of the mobile phone.

'From Igor,' Itnashar said.

Igor. Clearly not his real name. They called him that because he was . . . it was hard to describe. Basically they thought he was an idiot and Igor just seemed like a silly name for him. He was in his forties with wispy hair and a whiny voice and a peg leg and he walked with a stoop and compared to many of the other men in the place he just seemed so harmless and odd.

He was, however, a brilliant scientist. A professor from some top university that Aydin had never heard of in Iran. All of the elders at the Farm were experts at something or other. Engineering, chemicals, small arms, bombs, computers, combat. Torture.

'How?' Aydin asked.

'Igor is a fool,' Itnashar said, shrugging. 'I took it from his pocket one day.'

'That's it?'

He shrugged again, as though it was nothing that he'd stolen from an elder. 'They taught us how to pickpocket.'

'How long have you had it?'

'Three weeks.'

'What! And it still works?'

'It's prepaid, so I guess it won't last forever.'

'But how do you even charge it?'

138

They didn't have any electricity in their room, not even lights, so there were certainly no electrical sockets to charge a phone.

Itnashar smiled. He reached under the bunk's painfully thin mattress and his hand came back clutching a bundle of wires. He unreeled them and Aydin saw one end of the two wires was attached to a regular 9V battery. At the other end the wires were each curled around an uncoiled paperclip.

'You made that?'

'I took the parts when we were doing electronics.' Aydin watched as Itnashar removed the back cover of the phone and took out the battery. He twisted and bent the ends of the paperclips so they straddled the charge points of the battery. 'It's pretty easy really.'

Pretty easy? Maybe it was, but Aydin wasn't sure he could have cobbled together the makeshift charger himself, though it didn't surprise him that Itnashar had so easily figured it out. It wasn't hard to see where his future specialism would lie.

'Why are you showing me this?' Aydin asked.

'You asked about my family,' Itnashar whispered. 'Whether I still think of them. The answer, the real honest answer, is all of the time. In fact, I use this to call them.'

'You speak to them?'

'Of course not! Imagine if the Teacher found out about that. I just . . . listen.'

He unclipped the battery and placed it back into the phone, then powered it up. After a few seconds he handed it to Aydin.

'The reception isn't good, sometimes it's not there at all, but you could try. You know their number, don't you?'

Aydin didn't answer. His mind was too busy thinking about his mother and sister. Their faces were still clear in his head, but when he really tried to hear their voices, they seemed distorted and he worried that what he heard in his head was just a false memory.

'Do you want to?'

'Do you think it will reach England?'

'Why not?'

'It might waste all of the money.'

Itnashar shrugged again. 'I can get another phone. Igor's not the only fool out there. And I don't mind doing this. For you.'

Before sense got the better of him, Aydin took the phone from Itnashar's grasp and dialled the number.

Was that even the right number now, he wondered? He had no idea if they'd changed number or even moved house.

He heard the dial tone and held his breath.

'Hello,' came the woman's voice, soft and warm in his ear.

He took a sharp inhale of breath. Her voice . . . it sounded just like he remembered. For some reason that made him feel incredible sadness.

'Hello, is there someone there?'

'Mumya,' he said. 'It's—'

'What the hell are you doing!' Itnashar hissed, snatching the phone away. Aydin looked at his brother's face, creased with rage.

'I'm sorry, I—'

'You weren't supposed to speak to her!'

There was a thud outside the door.

'Get out, get out!' Itnashar said, lifting the blanket and shoving Aydin to the floor.

He jumped across to his own bed as the thumping footsteps outside the door filled his ears. He threw the blanket over him just as the door burst open and a swathe of electric light swarmed into the room.

He squeezed shut his eyes; he was breathing quickly, his chest heaving, and whoever was at the door would surely know he wasn't asleep.

'Which one of you brats is it?' the growly voice asked.

It was Fardin, though the boys called him Qarsh. Shark. On account of his unyielding hostility to them all. He was one of

140

the guards. The one they all feared the most. It was pure rotten luck that he was the one who'd heard them tonight.

'I won't ask a second time,' he said.

Aydin opened his eyes. He was looking over at Itnashar, who was facing him and doing a much better job of pretending to be asleep.

'It was me,' Aydin said, locking on to Qarsh's perpetually bloodshot eyes.

'And?'

'I was trying to wake Itnashar. I was scared.'

Qarsh smirked and humphed. 'Scared? Talatashar, you really are such a disappointment.'

Aydin said nothing to that.

'Get up,' Qarsh said.

Aydin's eyes again flicked to Itnashar, who was now staring at him, a pleading in his gaze.

'I said get up!' Qarsh boomed, making both of the boys jump.

Aydin threw the blanket off him and stepped out of the bed. He flicked his gaze to Itnashar. Aydin was sure his brother mouthed 'Thank you' to him. Qarsh loomed forward and grabbed Aydin's arm, squeezing hard. He dragged him away, out of the room. Aydin was quivering with both cold and fright as they headed along the labyrinth of corridors and out of the door into one of the courtyards, the one where they often took their physical training.

It was freezing outside, and Aydin's hands and feet and face were stinging by the time they came to a stop. He looked around, shaking; the only light in any direction was the thin veil seeping out of the still-open doorway several yards away. Everything else all around was just black.

'You're scared of the dark?' Qarsh asked.

He pulled his hand out of his jacket and grabbed Aydin's wrists. He slung a cuff over, then yanked on the chain, pulling Aydin further across the black space. He grabbed Aydin's other hand and pulled it up and before Aydin knew it his wrists were clasped together, around one of the thick wooden poles at the outer edge of the courtyard.

'Goodnight, Talatashar. And good luck.'

Qarsh cackled to himself as he wandered off. He stepped through the door, shut it behind him and Aydin was plunged into darkness.

'Baba,' Aydin said after a few moments of absolute silence. 'Baba, Mumya, why won't you come for me?'

And as he fell down to his knees, his whole body shaking violently, he did nothing to fight the tears as they began to flow.

TWENTY-THREE

Bruges, Belgium

Aydin sipped the milky coffee. It tasted like crap. He had no idea why Itnashar took it like that. He set the steaming cup down onto the table and looked across at his brother on the opposite brown leather sofa. The apartment, although not exactly luxurious, remained way better than the hell-hole Aydin was given in Paris, and he wondered if Itnashar sensed his resentment – not that it was directed at him.

'You can't stay here,' Itnahsar said, the concern on his face clear. 'Haroun will be back soon.'

Aydin didn't know Haroun, only that he was an administrator. Like Khaled had been for him back in Paris.

'In fact, you shouldn't have come here at all,' he added.

'I've nowhere else to go.'

'I want to help you, Aydin.'

Aydin winced at the sound of his real name. Itnashar was the only person who'd called him that in years. A habit the two of them used to cement their bond in their later years at the Farm.

'But?' Aydin asked.

'But what do you expect me to do?'

Aydin didn't answer that. He wasn't sure of the answer, in fact. Did he really trust Itnashar? He certainly trusted that he wasn't about to whip out a gun and shoot him in the face right there, just like that. But he couldn't possibly fully trust that Itnashar would side with him now, against all of the others. They were too far down the road for that to be the case. As close as Aydin was to this man, they weren't thirteen-year-old boys bunking together in the dark any more.

Anyway, Aydin wasn't just there to see an old friend, or to ask for his shelter. There was something else much more important that he needed. He just wasn't yet sure how to go about getting it.

'You know they're after you now,' Itnashar said.

'Who exactly?'

'Wahid has spoken to us all.'

Who else. Aydin had never been close to Wahid. He didn't think anyone but the Teacher had. Wahid really was the epitome of what *they* had wanted to create. He may as well have been a machine for all of the empathy and humanity that remained inside him. A supremely clever, conniving, manipulative machine, that is.

'Wahid has put the order out to capture you. Capture, not kill, Talatashar. Do you understand?'

'Yes. They want to take me away somewhere so that my death will be extremely slow and excruciatingly painful.' For some reason Aydin found himself smiling at that horrible statement.

'No,' Itnashar said, not looking at all impressed with Aydin's nonchalance, though it wasn't his life on the line, so Aydin felt his sarcasm was perfectly justified. 'You're still one of us. Show them. Prove to Wahid that you can still be part of this.'

'Do you really believe that? That I can just turn back now and everything will be okay?'

'Don't you?'

'Not at all.'

'You know I'd never hurt you.'

'But you're happy to throw me out there for the sharks.'

Aydin looked towards the window as the words passed his lips and he imagined them all out there, already circling the waters.

'What does that mean?' Itnashar said.

'You start by saying I can't stay here. Now you're trying to tell me everything will be fine, if I just hold my hands up and stand back in line. That Wahid and the elders just want to know I'm still on board. So which is it, *friend?*'

'It's both. You'll always be my brother, but don't pull me into your mess. And you don't need me anyway. If you really want to keep running then I can't help.'

'Thanks.'

'You don't need me! If you care about me then why would you put me in danger too? You've already shown how good you are out there. You got here, didn't you?'

Aydin's eyes narrowed. He wondered just what Itnashar knew of his journey thus far. How connected were the other twelve over his disappearance and over their search for him?

'Wait, why did you come here exactly?' Itnashar said as though he'd had a eureka moment. He looked more unsettled all of a sudden.

Aydin didn't bother to answer the question. Now wasn't the right time. He took another sip of the coffee. It was now only lukewarm and tasted even worse. Itnashar's eye caught his.

'I'm sorry for what they did to your mother,' he said.

Aydin shook his head. 'You know about that?'

Itnashar looked at him quizzically. 'You haven't seen?'

'Haven't seen what?'

Itnashar got up from the sofa. He moved over to the door behind him and took a key from his pocket. He first typed a combination into the keypad next to the doorframe. Aydin couldn't see the number because he did a good job of screening

145

it. There was a click and Itnashar then used the key to release the manual lock and pushed open the door. Beyond him Aydin spotted his equipment. Computer terminals, screens, wires. All sorts of homemade electrical devices. Aydin thought he knew what most of them were, but not everything. Electronics remained Itnashar's unrivalled area of expertise. His work, his knowledge, was essential to their plans.

Their plans. Like Aydin was still part of it.

Itnashar grabbed a tablet from the shelf in front of him then moved back into the lounge, closing and locking the door behind him. He stood there, tapping away on the tablet's screen before turning it round for Aydin to see.

Aydin was left staring at his own face. A candid picture of him. Not CCTV. He was well used to keeping his face away from street cameras wherever he went, and he knew that no camera in Paris or London would have a good capture of him. The image he was looking at was a high-quality colour picture, of him sitting on the bench in the recreation ground in London two days ago, across the street from his mother's flat.

He was both shocked and disgusted. Frowning, he got up from the sofa and moved over to Itnashar. He took the tablet. The picture was attached to an article from the *Daily Mail*'s website, describing in awful detail the murder of his mother, bludgeoned to death in her own home. A brutal murder during a home invasion gone wrong. An illegal immigrant who'd arrived in the country that same day was wanted for her murder.

An illegal immigrant. Aydin.

When he realised what he was looking at . . . no, there were no words to describe how that felt.

'I know it wasn't you,' Itnashar said.

But it really didn't matter what *he* thought.

Not content with just taking her from him, his own people, his brothers, had set Aydin up for the murder of his mother.

TWENTY-FOUR

'Are you ready?' Aydin whispered to Itnashar as they hunched up against the closed door to their room.

Aydin looked over to his brother, who just nodded, though his face suggested he was less than sure about what they were going to do.

'You have it?' Aydin asked.

Another nod.

'Come on then.'

Aydin took out the two forks that he'd stolen from the kitchen a few days earlier. Using a knife he'd taken at the same time, he'd slowly sawn and twisted and bent and cut through all but one of the prongs on each of them. Itnashar pressed his ear to the door and listened as Aydin stuck the two remaining prongs into the lock and began twisting and prodding, trying to release the latch.

'Stop!' Itnashar said.

Aydin froze. He listened. He could hear nothing other than his own calm breathing and Itnashar's much more erratic breaths.

'What?'

'I heard something.'

'No,' Aydin said, shaking his head. 'There's nothing.'

He carried on. He jerked one of the forks and it clanked inside the chamber and both boys' eyes went wide at the unexpected sound, which echoed all around. But, after a few moments, all was quiet outside.

'Are you sure you can do it?' Itnashar said.

'Just one more twist,' Aydin said, grimacing as he tried to lever the fork around in the confined space.

There was a click. Itnashar looked at him expectantly.

'I did it!' Aydin said.

He twisted the handle carefully until the latch released then he carefully pulled the forks out and put them into his trouser pocket. Aydin pulled open the door.

The corridor outside was dimly lit, yet it caused the boys to squint as they peered out from the darkness of their room. The corridor was all quiet.

'Come on, we need to be quick,' Aydin said, moving out of the room and pulling up against the bare stone wall outside.

He crept along, past one closed door, then another, then another.

'Aydin!' Itnashar whispered. 'It's this one. Where are you going?'

'I can hear them,' Aydin said, cocking his head and concentrating on the faint noise coming from further down the corridor. Chatter. A TV?

'Just get us into the room.'

'No,' Aydin said. 'I've got a better idea.'

Itnashar tutted but Aydin ignored him and began moving again. He was soon at the T-junction at the end of the corridor. Off to the left was another long corridor that eventually led out into the yard. To the right was a much shorter corridor with just two doors off it. One of them was the toilet and shower room. The other was the guards' break room. The door was ajar, and now he was close the sounds were clearer.

'They're watching football,' Aydin said.

He crept further towards the open door.

'No!' Itnashar said.

148

Aydin ignored him. He reached the edge of the doorway and looked behind him to see Itnashar still cowering by the junction. That was fine. He could do this alone. He peeked into the space beyond. There were two sofas in the room, both facing away from the door. He spotted the backs of three heads sticking up. Qarsh was one of them. The nearest to Aydin. As well as the two sofas there was also a table with four chairs in the room, where the guards ate, and a small kitchenette. Both of those areas were empty. Just the three guards. The same as every night.

Aydin jerked back when the men suddenly erupted in shouts and calls. A bad refereeing decision by the sound of it. They all remained seated, and soon they quietened down again. Aydin scanned the room. He spotted what he was looking for. Midway between the door and the back of the nearest sofa was a row of hooks, from which two sets of keys were dangling.

Aydin wanted those keys.

He took a lungful of air, then ever so slowly exhaled. He was surprised, and impressed, to note that his heart was calm. He crept forward on his haunches, his bare feet silent on the stone floor, his eyes not once leaving the back of Qarsh's head. As he got closer to the keys the TV came into view. Aydin's eyes flicked to it. He remembered watching football with his father back in England, but he'd not seen a game in years. He didn't recognise who the teams were, but the commentary was in Arabic. For a few seconds he was enthralled by the somewhat simple sight of men kicking a lump of leather around a green field. But he couldn't just stay there all night.

He stole his eyes from the screen and looked over to the keys. Two sets. Were they just duplicates or did they have different purposes?

He decided he wouldn't take both. Two missing sets was far too suspicious. Best to just grab the nearest ones. Imagine the freedom of having the keys to the Farm.

He reached out . . .

Then jumped, and his heart skipped a beat, when Qarsh shouted out in anger. Aydin daren't even look, as ominous thoughts crashed through his mind, but he soon realised he hadn't been spotted, it was just the game – one of the teams had scored, judging by the raised octave of the commentator. Apparently it wasn't Qarsh's team. Still none of the guards looked round, and Aydin wrapped his fingers around the keys and slowly pulled them up off the hook.

He had them! He backtracked, his heart no longer calm, though he was sure it was just the rush of adrenaline that caused it to race.

When he stepped back out into the corridor he locked eyes with Itnashar and held the keys aloft victoriously. Itnashar initially looked shocked, but then his face opened out in amazement.

Aydin stared at the keys in his hand, then looked down the corridor. The exit was right down there . . .

Could he do it? Could he just open the door and step out into the night and leave the Farm behind?

'Aydin, come on, we need to finish this now!' Itnashar hissed, perhaps sensing Aydin's moment of deliberation.

Aydin slumped a little at the realisation that he simply wasn't brave enough to do what his head was willing him to. But then just look at what he'd achieved already.

He squeezed the keys in his hand and moved back over to Itnashar, then they headed along the corridor back to the door for Wahid and Itnan's room.

'Which key is it?' Itnashar said.

Aydin didn't answer as he thumbed through the selection. He'd long paid attention to the keychains the guards carried, and he knew the shape of the one that was used for their door – would the same key open the doors for all of the boys' rooms?

He found the one he was looking for and stuck it into the lock and turned. It worked.

'Ready?' Aydin whispered.

Itnashar nodded and Aydin turned the handle and pulled on the door, which let out a tiny creak as it opened. Inside, the room was black, and Aydin could hear the soft breathing of the sleeping boys.

'Go on then,' Aydin said to Itnashar.

Itnashar brushed past him, into the room which Aydin could just about make out from the faint light seeping in from the corridor. He watched as Itnashar slunk up to Wahid's bed and lifted the device out of his pocket. He pushed his arm forward, under the bed, and took a few seconds as he tried to attach it in place. Now that they were so close to finishing, Aydin could finally feel his nerves building. He was willing Itnashar to just get this part over and done with so they could head back. What the hell was he doing?

Finally Itnashar pulled his hand back out from under the bed and turned round. Aydin expected to see a smile on his face. Or at the least a look of relief. Instead he looked petrified. Though he wasn't looking at Aydin; he was looking over Aydin's shoulder.

Aydin spun round and was staring into the angry face of Qarsh.

'You stupid little—'

Qarsh smacked Aydin across the face, causing him to reel back. He grabbed Aydin's hair and pulled him off his feet. Another guard came forward, turning on lights and rushing forward to grab Itnashar. Wahid and Itnan both shot up in their beds.

'No!' Aydin pleaded. 'You don't understand, it was just a task. Teacher told us to!'

But Qarsh took no notice. He slapped Aydin across the face again, harder this time, and Aydin fell to the ground. Qarsh lifted his boot and drove it into Aydin's gut, knocking the wind from him and causing his vision to blur.

There was shouting all around. Itnashar was flung forward and crashed into a heap by Aydin's side.

'You two will pay for this,' Qarsh spat.

'Please,' Aydin pleaded. 'We were told to spy. It was just a task. Ask the Teacher. Please!'

Qarsh smashed his boot into Aydin's gut again and it was an effort for him to fight to stay conscious. When his vision returned he looked beyond Qarsh and saw the looming figure of the Teacher.

'Tell him!' Aydin shouted. 'You told us to spy. We didn't do anything wrong.'

Qarsh stepped to the side and the Teacher, clearly pissed off at having been disturbed, came forward into the room. Aydin pulled himself up onto his side. The Teacher looked around, then turned to the two boys on the floor.

'Well?'

'Under the bed,' Aydin said.

The Teacher moved over to Wahid's bed and hunched down and stuck his hand under. He rummaged about for a few seconds then tugged and his hand came back out holding on to the device.

'It's a microphone,' Itnashar said. 'With a radio transmitter.'

'You made this?' the Teacher asked.

'You asked us to spy!' Aydin said again, for which he received another clip around the head from Qarsh.

The Teacher said nothing to Aydin. He turned to Wahid, his pet, who was looking more sheepish than Aydin had ever seen him look before. The Teacher said nothing to him, though Aydin could sense his disappointment. But then the Teacher turned back to Aydin and Itnashar again and Aydin wished he could shrink away to nothing.

'You broke out of your room?' the Teacher said. 'And into here? How?'

Aydin pulled out the forks. 'These,' he said. Then he lifted up the keys. 'And these.'

The Teacher pursed his lips and nodded – was that a sign of satisfaction?

'You took the keys?' he said to Aydin, before looking to Qarsh, who looked stunned all of a sudden.

Aydin just nodded.

'Very good. I'm impressed,' the Teacher said, though his tone didn't at all match the words. He strode back towards the door. Aydin felt himself cower away. 'But you failed.'

'No!' Aydin shouted.

'You were caught. It was all wasted because you got caught. You failed. Take them both away.'

As both Aydin and Itnashar shouted and begged, Qarsh reached forward and grabbed Aydin by his hair again. He tugged hard and dragged him away. The last thing Aydin saw before they were out in the corridor was the snide grin on Wahid's face.

TWENTY-FIVE

'I know it wasn't you,' Itnashar said again, though Aydin wasn't sure why he bothered. He knew Aydin hadn't killed his own mother? Well, what a genius.

The British police too, surely, would know that Aydin hadn't killed her either, if they actually knew Aydin's true identity and that he was the victim's son. But they didn't know his identity, at least not according to the article he was reading. The set-up by his brothers was simply to add pressure on him. He was already being hunted by his people, and now he had the British police, and maybe very soon Interpol, on his case too.

Which planted a seed of doubt in his mind. What did his brothers have to gain from the deception? If the British police caught up with him, they'd simply haul him into jail, wouldn't they? Where was the benefit to his people in that?

Unless . . . Just how far did their reach now spread?

He couldn't rule out that the British police and the intelligence services had been infiltrated at some level, and he shivered at the thought.

Itnashar took the tablet back from him.

'Like I said, you can't stay here,' he said. 'Even if you do the right thing now and prove that you want to get back on side with Wahid, you being here could blow everything open. I can't afford for the police to come knocking on my door.'

'I understand,' Aydin said. 'I'll go. But I need something from you first.'

The way in which he said it made Itnashar squirm, and Aydin could tell that, for the first time, his brother sensed the threat in the man standing before him.

'Tell me what it is,' Itnashar said.

Before Aydin could answer there was a soft electronic chime, coming from over by the door to the apartment. Itnashar's eyes flicked to where the noise came from, but Aydin's stayed fixed on his brother.

'It's Haroun,' Itnashar said. 'You have to go.'

Aydin stepped back, increasing the space between him and his closest companion to a safer distance, and then turned his gaze to the small monitor mounted next to the door frame. Sure enough he saw the dark figure of a man stepping through the entrance doorway. There was another single bleep as the door closed behind him.

In the corner of his eye Aydin saw Itnashar moving towards him. Aydin was ready to attack, but he quickly saw as he turned back that Itnashar had his open hands up to his chest to show he wasn't a threat.

'Come on,' he said, moving for the door. 'Go up the stairs. When Haroun's inside, you go back down and out.'

'What if he sees me on the monitor?'

'Why would he look? Just keep your head down. You could be anyone.'

Itnashar pulled open the door without making a sound.

'We're not done,' Aydin said quietly.

'Go now,' Itnashar whispered. 'Meet me at six p.m. at Markt. It's busy, you'll feel safe there. There's an Italian cafe called Gino's on the Eastern corner. Somewhere near there.'

Before Aydin could either protest or agree, Itnashar shoved him towards the open door. Aydin didn't resist. He didn't need the fight with both Itnashar and Haroun.

He walked out and moved up the staircase, not risking taking a peek below to see how far away Haroun was. He bounced softly up the stairs, his springy knees and the rubber of his trainers allowing him to move silently. As he turned a hundred and eighty degrees with the staircase he looked back down below to see the door to Itnashar's apartment was shut again. He hadn't heard the door close at all. Further below Aydin could hear the plodding of Haroun's feet as he headed up the stairs.

When he reached the top of the staircase, two floors up from Itnashar's apartment, Aydin pulled up against the far wall. There were two apartment doors in front of him. He could hear noises from behind both. A baby crying, its mother singing a soft lullaby to try and calm it. From the other he could hear a TV. There was no indication that anyone up there had been alerted to his presence.

He refocused his hearing to Haroun's footsteps. They stopped. He heard a key in a lock, then the clicking and creaking as the handle was pressed down and the door pushed open. There was a soft thud as the door closed again and then all was silent down below.

Not a second later, though, Aydin's attention was grabbed by the noise coming from the apartment right next to him. The baby's cries were getting louder and he could hear footsteps beyond the door. Whoever was in there was coming out. Had the mother heard him outside, or were they leaving anyway?

As he heard locks clicking, Aydin spun away from his position and glided down the stairs. He was several steps down before he heard the door open and the cries of the baby growing louder still. He didn't look back up, just kept on going down. He didn't slow at all as he passed Itnashar's

156

front door, though his hand did brush against his hip, feeling the hard form of the gun that was stashed there.

No need to draw it. There was no sudden ambush. Not this time.

He continued down, taking a momentary glance up at the ceiling as he reached the ground floor, looking to where the camera that Itnashar had a feed for must be located. He couldn't see it, but there was an air-conditioning duct up there where he must have stashed it. He moved his head down again as he entered the camera's field of vision. He pushed open the door at the front of the building and exited onto the cobbled alley.

Outside in the fresh air Aydin looked left and right before he moved away. He quickly spotted the candidate he was looking for. It was perfect. The other buildings opposite Itnashar's were too close, but the twisting alley meant there was an apartment block less than a hundred yards back towards the canal whose frontage had an almost direct view back to where he was standing.

He moved off in that direction, keeping his head low. He checked the time. Not quite one p.m. so he had a few hours before the hastily arranged rendezvous. It hadn't escaped his mind that the whole thing was most likely a set-up. He needed the few hours to decide what to do.

As he walked along the alley he fished in his pocket for the wireless earbud. He flicked the tiny switch to the on position then put the bud into his ear. The battery should last at least until the planned meeting later on.

He took out the new phone he'd purchased in an electronics shop in Bruges just before he'd headed to Itnashar's apartment. There was a decent 4G signal in the city and he'd already managed to download the app he needed to connect to the tiny microphone that he'd just placed down the side of Itnashar's sofa.

He checked in the Bluetooth menu that the earbud was connected to the phone. It was. He'd earlier spent a good chunk of the cash he had on the various pieces of spy equipment, most of which were now stashed in the backpack slung over his shoulders, but it was worth it. He was on his own for this mission and needed all the help he could get, and he would eke out every advantage he could, however he could.

He didn't know why, but he held his breath as he turned the volume up one notch at a time. There was a chance it wouldn't work, that he'd made a mistake or that the equipment was simply sub-standard, but then the silence in his ear was soon replaced by crackly static.

Moments later, above the crackling, he heard muffled voices. He turned the volume up two more notches, frowning as he listened. He could pick out the tone of Itnashar's voice, and that of a second man – Haroun? The reception was too muffled though to clearly hear their words. Then a third, more distant voice crackled into his ear.

They were speaking to someone else, someone not in the apartment. Wahid? The Teacher?

Of course Aydin immediately suspected the worst. That his closest friend was already stabbing him in the back even as he walked the few yards away from the apartment. But a part of him thought – *hoped* – that perhaps they were just making a routine progress report. Or maybe the third person had contacted *them*.

Unfortunately the microphone reception simply wasn't good enough for Aydin to make out the conversation in any detail, save for the odd word here and there. Certainly he heard no mention of his own name.

He cursed himself under his breath. Back at the Farm he and Itnashar had been such a good team. Aydin was creative and stealthy and ballsy. Itnashar on the other hand could fashion

158

just about any piece of electronic equipment a person could imagine. Aydin had no doubt that in minutes his brother would have been able to cobble together better working devices than the ones he'd just bought. But that had never been Aydin's core skill, and he'd had no choice but to opt for the cheapest miniature microphone the store offered. Despite his stealthy move, in an effort to conceal the device he'd possibly wedged it too far into the sofa's crevices for it to pick up any audio.

He couldn't change it now, though.

Frustrated at what felt like a blown opportunity, Aydin reached the building he was heading for and took a look around outside. No sign of anyone following behind him. He moved over to a souvenir shop a few yards away and rummaged through the racks of postcards on the stand outside. From there he was out of view from Itnashar's building, and he had the front door of number twenty-four in his sights.

Luckily he didn't have to wait long. As he continued to listen to the distorted conversation in his ear, he saw the blue door of the building open, and out stepped a young man, early twenties and scruffily dressed. With a set of big can-like headphones over his ears he was oblivious to everything around him as he walked away, and the door behind him slowly swung closed.

Aydin waited until the last second before he darted forward and slipped through the narrowing gap and into the building.

The interior was gloomy, with no natural light, and it was cold. It was quiet too, and he neither saw nor heard any signs of anyone else. He moved over to the bare stone staircase and made his way up. He'd seen from the outside that the building had five floors, but he'd also noticed that unlike many others around, this one had a flat roof. He didn't know if there was a roof garden up there or if the roof just had access for maintenance, but that was where he was headed.

As he reached the fifth floor he saw there was just one apartment door there, and no more staircase leading up, and he had to concede that the roof was likely a private terrace for the building's penthouse. He was there now, though, and willing to do whatever was needed. If he had to gain entry to the apartment forcibly and subdue whoever was inside, then so be it.

But then he realised that wouldn't be necessary, and there was no doubt that was a relief. Tucked away in the corner was a bland white painted door with a security bar across it. He moved over to it and pushed the bar down. As he slowly swung the door open he wondered whether doing so might trigger an alarm, but once again he needn't have worried. He was greeted only by silence and a narrow staircase. He moved up the stairs and came to another similar door at the top. He opened that one and stepped out onto a rolled lead roof that looked unused. There was a brick wall around the outer edge, less than three feet high, and he crouched down as he scuttled across the top towards the north side of the building.

He came to a stop by the wall and pushed himself up against it before peering over the top and looking back along the alley to Itnashar's building. He was prone with his head sticking up over the parapet and it'd be stupid for him to sit like that, so exposed, for the next few hours. Instead he took out the tablet computer he'd bought and the CCTV camera which he plugged into the tablet with a USB cable. He pushed the camera onto the brick ledge and used the controls on the tablet to zoom in. The picture quality wasn't great, and he was probably twenty yards too far away to be able to make out people coming and going in great detail, but it was good enough for what he needed.

He took out the roll of gaffer tape from the backpack and used a stretch to fix the camera into position, then he sat back against the wall to wait, his eyes on the screen of the tablet as he listened to the crackling voices in his ear.

TWENTY-SIX

Ankara, Turkey

The journey from Syria and onwards to Turkey was just as horrific as Cox had expected. Well, perhaps horrific was the wrong word because there were no more roadblocks with armed combatants wielding assault rifles and rocket launchers, but the trip was nonetheless tiring and gruelling. Having arrived at the US air base in Syria in the middle of the night, Cox had to wait several hours for a flight out of the country, spending the time in a military bunker with copious amounts of crappy coffee while she scoured Nilay's files.

With a decent Wi-Fi signal there, and hoping they could help put some of Nilay's findings into context, she'd fired off several emails to the SIS's Data Ops team back at Vauxhall Cross. They weren't exactly Trapeze, but the data analysts there were the best SIS had to offer, and they had access to – and knew how to search – vast swathes of electronic data, including the databases of many law enforcement and intelligence agencies the world over.

Now it was just a waiting game.

Quite literally.

The flight from Syria into Turkey on the military jet was bumpy and uncomfortable, and gave Cox no chance for either work or sleep. She arrived in Ankara after sunrise, bleary-eyed

162

and feeling beaten up. She was, however, alive and breathing. Which was quite a big plus point considering what she'd been through already.

In Turkey she was taken on a much less nervy car journey from the military base where they landed, to Esenboğa International Airport in the nation's capital, Ankara. As Flannigan had told her on the phone – God knows how many hours before – she was travelling civilian class back to London. That meant going through bog-standard check-in and queuing in the ridiculously long bog-standard security queue. Not quite what most people would expect for international espionage.

It also meant she'd had to give up the guns she'd been carrying through Syria, but that was no big deal really. She was pretty sure she wouldn't be needing them on the British Airways flight.

Several hours later, with the flight to London delayed, Cox was still sitting on a painfully hard metal chair in the departure lounge when she spotted two uniformed policemen making a beeline for her. She sat up in her seat and held their gaze.

'Mrs Taylor?' the shorter, older man said as they reached her, using the alias name Cox had travelled under.

'Yes?'

'Please can you come with us.'

'Is there a problem?' she said, looking around and noticing several other passengers nearby were trying their hardest to pretend they weren't being nosey. In fact, one or two were beginning to skulk away as though they sensed the scene might turn ugly. Cox guessed there was good reason why so many people were jittery travelling through airports.

'No problem, ma'am. We just need to speak to you.'

The man's English was good, though heavily accented. There was no particular tell in his tone. His demand was firm, but not in any way hostile.

'Sure,' Cox said, getting to her feet and picking up her backpack.

'Here, let me take that,' the second policeman said, taking the bag from her grasp with a firm hand.

Cox eyed him up, not quite sure what his gesture was about, but there was no further reaction from him and the older guy stepped to the side and casually indicated with his hand.

'This way, please.'

Cox followed along. The short guy in front, the one holding her bag to her side. They reached a door with a No Entry sign and the policeman in front knocked then stepped back. The door opened to reveal an identically dressed policeman on the other side, who took one look at the old guy before nodding and waving them all through.

Inside they headed further down a warren of bland corridors, the off-white walls all cheap partitions as though the whole structure was temporary. They eventually stopped at a closed door and the old guy once again knocked and waited. The door was opened a few seconds later by a policewoman. Cox peered inside the windowless room.

'Please, Mrs Taylor,' the old guy said, waving her in.

Cox did as she was told. Her mind was still buzzing with thoughts as to what was happening, but even if she was in trouble for some reason, she wasn't exactly in a position to start attacking and taking down each and every one of the officers to make a miraculous escape.

The room she found herself in was a ten-foot by ten-foot square, no windows, but with a wide mirror on one wall. An interview room. In the centre was a simple plastic-topped table and two metal chairs.

'Please take a seat,' the old guy said.

This time Cox didn't do as she was told.

'Why am I here?' she asked him.

The policeman simply gave her a strange and crooked smile before he turned and walked out and the policewoman shut and locked the door behind him, then stood guard in front of it.

'So can *you* tell me?' Cox said.

No answer. So she repeated the question in Turkish. Then Arabic. The policewoman briefly locked eyes with Cox but then looked away, staring back to the wall without saying a word.

Cox stayed where she was, at the other side of the table, not bothering to take either of the seats. Several minutes passed, Cox's brain not once letting up during that time. She was trying to recall all of the times she'd been through the country. Had she made a mistake in the past that was now coming back to bite her? Had she been rumbled because of the identity she was using? Joanna Taylor. She didn't know whether she'd used that passport in Turkey before, or why doing so this time would have triggered any sort of alert.

Or was this somehow connected to the problems in Aleppo? Was that possible?

The longer the wait went on, the more nervous Cox felt. She looked over to the policewoman again. She had a sidearm in a holster by her hip, just like the other police officers had. Cox felt sure she could easily disarm her. And the door was only locked with the standard latch that the policewoman had turned from the inside. This didn't exactly feel like maximum security. Which meant Cox could comfortably make a run for it.

But was that the point? This place wasn't maximum security because there wasn't a *threat*.

There was a rap on the door and Cox stiffened as she was shaken from her thoughts. She looked over at the police officer, who calmly turned and looked through the peephole then released the lock and opened the door. Once again on the other side was the old guy. Except standing beside him now wasn't his colleague, but another man.

165

Henry Flannigan.

'Bloody hell, sir,' Cox said, without thinking.

He raised an eyebrow then came into the room and shooed out the policewoman before closing but not locking the door.

'Bloody hell, what?' he said, taking a seat at the table and slapping down a bundle of papers.

'For starters what are you doing here? I thought I was about to be handed over to MİT so they could take me to some dark site and string me up.' Millî İstihbarat Teşkilatı. The Turkish intelligence services.

Flannigan snorted, a mix of incredulity and amusement. 'Why on earth would you think that?'

'Why do you think! You could have told me you were coming.'

'But I didn't know I was coming last time we spoke.'

'So what changed?'

'Why don't you take a seat.'

Cox did so and sat forward in the chair while Flannigan stared at her.

'I heard what happened on your way out of Aleppo.'

Cox just shook her head at that, not sure what to say.

'I've spoken to people on the ground,' he said. 'There's nothing to suggest they were targeting you in particular.'

'It doesn't really matter much whether they were or weren't. They would have kidnapped or killed us either way.'

'Yeah. Maybe,' Flannigan said without any real feeling.

He rifled through the papers on the desk. He found the one he was looking for, slipped it out and passed it across the table.

'This is the man you referred to as Talatashar,' he said.

Cox stared down at the black-and-white picture. It was the same one she'd come across in Nilay's files, all of which she'd passed to Flannigan before she'd left the safe house in Aleppo.

'Yes,' she said. 'Number thirteen.'

'There's been a development.'

Cox frowned. 'Go on,' she said.

Flannigan let out a long sigh. 'We discussed the possibility that this Talatashar is now in London.'

'Yeah. And?'

'And the data you sent me suggested that Talatashar's real name is in fact Aydin Torkal. Now that boy hasn't been seen for over fifteen years.'

'I know.'

'Until yesterday. When he paid a visit to his old family home. His mother still lives there. *Lived*, actually.'

Flannigan pushed some other papers across. The first was a colour photo of the same man, a candid of him sitting on a park bench. The other was a gruesome crime-scene photo showing the bloodied body of a middle-aged woman.

'What happened?' Cox said, feeling revulsion as she looked at the sorry image.

'That's Torkal's mother. We think he killed her.'

Cox found herself shaking her head. 'No,' she said. 'That doesn't make any sense. Why—'

'Of course it makes sense. The man is deranged. It was *you* who told *me* about these people. Trained from nine years old to be some sort of unhinged, unfeeling jihadi warrior. He's left a trail of destruction from Paris to London and three dead bodies in the process.'

'It just doesn't—'

'It is what it is. Whatever the story, *you* need to help find him.'

Cox felt a hard-nosed resolve break out into her face. 'I will,' she said. 'But I still don't understand why you came all the way here to tell me this?'

'We haven't got an active trail on Torkal, but we believe he smuggled himself onto a container ship at Felixstowe. My

167

guess is he's already skipped England for his next port of call. It could be anywhere on the damn continent.'

'Germany,' Cox said, putting the pieces together in her mind.

'Germany?'

She bent down and lifted the laptop out of her bag. She flipped the lid and, using the weak 3G signal in the airport, she scrolled through to the news reports she'd been scouring while waiting for her London flight to board. She turned the screen round for Flannigan to see.

'Roman Asrutdinov,' Cox said. 'Recognise the name?'

Flannigan's eyes narrowed. Cox thought she could see the flicker of recognition.

'Of course I do,' Flannigan said. Asrutdinov had, after all, been an SIS asset of sorts, delivering intel to the West about North Korea's Internet espionage. 'But everyone believes it was a hit by the North Koreans, or if not them then the Russians.'

'Maybe it was,' Cox said. 'And probably under any other circumstance I'd agree. Except this also happened in Berlin, two days ago.'

Flannigan's eyes flicked about as he read the report. 'Six dead bodies in a burned-out van outside an abandoned warehouse?' he said, sounding even more sceptical. 'What are you trying to tell me, Cox? You think this is the work of Torkal?'

'Probably not. He was still in London when these deaths occurred. But Germany was hinted at as one of the locations for the Thirteen in Nilay's documents. I've included details in the information I sent to Data Ops, and maybe Germany is where Torkal has gone now. You said yourself he could be anywhere on the continent. Most likely he'll be in one of the twenty-six Schengen countries still, wouldn't you say?'

'At this stage, yes. He'd need more time to go anywhere else, both geographically and logistically.'

'Then I think it's worth taking a closer look at these deaths in Berlin.'

'I'm not sure I get how you think this is linked?'

'Preparations. What if they were working with Asrutdinov? They've got what they need from him now so they've dispatched him.'

'And the six dead bodies in a van?'

'Still unidentified so it's hard to say, but the circumstances aren't exactly normal. It was no accident. If we can identify the corpses, it'll tell us a lot more.'

'I can't help but think you're making too much of this.'

Cox glanced at her watch. 'I already checked and there's a flight to Berlin leaving in less than an hour. I can be there by early evening. If it turns out to be nothing I can be back here, or wherever else you want me next, in the morning.'

Flannigan mulled over that one for a few moments. Cox knew it was a long shot, but it didn't feel like there was much else to go on. Yes, she could go back to London as planned but they both agreed Aydin Torkal had more than likely already left. Perhaps he wasn't in Berlin either, and never had been, and she would just end up chasing more shadows. But unless Flannigan had a better idea . . .

'Okay,' Flannigan said. 'We'd better see about getting you a new ticket.'

TWENTY-SEVEN

London, England

Obbadi had picked the car up from a prestige rental company five miles outside Heathrow airport. It was the first time he'd taken a commercial airline for months, and would most likely be the last for quite some time. This, though, was a hastily arranged trip and there hadn't been enough time to properly organise all of the paperwork to charter his private jet. Sometimes it was easier to just travel like everybody else.

That didn't mean, however, that he couldn't still have some fun. Hence the car. A very nearly brand new Bentley Continental GT. He was in England after all. The V8 engine – he'd opted for that model rather than the slightly more powerful W12 simply for the more racy noise – growled happily as he pushed his foot down and the two-tonne beast lurched forward at speed. The quiet and twisting A-road he was travelling down with neatly trimmed hedgerows either side gave him ample opportunity to test the machine's capability. And work out just a little bit of the tension in his mind following the ongoing problems with that imbecile Talatashar.

It wasn't long before he hit the upmarket town of Burnham in Buckinghamshire, where he'd arranged to pick up his companion and guide for the trip. He spotted his brother standing outside the town's post office and pulled the Bentley over to the side of the road. Arab'ah – number four – opened the door and sunk down into the damson leather seat. He snorted.

'Nice,' he said.

Obbadi put his foot down and the engine revved freely again as the car shot away.

'Very nice,' Arab'ah said.

Obbadi said nothing, just carried on driving. Only once they were out of the town and back travelling at a heady speed did he decide it was time to get back to business.

'How is our brother?' Obbadi said, referring to Hidashar. He'd suffered two cracked ribs in the fight with Talatashar in London, though really Obbadi knew Hidashar was made of steel. It took a lot more than two broken ribs to stop him.

'I think his pride is hurt more than his body.'

Obbadi huffed in agreement.

Arab'ah gave the directions as they carried on the journey through the lush English countryside. It was the first time Obbadi had been to this part of England – his presence required to ensure the preparations were in place and satisfactory. Not that he doubted Arab'ah's planning, who was as meticulous as anyone Obbadi had met.

They'd been travelling for well over an hour when they turned onto narrow and even quieter roads.

'Okay, if you take the lane on the left here, it's just a few hundred yards further down.'

Obbadi turned in, moving from tarmac onto a dirt track that had two wide grooves either side of a run of green grass. The low-sitting car bounced and banged across the uneven ground. When he spotted a secluded turn-in he pulled the car over.

'Maybe we should just walk the rest of the way,' he said. No reason to beat up such a nice machine.

Arab'ah just shrugged. Obbadi turned the engine off and they both stepped out into the murky and humid afternoon.

When Obbadi had arrived at Heathrow the sun had been shining, but it now felt like a rainstorm was imminent.

Welcome to England, he thought.

'This way,' Arab'ah said, moving off and further up the track.

Obbadi followed and they soon came to a large metal gate beyond which was an old red brick structure – two storeys tall and fifty yards wide – that was clearly now abandoned, evident by the severely overgrown grounds and the cracked and missing windows in the stone frames of the building. The gates had a thick and rusted padlock holding them together but there was a gap about a foot wide between the left gate and the wire fence that trailed off from it – easily enough to slip through.

'This place was built in the Victorian times,' Arab'ah said as he squeezed through onto the weed-filled grounds. 'It was one of several pumping stations needed to take raw sewage from the towns, but these places haven't been used for years. All the modern equivalents are underground.'

'Glad to hear it,' Obbadi said. 'I don't really want to be wading through shit today.'

'You won't be. I promise.'

They worked their way round the outside of the main building until they came across a large manhole cover protruding from the ground. Arab'ah dug into his backpack for the foot-long key that he used to lift up the thick metal cover. As he clanked the manhole cover onto the floor next to them the sound echoed down the brick chamber by their feet.

'You first,' Obbadi said with a wry smile.

Arab'ah nodded and lowered himself down into the hole, using the dilapidated-looking metal ladder that was attached to one of the side walls. When he was out of sight Obbadi peered over, looking into the depths, before he followed his brother down. He initially held his breath, expecting a foul stench, but when he was finally forced to inhale there was nothing but the smell of damp and mould. Quite a welcome smell compared to what he expected.

He reached the bottom where the entrance opened out into a tunnel that trailed off into the distance to his left and right. Arab'ah was holding a powerful torch that shone some hundred yards in front of them, lighting up the spooky space in a yellow electric haze. The rounded tunnel was only six feet high at its peak and standing at the side to avoid the pooled water in the middle of the floor meant both men had to stoop.

'Come on,' Arab'ah said, 'it's this way.'

They traipsed along, Obbadi looking behind him every now and then, into the darkness. He certainly wasn't one to be scared either of the dark or of confined spaces, but still, this was hardly his choice of a fun way to spend time. Yet he was filled with quiet anticipation as to what lay ahead.

'This sewer hasn't been used for about twenty years now,' Arab'ah said. 'A new treatment plant opened up a few miles away and this was one of a handful of tunnels that were no longer needed, and the original pump house was left to nature. But the Victorians knew how to build. This place'll last for centuries yet.'

They walked on for over twenty minutes. More than once Obbadi heard the sloshing of water and the padding of little feet as rats and whatever else lived down in the depths scampered out of the way of the new arrivals.

'Are you sure you can carry the equipment this far?' Obbadi asked.

'Hidashar will be with me,' Arab'ah explained.

Obbadi guessed that was sufficient. The big man was like a mule. He could probably haul a ton weight this distance without breaking a sweat.

They reached a junction in the tunnel and Arab'ah stopped. Off to his left was an opening where a rounded pipe about three feet in diameter trailed away.

'I hope you're not about to tell me we need to crawl through that.'

'That?' Arab'ah said, pointing the torch down the pipe. 'No. That's an overflow pipe from the water system, to relieve flooding.'

'Better hope that rainstorm doesn't hit, then, or we'll be washed away with the rats.'

Arab'ah huffed as though that was a ridiculous statement. 'Actually, flooding is usually caused by rain much further down the line. The main water supply is nearly a hundred miles from here. This whole area of the country is supplied from a man-made lake in Wales. In the 1960s they dammed up and then flooded a huge valley there to supply water to the region.'

'Thanks for the history lesson,' Obbadi said, sounding uninterested, though he was impressed with Arab'ah's level of research and knowledge.

'Anyway, we're here,' Arab'ah said. He lifted the torch and pointed upward and Obbadi saw a chamber rising up twenty feet.

They climbed the ladder one after the other and once Arab'ah had forced away the manhole cover they were soon both stepping out into thick rain. Obbadi clambered out and looked around. They were in a narrow clearing of grass that stretched off for several hundreds yards in either direction, flanked on one side by a dense tree line and on the other by a small hill, fifteen feet high – its neat form suggested it was man-made.

'Keep down,' Arab'ah said, hunching over and moving on his hands and feet up the mound. 'It's usually quiet this side but you never know.'

174

Obbadi followed and a few seconds later when he was halfway up, the roar of jet engines blasted into his ears a moment before he saw the giant hulk of a passenger plane sweeping through the air almost within touching distance above him. The noise and vibration of the aircraft so close made his insides curdle as it passed overhead. The next step Obbadi reached the top of the mound and lay down on his belly with Arab'ah next to him to look out over the sprawling airport in the near distance. The arriving plane bounced down onto the tarmac runway, sending up a plume of tyre smoke into the air.

Obbadi looked over to his brother, who had a satisfied smile on his face.

'Perfect, right?' Arab'ah said.

Obbadi smiled and nodded.

'Twelve million passengers a year,' Arab'ah said. 'At this time of the year there'll be thousands in the airport at any one time. And the exit route for us from here couldn't be better. The plan is to head back the way we just came, but if we feel we need to I've pored over the whole network. There are three other escape routes that I know we can get to easily.'

'Good work, my brother,' Obbadi said, reaching over and patting Arab'ah on the back.

'So we just need the rest of the equipment now,' Arab'ah said. 'Have you heard from Itnashar?'

'As a matter of fact I have,' Obbadi said, gritting his teeth in anger as he thought about the last conversation he'd had with Itnashar not long ago.

'Talatashar?' Arab'ah said, picking up on Obbadi's mood change. 'He's gone to Bruges?'

'Yes, that's where he's gone. But the plan is that he'll never leave there alive.'

175

TWENTY-EIGHT

Bruges, Belgium

Aydin stayed in position up on the rooftop for more than an hour without seeing or hearing anything of interest. After the initial flurry of activity there had been virtually no chatter coming into his ear. No one had left the building either, and just two people had entered; a young mother with a baby in a pushchair. He wondered if it was the same mother and baby he'd heard leaving earlier when he was on the top floor.

It was nearly three p.m. when finally his attention was grabbed. He spotted the two men, their backs to the camera, walking along the alley. Even before they stopped outside the door to Itnashar's building Aydin sensed they weren't just two passersby. He risked a glance up over the edge of the wall. He wanted to set his eyes on the men properly, pick out any detail that the camera wasn't giving him.

As he looked over the edge he heard the ringing in his ear as the intercom from Itnashar's apartment sounded out. The two men had their eyes working the alley around them, but they didn't look up to where Aydin was at all. They were quite nondescript in appearance. Both wore dark casual clothing, but they were neither particularly old nor young, tall nor short, nor thin, nor muscled. Basically they blended.

Exactly the type of men needed for what Aydin thought their role would be.

Looking back at the screen on his tablet Aydin watched as the two men stepped inside the building. In his ear he heard Itnashar's muffled voice again, and not long after there was the thudding and clunking as the guests arrived inside the apartment.

A conversation began and lasted for several minutes though Aydin shook his head again in frustration as he listened to the mostly indecipherable chatter. Every now and then there was a single word, two or three in a row at most, that he could pick out clearly, but it wasn't enough to take any great meaning.

Then he heard his name. Talatashar. All of a sudden it was as though his senses had renewed focus. He heard further snippets. *He's alone. Confront him.*

Or had Itnashar said *don't* confront?

Aydin simply couldn't be sure and wondered whether he'd even heard those simple words correctly or was just making what he heard fit.

Regardless, he had a clear choice to make. He could go and meet Itnashar as planned, even though it was odds on that his brother was setting him up. It wasn't a welcome scenario but at least that way he had a chance of getting the information he needed. He had no idea of the exact location of any of his other brothers. Itnashar did.

Or he could run again. Get out of Bruges and try to stay one step ahead of the chasing pack. Quite where he could go to next he didn't know. But at least he'd still be breathing . . .

No, he wasn't running, he decided with absolutely finality.

He remained on the rooftop until four p.m., then he unplugged the camera from the tablet and switched on its wireless capability. To save its battery he'd only turn the camera on again when he was next looking at the tablet's screen. He left the earbud in place then packed up the rest of his things and headed across the rooftop to the door.

When he arrived, just before half past four, Markt was busy with locals and tourists. The large open space was one of the city's busiest meeting spots with lines of cafes and restaurants, together with several historic monuments – pride of place being the thirteenth-century belfry, with its gothic spires, that rose up into the sky beyond everything around it. In the past the belfry had been used as an observation post for spotting fires and other danger within the city. It seemed quite apt to Aydin – or was it ironic? – that this was the place Itnashar had chosen to meet.

He walked through the bustling square, past the grand central statue that featured two heroic and proud warriors atop it, whose history he knew nothing about. He ducked out of the way of the tourists posing for pictures and headed to the east corner of the square where Itnashar was expecting to meet him later. Gino's was a popular Italian – judging by the number of people cramming onto its terrace – and his belly grumbled angrily as he walked past and the smell of grilled meat and tomato sauce and melted cheese filled his nose.

He did need to eat, but not there. Instead, having scoped out the whole of the square to his satisfaction, he bought a cheese and chicken baguette from a delicatessen and ate it on the move, then set up position on the opposite side of the square to Gino's, in a coffee shop, taking a seat inside, up against the front window.

He wasn't deeply hidden, but he was far enough removed. It was busy outside, and with the position of the sun in the sky, no one looking from the square to the windows of the cafe could see who or what lay beyond the glare. He also knew there were two good exit routes directly outside the cafe that led away from Markt, if he felt under threat and needed to escape quickly.

As he sipped through his first coffee he took out his phone and opened up the feed to the camera. The smaller screen made it even more difficult to make out the picture clearly, but it was good enough to spot the three men leaving the building just a few minutes after he had. Itnashar and the two others. No sign of Haroun, who he assumed, judging by the faint sounds still in his ear (a TV or radio?), had stayed in the apartment.

The three men were soon out of sight of the camera so Aydin once again turned it off and closed the screen and set the phone down. He also took out the earbud and switched that off to save its battery. Then he again contemplated what he should do next.

He could go back to the apartment, break entry and tackle Haroun, and hope he could find and take what he needed from Itnashar's equipment without him being there. The first part would be simple, but once inside he would not only have to contend with gaining access to Itnashar's equipment room, but then breaking through any passcode or encryption on his devices. Although it was tempting to try that, it felt like a risk, particularly as Itnashar hadn't even arrived at Markt yet. He should at least see how the planned rendezvous played out first.

So instead he waited in the coffee shop. He was just finishing his second drink when, across the square, he spotted Itnashar roaming around. He was alone. Or at least Aydin saw no sign of the other two men, though he had no doubt they were there somewhere. Having not seen their faces clearly made it all the more difficult to pinpoint them, so Aydin was busily scouring the crowds as Itnashar casually set up position against a lamp post ten yards away from Gino's terrace.

179

After a couple of minutes there was still no sign of the two men, no one else milling who caught his eye. Nervousness began to bubble up in him. He wondered whether the men were armed and in sniper position, up at the top of the belfry perhaps, ready to put a bullet into Aydin's head the moment he stepped out into the square.

Either that or they were just damned good at hiding.

Then, Aydin realised, there was always a further option. That perhaps Itnashar wasn't setting him up at all. Maybe the other men weren't even there.

Across the square he noticed Itnashar bringing a hand up to his face. Covering his mouth? It didn't take Aydin long to figure out that he was talking. Likely him and his chums were all wired in to each other.

Or were they?

Aydin frowned. Itnashar's hand was just far enough away, and the angle just right to allow Aydin to partly see his lips. What was he saying?

Aydin dove into his backpack and took out the earbud. He turned it back on and put it into his ear.

'Aydin,' he heard Itnashar say, his voice loud and clear as he watched from across the square. 'Aydin, I know you can hear me. I can help to get you out of this city alive. But only if you do exactly as I say.'

TWENTY-NINE

Aydin clenched his fists, his fingertips digging into and cutting his skin, the grip was so tight. He didn't need to listen another second. He pulled the bud from his ear, switched it off and shoved it into the backpack. He stood up and slung the bag over his shoulder and headed for the door. Outside he turned left and within seconds was walking away from Markt.

He didn't know how long Itnashar would stand there, blathering away into the microphone, trying to persuade Aydin that he was on his side. Maybe five minutes, maybe an hour. It made Aydin mad that Itnashar felt he could play him so easily. How long had it taken to find the microphone in the first place? Perhaps that was why the reception had been so crackly from the start – Itnashar had made it that way by smothering it, having found the damn thing the second Aydin left the apartment.

He didn't know for sure why Itnashar had chosen to reveal his cards like that. There was the slim possibility that he really was looking out for Aydin, but if that was the case why had he waited so long?

It didn't matter. Aydin decided it was time for a different approach. He'd rather play the game by his own rules, not anyone else's.

He retraced his steps back along the canal to Itnashar's apartment, taking the most direct route. There was no hint that either his friend or the goons were following, though Aydin didn't mind that much if they were. It was plainly clear that, if he was to get what he needed, then sooner or later there was going to be a confrontation; the only questions remaining were when and how.

When he reached Itnashar's apartment building Aydin pressed on the buzzer for one of the top-floor apartments. He waited a few seconds but there was no response. He pressed on the next button and waited. After a few moments a woman's voice came through the speaker and he pictured the mother with the screaming baby once again.

'I have a delivery for 4b, do you think you can accept it?' Aydin said in French. He didn't know any Flemish and hoped the woman could understand.

He could hear the unsettled babe in the background still. The woman tutted but then said, '*Oui,*' and the door buzzed unlocked.

Aydin headed inside and up the stairs and as he reached the third floor he leaned over the banister and peered upward. Sure enough the woman was up there, looking down for him.

'It's okay,' he shouted up. 'He's here after all.'

She shook her head in annoyance and disappeared to tend to the youngster. She was too preoccupied to think properly about the simple trick he'd just played, and why would she care anyway – he wasn't presenting a threat to her.

He stood outside the door to Itnashar's apartment and pressed his ear up against the wood. Inside it was quiet but not silent, and he heard the faint sound of the TV. He could only guess that Haroun was still home, though he'd not been checking the feed from the camera the whole time so couldn't be one hundred per cent.

The door had two locks on the outside, though Aydin had noticed earlier that Itnashar didn't secure the deadbolt while they were inside, and he assumed that Haroun hadn't either. The other lock, a tumbler device, was easy to pick and it took Aydin less than thirty seconds to work through the sequence of pins. When the last of the pins was released he held the handle with one hand and grabbed the butt of his gun with the other.

He took a couple of seconds to run through in his head the various sequences of moves for when he threw the door open, the exact actions he would take depending on where Haroun was in the room.

Satisfied that he had the most obvious possibilities covered, he pushed down on the handle and swung open the door, bursting forward and drawing the gun at the same time.

He was pleased to see the back of Haroun's head, poking up from the sofa in front of him. Haroun jumped up and turned when he heard the banging of the door as it crashed against the adjacent wall, but Aydin didn't give him any time to offer up a purposeful response. He pushed his arm behind to slam the door shut as he moved forward, and just as Haroun's eyes met his, he smashed the barrel of the handgun into the side of his head. Haroun fell back down onto the sofa, his heavy body bouncing on the cushions.

Thirty minutes later and Aydin was out of luck. He'd not even been able to gain access to Itnashar's lab in that time, never mind break any codes to gain access to his equipment. He had to expect that his brother would be returning to the apartment sooner or later, so it was time to ramp up the pressure while he still had the chance.

He threw a cup of cold water into Haroun's face to rouse him. The liquid did the trick and he jerked awake. He coughed and spluttered for a few seconds while his brain recalibrated. His steely glare fixed on Aydin.

'You're dead!' he said, anger the first emotion to hit him. '*Kess ommak*!'

He hurled a mouthful of phlegm that splatted on Aydin's chin. Aydin wiped it away without showing any feeling. Haroun's words were intended to provoke and derail, literally referencing Aydin's mother's vagina, but Aydin was just a little beyond playground insults, however raw the subject of his mother was.

'Interesting that you should mention genitalia,' Aydin said, before casting his eyes downward.

Haroun's eyes followed and Aydin saw the moment of realisation sweep across his face. He was naked, his hands secured behind him and around the leg of the bookcase. His ankles were roped together and tied to the radiator pipes. He couldn't move at all. By Aydin's side was a pair of pliers and a hammer he'd found in a small toolbox. In his hand was a knife. Just a regular chopping knife from the kitchen drawer, but it was plenty sharp enough if he needed to make himself any more clear than he already had.

Aydin jabbed the pointed end of the blade into Haroun's scrotum, causing him to writhe and grimace until he took the bloodied tip away. Haroun understood, and Aydin saw the look on his face change.

Recalibration complete.

'Now let's talk,' Aydin said.

THIRTY

It was two weeks since Aydin had celebrated his fifteenth birthday. Celebrated? Perhaps that wasn't the right term. It had been acknowledged by the Teacher that he was now fifteen, not fourteen, and Itnashar had sung him a birthday ditty as they lay in their bunks that night. He didn't feel any different because he was now older – even though the Teacher had told him he was no longer a boy – but he did feel different because of what they were doing today: it was the first day that Aydin had held a real, live gun.

For all of the teaching he and the boys had experienced at the Farm over the years, everything the elders had shown them and made them do, Aydin had never felt so powerful as earlier that morning when he'd first held that lump of metal and pulled on the trigger to fire at the imaginary targets.

They'd spent several hours doing that. With a handgun each, the boys had been taught how to aim and fire, and how to reload. Aydin had done okay. Not the best of them, but certainly not the worst either. It was what Wahid always said to him – as an insult. Aydin was a jack-of-all-trades, master of none. An English saying, Wahid delighted in telling him, as though it made him superior to Aydin to know a saying of the place where he came from.

185

The weather outside was stifling with not a breath of wind and the air was thick with heat as the intense sun beat down on them. They had stopped for water not long ago but the Teacher now had the fourteen boys lined up in the yard for the next task. Fourteen. Neither Aydin nor the others knew exactly what happened to the fifteenth, though everyone had a tale to tell of his sorry demise.

The Teacher paced up and down in front of them, next to that damn wooden pole in the centre of the yard that Aydin had spent many a sleepless night chained to. There was a little portable table set up in front of the pole. On it sat a shining black handgun. The yard they were in was enclosed by a simple wooden fence. No other security was needed. Beyond the fence, in every direction, was simply an endless expanse of rock and sand. There was nowhere to run or hide out there.

'Today you will become men in my eyes,' the Teacher said, without looking at any of the boys. 'You've already come so far here, it's now time to prove yourselves to me. This is your one chance to show you belong here.'

Across the other side of the yard, where the series of low-rise buildings stood, a door opened and Aydin saw Qarsh with his back to them. Aydin knew it was him, even without seeing his face, due to the unmistakable slope of his heavily muscled neck and shoulders. Aydin wondered what he was doing, then he saw that Qarsh was heaving something out of the doorway.

No, not something, but someone. It was a man.

The guy was naked, except for his dirtied underwear, and there was a sack on his head. His brown skin was covered in wispy black hair, his hands were tied behind his back, and Qarsh was coaxing him along. The man stumbled every few steps as though there was no strength or focus in his limbs at all.

'Each of you will face this same test,' the Teacher said, turning to face Qarsh and the man. He paused. Then looked over the boys. 'Sura five, verse thirty-three?'

Several hands went up. Naturally, the Teacher pointed to Wahid.

'The punishment of those who wage war against Allah and His messenger and strive to make mischief in the land is only this,' Wahid recited from memory. 'That they should be murdered or crucified or their hands and their feet should be cut off on opposite sides or they should be imprisoned. That is their disgrace in this world, and a great torment is theirs in the Hereafter.'

The Teacher nodded in acknowledgement. Aydin bit his lip. Now wasn't the time to debate that much of the rest of the Sura referred to Allah's merciful nature.

'The objective is simple,' the Teacher continued. 'The men you will see today have to die, for they have attacked us. It is down to you to make that happen.'

Qarsh brought the man over and quickly untied his wrists, then retied them around the pole. He then lifted off the sack and Aydin saw the bouncing eyes of the man underneath. His jaw was chattering with fright as he mumbled incoherently.

'Wahid,' the Teacher said, turning to lock eyes with his favoured student once more.

Without hesitation Wahid stepped forward and moved up to the table. No more words were said as he reached out and brushed his hand across the gun. He looked back up to his master and the Teacher gave the slightest of nods. Wahid picked up the gun and strode over to the prisoner, who fell to his knees and began to plead.

Wahid moved right up to the man and placed the barrel of the gun up against his forehead. Then he paused and turned to the Teacher. He simply nodded again and Wahid pulled the trigger and Aydin felt himself jump at the booming sound as the back of the man's head all but exploded. His body flopped forward, suspended in the air awkwardly with his wrists still secured to the pole behind. When Wahid turned back there was a wide smile on his face as his gaze found Aydin.

Every one of the boys had their turn. Aydin had no choice but to watch as one by one Qarsh brought a condemned man out into the sun and secured him to that pole. No choice but to watch as one by one his brothers stepped forward and took the life of another human with the simple pull of a trigger.

No reasons were given for who the men were, nor what their crime – if any – was, and not one of the boys opened their mouths to ask any such question. Despite the Teacher trying to tie the killings to the will of Allah, it was clear the exercise wasn't about punishing the men they were shooting, it was about the boys.

Itnashar moved forward from the line, to the table, and picked up the gun. He took two steps further forward to the man before lifting the gun up. Aydin had been keeping a mental note of how far each of his brothers stood from their victim. Only Wahid had pressed the barrel of the gun right up against the condemned's skin. Itnashar, so far, was standing the furthest away.

Aydin once again flinched as the gun fired and the bullet splatted into the man's left eye. Itnashar hung his head, turned, and placed the gun back onto the table. Aydin looked back to the Teacher, who had stopped pacing and was staring at Itnashar. He said nothing but Aydin saw anger in his eyes. He didn't know why.

Minutes later, with another soon-to-be-corpse in place, it was Aydin's turn to approach the table. The vile exercise had finally become real for him, and he struggled to find the strength to pick up that gun. He had told himself he would, that he had to. But now that it was right in front of him it was as if there was a force field around it, pushing his hand away.

He fought through it and grabbed the butt of the gun, checked it over like they had been taught to that same morning, then pointed the barrel to the head of the man standing just a few yards in front of him.

His finger was on the trigger. But he hesitated. His brain was screaming for him to just do it, to prove himself to the Teacher and to his brothers, but something else inside was holding him back.

The gun began to shake in his hand. Just a tiny, almost imperceptible stammer coming from his arm. But it got bigger. Within a few seconds he worried that he might even miss the target.

He imagined what the others behind him were thinking. Were they willing him on, wanting him to succeed? Or were they hoping he failed, hoping that the Teacher and Qarsh would punish him for showing weakness?

'Stop!' the Teacher yelled and Aydin jumped and sensed everyone around him was now holding their breath. 'Put that gun down, now!'

Even from yards away Aydin was sure he felt the Teacher's spittle spattering his cheek, such was the force of effort in his bark. Aydin shifted his eyes and caught the Teacher's gaze and saw the unabashed rage in his eyes. He lowered the weapon, moved over and put it down onto the table.

The Teacher reached to his side and unsheathed an eight-inch serrated blade, which he slapped down onto the table.

'Now pick up the knife.'

Aydin did as he was told without hesitation.

'Take it over to him.'

Aydin moved, though it was an effort. His legs felt intermittently like lead and like jelly.

'Be sure that it takes more strength of mind to take a life up close, than from a distance,' the Teacher shouted, and Aydin sensed he was talking to the others as much as he was to him. 'You are men now, never fail to show your enemy that. To feel another person's life-force drifting away as you stare into his *dying eyes, feeling his slowing breaths on your cheek . . . there is nothing more powerful than that. And your enemy deserves nothing more. Never be afraid to punish your enemy. He would certainly not show you any mercy.'*

The Teacher had said this before. In fact Aydin thought he quite delighted in reminding the boys of the barbarous acts carried out by Western countries over the centuries, from torture techniques used in Medieval England through to Nazi human experimentation during World War II. Those examples were, according to the Teacher, convincing evidence of why the non-believers couldn't be allowed to control the world — couldn't even be allowed to live in the world.

Aydin reached the man and looked into his sorry eyes and for just a flash he thought that even he was mocking him now. That at least allowed him to muster an ounce more strength and determination.

'Do it,' the Teacher said. 'Slit his throat.'

Standing there, with the man on his knees in front of him, the stench of his urine and the blood-soaked ground filled Aydin's nose, and as he held back bile he was having serious doubts whether he could stomach carrying out the instruction.

He clenched his teeth, tensed his muscles, summoning an inner rage that he hoped would see him through.

It was working.

His body was shaking again, no longer from fear, but anger, and it was driving him on. He grabbed the man's hair, pulled his head back to expose his neck. He lifted the knife, ready to swipe . . .

'Stop,' the Teacher said. But gone was his bark, he was now measured and calm. 'Very good, Talatashar. Very good. But for you, something different.'

Aydin didn't move. Not at all. The knife was still there, in prime position to take the man's life. He was ready to do it. A large part of him wanted to do it. He had to prove himself.

'A challenge for you, Talatashar. Can you hurt this man for me? I mean really hurt him? Can you look into his eyes while inflicting the most unimaginable pain?'

'Yes,' Aydin said without even thinking.

'Good. Now cut off his ear.'

'I . . .' is all Aydin said to that. He simply couldn't find any other words.

'Cut off his ear. Show your brothers how strong you are, Talatashar. Show them what it takes to be up close and to have someone at your mercy.'

The shaking was back again, though Aydin was now struggling to keep hold of the anger that had driven him on moments earlier. He let go of the man's hair, and took an ear in his grip. He pulled the appendage outward and the man moaned louder, his pleading becoming more desperate.

'Show me you deserve your place among us,' the Teacher said.

Aydin had to. There was no other way. He had to stay at the Farm. Not just because it was what his father wanted, but because they'd all heard the stories of what would happen to the students who failed. After all, there used to be fifteen of them. Now there were only fourteen.

Without any further thought, Aydin pulled the knife round and sliced it down against the man's ear. He screamed in pain and writhed and jolted his head and Aydin heard the flesh of the ear in his grip tear further. The Teacher had to come over to hold the man in place. Aydin locked eyes with his master and saw he was smiling at him.

'You can do this, son,' he said.

Aydin didn't hesitate, moved the knife back and forth, and the blade sank down slowly through flesh. He finally found that inner rage again and he roared as he took two more swipes. His hand was covered in blood and the thick red liquid poured down over the man as the gristly piece of tissue came away from his head.

191

'And now you're a man,' the Teacher said, pride in his eyes, and he grabbed Aydin's hand, the one with the dripping flesh still dangling from it, and hauled it into the air like it was a trophy.

Aydin's brothers cheered for him and applauded and he broke out into as wide a smile as he could remember.

This was his *moment.*

THIRTY-ONE

Bruges, Belgium

'I don't know!' Haroun screamed, his voice coarse and gravelly from the effort of his cries.

But Aydin didn't believe him. He knew how their operation worked. He knew what Khaled had done for him, back in Paris. There was no way that Haroun didn't have the access code to Itnashar's lab, and Aydin was almost certain he had the passwords for the computer equipment too. The administrators were like personal assistants, and what PA worth their salt didn't know their boss's log-in details?

Did Haroun really believe he could hold out? Did he not understand what Aydin was capable of?

By now the blood coming from Haroun's head wound had clotted and the lines of blood on his face were dark and solid, beginning to crack. His flabby body was shivery and he was shaking with fear. His left foot and the floor around it was covered in fresh blood as Aydin worked across each of his toenails, the discarded pieces on the floor next to them.

'Four down, sixteen to go,' Aydin said.

'No, please!'

Aydin pinched the nail on Haroun's big toe with the pliers and pulled up until he felt resistance. He looked into Haroun's eyes. They didn't know each other. Aydin didn't feel any real animosity towards him, yet he had barely blinked at what he was doing to him. This was how *they* wanted him to be. He wasn't sure if it made him feel incredibly strong, or incredibly weak any more.

'The codes, Haroun. And I promise I'll stop.'

'*Telhas teeze!*'

Lick my ass. Not nice.

Aydin tugged upward with a short, sharp movement and the tight grip on the pliers allowed him to easily prise off the large nail with a squelch and a suck. Haroun screamed again and Aydin quickly stuffed the sock into his mouth. Together with the TV on full volume it was plenty enough to muffle his cries. When it was clear he was calming down Aydin grabbed hold of the little toe on Haroun's right foot and got ready again.

Then a beeping rang out just feet from where Aydin was crouched, cutting through the muted cries and the noise of the TV. As he listened to the ringing phone, his eyes remained fixed on Haroun, looking for a reaction on his face.

There it was. A glimmer of hope. He thought he was being saved.

Aydin pulled the sock from Haroun's mouth and released his toenail and he groaned in relief as Aydin got up and fetched the vibrating phone from the coffee table. It was Itnashar calling.

'If I don't answer he'll know something is wrong,' Haroun said through heavy breaths.

'Then answer it,' Aydin said. 'Tell him everything is okay.'

Aydin knelt and opened the pliers wide around Haroun's testicle. He squeezed, hard enough to make the man's eyes water but not so hard as to cause him lasting damage. Not yet.

'You know I'll do it,' Aydin said, and Haroun gave the slightest nod.

Aydin accepted the call and pressed the button to activate the loudspeaker.

'Hey, friend, all good there?' came Itnashar's tinny voice.

'All good,' Haroun said, his voice sounding surprisingly sure and unruffled. 'Did he show?'

A pause. 'No. I'm coming back now.'

'Sure. See you soon.'

'I'll pick us up some food.'

'Sounds good. Whatever you want.'

The call clicked off but Aydin stayed in position, phone held out, looking for any read on Haroun's face. There was something about the conversation . . .

Aydin had already sensed something wasn't right even before the loud clunk as the TV went off and the apartment lights went out, but by then there was nothing he could do. Apart from Aydin's and Haroun's breathing, the room was now deathly silent. Gone even was the buzz of the refrigerator and the perpetual low-pitch hum of electricity in the walls. Gone too was the glare from the overhead bulb, and out of the corner of his eye Aydin saw no light seeping in through the small gaps between the front door and its frame.

It was a full electric cut-out.

The only light at all was the faint glow from the screen of the phone that was still grasped in Aydin's hand. He angled the phone away from him to pick out Haroun's face; the shadows made his features elongated and sinister.

There was a slight twitch on his face. The faintest outline of a smile?

Then, behind Aydin, there was a crash as the front door sprang open. He spun to his right, grabbing the knife from the floor – the gun was out of reach – and dove for cover behind the sofa as the thwack, thwack, thwack of a suppressed gun sounded out.

He wasn't hit, but the soft squelch that two of the bullets made told him that Haroun was. Aydin didn't have time to think about who was shooting or who the target was, instead he let his instincts guide him and when the blasting of the immediate assault paused a moment later, he burst up from the sofa and hurled the knife at the first thing he saw moving: the arcing beam of a small flashlight.

There were two lights in fact, he realised as he jumped forward over the top of the sofa, just as the knife hit home and there was a cry of pain.

Aydin was on the first dark figure immediately, grabbed him and twisted him round. Three more shots were fired. Two from the second man, and both the bullets hit the guy Aydin was holding. Together with the knife, Aydin was sure he was done for. The third shot was from the now dead guy's gun, either an accident or a shot of desperation as Aydin wrestled for control. A good shot, though, from Aydin's point of view, because he saw the torchlight of the second man collapse to the ground, and he knew exactly where the stray bullet had landed.

Aydin wrenched the suppressed gun from the man he was holding and the body dropped to the ground. He shone the light attached to the weapon over to his companion. He was on the ground, moaning and groaning and gargling. Aydin took a step forward and pulled the barrel up, pointed at the man's head, ready to finish him off. He didn't care much who he was.

Before he could pull the trigger there was a rush of air from his right, where the door was, and an unseen figure barged into him and the two of them crashed against the back of the nearest sofa and then to the ground.

'You idiot!' Itnashar yelled as they grappled on the ground.

Aydin quickly gained the upper hand and just a few seconds later he was in control, straddling his brother, the suppressor of the gun pressed up against Itnashar's forehead, the light underneath the barrel blazing in his eyes.

'I don't want to kill you,' Aydin said, the honesty in his words surprisingly strong given the position they were in. But it was true. Whatever had happened today, it wasn't really of their making. From nine years old they'd been through so much together and Aydin didn't blame Itnashar for what he'd done. Sometimes there really wasn't a choice. 'I don't *want* to kill you, Itnashar, but I will. Unless you do what I tell you.'

'You fucked up, Talatashar. Whether or not you kill me, there's no way back for you.'

'That doesn't mean it's over. Not for me, and not for you.'

'You're wrong.'

'No, I'm not. I'm going to get off you. And you're going to open that lab door. You're going to get your computer, and you're going to give me the addresses of every single one of our brothers.'

'What! How—'

'I know you have that information. Please. You don't want to end up like Haroun. Do you?'

Itnashar said nothing to that, just huffed loudly. It was still dark in the room and he hadn't yet seen what Aydin had done to his administrator – but he had seen what Aydin had done to others. Starting with that day back at the Farm.

'Get the lights back on,' Aydin said.

'You need my phone. It's in my pocket.'

Without moving the gun from Itnashar's head, Aydin shifted just enough to allow his hand to feel around his brother's waist, until it brushed the form of a phone under the material of his jeans. Aydin reached into the pocket and pulled out the device.

'Now what?' Aydin said, still not taking his eyes off Itnashar.

'If you free my hands I'll do it.'

'Don't be stupid. Just tell me.'

'Figure it out yourself then.'

Aydin ground his teeth in anger. Itnashar was playing for time. The longer the lights stayed out the more chance there was that the neighbours would start roaming and someone would happen over them and call the police. Or maybe he already had back-up coming. What Aydin needed was to get the lights back on and the apartment door closed so he could finish this. Quickly and in private.

But there was no chance he was giving the phone to Itnashar. Among his many other gizmos he no doubt had a red alert rigged in there somewhere and it would only take him a second to trigger it, perhaps without Aydin even knowing.

'Sorry,' Aydin said to him.

In a fluid motion he stood up and pointed the gun down and pulled the trigger and there was another suppressed crack and a flash of light as the bullet tore out of the gun and smacked into Itnashar's knee. Aydin dove back down to stifle Itnashar's harrowing scream. Still holding on to the phone, he clasped his forearm tightly over his brother's mouth as he fought through the agony – his other hand pushing the gun barrel against Itnashar's temple.

Aydin didn't trust that his brother wouldn't find a way to fight back if he took his sight from him for more than a second, so he flicked his eyes from the phone screen and then back to him, back and forth, over and over, as he quickly navigated through the phone. He found the homemade app in a few seconds, but he needed a code to open it.

'I'm going to take my arm away from your mouth,' Aydin said. 'No screaming, just give me the code. If you don't, I'll shoot the same fucking knee again and again until your damn leg falls off. Got it?'

Itnashar nodded. Aydin took his arm away.

'Four, four, one, eight . . . five, four,' Itnashar said, grimacing with each number.

Aydin punched the digits in and within seconds there was that clunk again and the lights were back on and the hum of electricity returned to his ears. Taking a calculated risk he jumped up from Itnashar and strode over to the front door. Out in the corridor he heard talking among the other residents, asking each other questions about what was happening, but no one sounded particularly panicked – just inconvenienced about the blackout – and he didn't see anyone on their level as he pushed the door closed and locked it.

With the lights back on Aydin quickly took stock of the two men on the floor in front of him. He saw now it was the same two from earlier. One was very clearly dead. The handle of the knife was sticking out from his chest and he had a bullet in his shoulder and in his neck, and a wide pool of blood underneath him. The other man had a circle of blood on his chest where his friend shot him. There was no sign of him being alive either, though Aydin didn't stop to check because out of the corner of his eye he saw Itnashar hauling himself to his feet.

Aydin marched over and reached out and took Itnashar's weight then helped him over to the sofa.

'I can't believe you shot me,' Itnashar said, grimacing, though his manner was surprisingly placid and almost jovial.

'I can't believe you and your goons tried to kill me,' Aydin said in return with less warmth.

Itnashar said nothing to that. Aydin grabbed Haroun's shirt from the floor and tore off the sleeve. Itnashar was staring over at his ex-administrator. Not at the two bullet holes in his abdomen but at the bloody mess of his left foot.

'I need the codes,' Aydin said to Itnashar, as if in explanation. He grabbed Itnashar's leg by the ankle and wound the

199

cloth around above the knee, tying it tightly. 'Get me into your computer. Once I have the addresses I'll leave.'

Itnashar shook his head. 'Listen to yourself. What do you expect will happen to you next? Where did you go so wrong?'

How could Aydin possibly answer a question like that?

'Just do it.'

Itnashar sighed. 'It needs my fingerprint, not just the code,' he said, looking over to the keypad by the lab door.

'Fine,' Aydin said.

He grabbed Itnashar under the armpit and lifted him back to his feet then helped him to hobble over. Itnashar first placed his finger onto the small pad before he typed in the six-digit code and there was a bleep of acknowledgement.

'Key?' Aydin said.

'Pocket.'

Aydin fished around and found the key and turned it in the lock and pushed open the door. He let go of Itnashar, who hopped forward, holding on to the metal racking to keep himself upright. He opened the laptop on the shelf in front of him and pressed the standby button. The screen flicked on and Aydin watched as Itnashar punched in yet another six-digit code.

'The information I have might not even be right any more. You know only Wahid has all the details.'

'Let me worry about that.'

Aydin heard movement behind him. He turned, holding the gun out. It was the man on the ground. He was still alive – just. Though he wasn't looking like he was about to jump up and tackle anyone, so Aydin didn't bother to fire. But the distraction was enough for Itnashar. Aydin heard the scrape of metal on metal as Itnashar picked up the hidden weapon, and he spun round to see the blade of a knife arcing towards his neck. He tried to step back but, stuck in the doorway to the lab, there wasn't enough space to escape, so he lifted up his arm just as the knife swooshed across. The blade cut into his flesh and a stinging pain swept through his limb and up his shoulder, all the way into the bundle of nerves in his neck.

Acting on pure adrenaline and survival instinct, Itnashar was quickly bringing the knife back round for a second attempt. Aydin kicked out, against the side of Itnashar's injured knee, and he screamed in pain as his leg buckled. The blow took all the strength from his attack and Aydin grabbed his wrist, twisted, and pulled the knife free. Itnashar was already falling to the ground from the leg strike, and Aydin dropped down with him, landing on top, both his hands around the grip of the knife as he plunged it deep into his brother's chest.

Aydin pushed the knife further and Itnashar gargled and spluttered as his chest swallowed up the blade.

'I'm sorry, my friend,' Aydin said to him, feeling an unexpected well of sorrow and regret as he watched the life fading from Itnashar's now goggly eyes.

'Your sister . . .' Itnashar struggled to say. 'She knew . . . too much. About . . . your father.'

The next second the dying man went still.

Aydin stayed there, looking into Itnashar's death stare for just a few seconds, those last words sloshing around his brain. But he was afforded no more time than that for remorse, or for wondering exactly how his trip to Bruges, like London, had ended so tragically, because he soon heard the faint noise of sirens. Police. Alerted by a neighbour, perhaps? Or had Itnashar somehow sent a call for help?

It really didn't matter. Aydin couldn't stay any longer. He dragged the knife out of Itnashar's chest and quickly wiped it clean on his dead brother's shirt. He stood up and slammed shut the laptop, grabbed it and moved across the apartment. He picked up his backpack and stuffed what he needed inside, then headed for the door.

THIRTY-TWO

Berlin, Germany

The interior of the police-run warehouse on the outskirts of Berlin was brightly lit and modern with shiny grey lino floors and white-painted walls and LED lighting. The remnants of the burned-out van were in front of Cox, the contents from the vehicle laid out all around it in neat lines on top of plastic sheets.

'How far have you got in identifying the victims?' Cox asked in German. Polizeikommissar Rahn of the Landeskriminalamt – the criminal investigation division of the state police – raised an eyebrow at Cox's near perfect pronunciation, though said nothing of it. Rahn was a similar age to Cox though she carried an air of superiority that was already grating and Cox had only been in the room with her for ten minutes. With short dark hair, Rahn was short and plump though her face was thin and, every now and then, there was a glimpse that a human perhaps lay beyond the usual hard glare.

'Not far,' Rahn said, replying in her native tongue. 'The bodies are all but cremated.'

Cox looked across the six small piles of ash and bone that equated to the entire remains of the six victims.

'We're hoping there may be some DNA still intact within the bone or teeth fragments but it's going to be hard to retrieve, and it will take us some time to do the testing.'

'Is there anything at all you've found so far?'

Rahn gazed over the findings as if wracking her brain. Cox knew Rahn was the lead investigator, so in theory she would know more than anyone else, but so far Cox had been hitting brick walls with her. Perhaps Rahn just didn't like that Cox was coming onto her patch. In her experience police officers were quite often like that. Cox's cover in Berlin was that of an Interpol agent – a legend she'd used previously in Europe. Flannigan had done the leg work to get Cox access to the crime scene evidence though it was clear her presence wasn't fully welcomed by Rahn, who was openly suspicious as to the reason for Interpol's interest – not that she'd questioned it. Yet.

'We believe each of the victims was an adult male. Simply because of the size of the bones and the teeth we have. But that's just a guess. And really it could even be less than six men. There were six piles of remains, we thought, but perhaps the bodies were already in pieces when they were burned and that's why the parts were separated.'

Cox felt herself shiver at the gruesome thoughts running through her mind. Rahn on the other hand acted as though this was the most normal thing in the world. Cox knew little of the policewoman, other than she was an inspector who worked largely in organised crime. As well as her unflinching manner, Cox also got the impression that Rahn wasn't overly fussed about the deaths of the men, as though she'd already written it off to gang violence and that nobody would really care about the victims or about catching the killers.

But Cox was still holding out hope that there was more to the story than that.

Her eyes scanned over the remains of the van and the contents that had been taken from the inside. She understood from Rahn that her team had been busy the last two days simply cataloguing the various fragments in a vain attempt to find something useful in the charred remains. They hadn't any tangible leads yet though.

'What do you think that is?' Cox asked, looking over to a rounded piece of metal sheet.

'A container of some sort,' Rahn said. 'What's left of it anyway.'

Cox had a blurred thought in her mind, but it didn't take hold and she quickly moved on, trying to find something else to follow.

'Was anything found inside the building?'

'Nothing obvious. There was an area of floor that had been bleached. Probably recently, given the smell. We've sent samples for tests, again looking for traces of blood and DNA, but we don't have results yet.'

'So it's possible the victims were killed inside the warehouse?'

'Possible. Or maybe they were burned alive in the van. But we very definitely did find some blood traces outside. It's much harder to clean the blood up from broken tarmac.'

'But you haven't matched that blood to anyone?'

'I'd have told you if we had. Do you understand the process of DNA identification?'

Rahn asked the question as though Cox was an idiot. 'Actually, yes I do.'

'Then you'll know that we can only identify someone from their DNA if we have it on record, or if we have something else to match it to – something that belonged to them, a hairbrush perhaps. Yes, it is likely we'll get some useful sequences from the blood traces; after all, we can amplify the DNA from as little as ten or twenty cells, but unless we have something to match against it's meaningless.'

'What about CCTV?' Cox asked, her brain whirring with different thoughts.

'What CCTV? Have you seen where this van was found?'

Cox hadn't, but she knew it was an abandoned warehouse on a road filled with abandoned warehouses. But still, the van had got there from somewhere. And whoever lit the fire had to escape somehow. If they looked in the right places there would be a trail that could help to identify both the victims and the culprits, and more importantly, *why*.

'Do you have a map of the area, of street cameras, of businesses nearby?'

Rahn sighed. 'I'm sorry, Miss Cox, I know my boss told me to look after you, but I really don't have time to be watching endless hours of CCTV tapes today. We'll get to it but I have much more pressing matters.'

Cox didn't bother to ask what was more pressing than identifying six murder victims.

'Then let me do it,' she said. 'Just show me how.'

Rahn glared at Cox for a few seconds as though she wasn't yet sold on the idea. Cox had to hope that at least this way Rahn would be satisfied that Cox was out of her hair. 'Fine,' Rahn said eventually. 'Come on, let's go back to the office.

Cox looked over to the van again and paused. The thought that had been gnawing away at the back of her mind returned.

'What colour did you say the van was?'

'The VIN number we found on the engine block indicates it was white.'

Cox walked over to the van. The metal panelling of the vehicle was crumpled and melted in places, though the basic shape remained. There was certainly no white paintwork visible any more, everything was simply black.

Well, almost everything.

'What would you say that is?' Cox said, pointing to a spot on the inside wall of the van where the soot looked like it had been washed away, revealing a blueish tinge on the bare metal surface underneath.

'It was raining heavily the night it was found. It's lucky because the rain helped to keep the fire under control. Sort of. Probably helped to preserve the little we have left. We covered the evidence as soon as we could but still, what you're seeing there is just the effect of the rain.'

'No, it's not the smudging I'm asking about. It's the blue colouring. It's a white van, so what's the blue?'

Rahn now looked confused. Cox wasn't sure whether the inspector had no clue what she was getting at, or whether she was deep in thought and on the verge of processing the potential significance.

'I said the van was registered as white,' Rahn said, clearly not yet there, 'but who knows what colour it ended up as. It was stolen. Maybe the thieves re-sprayed it.'

'On the inside?'

Rahn frowned.

'It was an old van, right?' Cox asked.

'Fifteen years old.'

'Probably heavily rusted.'

'Maybe,' Rahn said, shrugging in acknowledgement.

'So plenty of iron oxide on display. And what about that container?' Cox pointed over to the charred metal sheet. 'Can I pick it up?'

'Wear these,' Rain said, taking a pair of latex gloves from the back pocket of her suit trousers.

Cox pulled them on then walked across the plastic sheets to the twisted piece of metal. She lifted it up and rubbed at the layer of ash that clung to the surface. Sure enough as the black smudged away there was a definite tinge of blue, dotted about the metal surface.

Cox looked over to Rahn, whose face was now covered in concern.

'Are you thinking what I'm thinking?' Cox said.

'I hope not,' was Rahn's answer.

'Prussian Blue. A dark blue pigment known to be produced when iron reacts with—'

'Cyanide.' Rahn twitched, then shook her head. 'I think I'd better call my boss.'

THIRTY-THREE

Rome, Italy

Obbadi dragged open his eyelids. His head was pounding, a horrific stabbing pain right between his eyes. He fought through it, his lids doing their best to shut, but Obbadi eventually won the battle for control.

He realised he was on the sofa. In his lounge. He lifted his hand up to look at his Patek Philippe watch. It wasn't there, and instead he was left looking at the ring of lighter skin around his wrist. He tried to sit up, but only managed to get halfway before he gave up because of the throbbing in his head. His eyes shifted over to the windows. The blinds were closed. He could tell from the dark outline around them that it was nighttime outside.

Then he heard a noise in the kitchen that sent a wave of clarity over him. He looked over and spotted Katja, who was hunched over as she searched through a drawer.

Obbadi shot up from the sofa.

'What are you doing?' he said, more a statement of warning than a polite question. Katja bolted upright and spun round, the base of her spine smacking off the open drawer she was standing by. Obbadi saw her fight through the pain as she gently closed the drawer behind her.

'Honey, you're awake,' she said, sounding both surprised and concerned.

She moved towards him and Obbadi, as much as he was fighting to keep his weary mind focused, had to put a hand up to his head and press against his temple to try and ease the thumping pain. As she came closer Obbadi could see she was looking rattled.

'What were you doing?' he asked.

'Just putting things away.'

A clear lie.

She was wearing a long black dress, silver earrings and necklace with a drop pendant that ended in her pushed-up cleavage. Formal wear, for her. His brain began firing as he recalled. He looked down and saw his own clothes; black trousers, white dress shirt.

'You said you were feeling sick,' Katja said, answering one of the questions he was asking himself.

'The ambassador's dinner,' Obbadi said as the memories began to take shape. After the recce with Arab'ah in England he'd headed straight back to Rome for the event. He had to keep up appearances after all.

'I don't know if it's something you ate or if . . . well, it's not like you drank too much, is it?'

Obbadi stared at her, trying to figure out what was going on, and looking for any deceit in her eyes. Was it just tiredness from all the recent travel catching up with him?

Shit. Bruges. He realised he still didn't know how that had panned out. The last he'd known, Itnashar had been trying to lure Talatashar into a trap. When he and Katja had headed to dinner Obbadi had still been waiting on confirmation of how that had turned out. In this case he firmly believed no news was likely very bad news.

'What time is it?' he asked.

'About midnight.'

'We came home early?'

'I practically had to carry you out of there. You could barely walk.'

He couldn't remember any of it. He moved past her and towards the kitchen. What had she been doing in there?

Katja rushed past him, getting to the kitchen first and he saw her head bouncing this way and that. Double-checking everything was in place. What a piece of work she was.

'Here, let me get you some water,' she said, grabbing a glass from the dishwasher. Obbadi spotted it was full. *Putting things away*. I don't think so, he thought.

Quite what she was up to he didn't know. But he didn't like it. This wasn't the first time he'd had suspicion of her snooping, but would she really go so far as to drug him to render him unconscious so she could do it?

She poured the glass of water and turned around, ready to hold the glass out to him. When she saw the look in his eyes she paused, the glass staying pressed up close to her chest. Obbadi studied her, wondering what he should do.

His phone buzzed, over on the coffee table. Katja breathed a sigh of relief as Obbadi turned and groggily headed for the handset.

A message. And not the first he'd received over the last couple of hours. He was needed. Katja would have to wait.

He said nothing to her as he walked to the office door, took the key from around his neck and unlocked the door then stepped inside. He glared over at his girlfriend as he shut the door behind him, her face eventually disappearing out of sight behind the wood.

'I'm here,' Obbadi said, once he'd logged on to the encrypted call on his laptop.

'It's me,' came the voice of Tamaniyyah – the second of his brothers stationed in Bruges.

The fact that it was Tamaniyyah he was speaking to and not Itnashar was enough to cause Obbadi to slump.

'Your brother?'

'Itnashar is dead.'

'You fucked up,' Obbadi said, anger rather than disappointment clear in his tone. 'Is Talatashar still alive?'

A delay. 'Yes.'

'Then you *really* fucked up.'

'But we will make this right. He won't get far.'

'Yet he's already gone much further than he should have, and you still haven't stopped him yet.'

Obbadi's statement was met with silence and he was glad that Tamaniyyah had chosen not to further defend his poor performance.

'Go back to your position,' Obbadi said.

'You don't want me to keep on him?

'No. He won't stay in Bruges. Most likely he's coming for me next. You stick to the original plan. The operation is too important for you to abandon post. Is everything else in hand?'

'Of course. Itnashar completed what we needed. All the plans are in place.'

'Good. I'll come soon to collect.'

'Okay. So that's it?'

'No. You failed with Talatashar, and you know I have to pass that back to our father—'

'But brother, please!'

'I'm sorry, but there is no exception. Stay in position and await further instruction.'

'Understood.'

'It's not long now before you'll receive final word. That will be your chance to redeem yourself.'

'This is what I've been waiting for. I *will* redeem myself. I will make you and all the others proud.'

'I would expect nothing less, brother.'

THIRTY-FOUR

Berlin, Germany

The LKA building in the centre of Berlin was a six-storey sandstone structure on a corner of Tempelhofer Damm – a long straight main road leading from the city to the defunct Tempelhof airport. The windowless room Cox had been plonked in was tiny, though she was happy enough – it was now dark outside anyway as the clock wound slowly towards the convergence of night and morning, so she didn't care about having a view.

Following the discovery at the evidence warehouse, the LKA's response to the investigation had ratcheted up several notches given the alarming and unusual circumstances of the deaths of the six men. Cox's knowledge of hydrogen cyanide and the effect of the gas when it reacted with iron was one of many previously useless facets of knowledge stored deep in her brain. On this occasion, the knowledge had come from her longstanding interest in twentieth-century warfare, though it didn't surprise her that the police in Berlin were also acutely aware of the poisonous gas and its heinous history.

Hence the heightened interest in the case. Cox knew that in the rooms next door to her there were half a dozen other police officers now helping on the expedited search to identify the victims and culprits. Cox's hypothesis that cyanide was somehow involved in the crime was far from proven, but based on the evidence had been enough to kick-start the LKA's big machine. Forensic scientists were busy scraping samples from the remains of the van to confirm Cox's theory, but in the meantime she was busy helping the LKA with other avenues as they accelerated their efforts to determine who the victims – and perpetrators – were.

A colleague of Rahn's had set Cox up with the recordings of all the CCTV cameras in the area that the LKA had access to, and other officers were working on gaining access to other recordings from private businesses to add to the mix.

Cox had been steadily analysing the data she had for the best part of two hours, working backward from the site where the van was found and looking over a twelve-hour time period. She needed to identify the victims as they arrived at the crime scene, and the assailants as they left.

In the dimly lit room the lack of proper sleep was quickly catching up with her and her eyelids were becoming heavier and heavier. Through a combination of sugar and caffeine she'd kept herself going, though she knew sooner or later she'd crash.

But it felt like she was getting closer to something. She'd honed her search onto six vehicles in particular; each had followed a similar pattern of travel during the relevant time period. But she needed a way of whittling that down further. So far, none of the CCTV shots had provided clear enough images of the occupants' faces, and certainly none that any image recognition software could work with.

There was a knock on the door and Cox turned to see Rahn standing in the doorway.

'We have some more data coming your way,' she said.

'Perfect,' Cox said. 'Actually, you can come and have a look at this. I need some help with these vehicles I've found.'

Rahn came over and hovered over Cox's shoulder. Cox clicked through the various files where she'd saved the relevant snippets.

'I think this could be the white van,' Cox said, showing the grainy still taken from a camera on a busy road junction about a mile away from the warehouse. 'This was at eleven twenty-nine.'

'There's no shot of the front to see the driver?'

'Not here, no, but I've got some other vehicles that may or may not be relevant too.'

Cox quickly clicked through the files to bring up images of each of the vehicles. When she turned to Rahn the officer's mouth was wide open.

'What?' Cox said.

'*Heiliger Strohsack!*'

Cox raised an eyebrow. 'You recognise one of these?'

'The BMW. Give me a second.'

Rahn walked out and Cox was left waiting, wondering what on earth she'd just found. Less than two minutes later Rahn was back with a look somewhere between satisfaction and fright.

'The car belongs to an associate of Tomas Streicher,' she said. 'Streicher is a well-known neo-Nazi. A white supremacist. Basically the leader of an organised criminal splinter group with close ties to the NPD. I suppose you've heard of them, too?'

'The National Democratic Party of Germany. Yeah, I've heard of them.'

Cox's heart sank as she stared at the picture of the man. Neo-Nazis? That was hardly what she'd expected or wanted to hear. She could imagine Flannigan's reaction to her having spent the best part of twenty-four hours chasing down a domestic issue involving the far right.

214

'So, is he one of the dead guys, or the man who did this?' Cox asked. If it was the latter then her time in Germany had been a waste.

'Have you found any more images of that vehicle leaving?' Rahn asked.

'Yeah,' Cox said, 'but again there're no clear pictures of the driver or passengers.'

'What time?'

Cox opened up the file. 'Three twenty-four. The same junction.'

'Wait there,' Rahn said before again disappearing.

Cox sat staring at the picture for a couple of minutes, part of her already planning how soon she could leave Germany. Rahn came back into the room with a weary-looking man traipsing behind her. He looked to be in his fifties with a thin frame and thinner white hair, a bedraggled appearance and a pair of glasses hanging off the tip of his pointed nose.

'This is Polizeiobermeister Bierhoff.' Cox nodded in greeting. 'I think he can help you find a face for the white van driver and for the BMW.'

Bierhoff nodded and walked over. Cox leaned out of the way as Bierhoff bent over the keyboard and began typing away. Cox held her breath as the stale odour from his armpit hit her.

'This is the data I sent you just now,' Bierhoff said. 'There's a camera near there, for a nightclub. Oxygen it's called. Here, just give me a minute.'

Bierhoff opened up a video file and quickly began fast-forwarding. Cox watched the time stamp in the corner of the screen whizz forward.

'Stop!' she snapped.

Bierhoff clicked and the screen froze.

'A minute after that,' Cox said.

Bierhoff pressed play and left the screen running as he delved into another folder. Within seconds he was fast-forwarding through that one too.

'Three twenty-four, you said?' Bierhoff asked.

Cox nodded.

'There it is,' Cox said a couple of seconds later.

Bierhoff hit pause and the screen froze on a clear image of the front of the BMW. He went back to the first video and seconds later the BMW came into view on that one too and he hit pause. Cox stared at the two images. On the earlier video there were two men in the front. Two white men.

'That's definitely Streicher,' Rahn said.

But it wasn't Streicher on the second video. The man who'd driven the BMW away from the crime scene looked very different indeed. For starters, he wasn't white.

'Streicher was one of the dead men,' Cox said.

'And we have to assume that man is the killer,' Rahn added.

'Okay,' Cox said, feeling a wave of first excitement, then of concern. 'And now I really think I need to call *my* boss.'

An hour later, back at her hotel, Cox sat by the window looking out over the lit-up bombed remains of the Kaiser-Wilhelm Memorial Church on the corner of Kurfürstendamm. She had her head in her hands as she spoke to Flannigan. Sunrise wasn't far off and both of them were tired, and both of them were edgy, though Cox was getting to the point where she might just roll over and be done with it. More than anything, she just wanted to sleep.

'Seriously, Cox, listen to yourself. Cyanide? What the hell are they going to do with cyanide?'

'Kill people, I'm assuming.'

'Where? How?'

'I don't fucking know!' Cox shouted. He'd asked the same damn question three times already. 'I'm just telling you what I've found. Come on, you can't tell me this is all meaningless.'

'I'm not saying that at all. You've got six dead neo-Nazis, one of them a very prominent member of their organisation. It's a serious crime, certainly, but you're going to need to give me more to link this to your investigation than just a crappy image of a face.'

'I'm trying,' Cox said. 'Data Ops have that picture. They're doing everything they can to identify the driver. But you have to accept the possibility that the Thirteen have somehow equipped themselves with a deadly chemical weapon. Maybe they sourced it from this Streicher, or maybe he was just a guinea pig. Possibly it was both.'

'Or neither.'

'Do you really believe that?'

Flannigan didn't answer the question immediately.

'Either way there's no need for you to waste any more time there. The German police have the lead, they can figure out where it goes. I'd suggest you leave in the morning.'

'Leave for where? Bruges?' They'd already discussed the news coming from Belgium. The dead bodies there. The man escaping whose description bore more than a passing resemblance to Aydin Torkal. 'Don't you get it? We've missed him again. He'll be long gone by now.'

'Which is why I'm not suggesting Bruges. We already have a clean-up team there. I think you should head back to Turkey while we wait on the results from Berlin.'

'But why Turkey?'

'You passed a series of requests over to Data Ops last night.'

'Yeah. You've got the results?' Cox asked, not bothering to question how Flannigan had come across her requests – she certainly hadn't passed them through him herself.

'Did Nilay Torkal ever talk to you about her father?' Flannigan asked.

'Yes. It was what initially took her to Syria. She was looking for both her father and her brother. I think she was killed because of the questions she was asking about them.'

'It seems she shouldn't have bothered,' Flannigan said, and Cox felt riled at his heartless tone. He'd never met Nilay, to him she was just another name, but to Cox she had been more than that – a friend. 'SIS have files on Ergun Torkal dating back years. He was a known affiliate of Al-Qaeda in Afghanistan back when the war there first started after nine-eleven. But him and his chums were killed in an American drone strike eight years ago.'

'You know that for sure?' Cox said.

'This is based on *your* intel, we're just following it through. Ergun Torkal is dead, and has been for a long time.'

Which only made Cox feel all the more terrible about Nilay. She'd been killed looking for a dead man.

'So, what am I missing here?' Cox asked. 'Where's the link to Turkey?'

'Ergun Torkal had a brother. Kamil. Now he's most definitely still alive. And he lives in Turkey. Istanbul to be precise.'

Cox sat back in her chair, a sense of victory passing through her, though it didn't last long. Yes, this could be another small, seemingly unconnected breakthrough, but it really only added more questions to the murky mix than answers.

'You want me to track him down?'

'I do. We know that Nilay was in Turkey just a few months ago. It's not hard to see now who she was probably visiting. Which suggests this Kamil may well know something about Talatashar.'

'Even better, Istanbul might be exactly where he's headed next.'

'It's got to be better than chasing shadows.'

'There's only one way to find out.'

218

THIRTY-FIVE

Aydin had never seen anything like this in his life. The blazing sun beat down on him as he stared in wonder across the crowds, mostly men and boys, as far as the eye could see. Tens of thousands, possibly hundreds of thousands travelling to the Great Mosque in Mecca. He and three other boys from the Farm had made the trip in a rickety minibus that had taken several days, with their imam and Qarsh as chaperones. Being the youngest, Aydin and his brothers were the last of the boys to have performed the Hajj, an obligatory pilgrimage for all Muslims to the holiest of cities. This was a rite of passage that Aydin hoped would finally make him a man. Yet this was also the first time he'd been outside the barricade of the Farm in years. If ever there was a chance to run . . .

Since arriving in Saudi Arabia they'd already passed through the Miqat, one of several stations around the outside of the city where people prepared themselves for the Hajj, entering the spiritual state known as Ihram. Aydin and all the others had undertaken the necessary cleansing rituals and were now dressed in the traditional prescribed clothing consisting of two pieces of plain white cloth; one wrapped around the waist reaching below the knee and the other draped over the left shoulder and tied at the right side. Together with the thousands of others, they were now slowly converging on the Great Mosque, its towering minarets visible several hundred yards in the distance.

Once inside Aydin and the others would perform Tawaf, the first of several rituals. Of all the rituals he was to face, Sa'ay was the one he looked forward to the most, which involved running or walking seven times between the hills of Safa and Marwah, and was derived from one of his favourite stories.

According to ancient texts, Abraham had left his wife, Hagar, and son, Ishmael, in the desert on the instruction of God. The mother desperately sought water for her infant son. To make her search easier she went alone, leaving the infant on the ground. She first climbed the nearest hill, Safa, to look over the surrounding area. When she saw nothing, she then went to the other hill, Marwah, to look around. While Hagar was on either hillside, she was able to see Ishmael and know he was safe, but in the valley between the hills she couldn't see him at all, so decided to run through the valley, back and forth through the searing heat, getting thirstier and more desperate by the second. She found nothing, but when Ishmael began to scrape at the land with his feet, water suddenly sprang out. That spring became the Well of Zamzam, from the phrase Zomë Zomë, meaning 'stop flowing', a command repeated by Hagar during her attempt to contain the spring water.

The story of survival felt both personal and relevant to Aydin. The story of a father who'd abandoned his wife and son, and of a mother and her unbridled sacrifice for her child.

Aydin clenched his fists and chastised himself for so arrogantly comparing his own situation to Hagar and Ishmael. He looked over and saw Qarsh was glaring. At the Farm there was no doubt that Aydin was terrified of Qarsh. But out here? He was just another man. And one of the key conditions of Ihram was that no one could carry weapons of any sort. What exactly could Qarsh do if Aydin decided to suddenly break away from the group and run? He didn't even need to do it overtly. With the masses of people all around he could just slowly separate himself and wait for the right moment.

'Whatever you're thinking, Talatashar . . . don't,' Qarsh said with a ghoulish smile.

Aydin looked away, trying not to show any reaction. Was he really that obvious? Then Aydin remembered something else. There used to be fifteen of them, now there were only thirteen. None of the boys knew the full truth of what had happened, but they also didn't believe in the coincidence. One of their missing brothers had successfully completed the Hajj, had even returned to the Farm, but the very next day had vanished without a trace. The rumour was that during his time in Mecca he'd managed to send a message out. What the message was, or who he'd given it to and how, none of the boys knew. Some believed it was a letter home, others an SOS to the Saudi authorities. Whatever it was, he'd paid for his indiscretion with his life – or so Aydin and his brothers believed.

Up ahead the calls of an imam blasted through loudspeakers, catching the attention of the many pilgrims. Aydin and the other boys all looked at each other. Aydin saw the wonder, the hope and expectation in his brothers' eyes.

He felt his shoulders drop. No, he couldn't run. Not at such an important transition in his life. God had brought him to Mecca – how could he ignore that? If this life was the path that had been chosen for him, then he saw no choice but to follow, wherever it took him.

THIRTY-SIX

Rome, Italy

Aydin once again used a variety of public transport to leave Bruges and travel further south through Europe. After events in Belgium his paranoia was growing by the hour, and more than once he'd halted his plans abruptly, leaving a train or a bus at the first opportunity each time someone had inexplicably looked in his direction for a second longer than seemed necessary.

On the train crossing the border into Italy he'd been a second away from slitting a man's throat, pulling the emergency stop cord and jumping from the train to escape through the pine forests of the Alps. The dark-skinned man playing on a high-end smartphone had caught Aydin's eye one time too many from across the open carriage. When Aydin had passed him to go to the toilet he was sure the man had tensed and twitched, as though readying for a confrontation. Then, when Aydin emerged from the toilet, the man was coming towards him, just yards away, and Aydin's hand had slunk inside his jacket. His fingers were coiled around the grip of the blade when the man simply looked up and smiled and said, '*Mi scusi.*' Aydin, hand still on the knife, had stepped out of the way and then watched as the man made his way through to the next carriage. Minutes later, with Aydin back in his seat, the man had returned with a paper bag containing a sandwich and small bottle of wine from the restaurant car.

Aydin jumped from that train at the very next stop. The man hadn't.

The occasional jitters had slowed Aydin's progress, but he made it to the Italian capital unimpeded. Coming into Italy from the north, he stepped off the Rome metro at Colosseo. As he walked up the stairs to the outside, his eyes busy as ever, the knife wound he suffered on his leg in London twinged with each step he took. Having done his best to stitch the wound himself, he'd put antiseptic cream on daily, and replaced the dressing whenever possible, but the whole area around it was a swollen mess and he worried it might be infected. The wound on his arm from Bruges was faring better, but caused him serious discomfort nonetheless. Regardless, he would have to make do with the limited recuperation afforded from the stop-start journey he'd just endured. There was no time for resting now to let himself heal.

He reached the top of the stairs and limped across to the exit, out onto the stifling streets of Rome. The temperature was much warmer than in Belgium, the air thick and heavy with exhaust fumes. He pushed past the throngs of tourists cramming the pavement who had come to see the Colosseum, its monstrous structure with its stacked rows of archways looming into the sky just across the road. As he passed the historic stadium, where gladiators had battled ferociously all those years ago, he compared his own predicament to theirs. Gladiators. In a way that's what he and the other boys were trained to be; nothing more than slaves skilled in all manner of combat and warfare, for the ultimate benefit of their masters.

The men he'd come to hunt in Rome were prime examples. But his brothers weren't just brutish brawlers. Like him, they were trained to be so much more than that. Each of them was cunning and resourceful beyond compare, and Aydin knew he had to plan his move against them with the greatest care. He knew Wahid was in Rome. The laptop he'd stolen from Itnashar would lead Aydin to his door. But he had no way of knowing what hell might be lying in wait to greet his arrival.

Just metres away from the Colosseum, Aydin walked down a narrow street with crumbling apartment blocks standing shoddily on either side. Cars and mopeds were crammed along the pavement, most of them grimy, with large dents and prangs speckling their bodywork.

The uneven slabs underfoot wobbled and clacked beneath his feet as he moved, but he was alone. He heard the high-pitched whine of mopeds snaking through the city streets all around. Two of the bikes grew louder. Without breaking his stride, he turned to see a pair of black mopeds hurtling down the road towards him. But the young, helmetless drivers barely registered him at all as they sped past.

Aydin only realised what was wrong with the picture as the mopeds headed away in front of him: on the lap of the second driver were two large handbags – one red leather, one chequered fabric. Seconds later Aydin heard the grating siren of a police squad car. He didn't look behind, just kept his head down as the siren howled louder on its approach. Did anyone know he was there? He continued apace and exhaled deeply as the flashing blue light of the Fiat raced past him without slowing, and then turned left up ahead on the tail of the fleeing mopeds.

Aydin took a left at the end of the street onto a wide, bustling pavement filled with tables and chairs for the many cafes and restaurants. Offices, apartments and eateries were crammed side by side, and, looking at the numbers, Aydin realised he was already close.

As he passed a bus stop he saw the building across the road. It had to be the one; a fifteen-storey, ultra-modern structure with huge panels of glass bisected with thin grey metal frames; modern Western high-rise architecture at its most pristine and showy.

To the left of the large double-doored entrance, the ground floor was taken up by a trendy wine bar, with hundreds of bottles filling the windows. On the right, an exclusive-looking restaurant and a gym visible through the windows of the floor above. Above that, all the way to the top, it was apartments.

Aydin didn't cross the road, but headed for the bar across from the building. It wasn't exactly a dive, but it was certainly more traditional than the modern block opposite, with a dusty wooden floor underfoot and more beer taps than he cared to count. The place wasn't too busy, so Aydin ordered a coffee at the bar and took a small table by the front window. Content that no one had followed him in, he removed Itnashar's laptop from his rucksack.

Since leaving Bruges, Aydin had already scoured the machine for information, hacking his way into messages and documents as best he could, but there remained areas of the hard drive where the encryption was simply too complex. Just like his own communications back in Paris, Wahid and Itnashar had used several layers of security for their conversa-tions – predominantly by using message boards on the Dark Web. By utilising the Tor network so that traffic from the host ISP was scrambled through numerous randomly selected relay networks, they could essentially muddy the waters as to where the beginning and end chatter originated.

But the breadcrumbs remained, and Aydin had long been trained in how to back-trace such communications, allowing him to follow tracks to an Internet exchange point in Italy, and finally to the originating ISP which was linked to an address in the building he was now looking at: Wahid's home. In fact he'd also discovered that Hamsah – number five – was also based in Rome. Aydin didn't have an address for him yet though. Only Wahid. That was okay, because it was Wahid that Aydin had come to see. He wanted answers. About his sister, his mother. His father.

After two hours in the bar, the dying words of Itnashar still ringing uncomfortably in his mind, Aydin had seen no sign of any faces he recognised outside, though he'd had some further luck in accessing the files on Itnashar's laptop. Not that he liked what he'd found: a link to a satellite map of his mother's street in London. But the file attached to the link was three months old. There was no context for him to understand what that meant, but he was left wondering whether he really was the cause of his mother's death, or had something else happened earlier that made it necessary for his brothers to target her?

Whatever the answer, Aydin couldn't hang around the bar all day. He suspected Wahid lived on the top floor of the building across the street, in the penthouse apartment. Craning his neck, he looked up.

In Rome, Wahid went by the name Ismail Obbadi. The legend had aided Aydin's brother in growing the group's modest wealth to breathtaking effect. Obbadi was not just rich but super rich, and in the few short years since leaving the Farm he'd built a business empire that ensured their operation was utterly entrenched in Western society – built from within it, even. They were hiding in plain sight – Obbadi was just another head of another corporation and making a killing. As number one in the group, this was Wahid's fate.

Around four p.m. Aydin felt a lull fall around him. Gone were many of the lunch-time drinkers and eaters, and it was too early for the rush-hour footfall.

226

Then he spotted Katja Bonetti. He recognised her, even at distance. After all, he'd been looking at a photograph of the young woman just moments before. She strode on tall heels, wearing a knee-length silvery dress over her lithe figure. A pair of aviator sunglasses were pushed up over dyed blonde hair that flapped on slender shoulders as she walked.

Katja Bonetti looked, and strutted, like a catwalk model. But from what Aydin had learned she was just a wannabe actress who'd found love – and a little bit of the limelight – by dating the wealthy Ismail Obbadi.

Aydin had found pictures on the Internet of the two of them together, attending various balls, ceremonies and dinners for the city's rich. With each picture he gazed at he felt a renewed sense of anger flow through his veins as he set eyes on the smiling face of his brother with his outrageously expensive suits, his manicured looks and the glamorous woman dangling off him.

He wondered whether Wahid genuinely enjoyed that life-style. Or did it leave a sour taste to know he was living the life of the people he had been built to destroy? Aydin certainly saw no embarrassment on Wahid's gurning face, but then that was the reason he was made number one; he was the best of them, in every sense – everything the Teacher wanted them to be. Wahid would surely have little problem pretending to be the type of man he was raised to hate.

Aydin kept Katja in his sights as she reached the large doors to 221 and dug into her purse for a keycard. She pushed the card up against the panel beside the doors then stepped inside.

Aydin kept his eyes on the building, looking up to the top floor. After a couple of minutes he saw the reflection on the penthouse windows begin to change, the glare increasing, sweeping from top to bottom. Electronic blinds lifting up.

So it looked like he was right. Wahid wasn't home. But his girlfriend was.

Aydin quickly packed his things up and headed for the exit. Outside he meandered for a while, moving down the pavement a few yards before crossing over the road and doing the same the other side. Number 221 was a big building, with lots of people coming and going, and he didn't have to wait long for his opportunity. Within a few minutes a smartly dressed man approached the door. Aydin increased his pace as he headed up behind, and by the time the man opened the door and stepped inside, Aydin was in tow.

A concierge desk was positioned off to the left with a single uniformed man sitting down behind it. The guard gave Aydin a customary moody glare, but when Aydin returned the look with a nod the guard turned back to his computer screen. No way he could recognise every face that came and went in a building that size.

Aydin followed the smartly dressed man into a lift. The man pressed floor ten, and Aydin fifteen. Was that a sideways glance? A glint of suspicion? Did the man know Wahid? Or perhaps he just didn't think Aydin looked the part of a penthouse owner.

Aydin exhaled in relief as the man departed at floor ten, and soon found himself at penthouse level. Outside the lift there were just two doors in front of him. One was plain white and led out onto the stairwell, the other much wider and sturdy-looking. He walked up, knocked and then stepped to the side so his face wasn't quite in clear view of the spyhole, but ensuring he wasn't fully hidden from the viewer either.

Soft footsteps shuffled from behind the door, followed by a couple of seconds of silence as Katja – he presumed – looked out to see who was there.

Then, one by one, the locks turned, the door opened, and he was looking into her twinkling green eyes.

'Katja?' Aydin asked before she could offer any questions herself.

'Yes?' she questioned, her eyes pinching as she eyed Aydin with distaste, visibly annoyed by the interruption.

'Lovely to meet you,' he said, reaching out to shake her hand. She returned the gesture dubiously. 'I've heard all about you. And . . . wow, you're even more beautiful than Ismail said.' She didn't react as he lightly pecked each of her cheeks. Aydin wondered for the first time how much this woman knew – of Wahid's other life, of where he came from. Had she been expecting Aydin? He was certainly never known for his charm or quick wit – after all, he'd spent most of his life at the Farm with no females and only his brothers and the psychotic guards for company – and his nerves standing in front of Katja confirmed this.

'I'm Aydin. An old friend of Ismail's, from back home.'

'Well, he's not here.'

'That's a shame. Do you know when he'll be back?'

'No I don't know when he'll be back. He's gone back home.'

'To Morocco?' Which was both Wahid's real home country, and the fake Obbadi's. Aydin sighed. 'And I find myself here. Can you believe it?'

'No. Not really,' she said. 'Well, yeah actually. He never gives much notice for these things.'

'Always the same, isn't he? How long will he be gone?'

She took an unusually long time to answer. 'He said he'd be back today.'

She was lying, Aydin knew. Was she afraid of him? A stranger she didn't want knowing she might be alone in the apartment for some time? She looked at her watch mechanically. 'I'm expecting him this evening.' She fell silent for a few seconds, but Aydin needed to keep the conversation going.

'I've been travelling all day,' he said. 'You can probably tell by looking at me.' He smiled as she glowered back. 'You don't think I could wait here a short while, do you?'

A flicker of panic in her eyes. 'Why don't you call him? You know, there's a bar downstairs. You could wait for him there.'

'Will you join me for a drink then?' he said. 'It would be nice to get to know the woman Ismail chose.'

Aydin could tell she hated the idea.

'I'm actually kind of busy,' she said. 'But it was really nice to meet you.'

She went to push the door shut. Aydin had a split-second decision to make: cut his losses and head away, or . . .

He lifted his foot into the doorway just in time, and the wood banged against his toes. Katja's face dropped.

Aydin lunged forward, into the apartment.

THIRTY-SEVEN

Istanbul, Turkey

Cox travelled by car through Istanbul, her journey from the hotel on the Asian side of the Bosphorus Strait taking her back onto European soil that she'd left behind just the day before following her brief trip to Berlin. She'd finally had the chance for a proper night's sleep in Germany, and was feeling refreshed for it, but was also left feeling slightly guilty as though she'd taken her foot off the gas. She needed to keep the investigation moving, because Aydin Torkal and his brothers certainly wouldn't be taking breaks.

There'd not yet been any further update from Germany on identifying either the killer or the victims found in the van, nor confirming if cyanide was indeed the cause of the blue smears at the crime scene. There also hadn't been any useful updates from Data Ops or Flannigan recently. Cox felt like so many elements of the investigation were up in the air, though she had to believe they were only one step away from everything falling into place. Sooner or later she'd get the break she really needed. She had to.

Driving in the rented Seat, she crossed the strait that divided the city at the Bosphorus Bridge. When constructed it had been one of the longest suspension bridges in the world, though in recent history it was more recognisable to millions around the world as one of the key sites of the 2016 failed military coup that had played out the world over live on TV.

Across the other side of the water, on the European side of the city, Cox could see the many ancient and ornate buildings rising up proudly into the sky. Minarets of the many mosques. Clocktowers. The wide baroque, white stone frontage of the Dolmabahçe Palace on the edge of the water, built for the Ottoman sultans in the nineteenth century. The spectacular old buildings of the city gave Cox just a glimpse of Istanbul's rich past that stretched back thousands of years, and blended – sometimes awkwardly – with the more modern. It fascinated her how places and peoples and cultures could recycle and remodel and change so significantly over time. Natural human instinct was to resist change, yet an outside observer would likely suggest that it was through destruction, in all manner of guises, that the human race had forged progress, again and again.

Following the in-car sat nav Cox soon found herself out of the city proper and travelling through lesser populated suburbia. The relative wealth of the area was confirmed not just by the size of the individual houses, but the amount of greenery she saw at the sides of the road. When the sat nav indicated she was just half a mile from her destination, Cox slowed and began looking more keenly out of her window. With tall hedges and walls and gates, there were only glimpses of the properties that lay beyond. One thing was clear, though, they were big.

Cox took a right onto a much narrower and twisting road – wide enough for only one car. After a couple of hundred yards the sat nav bleeped to indicate she'd reached her destination, though all Cox could see were trees and hedges.

But a few yards further up the road she spotted a discreet gap between two tall date palms. She turned in and soon found herself in front of arched brown-painted metal security gates, more than eight feet tall. Either side of the gates a white wall ran off into the distance, colourful bushes and flowers screening much of the outside of it, and in some places spilling over the top from the inside.

Cox wound down her window, the sweet smell of the date palms and of lavender and other scented flowers tickling her nose as she pressed the buzzer on the intercom.

'*Merhaba*?' came a croaky female voice moments later.

'Hi,' Cox said, moving straight into English. 'This is Rachel Cox from the British Consulate, I'm here to speak with Kamil Torkal.'

There was a click and then silence and Cox frowned and wondered if her plans had already been scuppered so soon. She'd pre-arranged to meet with Kamil, posing as a legal liaison from the British government, there to discuss Nilay's untimely death in Aleppo. Kamil had agreed to that by phone, but perhaps he'd had a change of heart.

After a couple of minutes of waiting, with Cox torn between pressing the intercom again to check what the issue was, and just driving away to rethink, the gates in front of her clunked and then whirred open.

On the inside she was greeted by a glorious yellow gravel driveway that led up to a white Roman-style villa, a turning circle in front, complete with fountain topped with water-spitting cherubs. Cox parked the car and before she'd stepped from it the large wooden door to the villa was opened to reveal a plump middle-aged woman in plain blue linen trousers and matching top – a uniform by the looks of it, a nurse or maid perhaps, though which it was Cox wasn't sure.

She smiled at the woman.

'Please, he's inside.'

Cox nodded and carried on in, breathing a sigh of relief at the welcome moderate temperature inside. The last reading on her car's thermometer had been thirty-one celsius. Inside the villa it felt half that, though Cox didn't note any air-conditioning units, the cool ambient temperature achieved the old-fashioned way through the design of the building itself, with overhead fans keeping air moving through the shaded spaces.

Cox followed the woman across tiled floors, through airy rooms, taking in what she could of the elaborate layout. As well as crammed bookcases almost everywhere in sight, there were statues and ornaments and paintings depicting and originating from a wide range of different times and cultures; Ancient Egypt, Ancient Greece, Ancient Rome, Persia, the Far East among them.

They moved through into a garden room where the shuttered doors were wide open to reveal a cascade of water features in the manicured garden outside. There were two wicker seats in front of the open doors, the straggly white hair of a balding man poking up over the top of one of the seat backs.

'Would you like a drink?' the lady offered.

'Just a water, please.'

The lady gave a slight bow and walked off, just as the man turned his head.

'*Selamünaleyküm*,' he said. May God's peace be upon you. His voice was hoarse and wheezy.

Cox continued to step towards him. '*Aleykümselam*,' she said in response.

The man gave a half-smile before turning back around in his seat.

'Please, come and sit with me,' he said, changing to a barely accented English.

Cox did so, putting her handbag on her lap. She'd brought the Glock pistol that Flannigan had given her in Ankara with her. Looking at the frail man in front of her, she now felt a bit foolish about that, though given recent form it was still good to have the extra security at her fingertips.

'I'm so glad it's cool in here,' Cox said. 'I spend a lot of time in some very hot places but I can never get used to heat. It's the Celt in me.'

'I'm the same, my dear. This is too hot for me. Istanbul is about the coolest place in this country, though. It's one of the reasons you find me here.'

Cox smiled at that, more because she could see Kamil himself relaxing than because of what he'd said.

'It's a glorious home you have,' Cox said. 'And the garden . . . it's incredible.'

Kamil nodded. 'It's taken many years.'

'Ancient studies was your area of expertise,' she said, looking at the bookcase behind Kamil, across the many over-sized books and the knick-knacks carefully arranged there.

'Not *was*. It still is. What are we without knowledge? I was a working professor for more than twenty years. I had to stop not because of my mind but because of my body, but I still study all the time.'

As if on cue he began to cough. Just a light, clearing-the-throat-type cough to start with, but after a few attempts it grew into an almost full body spasm with each exhale. When he finished he was panting and wheezing, his face grimacing in pain.

He sighed and sat back just as the nurse came scuttling over to his side. She whispered something to him, indicating the oxygen tank and mask over in the corner, but Kamil waved her away and, head down, she disappeared again.

Cox studied Kamil for a few more moments while he continued to compose himself. The man was sixty-two years old but he looked more than eighty with his withered features and mottled skin and yellowed eyes.

'What's wrong?' Cox asked, not caring about prying.

'What's not wrong,' he said. 'But it's the emphysema that will kill me.'

The nurse came back in and handed Cox a glass of icy-cold water. She again checked on Kamil but he just waved her away once more.

'Sometimes it would be nice to just be left alone for five minutes.'

'She's certainly very attentive,' Cox said. She took a sip of the water which was so cold it made her front teeth ache. She set it down.

'Don't get me started,' Kamil said. 'My wife insists she be here all the time. They both think I'm some old cretin.'

He laughed at that. Cox didn't.

'Is your wife home?'

'No. She went shopping. Hours ago. To be honest she didn't want to be here when you came.'

Cox frowned but said nothing to that.

'Perhaps we should stop the small talk,' Kamil said, his face turning slightly sour. 'You said this was about Nilay.'

'You've heard what happened to her?'

'Of course I heard.'

'I'm sorry for your loss.'

'Perhaps you are. But I'm not sure why her horrible death means you're here.' He sounded more bemused about that fact than confrontational.

'I'll be honest with you, Mr Torkal, I'm not here just to speak about Nilay. It's other members of your family too.'

'Family? Yes, she was my niece, but I haven't seen her in years.'

'Really?'

'No. The situation was . . . complicated.'

'But you did know she had been killed?'

'Her mother called me the day she found out.'

'So you were still on speaking terms with her?'

'I never said otherwise, did I? Yes, we spoke every now and then. Not often. We sent cards to each other on birthdays.'

'And you've also heard what happened in London? To Nilay's mother.'

Kamil hung his head. 'Yes.'

'Do you know why someone would hurt her?'

'Someone? This wasn't just *someone*. That boy was always trouble.'

Cox frowned. 'Aydin?'

'Sometimes you just know. Even in children. You sense they're different. That was always the case with him. I knew him from when he was a baby, of course. There was always something hiding in there, behind those innocent eyes.'

'So you believe Aydin killed his own mother?'

'I absolutely do. Are you saying otherwise?'

The information about Aydin being the man wanted for murder wasn't public. Yes, it was his picture plastered all over the newspapers, but he hadn't been formally identified as Aydin Torkal by the media, even though Cox was convinced it was him. So how and why was his uncle so sure? This was a boy he hadn't seen for at least fifteen years.

'What happened to Aydin?' Cox asked.

'How do you mean?'

'Your brother, he kidnapped Aydin when he was only nine,' Cox said, a fact she'd long ago confirmed both with the Met and with Nilay, though what happened after that she still had little knowledge of. 'Why did he do that? And what happened to them?'

Kamil scoffed. 'There were many things wrong with my brother, but one thing is for sure, he didn't kidnap his son. He loved that boy. What he did was *rescue* him. My brother

237

did everything he could to help that runt, but it seems like whatever he did it wasn't enough. The only question in my mind with Aydin was always *when*, not *if* he would kill. Put simply, Miss Cox, Aydin Torkal is nothing but a monster.'

THIRTY-EIGHT

Rome, Italy

Katja was sitting on the floor in the middle of the lounge, gagged, with her ankles and wrists bound with plastic cable ties. Since the moment he'd forced his way in, she'd looked more angry than scared.

The situation was far from ideal, Aydin knew, but he had to get inside the apartment – he desperately needed leads, any clue as to where Wahid had gone. Had his brother already disappeared into the shadows? Had he set the operation in motion?

Aydin gave the apartment the once-over. The rooms were huge, but there weren't many of them: a bathroom; two en suite bedrooms; a gigantic open-plan kitchen, diner and lounge. There was no indication that the second bedroom was regularly occupied – it was clear neither Hamsah, nor any administrator, lived there with Wahid. He was too important to have to share.

One door that led off from the lounge was closed and locked. Much like in Bruges, Aydin guessed what he wanted was most likely behind there.

He kneeled down next to Katja, and she squirmed and growled as he pulled the gag from her mouth. She yelled and swore.

'I can put the gag back in, if you like?' he said, his hand now pressed against her mouth. The threat quickly shut her up and he took his hand away. 'Some honesty, please? Do you know where Ismail has gone?'

'I told you already!' she shouted.

'But what you told me isn't true. So either he lied to you, or you lied to me.'

She didn't reply.

'Where's the key for that door?' he said, pointing to the closed door that led off from the lounge.

'I've no idea,' she said.

'You think telling me lies will help you right now?' Aydin thought for a moment. An idea sprang into his head. 'He doesn't know, does he?'

Aydin saw the look of doubt creep across her face.

'How many times have you gone snooping?' he asked. 'Is that why you came today, when you know he's not here? Probably you're stealing from him too. Cash, jewellery?'

'I am not!' Katja screamed, and Aydin could see he'd really pissed her off.

He smiled. 'Yeah, that's you, isn't it. Sneaking around behind his back. You like the money, don't you?' He reached out and took the large diamond pendant around her neck in his hands. 'But you like it on you more than you like it on him.'

She pulled her body back, taking the stone from his grasp.

'You have no idea what you're talking about.'

'What do you think Ismail would do if he knew?'

Aydin saw the look of panic in her eyes. It made him worried too, because it suggested she was scared of Wahid, but why? A slim thought remained that maybe Katja was more than just a prying girlfriend – an undercover agent of some sort, perhaps? Or could Wahid have possibly let slip to her about their plans?

240

'I'll ask one more time, nicely, and then we'll try something else,' Aydin said. 'Where's the key for the door?'

'He keeps it around his neck, on a chain,' she sighed. 'But there's a spare. In the kitchen. At the back of the cutlery drawer.'

'Thank you,' Aydin said.

He stuffed the gag back into her mouth, and she moaned and blathered again as he walked into the kitchen to find the key.

The room it unlocked turned out to be an office, exuberantly decorated, with a crystal chandelier dangling above an oversized dark, lacquered wooden desk. He looked back at Katja before he stepped in. Despite being tied up, Aydin didn't trust leaving her out of his sight, so, taking hold of her ankles, he dragged her into the room with him to renewed whining.

'I'm not going to hurt you,' he reassured her, quickly averting his eyes from her bare legs, her dress having ridden up over her thighs. 'Not unless you give me a reason to.'

Aydin let go and she quietened down, and he got to work.

It didn't take him long to discover there was nothing for him to find. It looked like a clean-up job. Either Wahid never kept anything in there of importance to start with, or he'd already shipped everything out. Was he even planning on coming back to the apartment at all, or was he gone for good?

He moved over to the desk. It was bare on top except for a chrome lamp. Aydin ran his fingers along scuff marks in the shiny finish, to the small round blotches from the rubber feet of a laptop computer. He wouldn't have expected Wahid to be stupid enough to have left that out in the open.

Aydin tried the top drawer – locked. Within seconds he'd prised it open with his multi-tool, using the screwdriver as a lever to pop the cheap lock. Inside, the drawer was neatly arranged with pens and pencils, a stapler, hole punch, an old-fashioned ink-pot. As though Wahid sat there with his quill pen to handwrite letters. All the fixtures and fittings, all the money and glamour and material nonsense painted such a different picture from the boy Aydin had grown up with.

The second drawer was empty, as was the third, save a couple of loose paperclips and the last few pieces of plain white printer paper from a pack of five hundred.

The printer. Aydin spotted the machine atop an ornate table in the corner. It was a professional piece of kit, designed for a small office with multiple terminals. Aydin hoped he might be in luck after all.

He grabbed his backpack from the lounge and brought it back into the office, pulling out the laptop as he moved. He didn't need any specialist equipment. Most office printers routinely received large batches of documents throughout the day. Computers didn't transfer those documents one page at a time, it all went to the printer in one go. Printers therefore needed a small memory to store those documents while they spat out the paper. Spool data was quickly overwritten by subsequent jobs once printing was completed, though some machines had bigger memories than others. Regardless, the data on the printer could prove useful, and he connected the laptop, navigated into the printer's memory, and located the spool data of all recent activity.

With the laptop busy downloading, Aydin moved back to Katja and again took out her gag.

'Where's Ismail's safe?' he asked her. He was certain Wahid had one. He thought he might have found it in the office but there was nowhere it could be, unless it was well hidden under the floor or in a wall recess.

Katja said nothing. Aydin brought his face closer. He felt her soft, warm breath on his cheeks.

'Is it in here?' he asked, staring at her face for any tell. She didn't answer and her eyes gave nothing away. 'The bedroom?'

242

Just the slightest flicker on her face gave the answer away. Despite everything, he was occasionally grateful for the skills he'd developed at the Farm.

'Thank you,' he said, and began dragging her through the apartment and into the bedroom.

Rummaging around in cupboards and drawers, he found nothing other than expensive clothes, shoes, watches and other fashion accessories. He got on his hands and knees and examined the carpet around the edges of the room. He pulled a bedside drawer out of the way. And there it was. A corner of the carpet was up just slightly. Not even an eighth of an inch, but the difference was noticeable with the frayed material around the edge not properly tacked underneath.

Aydin pulled the corner up, and then the green underlay, to reveal the concrete floor. Mostly concrete, anyway – except for the square of sheet metal that sat flush. Lifting it revealed the safe door, and its keypad. Not a particularly sophisticated unit, just the type generally seen in hotels. He used his multi-tool to prise off the front panel of the keypad. He saw the USB port, tucked away, revealing exactly what kind of override measure the safe had. With the laptop and a bit of time he could crack the code himself. But he'd rather Katja just gave it to him.

'What's the code?'

No response.

'No one's coming for you,' he said. 'It's just you and me here. Give me the code and I'll be gone in minutes. If you don't, it's going to be a very long evening for you.'

Still nothing, but he could see her resolve was cracking.

'The last person I tortured was trained to resist. You don't want to know what I did to him. What I *had* to do to break him. He only lasted a few minutes. Now he's dead. Do you really want to find out if you can do better?'

'I think I know it,' Katja said as a tear fell from her eye. 'But it's easier if I type. You know how it is, I can't remember unless I'm typing it.'

Aydin scoffed at that.

'I'm serious. Help me up. I'll do it.'

He sighed then moved over and put his hand under her armpit and pulled her up. With his help she hobbled across the room towards the safe. But just before they got there she made the dumb move he'd hoped she wouldn't. She swung her elbow into Aydin's gut and tried to shove him away. The full-force blow knocked the wind from him and he side-stepped to keep himself upright and reached out to grab her as she lurched away, towards the wardrobe. He couldn't get to her quickly enough. She hauled open a door, pulled out a drawer and reached her arm inside just as Aydin grabbed her by the shoulders.

A piercing alarm blared.

'No—!' Aydin growled, anger rising up. He wrenched her away from the drawer and flung her to the side. She crumpled over and her head smacked off the wooden end of the king-sized bed, her body going still.

Aydin's body twitched. Should he just go? No, he had to get into that safe.

He dashed back to the office and checked the laptop. The spool data had downloaded. He pulled the cable from the printer and ran back to the bedroom, skidding down to the ground by the safe. He plugged the cable into the port on the safe and as quickly as he could found the online software that would read the safe's memory and reveal the override code.

He glared over at Katja. She was beginning to stir. He realised his leg was tapping furiously. He looked at the laptop's clock. A minute had passed already. He wondered who would arrive on the scene first. The building's security team? The local police?

Or was it his brothers who would come bursting in?

Aydin checked the clock again. He couldn't wait another minute. Then a ping came. He looked at the small window in the corner of the screen. The swirl of numbers stopped, revealing the six-digit code. Aydin hit enter and the signal transmitted through the cable to the safe. A green light flicked on the box and he heard the lock release.

Aydin reached inside and grabbed everything there was and flung it all into the backpack: rolls of money. Two passports. A thumb drive. A brown envelope. He zipped up the backpack as he rose to his feet. Katja was still lying on the floor, but her eyes were open and she was staring up at him. She looked terrified. Perhaps it was the rage she saw on his face. But he wasn't interested in her. He had to get out of there as quickly as he possibly could.

THIRTY-NINE

Aydin crashed through the stairwell door and clambered down the steps two at a time. He contemplated breaking into one of the other apartments to hide out, but he didn't know exactly who Katja had called, or how big the response would be. It was possible the police would sweep the entire building if they understood exactly who it was they were after.

Staying inside was too big a risk, so he kept going to the bottom then slowed down and took a deep breath to try and calm his pounding heart. He calmly pushed open the door that led out onto the main foyer, glancing left and right. Off to his left were the entrance doors, but it was the two men standing closer to him, by the concierge desk, that his eyes found first. Dressed in their grey-blue uniforms, their jackets had *Polizia* emblazoned in large letters across the backs. Aydin spotted their blue Alfa Romeo patrol cars outside. Two in total.

There was another exit to his right – perhaps a service route, or the entrance to an underground car park. But the moment he turned towards it the officers' shouts came.

'*Arresto!*'

Aydin had no intention of stopping. Instead, he slammed through the door and into another stairwell, racing down before banging through another door and skidding into a car park. He stopped momentarily. A smattering of shiny black and silver and white cars gleamed back at him. He raced across the concrete, looking for the ramp that would lead to the exit as the policemen burst in behind him, panting and yelling in Italian.

He didn't heed their warnings. They were armed but would they really shoot? The problem was that he was armed too – he needed to dump the gun. He'd try his hardest to escape them, but if he was to get caught the last thing he wanted was to be found with a weapon on him.

Darting between the parked cars, he was up the exit ramp, the glare of the outside daylight getting closer with each step. Fresh sirens whirred. Were there more police cars in the chase or the same ones from the front? He reached the top and ducked under the barrier before he saw any sign of the vehicles. As he moved to the left he saw a Fiat patrol car speeding towards him. That was three cars now: quite some response to a burglar alarm.

The police car screeched to a halt and the doors opened and two more men stepped out, their pistols drawn. Aydin raced across the street and scaled a fence onto a small square that contained a bare patch of grass and a children's play area; mums and dads yelled and cowered around their children as he sprinted by.

Aydin weaved in and out of the people and around trees as he burst across to the other side, over another fence. The officers were closing in, he could hear them pounding through the play area behind. Satisfied there were no witnesses, he dropped the gun into the bin nonchalantly and then hit a crossroads at full tilt, jumping awkwardly across the bonnet of a car as it screeched to a halt. A moped driver buzzed round the turn, and, to avoid Aydin, twisted the bike's handlebars away so the small machine wobbled viciously and, lurching sideways, spat the driver off, sending both him and the bike clattering across the tarmac to a stop at Aydin's feet.

Aydin made for the bike. It was battered but the engine was still running and the wheels didn't look buckled. With the driver groaning on the ground, Aydin heaved the moped to its wheels. He heard sirens behind him; to the side too. Tyres screeched, and the shouts of policemen and women came from all angles. Aydin jumped onto the bike and pulled the throttle. The engine of the moped whined but the wheels didn't move.

Out of luck, Aydin dropped the bike to the ground and was just about to move off to restart his escape when a gunshot boomed, the ricochet not far from his feet. He stopped dead. There was no exit. There were now six police officers within yards, all with guns drawn, fanning out in a circle around him and closing in.

Aydin saw no other option. This wasn't a fight he could win, and he had no reason to try and kill all of the officers – a chance to escape, he had to hope, would come later. So he did exactly what they were telling him to do. Hands above his head, Aydin sank down to his knees.

FORTY

Istanbul, Turkey

Cox felt derailed by Kamil Torkal's forthright opinion of his nephew. He seemed so certain of Aydin's guilt over his mother's death, and of the young man's psychotic nature. If Aydin really was part of the Thirteen, as Cox believed he was, then he was absolutely a dangerous man capable of extreme violence. So why was she finding it so hard to buy Kamil's story? Was Kamil seriously misguided and misinformed about his nephew, or was he an outright liar?

'Neither Aydin nor Ergun were seen again after they left London in two thousand and three,' Cox said to Kamil. 'Where did they go?'

'You need to understand about my brother. You never met Ergun, but he was a good man. He didn't have the same lucky breaks in life that I had. He didn't go to university, and for years he felt lost in this country. He had the opportunity to move to England, and he took it.'

'Opportunity?'

'My brother was a deeply religious man. More so than me. While I took great pleasure in studying ancient civilisations, Ergun took great pleasure in studying the Quran. He went to England to teach others.'

'My understanding is that Ergun never found employment in England. He became disgruntled not just with his own position there but with the entire way of British life. He harboured great resentment.'

Kamil's face twitched.

'His decision to leave England wasn't about money and it wasn't about resentment towards English people, or non-Muslims. It was simply about his devotion to Islam, and to his boy. But you're right, he struggled. Ergun didn't fit in over there. I begged him to come back home to Turkey. I even offered to find him a job. But then . . .'

He looked away.

'Then what?' Cox asked.

'Then came the time for him to remove Aydin. Something had to be done about the boy.'

'But where did they go? What happened to them?'

'They went to Kandahar. The whole family agreed it was for the best. Kidnapped? Whoever said that is an idiot and a liar.'

'His mother said that, Mr Torkal. She went to the police soon after they disappeared, but, the way I understand it, the police did nothing to help.'

'She was just confused. She was grieving,' Kamil said. He was now becoming increasingly animated in his movements, gesticulating as he spoke. It was clear there was a lot of ill-feeling in the man, though it was hard to gauge who, or what, those feelings were directed at. Cox noticed, too, that the more rattled he became, the more fragile and frail he seemed, as if her being there was sucking the energy from him. 'This school, it was exactly what Aydin needed. But, it seems it wasn't enough.'

'What was the name of the school?'

'It was . . . Oh, I don't remember now. This was many years ago. I never went there myself.'

'You've never been to Afghanistan?'

'No. Never.'

'And did you ever see Aydin or Ergun again?'

'No,' he said, more sternly now, as though riled by Cox's questions. 'Perhaps that school was the right place at the wrong time for both of them. Ergun was killed over there, you know that?'

'I understand he was killed by an American drone strike. That he was actually one of the intended targets of that strike because he was believed to be a close affiliate of an Al-Qaeda cell.'

Kamil's face now twisted in disgust. 'You know absolutely nothing about what my brother was.'

'I'm just telling you what I've heard, the information I've seen.'

'My brother was a good man, a man of religion. That's all. He didn't have a hateful bone in his body. His death at the hands of the British or the Americans or whoever it was, what do you think that would do to a boy like Aydin? Do you think it would help him to become a better man, or do you think it would only further foster that burning need for revenge, for violence? Yes, he was born bad, but he could have been helped. We were trying to help him. It was the West killing his father – among many, many other things – that made him the monster he now is. And this isn't just about Aydin and Ergun, it's the same story across the entire Muslim world. When your guns and your bombs kill innocent women and children, exactly what do you expect the response will be?'

His words were strong but still measured. No venom or vitriol, more disappointment and hurt. But Cox wasn't about to let up. She wanted to push this man as far as he'd let her, see if the facade would eventually crack. What he was saying was so far from what she believed the truth of Aydin and Ergun to be. How were the lines so crossed?

'The school that Aydin went to. Is that the place commonly referred to as the Farm?'

Kamil looked bemused. '*The* farm? I know lots of farms. I'm not sure what you're talking about.'

'Aziz al-Addad is believed to be involved there. Have you heard of him?'

Kamil pursed his lips and shook his head.

'You've never heard stories, rumours, of a place where young boys are taken to be trained as elite jihadi warriors?'

'You want me to tell you about stories now?' he said, frowning. 'I know lots of stories.'

Cox didn't appreciate his scathing tone, and determined just to carry on. 'What do you know about cyanide poisoning? About its use in terrorism and chemical warfare?'

She didn't expect a straight answer, her questions designed more to eke out any tells in the man. He remained ice cold.

'Miss Cox, perhaps rather than asking me these silly, vague questions you could just come out and tell me what this is really all about, because it's quite clear you are not just some liaison from the Consulate here to talk to me about my late niece.'

'Please, there's no subterfuge here,' Cox said, holding her hands up. 'I'm simply trying to find out about Aydin. You think he killed his mother. He's now on the loose and he needs to be stopped.'

'So you agree it was him,' Kamil said, the anger in his tone now clear. 'And now you've just made it clear that it's because of *that boy* you're here, not Nilay.'

'I am here because of Nilay. This is about her too. I didn't lie to you. I think her death is connected to what's happening with Aydin.'

'Connected to what? She was a bright young girl killed in a cowardly suicide attack.'

'It's my job to find out if that's the truth.'

'What do you mean?'

'I knew Nilay. She was a friend.'

252

'Yet you just said there was no subterfuge to you being here. You were a friend of Nilay's, who just also happens to work for the British Consulate in Istanbul?'

'I'm not trying to trick you. I do work for the British government. But, Mr Torkal, this is personal for me, like it is for you. I want to find out what really happened to Nilay. I want to know why she was targeted, and I want to find those responsible for her death. Because I don't believe it was an accident.'

'If you're intent on pursuing what happened to her then you're in the wrong place,' he said before starting to cough, struggling to catch his breath. He was still angry, but the conversation was taking its toll. Cox offered no sympathies, just waited for him to carry on. 'I told you I haven't seen the girl for years. If you want to find out who killed her then you should probably be in Aleppo, not Istanbul. That's where she died after all.'

'Actually, that's where I came from. I'm just following the trail. And I know she was in Istanbul not long ago. She came to you, didn't she?'

Kamil held his tongue, but his cheeks were flushed and his breaths were wheezy, his chest heaving as he tried to appear calm and unfazed.

'Why are you lying to me, Professor Torkal?'

Just then footsteps caught both their attention. A smartly dressed woman entered the room wearing an expression of concern.

Cox stood. 'You must be Mrs Torkal.'

'What have you done to him?' the woman said, heading over to her husband and putting her arm around his shoulder. 'You can see he's not well.'

'It's okay, my dear,' he said, still wheezing, his weak head rolling about. 'I think she was just about to leave.'

His wife's beady eyes locked on to Cox.

'You heard him.'

'Of course,' Cox said. She had more than enough to think about already, and Torkal wasn't going anywhere fast. 'Thank you very much for your time, both of you.'

'Have a safe trip back to wherever you're going,' Kamil said, his voice now far more coarse and wheezy than it had been moments ago. 'London, Aleppo. Wherever.'

'Oh, actually, I'll be sticking around Istanbul a while longer yet. There's a lot to see here, and you've given me a lot to think about. No doubt we'll cross paths again soon. Have a good day, Mr and Mrs Torkal.'

Smiling, Cox turned and headed for the door.

FORTY-ONE

Rome, Italy

Being handcuffed and stuffed into the back of an Alfa Romeo police squad car was bad enough, but what was more worrying for Aydin was how long they'd been driving. The police had swarmed on Wahid's apartment block within two minutes. They couldn't all have been passing by; there must have been a police station nearby. But they'd been on the road for fifteen minutes already and heading out of the city, away from the tourist sites and hotel district.

So where exactly were they taking him?

On the plus side, the traffic was thick. It was rush hour and the multi-lane road was at a near standstill, save for the motorbikes and mopeds whizzing by on both sides.

'What were you doing there?' the policeman in the passenger seat asked in Italian, turning to face Aydin.

Aydin said nothing. As far as the police knew, he didn't speak the language.

'You haven't got any ID. No driving license, passport. Where you from?'

'England,' Aydin said.

He wasn't sure why he hadn't just stayed silent, but he was pleased to see the slight look of confusion, and annoyance, on the officer's face.

'Have you ever been to London?' Aydin asked him.

'Too wet.' He shrugged.

'That's why I came to Italy,' Aydin said.

'No. You came here to steal from Ismail Obbadi.'

The policeman turned his head again for a second and Aydin saw a confident smile on his face. Would a police first responder know of Obbadi?

Aydin really wasn't liking any of this.

'It's a long way,' he said.

'We're not far,' the driver responded.

'I think I'm going to piss myself.' Aydin clasped his thighs together and grimaced.

He didn't really need the toilet at all, nor was he expecting them to accommodate him. He was just fishing.

'Nothing I can do,' the driver said, shrugging. 'You'll have to wait.'

'For how long?'

Another shrug. Aydin didn't think he'd be getting anything more out of the two of them, and his mind was made up. He'd calmly and very deliberately let the men arrest him, but only because the numbers had been so stacked against him. He'd never had any intention of spending time in a jail cell, if that's even where they were headed.

None of the other police cars were with them now. Why would they bother giving an escort for a simple lone man? Aydin liked these odds much more. Two on one. His hands were cuffed behind him, and there were no door handles in the back. He needed to get them outside.

Suddenly screaming at the top of his voice, Aydin threw himself down onto his side, kicking out with his feet and legs. The back of the driver's chair buckled forward under the impact. He turned his attention to the door, the rear window. The driver yelled, and pushed on the brake to stop the car.

'Sit back up, now!' the driver shouted.

'Stop it!' the other one called.

Aydin did the opposite, ratcheting up the lunatic behaviour, going berserk as he writhed and thrashed, screaming so hard his throat roared with pain. The passenger lunged at Aydin from the front, trying to pin him down with his hands. His attempts only added to the strength and focus in Aydin's movements. He jerked his body and crashed his legs against the window again and again as the glass shuddered, shook and bowed.

The driver jumped from the car and opened Aydin's passenger door. Most likely he would drag Aydin out and either beat him until he co-operated or stick a gun in his face to achieve that same result. Either of those scenarios was fine with Aydin. The officer holding him released his grip and rushed out after his colleague. Both men livid, they made to drag him from the car. To them, Aydin was out of control and force was the only way to subdue him. But Aydin had been bucking not to smash his way out of the car, but to manoeuvre his handcuffed hands from behind his back to the front.

By the time the driver opened the rear door and grabbed hold of Aydin's ankles it was too late. Both cops hauled Aydin out. He made them work for it, grimacing in pain as the officers dug into the tender flesh on his leg wound. He was on the road now. Faces pressed up against windows in the stationary cars around them. Here was a sight they wouldn't see every day.

Unperturbed by their audience, the officers punched and kicked Aydin, trying to dispel his madness. Tired from the onslaught, the two men soon stopped and brushed themselves off. Aydin locked eyes with the driver. There was a brief flash of recognition on the man's face: he'd finally seen what Aydin had done.

It was too late for him.

Using all of the muscles in his core, Aydin bounced to his feet. Their victory short-lived, the policemen closed in. Aydin side-stepped and swiped his hands around the neck of the driver. He tugged sharply with his arms and the chain of the cuffs caught, the momentum whipping the driver to the ground with a crunching thud. Aydin swivelled and delivered a powerful elbow strike to the solar plexus of the second officer before he could get close, knocking him down to the ground, winded. He wouldn't get up again before Aydin was gone.

The driver was still in the fight, but only just. Aydin dropped his body weight and slammed himself down onto the prone policeman, digging his elbow hard into the man's chest. Most likely the blow cracked several ribs, or at the very least sent the officer's heart out of rhythm. He coughed and spluttered, barely able to breathe. Lying on the floor next to him, Aydin sank his hand into the driver's pocket and grabbed the key to release the cuffs from his wrists. Then he jumped to his feet and dived into the open door of the police car to snatch his backpack from the passenger side footwell.

A radio crackled from behind him, and Aydin turned to discover the driver painfully calling into the device, asking – almost *begging* – for assistance. Aydin left him to it – his only objective was to get away.

Behind them the road was still clogged up. Some people were out of their cars, gawking at what they'd witnessed. One or two had their camera phones held aloft. Not good for Aydin. But a few Internet videos of his escape from police custody was far better than being locked in a cell.

In the outside lane he saw a motorbike approaching. The rider gently weaved the machine through the stationary cars, but he hadn't yet realised what was happening in front of him. Aydin jumped across the police car's bonnet and swung into the bike's path. The rider skidded the bike to a stop and Aydin lunged forward. The young man sensed the threat, and took a half step off his bike as Aydin came for him, and it only took a small shove to clear him from the bike. He was shouting at Aydin angrily but there was nothing he could do as Aydin pulled on the throttle and the bike surged forward.

FORTY-TWO

Ostend, Belgium

It was amazing what you could make happen when you were rich, Obbadi thought to himself as he waited by the door of the Learjet. After a few moments the steps were lowered down towards the floor of the hangar. There were no security guards waiting, no police or border patrol to check who was arriving in the country. Obbadi had friends in the right places and he may as well have parked up in his own backyard for all of the scrutiny that was placed on his arrival.

He straightened out his cream suit then walked down, looking around the enclosed space in front of him that was lit by several fizzing strip bulbs above. The wide metal doors of the hangar were rolled shut, a silver Ford transit van a few yards away with two men standing by its side, and another sitting in a wheelchair. Obbadi knew the name of the man in the wheelchair was Omar, though they'd never met. One of the men standing by Omar's side was Obbadi's brother, Tamaniyyah.

Obbadi, sullen faced, walked up to his brother and the two men hugged, slapping each other on the back.

'Good to see you,' Tamaniyyah said.

'And you. Although the fact that Itnashar isn't here too . . .'

Obbadi trailed off as he looked over to Omar, who was unable to hold Obbadi's eye.

'Brother, this is—'

'I know who he is,' Obbadi snapped.

Omar was one of their key associates in Belgium. Little more than a foot soldier really. He'd been part of the team deployed to help Itnashar capture Talatashar. In the end he'd been the only one other than Talatashar to come out of the mess in Bruges alive – shot in the chest in Itnashar's apartment, the bullet slipping by the side of his Kevlar vest. Not only had he suffered a punctured lung, but the bullet had wreaked havoc with the nerves in his spine. The doctors said he might never walk again, but Obbadi didn't feel an ounce of sorrow for the man. They'd failed in bringing down Talatashar, and Omar spending the rest of his life in a wheelchair was just punishment.

'You said you wanted to speak with him?' Tamaniyyah said.

'I do. But first let's complete what we need to. Do you have the drones?'

'Yes,' Tamaniyyah said, and he indicated to the other man by the transit van, his administrator, Yasser.

Yasser nodded and moved to the back doors of the van. Obbadi followed and when the doors opened he stared inside at the two large crates, each about a metre cubed.

'Everything's been checked?' Obbadi asked.

'It's all exactly as planned. Itnashar did us proud.'

That was good enough for Obbadi. No point in repeating work.

'Good. Load them onto the jet please.'

'And your goods arrived just a few hours ago,' Tamaniyyah said. The twenty-five canisters of cyanide pellets, transported from Germany to Belgium – half of the order Obbadi had received from Streicher.

'So, you're all set?' Obbadi asked.

'Just awaiting the final word.'

261

'It will come soon, I'm sure.'

'And what of Talatashar?'

'What indeed. Let me speak with Omar for a moment.'

Tamaniyyah nodded and Obbadi, eyes pinched in distaste, walked over to the wheelchair-bound man.

'Wahid,' Omar said, bowing his head and gripping Obbadi's hand with both of his. 'It truly is an honour.'

Obbadi pulled his hand back. 'Yes, I'm sure.'

'I'm so sorry for what happened.'

'Perhaps you can try to explain it to me. Every detail. I need to know what my brother did there, what he took from Bruges. Where he will go to next. Anything you can think of, however small, you need to tell me.'

'Certainly,' Omar said, visibly nervous.

Obbadi continued to glare, barely blinking, as Omar gave the detailed account of the failed operation. Obbadi felt his anger rising. How had Talatashar managed to evade them so easily? When did that little cretin suddenly become so accomplished?

'So you're telling me you just lay there on the ground while he stabbed my brother through the heart,' Obbadi said, more or less spitting the words, when Omar concluded the story.

'Y-Yes,' Omar conceded. 'But I couldn't move. The bullet . . . I—'

'What did he take?' Obbadi knew Talatashar had an encrypted laptop but didn't know exactly what else his brother had stolen – only Itnashar would have been able to confirm that and he was now lying in a morgue.

'It was hard to see, I really don't know.'

Obbadi glowered, not sure what else to ask to the simpleton.

'If there's any way for me to help,' Tamaniyyah said, putting his hand on Obbadi's shoulder, 'you know I will.'

'He's not in Bruges any more. And I told you before I can't have you moving now. We're too close.'

262

'But do you know where he is?'

'Mr Obbadi!' came a panting voice from behind them. It was Mustafa, Obbadi's aide who'd accompanied him on the flight from Italy. Obbadi turned and saw the young man striding over, his eyes twitching as he held a phone out in his hand. 'I think you should take this.'

Obbadi glared daggers at the young man, the unspoken question clear enough: *Why are you interrupting me?*

'It's Katja,' Mustafa said by way of explanation. 'She's called several times already. I answered to see what the problem was. I really think you should speak to her.'

Obbadi sensed more bad news was to come. He snatched the phone from Mustafa then turned away from the others while Katja explained what had happened. Obbadi barely said a word. By the end of the call he was squeezing the phone so hard he thought it might shatter in his hand.

He passed the phone back to Mustafa.

'Talatashar was in Rome,' Obbadi said, first looking over to Tamaniyyah. 'He's been to my apartment. Threatened my girlfriend.'

Tamaniyyah stared back but said nothing. Obbadi turned to face Omar.

'He got away. Again.'

Omar shook his head. He knew what was coming – everyone in the hangar did.

Obbadi roared as he lurched forward towards Omar. He reached out and grabbed the injured man around the neck, the power of the move sending Omar – wheelchair and all – clattering to the ground, the structure of the chair failing under the force. Obbadi was on top, on his knees, squeezing Omar's neck with everything he had. His victim's eyes bulged, but when he tried to choke out words the grip on his neck, crushing his windpipe, was too much. Obbadi's nails dug into the skin, pinching around the throat. He squeezed harder and harder, his fingers sinking deeper. Blood poured. No one came to Omar's aid.

Obbadi saw the strip of metal sticking up by Omar's side. A strut from the wheelchair, six inches long. He reached out and twisted the thin metal off the frame then drove the spiked end down and through Omar's left eye. He heard a gasp from Yasser. Obbadi pushed, the metal sank, squelching further and further into Omar's face as blood and thick white fluid oozed out. Omar's body twitched and shuddered for a moment, before it went still.

Obbadi, chest heaving, released the metal and stood, staring down at the corpse while he brought his breathing back under control.

He turned to see Mustafa holding out a handkerchief towards him. Obbadi snorted and took it from him and casually wiped at the blood that dripped from his hand. The sleeve of his suit was also covered in speckles of red. He stripped it off and dumped it on the ground next to the corpse.

'Clean up the mess,' Obbadi said to Tamaniyyah.

'Yes, brother.'

'I'll be in touch soon.' Obbadi turned to Mustafa. 'Tell the pilot we're leaving for Italy. Now.'

Mustafa scurried off.

'I'm sorry,' Tamaniyyah said.

'I know you are.' Obbadi took one last look at what was left of Omar. 'Never underestimate the punishment for failure, my brother.'

FORTY-THREE

Istanbul, Turkey

'I think Kamil Torkal is lying,' Cox said as she lay on the bed in a hotel room in central Istanbul. Outside her open window the high-pitched voice of the *muezzin* screeched – a call to prayer trumpeting from the Blue Mosque in the old town across the Bosphorus Strait. Cox rose from the bed and moved over and pulled the sash window shut, and the noise of the *adnan* and the busy city streets below disappeared.

'Lying about which part?' Flannigan asked, his voice coming through an earbud. They were on a white-line call, and although the hotel room might be compromised, she would rather at least one half of the conversation was too quiet for any bugs or eavesdroppers.

'I think he's lying about most of what he said, to be honest.'

'What he said seems plausible to me.'

'Are you kidding me?'

'Not at all. This Aydin is a psychopath. He's leaving a trail of bodies everywhere he goes. Who knows where he'll strike next. Do I think he's capable of killing his own mother? Abso-fucking-lutely.'

'There's more to what's happening here than that.'

'Says you, Cox. You have to admit Kamil Torkal's explanation ties with everything we *know*. I mean, factually know, not what we can make fit into a wild theory about elite jihadis.'

Cox held her tongue, trying her best not to bite back too hard. She would never win a slanging match with Flannigan. He was too rambunctious for that. She needed to persuade him with cold, hard facts. Which, she had to admit, weren't exactly in plentiful supply.

'Sorry, sir, but I'm just not seeing the situation like Kamil described it at all.'

'What don't you see? We know Ergun Torkal took his son away from England. Okay, there's a question mark over the intentions of that, but neither theory has any solidity to it. We do know they went to Afghanistan. What happened after that? Who knows? You're saying Aydin went to a school to be trained as a ruthless jihadi warrior, but it's just as likely his father took him there to turn him into a bloody mullah. And the story of drone strikes and innocent victims . . . it's credible.'

'No. What's credible was the intel that led to the drone strike in the first place. Ergun Torkal was known to be affiliated to fanatics.'

Flanngian sighed. 'One man's religious fanatic is another man's devotee.'

'That's a load of crap and you know it. Since when have you ever thought that before about *our* intelligence?'

'Sometimes intel is wrong. Sometimes the wrong person is killed, even. We have to accept that. WMD ring any bells for you?'

Cox tried to respond but she just didn't know what else to say. Having been amenable to her in Ankara, Flannigan was back to his usual belligerent self with a vengeance, barely giving any of what she was saying even a second's thought.

'Look, Cox, I'm not saying there isn't something in why your friend Nilay was killed.'

266

'Friends,' Cox interjected. 'It was Subhi too.'

'Okay, *friends*. It's suspicious. And this Aydin character, he needs to be stopped.'

'And Germany?'

'And Germany just raised even more questions. I need answers, not questions. What I'm saying is you're still no closer to breaking out here and proving with any credibility that the so-called Thirteen are an imminent threat to society, or even that they exist.'

'If you believe that, then it's time to get your head out of your arse. Sir.'

Cox held her breath while she waited for her boss to respond to that. She was fifty/fifty as to whether he would explode or not.

'I could say the same to you,' he came back with, with absolute calm. 'I agree there is a problem here. A potentially *big* problem. But so far it seems to be confined to one man. Aydin Torkal. We don't know his full history, and we don't know what his plan is. What we do know is that he's on a mission, and that mission has already seen several people killed at his hands.'

'That very fact alone suggests something bigger is happening here! Who are these people he's gone after so far? Paris, London, Bruges. This isn't random. And he was never in Germany so how do you explain what happened there?'

'Which is what you need to find out. Help find this guy, before it's too late.'

They both went silent. Cox wracked her brain, trying to think of something to go back at Flannigan with. As rattled as she was, she knew deep down he wasn't being a dick to her for the sake of it. Not this time, at least. This time he genuinely didn't see what she was seeing and was simply challenging her findings. She *had* to find Flannigan the proof he craved.

'You have to reconsider my application to use the Trapeze team,' Cox said. 'We now have several locations where it's very likely some of the Thirteen are based. Using Trapeze to target those cities we would surely crack this. Identify the cells, their addresses, stop them before it's too late.'

'No,' he said almost immediately.

'Just like that?'

'It won't pass. Miles won't even think about it unless you give him more. Don't waste your time, Cox.'

'You said you want me to find Aydin Torkal. Using Trapeze will be the quickest way.'

'It's too much to find one man who's already in our sights.'

'In our sights? And it's not just one man we're trying to find, is it? It's all of them.'

'Do you even know why it's called Trapeze?'

Cox sighed, not really interested in the history lesson. 'A reference to the Circus, I'm guessing . . .'

'Exactly. MI6, the Circus. Commonly thought to be a phrase coined by John le Carré for his novels, but actually simply because the Dorset Square office used to belong to the directors of Bertram Mills Circus.'

'I think you'd make a good Smiley.'

'I'm not going to ask you why you think that. The point is, Cox, it's called Trapeze because that team sits above *everything*, and they see *everything*. It's a big deal to use them. They have the capability to do things that the man on the street can't even imagine. Tap into people's fridges and TVs to listen into their homes, for fuck's sake. They can hack your home Wi-Fi to record every single keystroke on your phone, your computer, your—'

'Sir, I get it.'

'Maybe you don't. The trapeze is traditionally the last act of the circus. For us they are an absolute last resort. Every application approval for Trapeze has to be taken with the utmost seriousness and rigour. We invade people's privacy beyond what many people can even comprehend. If we get it wrong . . . it's arses on the line time. Not just for us, but for our friends over in Westminster.'

'Friends? Never heard you call them that before.'

'I'm sorry, Cox, but I won't accept a new application. Not until you have something more. In the meantime, do everything you can to find Aydin Torkal.'

Cox opened her mouth to speak but before a word passed her lips, the call clicked off.

For a while Cox just sat on the fabric sofa in the hotel room, looking out over the bobbing water of the Bosphorous, the sky above darkening into a fusion of blues and reds and oranges as the sun set behind her. Her mind was in overdrive, thinking through what she could, and should, do next.

Eventually she got up and went back to the laptop on the bed. She pulled up the last report she'd sent Flannigan – three weeks ago – and to her previous sign-off sheet for her request for Trapeze support. How life had already changed so much in that time.

She didn't take her eyes off the request form for several minutes as her brain chugged away. All that was missing from that document was the signature of a level six director and the rudimentary SIS stamp. For all SIS's cutting-edge technology and sophisticated networks of agents and informants across the globe, dealing in all manner of threats, authority for operations still came down to nothing more than a scrawled name on a piece of paper.

Cox snorted at the thought rushing through her mind. Why was she even contemplating it? Even if it got her the answers she needed surely it would be the end of her time in SIS. She could even end up in jail on some trumped-up treachery charge. Or worse they'd bung her off to a black site and she'd never see the light of day again.

It had to be worth the risk, though. She couldn't live with herself knowing she could have done something but didn't. Knowing that her inaction cost hundreds, even thousands of innocent lives.

She pushed the doubt aside and went back through into her old emails. It didn't take long to find what she was looking for. Her promotion assessment. To fully convince herself of what she was contemplating, she had to feel truly aggrieved and disgruntled at the big machine.

She read through the document. At the age of thirty-seven she'd long been looking for a new path. Her application for level four supervisor nearly two years ago was both because she genuinely believed she deserved more internal recognition, and more reward for what she did, but also because on many levels she was becoming tired of the life of an undercover intelligence agent. She'd never seen herself as a pen-pusher, and the reality was she would probably hate the job Flannigan had, but how long was she going to keep up a homeless, globetrotting existence? The promotion would have changed her life. She would have been back in England, probably still happily married. Instead, all she had were her cover identities and the knowledge she was righting the world's wrongs. Or trying at least.

She first read through the promotion self-assessment she'd written herself. Then the assessment of her sponsor – Henry Flannigan. What a bloody joke. He'd actually sung her praises on the document she was reading, but she had to wonder if the words that had come out of his mouth to the panel had been quite different. Why else would the ultimate conclusion have been in such contrast to what he'd written? Finally she reached the end of the document. The reject decision, signed off by one Roger Miles. Seeing the document again was all she needed to get her blood boiling.

Thirty minutes later, with a bit of tweaking to her request form to take account of the events of the last few days, including Aydin Torkal's known movements through London, Paris and Bruges, and from her trip to Germany, it was done. Trapeze request authorised – kind of – and submitted. Within hours she'd have the most sophisticated surveillance team on the planet on her side, everything from live satellite imagery and real-time capture of CCTV in various locations, to the utilisation of cutting edge software to run keywords across real-time telephone and Internet communications, covering not just specific persons of interest at home and abroad, but hundreds of thousands of people in designated locations.

If there was evidence to find, Trapeze would find it. Screw the suits in Westminster if they didn't like it.

Flannigan and Miles would find out what she'd done sooner or later. She had to believe that, and she had to expect the worst for her when that happened. She just hoped she would get what she needed before then.

Cox sat back in her chair.

'You silly woman,' she said out loud, shaking her head, though a smile broke out on her face before she repeated herself in Arabic.

'I just hope you're worth it, Nilay.'

FORTY-FOUR

Sofia, Bulgaria

Aydin had originally intended on moving from Italy to Greece before taking a bus on to his next destination – his family's home country of Turkey. In the end his suspicions had got the better of him and he'd opted instead to move further east into Bulgaria to catch the overnight train. On a train there was more space, he could blend in and hide more easily than on a cramped bus. It meant, however, that he had to leave the Schengen zone, and in reaching Bulgaria he'd endured tortuous border crossings from Hungary and then Romania, traversing woodland, rivers and muddy fields out of the sight of authorities.

He was badly in need of rest as he walked through Sofia at dusk. But he fully expected the onward train journey to be just as fraught as the last two days since he'd left Rome. After the run-in with the police in Italy, and being wanted for murder in London, he not only had to worry about his brothers tracking him down, but also, most likely, the police and intelligence services of several countries.

Plan for the worst.

The journey from Rome had at least given him time to more thoroughly peruse the items he'd taken from Wahid's safe. Firstly, the two passports; different names, different countries, two slightly different pictures of Wahid. Aydin had sneered when he looked at the passports in more detail. One was Turkish, the other German. One of the most recent stamps in the latter was a trip to Turkey. Nilay had been there not so long ago as well. Which fitted uncomfortably with the contents of the brown envelope from Wahid's safe. A printout of an identity check on his sister, together with a residential address in Aleppo. He still couldn't fathom exactly how she'd got into Wahid's crosshairs, but he was determined to find out.

The thumb drive he'd pilfered was a different prospect, with yet more layers of security that would take Aydin time to break through. He would keep trying, at every opportunity he got.

With time to spare in Sofia before the train, he bought new clothes – some jeans, brown loafers and a smart roll-neck jumper – and a razor and scissors to tidy up his increasingly rugged appearance. Moving out of Bulgaria to Turkey would be the first time on his journey that he was passing through an official border crossing – the gateway between Europe and Asia. As such he knew it would be more substantially protected than most intra-European borders, and he wanted to rouse as little suspicion as he could.

Thirty minutes before the train was due to depart, Aydin headed to Sofia Central Station and bought a ticket for a single berth cabin on the overnight train to Istanbul. He waited in the huge central foyer that was framed by massive Brutalist-style concrete blocks and patterned with a multitude of straight lines and stars, a well-worn style that emphasised the country's recent communist past. Cyrillic script scrolled along the electronic boards in front of him. He didn't understand the language, but had bought a guidebook earlier to help with the basics.

As the local time approached nine p.m. he saw the platform announcement for his train and headed through the station, his eyes working overtime as he scanned the people and the security guards and the blue-uniformed policemen. No one he saw caused him any concern.

Aydin boarded the train at the front, right next to the block-shaped red engine carriage that looked at least fifty years old. The first carriage was one of the two air-conditioned sleeper carriages. He walked all the way through and took the first cabin in the second carriage – the closest to the exit doors. Before he closed the cabin door he glanced quickly into the corridor. A man and a woman – both in their thirties, casually dressed – were standing at the other end of the carriage. They looked Northern European, with light skin and blonde hair. The man paid Aydin no attention, but the woman caught his eye before the two of them disappeared inside a cabin. Aydin realised his heart was pounding as he closed and locked his cabin door. Was it exhaustion that made him feel so on edge? That sense of being watched?

At one minute past nine the train slowly crawled out of the station. Peering out of his window, Aydin had only spotted about twenty or so other passengers boarding the four carriages. Satisfied that he was as safe as he could hope for, he sat down on the garishly patterned fabric bench and looked around. The tiny cabin had a washbasin and mirror in one corner. Other than the communal toilet at either end of each carriage there were no other facilities on board – no restaurant car or even a snack bar. Not that Aydin would have dared venture out to those anyway, and if he needed the toilet he'd do it in the sink.

He stared out of the window, barely able to see anything in the black night. The train would arrive in Turkey in the morning, just in time for sunrise. He wanted nothing more than to shut his eyes and sleep, but his brain refused to allow him. After half an hour, though, it became increasingly difficult to keep his heavy eyelids open. A loud knock on the door caused him to jerk and bang his head against the wall behind.

Had he actually been asleep, or lost in some fatigue-induced trance? Through the frosted glass of the door he could see the form of a person – a tall man, given his head reached above the top of the doorframe.

'*Bileti*,' came the loud and gruff voice from the other side of the door.

Aydin got up from the bench and reached for the backpack on the floor. He took the ticket in one hand, and the large hunting knife he'd bought in Sofia in the other. He hadn't yet had a chance to re-arm himself with a gun since leaving Rome, and it would have been too risky given the various borders he was crossing.

He moved to the door and stood to the side as he unlocked it and slid it open a few inches to stare up at the weather-beaten face of the bearded mountain outside, the knife held behind his back, ready to attack. The guy was a beast, but a uniformed beast. Aydin passed his ticket through the gap and after a long, suspicious study of the ticket the man stamped it and handed the stub back.

'*Leka nosht*,' the man growled before he turned and walked to the next cabin.

Aydin's eyes didn't leave the oversized guard until he'd gently shut and locked the door. He slumped down on the bench as he heaved all of the air from his aching lungs. Barely breathing, he waited until the guard was well out of earshot further down the carriage before inhaling sharply. He wasn't sure how much more of this he could take.

The screeching of the train's wheels was enough to drag Aydin back to the real world. Without intending to, he'd succumbed to sleep. It was midnight – he'd been out of it for a couple of hours, yet his head was pounding and his body was aching even more than when he'd boarded.

The darkness outside poured into the cabin and Aydin stared back at it, his head throbbing, as the train pulled to a stop at Kapikule on the Turkish border. Seconds later the booming voice of the guard could be heard as he stomped along the carriage, banging on the doors as he barked at the passengers to wake up and prepare themselves for the border check. Aydin was still clutching the knife, so he slipped it into the bag and took out Wahid's Turkish passport, stolen from the safe in Rome, before opening the cabin door.

On the platform, the cool night-time air hit him. He quickly scanned the passengers. The same light-haired man and woman again, standing alongside a handful of other passengers. There was a collective weariness to the group, put out by the late-night interruption – everyone, that was, except for the Turkish border guards. They were more alert than Aydin had expected, their watchful eyes scanning, hands clasped at their fronts, a baton and sidearm adorning their belts. Aydin kept his head down as the passengers were corralled into the small, ageing platform building that smelled of an unusual concoction of bleach, varnish and sweat. The passengers waited in line to have their passports checked and visas paid for, Aydin about halfway along the queue. He felt surprisingly calm as he waited – perhaps the sleep, although short and disturbed – had done him good after all.

When it was his turn he smiled at the expressionless man behind the Perspex glass, holding out the passport in the name of Mehmet Kahveci. The guard snatched the passport and studied the photograph, before placing it under the scanner in front of him and switching his eyes to his screen.

Aydin knew this part was by far the biggest risk he'd taken since leaving Paris. He'd done his best to clean up his appearance, to make himself as convincing a lookalike of Wahid as he was able. But if the guard looked close enough he'd surely realise it was someone else in the picture. That wasn't Aydin's only worry. He knew from experience that there were varying qualities to passport forgeries. Some were basic – sufficient to pass a casual examination – but had no link to any official identification database, which meant they were useless for modern-day travel through airports and across borders in any country that used basic scanning software. Aydin had to assume that Wahid's passports were the best. Wahid was a man who left nothing to chance, after all.

Even though he was doing his utmost to appear calm, Aydin still found himself clenching his fists tightly, digging his fingernails into the palms of his hands as he waited for the verdict.

'Mr Kahveci, I notice this is the first time you've returned to Turkey since your last trip to Damascus. What was the purpose of your visit to Syria?'

Aydin had noted the stamp from Syria, dated some six months previously. He'd expected the question. Still, he'd decided it was better to use the Turkish passport for this trip than Wahid's German one.

'I'm a journalist,' he said.

'And why are you returning to Turkey only now?'

'I'm visiting family.'

'And you live in . . .'

'In Italy.'

'Strange that you came to Turkey by train then. From Bulgaria. Much quicker to fly from Italy, I would have thought?'

'I was working in Sofia,' Aydin said, giving a casual shrug. 'I travel a lot for my job.'

'Very well.' The guard closed the passport but didn't hand it back. He began typing away on his keyboard and a few seconds later Aydin spotted movement off to his right. He glanced over and saw two other uniformed guards coming his way.

He felt his legs twitching, as though they were willing him to run.

'Mr Kahveci, we just need to ask you a few more questions,' the guard behind the glass said. 'Then you can go. It shouldn't take long.' He handed the passport to one of his colleagues, who gestured for Aydin to follow.

Flanked by the two guards, he stepped forward, scoping out the building further, on the lookout for potential escape routes. Could he feasibly make a dash for the platforms – perhaps slip across to the other side of the tracks and break free of the station? Darkness would help him greatly, but something was willing him to stay calm. To see how the situation played out. Surely Wahid would not have let one of his identities become compromised. This was likely just a routine check, born in part out of Turkey's recent tensions with its neighbour, Syria.

The other possibility was that Wahid had somehow put the measures in place for the very reason that he knew his passports had been stolen.

It was too late now. They'd made it down a narrow corridor to an interview room, which the guards shepherded Aydin into. One of them pushed him down onto a creaky metal chair.

'Wait there.'

The guard left, leaving Aydin with the shorter and stockier of the two. He closed the door, took one quick look at Aydin, and then turned back to face the wall.

Something felt wrong. Who exactly *were* they waiting for? If this was a routine check, wouldn't it just mean a simple set of questions?

Five minutes passed by. Then ten. After twenty minutes Aydin heard the chug-chug as the train on the platform slowly moved away into the night.

'And what am I supposed to do now?' Aydin said, his bitterness showing, deciding it was better to play the role of innocent-man-unnecessarily-inconvenienced than guilty man awaiting punishment. Despite feeling much more like the latter.

'You wait, like you were told.'

'And when's the next train, exactly?'

The guard shrugged.

A few minutes later there was knock. The guard unlocked and opened the door. Yet another uniformed border guard was standing on the threshold. He was short and wiry, in his forties, Aydin guessed, with an air of superiority that suggested he was more senior than the others. He struck up a hushed conversation with the guard in the room, who, after a few moments, glared at Aydin before scurrying out of sight.

The older guard bounded over. '*Selamünaleyküm.*'

'And may peace be upon you too,' Aydin said, as the guard put his hand under Aydin's armpit to lift him up.

'It's such an honour to meet you, Wahid,' the man said, his voice barely more than a whisper.

'The honour is mine,' Aydin said as his brain quickly re-calibrated.

'We don't have much time. Come on, we need to go.'

The guard tugged on Aydin's arm and pulled him out of the room and they soon came back out into the waiting area. They took a hard right, heading for another door that had a No Entry sign on it. Aydin noticed the waiting area was now deserted, just the outline of a couple of guards standing on the platform outside. The guard holding on to Aydin took a keychain from his hip and unlocked the no-entry door then shoved Aydin through before following and closing it behind them.

'You're lucky I was here tonight,' the guard said. 'Otherwise I'm not sure how long it would have taken to get you out.'

Aydin said nothing. He had no doubt the guy must be a genuine border guard. Just how far did the organisation's claws reach now? And yet the man, although he knew of Wahid, had certainly never met him before. How could he have?

They scuttled down the corridor through two more doors before finally they were out in the cold, dark of the night once more, having exited through a service entrance that led onto a deserted road.

'Don't worry, I'll make sure the record of your arrival is made properly. I'll get in some trouble, but I hope you'll tell your father how helpful I was. And you'll have no problem leaving the country when you're ready.'

The guard pushed Aydin a step further away from the door, at the same time himself moving back inside. He moved to pull the door shut.

'But—' Aydin said quickly.

'Take this road,' the guard said, pointing off to the right. 'There's a verge you can stay hidden in though there won't be much traffic now anyway. In less than two miles you'll hit the next town. You can take a bus from there at daylight. You'll be fine.'

'Thank y—'

'It really was a pleasure to finally meet you. Good luck.'

The door shut with a slam, leaving Aydin to consider – for a change – his unusual slice of good luck.

Allowing himself a small smile, he turned to his right, took the knife out from his backpack, and began his trek through the dark.

FORTY-FIVE

The Mediterranean

Italy had faded into the distance behind Ismail Obbadi several hours ago. He had mixed feelings about leaving Rome again so soon. Of course, he would be back, but the world would be a very different place next time he set foot there. The plan had always been to depart Rome before the operation went live, so doing so early was far from a capitulation, merely a minor deviation.

Still, the circumstances behind the change of plan were increasingly irksome to Obbadi, knowing that it had been caused by Talatashar's continued heroics. He ground his teeth at the thought.

At least Obbadi hadn't left Rome empty-handed. He felt himself relax a little at that, as he sat on the top deck of *La Signora Tranquilla* – The Quiet Lady – looking up at the stars above. The one-hundred-foot yacht, that had cost nearly as much to build as the entire apartment complex in Rome, gently bobbed up and down on the dark waters below. Tired, and with the gentle rocking of the yacht and the lapping of the waves, Obbadi drifted off before he was rudely interrupted by Mustafa's squeaking voice.

'Mr Obbadi, it's time.'

Groaning, Obbadi got up and followed the young man, one of several staff Obbadi had on board, two floors below to the office where the laptop computer was set up and the call already connected. He waited for Mustafa to disappear before he closed the door and sat down by the computer. He put the bulky headphones on.

'Hello, my son.'

Obbadi flopped back on the chair. 'I'm sorry,' he said, feeling genuinely ashamed by how matters were going against him. But shame quickly turned to anger.

'You could not have predicted this.'

Yet Obbadi believed he should have. Talatashar had always been something of a black sheep in his eyes.

'We will find him,' Obbadi said.

'Maybe he will find you first.'

Obbadi grimaced. His and Talatashar's paths had so very nearly crossed in Rome. Obbadi clenched his fists, enraged not just knowing that Talatashar was evading his pursuers so well, but that he'd been to *his* home, had threatened *his* woman.

'How much do you think he knows?'

'Not enough to stop us now,' Obbadi said.

'How can you be sure? You know what he did in Bruges. Why do you think he went there? And now he's been to Rome too. He's everywhere we are.'

'No, Itnashar was too careful. Talatashar won't have found anything useful from him.'

'And you? Are you careful?'

'We all are.'

'I can only pray so. But Intnashar was his best friend, and Talatashar still saw fit to kill him to get what he needed. If he has our full pl—'

'He doesn't. And even if he did, he can't stop us now.'

'I wish I shared your confidence, son.'

'Trust me.'

'I do. But I also know Talatashar. He's dangerous for you, for me, and for all the others. We need to move faster.'

'Move faster?'

'Asrutdinov is dead. Phantom is ready. You told me that yourself. And your brothers have each confirmed they have all that they need now, even Paris.'

Obbadi clenched his fists even tighter. Why had the Teacher been speaking to the others behind his back?

'It's time to set the clock ticking.'

'That gives us less than three days,' Obbadi protested. 'I—'

'Just get it done.'

The line went dead.

Ten minutes later Obbadi was still in position as he listened to the intermittent bleeps, one after the other, as each of his brothers joined the call. There was no preamble, no pleasantries as each man joined – just a thick silence as the group awaited news.

'It's time,' Obbadi said without feeling. 'The clock starts at midnight. In three days, this will all be over. You each know what you have to do from here.'

That was all that needed to be said. Obbadi was done. Neither wanting nor expecting any response, he reached out to end the call,

'What about Talatashar?' a voice piped up just in time. Itnan. Number two.

Obbadi was surprised. Itnan wasn't usually one to question.

'Talatashar's not important now,' Obbadi said.

'He's already killed Itnashar, how—'

'Yet he hasn't succeeded in stopping our plans in France or England or Belgium or anywhere else. We—'

'Three days is a long time. If he continues to disrupt us we may not be able to see this through.'

'Then what do you suggest?'

'We put all our efforts into finding him. Killing him. Before the clock starts.'

'No. It's too late for that.'

'I beg you, don't start it yet.'

'The decision has already been made. Let me worry about Talatashar.'

Obbadi killed the call and held his breath until his lungs burned. It was the only way he could keep his rage from exploding there and then. When he felt calm enough to move he took the headphones off and stepped outside the room. Mustafa was hovering in the corridor.

'I wondered if you needed me to do anything?' Mustafa asked.

Obbadi ran his fingers through his hair as he thought. He'd been putting this next part off as long as he could, savouring the moment for when he truly needed it. The wait had been long enough.

'Go to bed. It's late. I'll see you in the morning.'

'You're going below?'

Obbadi nodded. 'Don't disturb me. Not for anything.'

'Of course.'

Mustafa turned and left.

Alone, Obbadi made his way to the depths of the hull.

He released the padlock on the door of the box-like cabin. A desktop lamp illuminated the sparse space, its light reflecting sharply off the clinically white surfaces. Thick plastic sheeting ran all the way up to the feet of the forlorn figure who was tied to a chair, his head covered with a sack. Obbadi's face slap roused him to life, and the man's panicked gasps and wheezes filled the room.

'Massimiliano Cabrini,' Obbadi said. 'Welcome aboard *La Signora Tranquilla*.'

The sack was whipped from the man's head.

A wave of clarity flooded Obbadi as he saw the fear in the man's eyes.

'Remember me?' Obbadi asked as he straightened up. Cabrini said nothing. The man's chest rose in panicked breaths. 'Hey, hey, take it easy. Big breath in.' Obbadi took a long slow inhale. 'And a big breath out.'

Cabrini began to breathe less erratically. Obbadi approached the table and unbuttoned his blue Brioni suit jacket, slipped it off and placed it carefully onto the padded coat hanger dangling from a hook on the cabin door.

'I do hope you enjoyed your evening at Purity, *my* bar, and the free drinks I afforded you and your companions the last time we met.'

He rolled his shirtsleeves up past his elbows. Cabrini paid Obbadi his full attention as he slipped on an apron and tied it in place.

'You're such a good customer I thought it was only right that I should extend my hospitality to you once again, now that I've left Rome behind. Tell me, have you ever been to Spain?'

Obbadi pulled the thin blue latex gloves over his hands. Cabrini, confused, shook his head wildly.

'No? Shame. That's where we're headed. A wonderful country actually, so much history. I'm from Morocco myself. You know, the history of my people is so very strongly linked with those of Southern Spain. The Moors. You've heard of them? A truly magnificent civilisation.' Nothing from Cabrini now. 'Anyway, that's where we're going, but I'm so sorry you'll never get to see Spain for yourself. Don't worry though, there's plenty of time for me to tell you all about its rich history. We've a long journey ahead, after all.'

Obbadi stepped over to the table, upon which two shining stainless steel trays were arranged with a tidy array of silver tools. Gloved fingers brushing across the instruments, he fixed his eyes back on the man in the chair. The look in Cabrini's eyes . . . an understanding. It was exactly the look that Obbadi had hoped to see.

'But first,' Obbadi continued, 'perhaps I should tell you some more about *me*. After all, very soon we're going to be intimately acquainted.'

He picked up the miniature bone saw and stepped forward, his heart thumping in gleeful anticipation.

FORTY-SIX

Istanbul, Turkey

On Flannigan's advice Cox had spent the previous two nights in the hotel. Sparse intelligence suggested Aydin Torkal had been in Rome a number of days ago, in an apartment that belonged to a wealthy entrepreneur, but Aydin had fled and hadn't been seen or heard from since. Flannigan had deemed it pointless for Cox to chase him where he'd already been, and she'd agreed. The entrepreneur – Ismail Obbadi – had himself gone missing, and Cox felt sure he at the very least had links to Aydin and the Thirteen. Why else would Aydin have targeted him? She was still waiting on results from Trapeze and Data Ops who were doing what they could to pick apart Obbadi's life. So far he appeared squeaky clean, at least as squeaky clean as the mega rich could be, though everything Obbadi touched would now be heavily scrutinised by SIS.

The previous day Cox had met up with an SIS asset – a Turkish native who worked for a local government off-shoot. She'd given Cox quite the lowdown on the comings and goings of some of the most prominent figures in the city. Kamil Torkal, a well-respected professor who was wealthy not from his university career but from his dealings with various government-backed property development projects, was among the people she had talked about.

Interestingly though (or was it more surprising?) there was no hint at all that Kamil Torkal was in any way connected with any extremist groups, nor that he ever had been. The only dirt on him seemed confined to those property deals, where it was almost certain that palms had been greased and public money diverted into certain people's back pockets. As far from lily-white as the professor was, there was a hell of a difference between corrupt fraudster and terrorist. What was the real story with the professor? Was his only link to the Thirteen the fact that he was Aydin's uncle?

Cox looked at her watch. Nine fifty-nine. She opened up the call on her laptop, put her headphones on and leant back in the armchair, looking out across the sea that, on this unusually grey day, blended into the sky so there was no horizon.

'Rachel Cox here,' she stated when the call connected.

'Clarissa Poulter,' came the sharp voice of the Trapeze supervisor assigned to Cox's operation.

'You said you had an update?'

'Is Henry Flannigan on the line too?'

'No. Just me,' Cox said.

'Oh. I would have expected a level four to want to hear this.'

'I can fill him in later.'

'That's not really the way we work here.'

Cox had never met Poulter, hadn't even spoken to her before, but she immediately had an image of what the woman looked like based on the sound of her voice and her arsey tone. A witch, pointy nose and hat, warts, striped stockings and all.

'Sorry, Clarissa, but I'm in Istanbul. I don't even know where Flannigan is right now. Possibly he's on a flight back to London. I'll absolutely update him next time we speak.'

Poulter sighed.

'Very well. This is your first time using Trapeze, then?' she asked, in a tone which suggested she saw Cox as something of an idiot.

'Yes.'

'Okay, well I'll tell you how this works best. I'm not going to bore you with everything we've done, and everything we've seen and heard. Ninety nine per cent of our activity turns out to be fruitless so what I'm going to give you is the snapshot.'

'I understand all that. I'm not unschooled in how surveillance works, or in how to pull a story together from snippets.'

'Of course not. Anyway, of the persons of interest you've been looking into, we have several direct hits, by which I mean intercepted communications, in the locations we're covering; namely London, Paris, Bruges, Berlin and Rome. But from there we've also linked communications to Barcelona, Tel-Aviv and, lastly, Aleppo.'

Cox frowned. 'Sorry, what do you mean? How are the communications linked?'

'They're using large numbers of relays to effectively encrypt the data, but we've been able to pull apart the layers of the communications to identify the originating active servers, which are based in those locations I just mentioned. Needless to say, though, the security measures in place here are thorough and very deliberate, so it's possible we're not seeing everything, that not all of the cities I just mentioned are the bona fide locations of the people involved. We do however have strong secondary evidence in most of those locations. Hence the conclusion we've come to is that your target list of people are spread throughout those cities, and possibly others.'

'Do you have anything on their plans? When, where and what the possible attacks might look like?'

'I'm sorry, but no. You said you believed your persons of interest to be plotting attacks in Western Europe. I'll make this absolutely clear to you – we have no firm evidence so far that that is the case, though it would normally take us many days if not weeks to find such conclusive evidence.'

'I understand that.'

'However, we do have reams of data tracking the people we've identified – some thirty people now and counting – both over our active time period, and going back in time. That includes CCTV and satellite imagery of their movements, tele-communications and other electronic communications. Using what we've found, we've also linked in to historic data of these people's identities. Most telling is what we've found on Ismail Obbadi.'

Cox's heart raced in anticipation.

'Apparently he's a Moroccan national, and although his identity is registered in all the right places, we're struggling to piece together his full history. Family, where he was brought up, schools etc.'

'Meaning the identity may actually be bogus?'

'Meaning we don't yet know. But we'll keep digging. What I would say is that this guy certainly isn't afraid to get his face in the papers. It didn't really require Trapeze's firepower to find pictures of him and his girlfriend wining and dining in Italy's capital.'

Cox wasn't sure whether that comment was a dig at her.

'Any links between Obbadi and Turkey?' Cox asked. 'Or to Aydin Torkal or the others we identified?'

'Yes to the first question, no to the second. There are various money trails that we're still following but more than one of them does pass through Turkey. We've not yet found the purposes of these transactions, or in many cases the original source or end beneficiary. However, the trails do largely

290

appear to relate to assets controlled by Obbadi, or to parties who are involved with his businesses.'

'I need details of those transactions. Of the assets, of the names of his business partners too.'

'You'll get it all.'

The finding was potentially huge. If Obbadi was directly involved, he could be bankrolling the activity of the others in cities across Europe. If she followed the money, it might lead to addresses, locations, and to each of the members of the Thirteen.

Was Obbadi even one of them?

'Have you found anything to link Kamil Torkal to that activity?'

'Other than the fact he's in Turkey, nothing at all. In fact, from the limited information we've returned on Torkal, I'd say he's not linked to your other persons of interest at all.'

Cox sighed. She was certain Kamil hadn't given her a truthful account of what had happened to his brother and Aydin.

'One other thing,' Poulter continued. 'Obbadi has now left Rome, and last we knew he was heading across the Mediterranean on a yacht. Last night Obbadi, from that yacht, was involved in a multi-participant VoIP call. We know that call took place, however we weren't able to intercept the communication itself.'

'What do you mean *last we knew*?'

'I was just coming to that. The most alarming thing, however, is what happened almost immediately after that call. At midnight, Central European Time, to be precise.'

'Which is what?'

'To put it simply, absolutely nothing.'

'Nothing? As in—'

'As in every single one of our persons of interest has been dark since then.'

'Dark even to Trapeze? But that would mean—'

'That means, Miss Cox, that these people are incredibly careful, and knowledgeable in surveillance techniques. As far as we're able to see, these people may as well have now dropped off the face of the earth.'

Cox thought for a minute. 'This was probably all caused because of Aydin Torkal. He's tracking the others down. I don't know why he's doing that, but he's done enough to seriously spook them. Maybe they've dropped off the grid in response? Or maybe . . . they're getting ready to attack.'

Poulter went silent. Was that agreement?

'And you don't even know where Obbadi went?' Cox continued. 'He was on a boat in the Mediterranean and just disappeared?'

'It's a pretty big place.'

Cox said nothing to that. She was too busy thinking still. 'Is there anything else? Anything from Germany?'

'We've identified your man in the white van. Goes by various bogus aliases and we don't know his real name or origins, but we believe he is part of your group, and has been referred to as Sab'ah.'

Cox felt like giving herself a high five. 'Number seven. And what about the cyanide?'

'Nothing we've seen references cyanide, or any details about any imminent attack, for that matter. In terms of headline useful and credible evidence, I've given you all I have. We will of course forward you fuller details of the various parties. Names, historical addresses where possible, what we've identified.'

'Absolutely. Please do.'

'I'm sorry we haven't been able to provide you with anything more conclusive.'

'But you will keep searching?'

'Of course. And I'll pass the findings on to Henry Flannigan too,' Poulter said. 'Speak later.'

There was a click as Poulter left the call, and Cox winced at the parting comment. Poulter had no way of knowing the damage that would be caused once Flannigan found out what Cox had done. Cox just had to hope that Poulter's findings would be enough to defuse him. Otherwise she could kiss her career goodbye – and, more than likely, her freedom too.

FORTY-SEVEN

Aydin encountered no more setbacks on his journey through Turkey to Istanbul. The knife wounds on his arm and leg looked no closer to healing. Proper medical attention was required – antibiotics, antivirals – but turning up to a hospital was out of the question. The other option was that he stole the drugs he needed himself, but he hadn't become that desperate. Yet.

Instead he dressed and re-dressed the wounds with basic supplies from various pharmacies, and the antiseptic had at least stopped the wounds becoming deeply infected. He'd filled his body with all manner of painkillers, copious amounts of caffeine and some cheap lab-created opiate he'd purchased from a street dealer in a less than salubrious part of the city. In big cities, such people weren't hard to find, if you knew what you were looking for.

Sitting at an Egyptian cafe on the European side of the city, the deep blue of the calm Sea of Marmara directly across the road, his heart beat erratically, and his body felt oddly distant. Persevering was the only option – if he stopped, the hounds would close in and do everything they could to finish him off. It was down to him to get to *them* first.

The weather in Istanbul wasn't making him feel any better.

294

Not only was it hot as hell but it was humid too; the sky thick with cloud, the salty air wet and suffocating.

He took his time and eventually finished the *aish baladi* and water and left some coins on the table. A motorbike had cost him one hundred US dollars earlier that morning in northern Turkey – a twenty-year-old machine that somehow ran as smoothly as any other vehicle he'd been on the last few days. As he perched on the worn leather seat, the engine grumbled to life, and he pulled out onto the wide carriageway that ran along the coast.

He was confident of where he was going.

Aydin's family had come to Istanbul when he was a child, and some of his most cherished childhood memories were of the four of them in their native country. And it was his family roots that had brought him back once again: he knew his sister had visited in the last few months. Wahid too had been, given the stamp Aydin had found in Wahid's German passport. Aydin didn't know why either of them had come, but it was a lead.

The encryption on Itnashar's laptop was solid. But, for the first time, Wahid had been careless. Aydin found the encryption key contained within hidden files on the thumb drive stolen from Wahid's bedroom. After all, Wahid needed the key to decipher encrypted documents sent to him regularly by Itnashar and the other brothers.

On the long journey to come, Aydin would see everything Itnashar knew of the plan. It wasn't *everything,* but it was significantly more than Aydin had been told. Plus, it had already given him a much more conclusive link to Istanbul, and to one man in particular.

It was time to pay a visit to his uncle.

FORTY-EIGHT

Two hours after the call with Poulter, Cox pulled the rental car to a stop outside the gates to Kamil Torkal's home. Her phone had been buzzing in her handbag the whole way there, though she'd not yet been able to bring herself to answer it, certain it was Flannigan calling, and she wasn't ready to have *that* conversation with him.

Before she wound down the window to press on the intercom, Cox let out a long sigh then reluctantly took the phone out of her bag and scrolled through the notifications. Seven missed calls. One voicemail. As expected it was from Flannigan. As expected he sounded like he was halfway up the wall as he yelled down the line. The message was short, but far from sweet.

Cox's finger hovered over the call-back button. Thinking better of it, she put the phone on her lap, wound the window down and pressed on the intercom's buzzer. The little box chimed away for a few seconds. No answer. She frowned and pressed the button again but only got the exact same response.

This was all she needed. At the very least she'd hoped to be able to use her time in Istanbul productively before Flannigan shipped her off to jail. She hadn't pre-arranged to meet Kamil Torkal this time round, hoping to catch him more off guard. That plan seemed to have backfired already.

The phone once again vibrated. As much as she'd rather have nails driven through her eyelids, she found herself picking the phone back up and accepting the call.

'You stupid, crazy—'

'Sir!'

'Have you any idea how much shit you're in?'

'Actually, kind of, yeah. I'm sorry, sir.'

Flannigan went silent and Cox knew it was best to just give him a few moments to defuse.

'Something's happening here, sir. And whatever it is, it's coming soon,' Cox said, when she heard his breaths slowing, hoping to pre-empt his next barrage. 'You have to see that now.'

'I'm not sure exactly what I see,' Flannigan said, sounding only moderately pissed off. Quite a result, Cox felt.

'I told you – the Thirteen are real. Based on the intel I gave them, Trapeze have identified nearly all of the men I believe form the group. And located some of them too. We have names, faces, addresses—'

'No, Cox,' Flannigan bit back. 'We *did* have all that. Until each and every one of those men went dark. And it's highly possible that they went dark because of *your* antics. They realised they were under surveillance.'

'That's rubbish! They couldn't possibly have kno—'

'If they're as sophisticated as you've been saying they are then of course they could have bloody known. You may well have sent them underground for good.'

'That's not it at all. We've finally made progress in identifying the whole group. And those dead bodies in Germany? The guy driving away from the scene is Sab'ah. Number seven. He's one of *them*.'

Cox gave Flannigan a few moments to take that one in. She hoped for a response. She realised none was coming.

'I don't think they've gone into hiding. I think they're getting ready to attack.'

'Cox, you don't even know they have a *plan* to attack! This is still completely hypothetical.'

'I know you don't really believe that.'

'What I believe is that, as well as the dire consequences for your life and career, your gung-ho tactics may have scared these guys off. We may never find them now.'

'No, sir. I don't believe that at all. I think even if they know we're on to them they don't care. They've planned too well, they've been setting this up for years. And they're too close to their goal now. They've gone dark because the attacks are coming.'

Flannigan fell silent again and while Cox gave him time to compose his comeback, she once again pressed on the intercom. Still no answer. She stepped from the car and approached the metal gates. There was a small gap where the two gates met and Cox pressed her eye to it, peering past the gravel drive to the villa beyond. The view through was far from clear, but she was sure she could see a car parked up on the drive – the same car Torkal's wife had returned home in the last time Cox had visited. There hadn't been a second car at the house that day so someone was home.

'The simple fact is we just don't know,' Flannigan eventually said. 'But I agree that it would be a big risk to ignore what we've found.' Cox said nothing about his use of *we*. 'We'll have to work with the other countries on this one, in order to raid each of those locations. The evidence isn't strong enough for us to get clearance to take this on ourselves. Can you imagine the political fallout if our black ops teams swarm over each of those cities? Especially if they find nothing.'

'Sir, any delay now could be catastrophic.'

'There's no other way, Cox. You should be happy with this. With local co-operation we'll do our best to organise raids for each of the addresses Trapeze has given us for your *Thirteen*.'

Cox breathed a sigh of relief at her small victory, as she walked from the gates and over to where the white perimeter wall headed off into the dense foliage.

'Don't sound so relieved, Cox,' Flannigan scoffed. 'Now I'm going to *try* and help you, because I get why you did this, and I do . . . care about you.' He coughed awkwardly. 'But Miles is going to be far less amenable, trust me on that. He's got the politicos hounding him over this already and regardless of what we find down the line, he's going to need a scapegoat.'

'I get it.'

'Like I said, I'll try to help you, but I can't make any promises.'

'I appreciate that.'

'But you need to stand down.'

'What—'

'You will stand down! Now. Gather your things and head back to Istanbul airport. You'll be met there by an agent who will escort you back to London. Don't do anything stupid. Or, more aptly, don't do anything *else* stupid.'

But Cox barely heard him, focused as she was on the villa, tracing the wall with her eyes into the thick green where a glint of light sparkled through the gently flapping leaves. Doubling back, she reached into the car and grabbed the handgun from her bag. With the phone still pressed to her ear she clambered through the undergrowth.

'Cox, for Christ's sake, are you even listening to me?'

'Yes, sir. I'll come back. Just as soon as I can.'

'No, not as soon as you can. Now!'

Cox pushed her way further through. A gust of wind blew through the branches in front of her revealing a glimpse of shining black metal.

'Don't screw me, Cox. Or you can forget about my help.'

'I'm not messing you about, sir.'

Cox lifted a branch, stooped beneath it, and there, concealed in the foliage, was a motorbike. She looked around. The road was yards behind. The bike had very deliberately been pulled through the foliage, and pressed snug to the wall.

The engine was still hot.

'I've got to go,' she said, and ended the call before Flannigan could shout back.

Cox crouched low as she made her way silently through the Torkals' garden. The bike, positioned where it was, proved the perfect leg-up to help her over the wall – someone else had had the same idea and, given the heat of the engine, only minutes earlier.

The gun gripped in both hands as she moved, she soon came out onto a gravel driveway. Avoiding the noisy stones underfoot she moved towards the front of the villa.

The front door was ajar.

She stopped dead. Should she call the local police? But what would she tell them? No. It was too much of a coincidence, surely. She had to know if this was all connected.

The house was quiet beyond the threshold, the whir of ceiling fans and the gentle whistle of the breeze the only sounds she could make out.

As quietly as she could, Cox used the barrel of the handgun to push the front door open – the hinges giving the slightest of creaks as she did so.

Still nothing.

She stepped into the cool of the terracotta-tiled hallway. Only then, with the tepid air on her skin, did she realise her blouse was sticking to her chest and back, damp from the humidity outside – or was it her nerves? – and sending a shiver through her entire body.

300

A quick check of each room leading off the hallway revealed nothing.

The final doorway led onto a narrow corridor, the opposite side of the house to where she'd been the last time. Bedrooms perhaps?

Drops of liquid dotted the floor and, slowly, Cox knelt down and touched one of them with the tip of her finger. On the terracotta floor she hadn't been able to tell what it was, but the red of blood on her skin was unmistakable.

Cox straightened up and for a couple of seconds felt faint from the rush of oxygen to her brain caused by her racing heart. When the feeling had dimmed she moved down the corridor. A creak, then a soft bang emanated from one of the doorways ahead.

Cox picked up her pace, feeling more confident in her movements. She passed two open doors, one on her left, one on the right, with only a moment's hesitation at each. Then she heard a murmur. A stifled moan. Both sounds came from the room at the end of the corridor. She couldn't tell if the sounds were made by a man or a woman. Or both.

As silently as she could, Cox stepped quickly to the last room and, gun held up, spun into the open doorway, ready to shoot.

But Cox didn't fire. Nor did she head for cover. Instead she found herself standing in the doorway, her gun pointed at the head of the man across the other side of the room. One of the men, anyway, because there was a second man – a petrified Kamil Torkal – at the first man's feet. Blood poured from Kamil's nose, and a large kitchen knife was pressed up against his throat.

'Aydin,' she said.

FORTY-NINE

When the woman spoke his name, it derailed Aydin for a few seconds as he stood frozen to the spot.

'Aydin, put the knife down,' she said, her voice calm, though Aydin sensed her nerves. 'Please. He's your uncle.'

At her words Kamil whimpered pathetically. Was his show of fear genuine, or an attempt to make Aydin reconsider what he was going to do to him? Aydin didn't care – he had to get the truth from his uncle, and he would do that however he could.

'Where's your aunt?' the woman asked.

Aydin said nothing, but the woman's eyes moved down to the floor, where she could see the feet of his aunt poking out from behind the bed. She was hogtied and unconscious. Aydin had no quarrel with his aunt, he only needed to subdue her – just like the frail, old nurse who was tied up inside a locked cupboard. They'd both get out unharmed, as long as he got what he needed from his uncle.

'Is she alive?' the woman asked.

Aydin gave the slightest of nods.

'I can help you,' she said. 'In fact, I'm the only person in the world who will right now. Aren't I?'

Aydin didn't bother to point out that the last person who

said something similar had ended up with a knife in his heart. And that man had been a friend.

'Aydin, listen to me!' she said, her voice more purposeful. 'I know everything. All about the Farm. All about your group.'

'You can't stop them.'

'No. But maybe *you* can. You're not one of them. That's why you left. It's why all of this happening, isn't it?' Aydin held his tongue. 'That's why you've travelled across Europe to get here. What are you searching for, Aydin?'

'He's a psychopath – I told you! What are you waiting for?' Kamil blurted out.

Aydin drove a heel into the man's neck, sending him flying forward, his head cracking off the floor and knocking him out cold.

Now it was just Aydin and the woman, face to face. If she wanted to shoot, he had little chance with only the knife in his hands. Was this how it needed to end – rightful comeuppance for the things he'd done? He wasn't sure he deserved anything better.

Yet dying without knowing the truth – about his father, or sister, and why it was all happening? That couldn't happen.

'Drop the knife,' the woman repeated.

'And then what?'

'I'll lower my gun. Then we can talk.'

'You expect me to believe that? Who do you work for? MI6? Interpol?'

'I said drop the knife, and then we'll talk. Aydin, I was a friend of Nilay. I know she was searching for you. Looking for answers, just like you are.'

'What?' he spat.

'Help me find who killed her.'

Aydin didn't move; his brain felt like it was on fire.

'Think about Nilay, your mother. They wouldn't want you to do this.'

'You know nothing about them.'

'I know a lot, actually.' She looked down at his arm, at the white bandage. 'You're hurt. You must realise it's time to stop running. I know you didn't kill your mother. You're not one of *them*, Aydin.'

Before he could think better of it, Aydin dropped the knife and it clattered against the stone tiles. Out of the corner of his eye, Aydin noticed his aunt's head bob groggily and her eyelids flicker.

'So, what now?' Aydin said, taking a step towards the woman. 'We have a cup of tea and a quiet chat?'

The woman looked nervous with Aydin on the move, even though his hands were empty and she had a gun barrel pointed at his face.

'You said you would drop that gun,' Aydin said. 'I can't do this with you pointing that at me.'

'And I can't trust you just like that, Aydin. First you have to prove you can be trusted.'

'How then?'

'Untie your aunt and uncle. One of them will call the police. Once everyone here is safe, then we'll talk.'

'I won't be locked up.'

'You won't be. But it has to happen like this. Once the police are here I can call my people. They'll straighten this up, get us both somewhere safe. Then we can figure out what to do next. Figure out how to stop the others before it's too late.'

'That sounds like I've got to place a lot of trust in you first.'

'Aydin, for fuck's sake! Wake up. The attack is coming. You know it is.'

Aydin felt his face twitch as her words swam in his head. They'd been weeks away from completing their plans – had his running caused this? But then, how could she know? Was she bluffing to get him to surrender?

'It's not true,' Aydin said, rattled.

'How many lives will be lost if we don't stop them. Hundreds? Thousands? Don't have that blood on your hands. Please.'

Her words hit him like a brick. He was overcome with shame. Not because of who he was – he had no choice in that any more – and not because of what he'd done in the past. But because of what he *hadn't* done. Since leaving Paris he'd been hell-bent on catching Wahid, in order to find his sister's and mother's killer. And making them all pay. He'd not once stopped to think about the attacks. The woman was right. He was surely the only person who could stop it.

'You were just a boy,' the woman said. 'None of this is your fault. *They* made all of this happen. Help me now. For your sister. For your mother.'

'His mother?' Kamil shouted, taking both Aydin and the woman by surprise. 'He killed his mother! The boy is a monster, just shoot him!'

The woman's eyes flicked to Kamil, giving Aydin the split-second distraction he needed. He crouched low and burst upward, lifting his arm above his head. The woman pulled the trigger but Aydin's wrist had already slammed into her lower arm, pushing the gun up and sending the bullet into the ceiling above them. The woman moved quickly to defend herself, taking another step back, but even with Aydin's injuries she was no match for his speed. He snapped the gun from her hand, twisted behind her and kicked out her legs. Before she could respond she was on her knees with one of his arms locked around her neck, choking her, the gun pressed up against the side her head. She pulled on Aydin's arm, trying to get the room to breathe.

'No, Aydin, don't!'

It was his aunt. He looked over. Still hogtied but conscious, she was leaning against the edge of the bed to hold herself upright. His uncle was lucid too and staring at him – well, more like glaring daggers. The hatred coming from the man was unmistakable.

'Please?' his aunt begged.

Aydin had no more time for any of their crap. He lifted the gun then brought it down and smashed it against the woman's skull.

FIFTY

Minutes later Aydin had his uncle and the woman shackled in the kitchen. Each of them was tied to an oak dining chair, the chairs tied together, side by side. A line of dried blood snaked down the woman's head. His aunt was secured in the bedroom, locked in a cupboard, just like the nurse. Aydin just needed those two to stay put, because it was his uncle and this woman who he needed answers from.

He had the woman's handbag on the worktop in front of him; a passport in his hand, British, in the name of Joanna Taylor. The picture was of her, but he was certain the name wasn't real.

'You said you were searching for the truth,' Aydin said to the woman. 'Mrs Taylor?'

She shook her head and mumbled. Aydin moved forward and pulled the tape from her mouth.

'My name . . . is . . .' She gasped for air as she tried to speak. 'Rachel Cox . . . I work for SIS. MI6.'

Aydin thought hearing that would have troubled him more. It wasn't that he was feeling confident about his situation, more that he, for the first time, felt resigned to his fate. Between his brothers and the security services, he surely didn't have much time left.

'You're alone?' he asked.

'Do you think if I had a partner they'd let me be tied up like this? I was sent here to find you, Aydin. I want to help you. Don't do something you'll regret.'

Aydin snorted. 'Something I'll regret? Have you *any* idea of the things I've had to do?'

'You were taken as a child, weren't you? You were forced to do things. But you aren't like the others. You couldn't accept the things you were being told to do – then or now. It's not too late.'

'You don't know what you're talking about.'

Cox's phone vibrated on the worktop.

'That's HQ,' Cox said. 'They know I came here. If they don't hear from me they'll know something is wrong. They'll send help. They won't think twice about killing you now, Aydin. Unless I call them off.'

'Then I'd better be quick.'

Aydin snatched the pliers from the marble counter. Cox's eyes widened in surprise, but she needn't worry – he wasn't going for her yet.

His uncle began panting in horrified expectation. Aydin knelt down and pulled the sock from Kamil's left foot as the man rasped and begged. He couldn't move his foot at all, and the skin around his ankle was heavily discoloured from the strength of the ties, but he would still be able to feel the pain.

Aydin took Kamil's big toe and clasped the pliers over the edge of the thick nail. This wasn't just about finding the truth, it was about revenge too – but he had to push the primal need for vengeance away.

'I only want to know why,' Aydin said.

'No!' Cox shouted. 'Please, Aydin.'

'Why what?' his uncle blubbered.

'You knew about the Farm, didn't you? You knew what they'd do to me there.'

'I don't know what you're talking about! You . . . her . . . she said the same thing. You're both crazy!'

Aydin looked to Cox, who nodded, as if confirming what his uncle was saying.

'Nilay came to visit you,' Aydin said. 'Why?'

'I haven't seen her in years.'

Aydin tugged on the nail, just enough to tear the edge away from the skin. Enough to remind his uncle of the position he was in. He screamed – perhaps more in anticipation of what was still to come.

'And what about Ismail Obbadi?' Aydin asked. 'Or perhaps you know him as *Wahid?*'

'What . . .' Cox said. Aydin saw the look of confusion on her face. But she didn't say anything else about it. He turned his attention back to his uncle.

'Aydin, don't cross this line!' Cox screamed.

'You're a liar!' Aydin shouted at Kamil as he struggled to keep his growing rage inside. Yet the look of confusion in his uncle's eyes . . . Could Aydin really be so mistaken?

'He's telling the truth,' Cox said. 'He hasn't seen them – he told me the same thing. He wouldn't lie to you now, Aydin, like this.'

'What would you know?' Aydin said, spitting the words.

'More than you realise. I'm serious, this isn't the way. I want to find out who killed Nilay just as much as you do, but not like this.'

'I'm not lying to you,' Kamil butted in, his words quivery as the tears flowed down his face. 'We were devastated when we heard about Nilay. And when we heard about your mother.'

'I didn't kill her!' Aydin screamed, so loud it made his throat sting. 'But you know that, don't you? Because it was the people you work for who did it!'

'No! I don't understand—'

Aydin couldn't believe either of them. The truth would out.

He gripped the pliers on Kamil's toenail once more. Two or three nails would be all it took before the man crumbled and spat out everything he knew.

Just then, a bang and a clunk from somewhere outside the house made Aydin freeze. Both his uncle and Cox took notice. Kamil's eyes darted about. Cox looked wary. There was no way his aunt or the maid had freed themselves and raised the alarm. Someone else was out there.

This was down to Cox.

Aydin growled in anger and scrambled to his feet. But the next second the kitchen window smashed and a small metallic canister clattered and rolled across the tiles towards them.

Aydin had only enough time to cower and cover his face before the grenade exploded.

FIFTY-ONE

Aydin heard noises. Tinny and distant, the sound swirled in his brain without any sense of direction, as though he was caught in an endless spiral, twisting round and round and out of control. All he could see was white – an intense white that seemed to set his eyeballs alight.

The seconds passed as Aydin slowly regained his senses. The wall of white faded and he saw shapes, both moving and static. The sounds gained focus and direction, and he realised they were voices. Men shouting, giving orders.

It was a flash-bang grenade, he realised. Non-lethal, flash-bangs delivered a thundering boom and a bright flash or light to incapacitate rather than to kill. The perfect assault weapon where hostages were involved, but certainly not the type of weapon a regular police team would carry.

So who the hell was attacking?

Aydin battled through the torment in his head and scrambled to his feet. He saw Rachel Cox and his uncle in front of him, still bound to their chairs. Cox was stirring, his uncle was still. Aydin sensed movement behind him. As he crawled for cover, he realised the gun he'd taken from Cox had come loose. He managed to scoop it up from the floor and fire one shot back to the kitchen doorway as he skidded along the ground, just as a black-clad figure came into view through the smoke.

Was it smoke? Or just the effect of the wall of white that was still burned onto his retinas?

He expected raking gunfire to follow his moves. But no, these men were too careful, and the figure simply ducked back out of sight. With captives inside they weren't going to fire indiscriminately.

Instead, possibly worse for Aydin, he heard that same clatter again as another grenade was lobbed into the room. His brain couldn't take another blast like that. He'd be out for the count and dragged from there before he even woke up.

Aydin lunged towards the broken kitchen window just as the grenade exploded behind him. The shockwave shoved him forward and, as he lifted up his arms and smashed through the remainder of the window, something tore at the flesh of his upper arm, before he found himself tumbling into a hedge in the daylight outside.

It was a struggle to fight through the pain and the debilitating effects of the blasts, but he didn't have time to wait for recovery. Plundering the depths of his reserve, he dragged himself upright, lifted his gun and looked left and right. There was a man barely three yards away from him, dressed in heavy combat gear – and he'd spotted Aydin.

Aydin opened fire. Two shots. One high, one low. The high shot hit the man's Kevlar vest and was enough to send him off balance. The low shot hit him on an unprotected thigh, and he crumpled to the ground.

Aydin re-aimed and fired at another black figure, several yards further away on the gravel driveway. Two more shots. One miss, one leg shot. Neither man was down for good, all Aydin needed was breathing space.

Hauling himself to his feet, he burst into a sprint, scanning for more dark masses as he moved. He reached the first guy he'd shot, grabbed under his vest and dragged him further into the tree line to the side of the house. He was still awake, and groaning. Aydin stomped on his face to shut him up. As quickly as he could he removed the vest and took the man's sidearm. The assault rifle was too unwieldy – he just needed more ammo.

Just as he was putting on the vest two more black figures came into view in the distance, searching the grounds. They knew Aydin was out of the house. Pretty soon the whole team, however many there were, would be swarming around him.

Maybe he'd be better off going back inside and grabbing Cox or his uncle. A hostage could help him. But where would he go after that?

He cast the idea away – he just needed to escape. He grabbed a grenade from the belt of the wounded agent, pulled the pin and hurled it towards the house, hoping the effects of the explosion would buy him a few more seconds. He turned and quickly moved further into the thick of the garden, away from the house and closer to the outer wall, just as the blast erupted. He was at the opposite side to where he'd left his motorbike but he just needed to get off the property as soon as possible.

Shit. Only then did he realise he'd left his backpack in the house. Itnashar's computer. The thumb drive. The money. Wahid's passports. Everything that had got him this far. But he couldn't risk going back. Somehow, he'd have to make do.

He reached the wall. The trees and bushes gave him good cover from the house, but the outline of several dark figures loomed in the distance, moving in and out beyond the bushes as they closed in.

Aydin grimaced in pain as he scaled the wall. The fresh wound on his arm was bleeding badly, and it felt like he'd re-opened the cut on his leg again, or perhaps sustained a fresh one during the escape.

Dense foliage cushioned his jump from the top, and he immediately moved forward, the gun he'd just pilfered held in both hands – the spare tucked into his waistband.

There was no sign of the assault team as he reached the track that led back to the main road – no vehicles, no men, no sounds. But he knew they couldn't be far behind.

He hobbled down the road as fast as he could, looking back every couple of steps. When he reached the crossroad he headed right, opposite from the way he'd come, and moved into the middle of the road. He needed a vehicle, and the best bet was to simply stop one. He heard a car engine behind him, looked and saw a black SUV. It wasn't racing towards him, ready to mow him down. It wasn't *them*.

Aydin pointed the gun at the windscreen. On seeing the weapon the driver panicked and pushed the accelerator and Aydin fired twice as the SUV veered and screeched past him before speeding up and away down the road.

Brave driver.

It didn't matter, another car was coming his way, and the driver had taken the opposite approach. On seeing the gun she'd stopped the car and was fleeing, hands over her head, within seconds.

Aydin jumped into the drivers's seat.

That was when he heard the *thwap thwap thwap* of a helicopter above. He slammed shut the door and thumped on the accelerator. There was a junction up ahead but he wasn't about to stop. Unfortunately, someone else had the same thought – an armoured personnel carrier hurtled towards the junction, and by the time Aydin spotted it, there was no time to manoeuvre out of the way. The only thing he could do to attempt to avoid the collision was to swerve away and hope they missed.

They didn't.

The massive vehicle ploughed into the back end of Aydin's car, virtually cutting the thing in two. The force of the blow caused his head to snap to the side painfully, sending a searing jolt down his spine. What was left of the car was launched into a spin that only relented when the lump of metal crashed into something hard – a wall, a lamp post, another vehicle, Aydin had no idea.

This time he was dazed. His body had had enough, and as much as he tried to once again battle through the sense of disarray, there was simply nothing he could do to recover in time. Within seconds several black-clad figures were outside with their guns pointed at his head.

With no strength to offer up any protest as the car door was forced open, Aydin finally gave up as two hands grabbed him and pulled him from the wreckage.

FIFTY-TWO

Aydin wasn't sure if it was the noise that woke him when the door to the dorm burst open, or if he was already half-awake, sleeping with one eye open like he'd become used to. Either way, he was only semi-lucid when it happened, and he offered up little response as the boots stormed across the concrete floor and the hands jerked him ruthlessly from his bed, sending him crashing to the cold ground.

A sack was pulled over his head with hands that were thick and strong and anything but delicate. In the process a bony knuckle smashed across his nose and he felt blood pour. The open end of the sack was tied tightly around his neck, and as the blood flowed he wondered whether it might fill the hood and drown him.

He was dragged by his ankles out of the dorm, his back scraping across the pockmarked surface. No words were spoken, the only sounds he could hear were his own panicked breaths and the rustle as the skin was rubbed and torn from his back.

Which direction they took him in he had no idea. A minute later he was lifted up and thrust down onto a hard chair. He wasn't tied in place, not handcuffed or shackled, but he didn't attempt to move from that spot. There was no flight or fight response, only panic and silence.

316

His head twisted with questions: why they were doing this to him? Was it a punishment? Had he done something wrong again? Or was this yet another of the Teacher's unyielding exercises, designed to build him and the others up, to make them stronger men through pain? After years of it, he felt broken — like he could never be fixed.

'This is not an exercise,' came a male voice, as if reading Aydin's mind. The words were English, the accent American. It wasn't just the language that was unfamiliar for the Farm, but the tone of the voice too. Not someone that Aydin knew. 'This is really happening to you. Do you understand?'

Aydin didn't say anything, or give any indication of a response. He was so scared he wasn't sure he'd be able to even if he wanted.

'What is your name?' the man said.

There was a lengthy pause where Aydin heard nothing at all. He had no idea which room they were in, how many men were there, or — more disturbingly — what they were planning next. Yet he didn't respond. He knew the rules.

'We have every person in this facility locked down,' the man said. 'Nobody is coming to help you. Some of your people are already talking. They're going to be the lucky ones. You can join them. The choice is yours.'

Aydin whimpered. He was so confused. Had the Americans really raided the Farm? If so what should he do? Until he was brought to the Farm he'd never seen himself as an enemy of the West. But . . . the things he'd been told, the things he'd seen . . . and he didn't want to betray his brothers. Nor could he betray his religion, but if it really was all over for the Farm, then wasn't he now simply into self-preservation mode? Saving himself didn't have to be the same thing as betraying the others.

'What is your name?' the man asked again.

But despite his conflicting thoughts, Aydin still didn't answer. More than a minute passed with no response and no more questions.

317

'Okay. You had your chance. Let's take him out of here.'

With that the thick hands grabbed him once again and he was hauled off the chair. Moments later he was being dragged across the floor once more.

They drove for what seemed like hours. They were in a high-powered military style 4x4 – Aydin could tell from the unmistakable sound of the V8 engine and the rigid metal bench he was sitting on. They weren't travelling on roads, but across uneven dirt tracks, loose dust and stones spitting up in their wake, the vehicle bouncing and crashing on its heavy-duty suspension. With no belt holding Aydin in place, and no warning of the bumps, he was aching and dizzy from being bashed against the metal side of the vehicle.

A mechanical clamour above the grumble of the vehicle's engine whirred. It was coming from somewhere in the distance ahead of them, but growing closer and louder all the time. Soon the roar was drowning out the sound of the V8, and it wasn't long before the vehicle stopped and the engine shut down. Only then did Aydin realise what the other noise was: the whir of helicopter rotors.

Dragged from the vehicle and across the dusty ground, the high-pressure blast from the rotors bombarded him as he was lifted up and placed into the helicopter. The noise was hellish, making his insides curdle. A man shouted, but his words were drowned out by the din. Seconds later he felt the jolt as the helicopter lifted off the ground.

They were in the helicopter for little more than ten minutes. After that it was back to a Jeep, and then Aydin found himself in some sort of facility, but he had no idea where or what it was. They weren't outside, and they weren't moving, that was about all he knew.

No one had talked to him at all. He was certain he'd been in the room for several hours already – perhaps more than a day. In that time he'd been forced to endure some of the many torture techniques that the Teacher had warned him about – that he and the other boys had been trained to resist: stress positions, white noise, water-boarding. All designed to disorientate, to instil fear and to gradually break a prisoner's resolve. But this was far more severe than the training they'd been given in the past. His body was heavy and weak, his mind a bumbling mess. He was finding it hard to keep his eyes open, and every time they closed he wasn't sure if it was sleep or unconsciousness he was then waking up from.

So when he next opened his eyes – perched atop a hard metal chair, a sack covering his head – it took a few seconds to adjust and regain any focus.

'What is your name?' came the American voice again. After everything that'd happened to him since he'd last heard the voice at the Farm, it was surreal to hear the same measured tone, the same question.

'Do you know where you are?' the man asked, when it was clear he was getting no response to his original question. 'You're no longer in Afghanistan. Your people have no power here. You're now at a site operated by the US military, and you'll stay here, under our care, like this, as long as it takes. No one is coming for you.'

Aydin was quivering with cold, exhaustion and fear. The questions kept on coming, the threats escalating. He was getting closer and closer to the edge. But he didn't say a word. Not anything at all. Yet he knew that everyone had a breaking point. Was it really worth holding out?

'Your name is Aydin Torkal,' the man said. 'Seventeen years old. Is that correct?'

Aydin held his tongue, but his fear had gone up several levels. How did they know his real name?

319

'You're English. I'm curious, how exactly does a teenager from England end up in that place?' The man paused while Aydin's brain swam. 'The thing is, Aydin, we know what that place is. They call it the Farm. We know all about it. Like I said to you before, some of the other boys are already talking. We'll help them, like we'll help you. You're not the bad guy here. It's the men who are holding you that need to be stopped. And they will be stopped. They can't hurt you any more. Do the right thing, help us.'

He stopped talking again, and Aydin realised that, for the first time in a long time, both his breathing and his heart were calming.

'We've been speaking to your family. Your mother and sister. You can see them again. Don't you want that?'

Aydin realised he was crying. The images of his mother and Nilay glowed in his mind. He still longed to be reunited with them, even after everything he'd been put through and all the things the elders had done to change him. Every night he dreamt of being able to hold them both.

'This is the last time I'll ask this question today. If you don't give me a response, we're not going to stop. We're going to keep going. This is just the start. You have no idea of the lengths we're prepared to go to. We will get through to you eventually, no matter how long, and no matter how many pieces of you it takes.'

'Okay,' Aydin said, and as the word passed his lips the pictures of his family disappeared. 'Okay. I'll talk.'

His voice was weak and coarse, quite alien to his own ears, as though it was coming from someone else.

'Good. Then let's start at the beginning. Your name is Aydin Torkal. Is that correct?'

'My name . . . My name is . . . Talatashar.'

FIFTY-THREE

Ankara, Turkey

Cox watched Aydin Torkal on the CCTV monitor in front of her. He'd been in the locked room inside the Ankara safe house for several hours following the trip from Istanbul. Initially unconscious from the assault that led to his arrest, he'd subsequently been in and out of consciousness as a result of the drugs they'd plied him with. Now fully awake, he stared into space in the windowless room.

All in all, it was nearly twenty-four hours since his arrest outside his uncle's home at the hands of the PÖH – the special operations department of the Turkish police. Cox was grateful that Flannigan had been able to so quickly organise the raid, though disappointed with how the confrontation with Aydin had ended so abruptly, and ultimately fruitlessly. She still felt sure that she could break through to him, and that doing so was likely now the only way to stop the Thirteen.

Although the Turkish government had been easily persuaded to lend a hand in capturing Aydin Torkal, they'd had no interest in holding on to him, preferring to wash their hands of the terrorist who held such close ties to their country. As such, Aydin had quickly been passed from the custody of the police and into the hands of Cox and Flannigan in Istanbul. But Flannigan wasn't going to let Aydin stay in the safe house long. He was already putting into place the plans to extract Aydin out of Turkey and to a black site across North Africa in Algeria. Once that happened, it really was the end of the line for Aydin. Cox still held hope that she could force a break-through before then. But she had to be given the chance first.

'He's awake now. Let me speak to him,' Cox said to Flannigan. He was sitting on a worn brown fabric sofa in the corner of the room, playing on his phone. Despite it being light outside, the curtains were drawn and the overhead bulb was barely bright enough for the room, the dimness making Cox feel sleepy.

'And say what?' Flannigan said, looking up and sounding irritated by the interruption.

'I'll try to get through to him.'

'If I understand it correctly, the last time you tried *getting through to him* he ended up tying you to a chair so he could rip your toenails out.'

'Actually, it was his uncle's toenails,' Cox said, with a wry smile. Flannigan didn't return the look. He'd seemed perpetu-ally pissed off ever since Cox had met up with him in Istanbul shortly after Aydin's arrest.

'Cox, what don't you get here?' he said. 'This guy is a fanatic. He's not one of us. He's not going to help you – he *hates* you. Pretty soon, he'll be exactly where he belongs.'

'You think taking him to a black site and torturing him will get him to talk? And how long will that take? Weeks? Months?'

'It's the best chance we've got. We need to do everything we can to get him to spill the beans on his . . . group's plans. Before it's too late.'

'Well there's the thing, sir. We don't even know how much time we have left. It could be days. Hours even.'

Flannigan stared past Cox to the small CCTV monitor on the round glass dining table, his eyes squinting in suspicion. Cox turned and saw Aydin, on his knees, his head bowed as he prayed. Or at least he did his best to, given he was shackled to the radiator.

'Have you had any further word from Trapeze?' Cox asked. 'Anything on Obbadi or the others?'

Ismail Obbadi. Who, following the run-in with Aydin, Cox now knew to be Wahid. The mega-rich businessman wasn't just a financier, he was one of *them*.

'I would have told you if I had.'

Since Aydin's arrest, Flannigan and Miles had together re-approved authority for Trapeze oversight, but so far despite the far-reaching power that the surveillance team had, there'd be no further useful intel on any of the Thirteen, what attacks were coming, or when. On a personal level at least, Cox was relieved that Flannigan still had her on the operation, and there'd been no further threat from him about the consequences of her original deceit over the Trapeze approval, nor over the fact that she'd again disobeyed orders by going to Kamil Torkal's home instead of heading straight back to England. She could only assume those indiscretions would rear their ugly heads when the dust had settled – and certainly if the operation went further south. Cox would do everything in her power to make sure that didn't happen.

'Sir, just let me talk to him,' she said, more insistent. 'Seriously, I know more about Aydin, about the Thirteen, than anyone else. What harm is there in trying? All we're doing is sitting here waiting. We've had absolutely no further noise from any of his people.'

'We've still several addresses yet to raid,' Flannigan said impatiently.

'And you know as well as I do that more than likely we'll find nothing. We've already had teams raid in London, Paris, Berlin, based on what was credible intelligence. We were too late. What makes you think the other locations will be any different?'

'You might be right, but we still have to try.'

'I'm not saying otherwise. But whatever we thought we knew about the Thirteen, whatever intel we had on them, we now need something more. Even with Trapeze, the movements of the Thirteen are currently completely dark to us. Something is up. We need to know where they are *now,* and what their next moves will be.'

'Which is why you and Torkal sitting and having a pleasant chat is not exactly top of my list of priorities.'

'But it's worth a shot.'

Flannigan sighed, but Cox sensed he was coming round to the idea.

'One shot,' he said. 'It's worth *one* shot. After that we're moving him out of here, and it'll be time to put some real pressure on him.'

FIFTY-FOUR

When the sack was wrenched from Aydin's head moments later, he was still brimming with confusion. He'd been in the dark for who knew how many hours. They wanted him to feel that way – disorientated and truly alone. It took his eyes a few seconds to adjust to the sudden intrusion of light that seemed to bore a hole into his brain, but when he could finally see the face in front of him . . .

'Teacher?' he said.

He realised he sounded relieved – indeed he was relieved. But the Teacher wore an expression somewhere between disappointment and quiet fury. Sitting next to him was a white man Aydin didn't recognise. The American voice? But they weren't at an American facility – that much was clear to him now. Beyond the man, standing in the background, was a much younger, fresher face. A smiling face. Wahid.

Aydin continued to look around the room – just four plain walls, but walls he somehow recognised.

They were still exactly where they'd started. The Farm.

'What is this?' Aydin asked, his anger clear.

'What do you think?' the Teacher said.

Aydin shook his head in disbelief. 'An exercise? This was all just a test?'

'Yes, Talatashar. A test. All of your brothers have endured the same.'

'But . . .'

The Teacher held up his hand to stop him.

'I'm sorry to say, son, but you failed.'

'Failed? What . . . No! But I—'

'You talked.'

'No! Just one thing, I . . . I would never give anything away.'

'You gave your name.'

'Not my real name!' Aydin turned to the American. 'You called me Aydin. You talked about my family. I never gave you anything, about them, about this place.'

Aydin was surprised by his own strength of mind, by the raw feelings that were pushing upward within him, his resolve and determination to argue his position. He was furious that they'd put him through all of that, only to tell him that he'd failed.

'Your family?' the Teacher said, rising to Aydin's challenge. 'Talatashar, you have no family. Just me, and your brothers. And you never talk. Not a word. Not ever. Do you understand?'

Aydin said nothing; he simply couldn't find the words.

'I'm sorry, Talatashar, but you failed. And you know there has to be a consequence for failure.'

Wahid got to his feet. The smile on his face grew. Aydin saw the cloth sack in his hand.

'No, please!'

But there was nothing left to say. The rules were clear, just as always. Failure must be punished. Whatever Aydin had just been put through, he knew it was nothing compared to what would come next.

'I'm sorry, son,' the Teacher said, just a second before his face disappeared as the sack was once again pulled over Aydin's head.

FIFTY-FIVE

The door to the room opened and Rachel Cox entered. Alone, unarmed, she was dressed casually in jeans and a loose-fitting blouse. Yes, Aydin was shackled – a set of cuffs over both his wrists and his ankles, connected by a metal chain. The chain was looped over radiator pipes. There was no escaping the hold. Yet both Cox and the place were unassuming compared to the menacing places he'd seen in his past.

Only this was *real*.

'How are you feeling?' Cox asked.

Aydin thought about the question but didn't answer. Physically he felt much better than he had when he'd arrived at his uncle's house, however long ago that was. Then, he'd been weary and debilitated by injuries, and since his capture he couldn't be sure how long he'd spent tied up in this dark room. Now, although still tired and certainly bruised, he felt lucid, stronger.

Cox took a seat on the wooden chair at the opposite side of the room to where Aydin was curled on the bare floorboards. She crossed her legs and Aydin looked away.

'You look better,' Cox said, pulling a thread of loose hair back over her shoulders. 'The wound you had on your calf is quite badly infected, you know. While you were . . . *asleep,* we had a doctor see to you. The antibiotics should already have started to take effect.'

'And the rest of the drugs you've given me?' Aydin said, and Cox looked a little surprised that he'd chosen to speak so soon.

Cox laughed. 'Well there is that, too. You took quite a battering. Two nasty gashes on your arms, one on your leg, not to mention the bangs to your head. The open wounds are now at least stitched properly.'

They both fell silent, and Aydin wondered what she'd come at him with next. This wasn't about his health. But in the end she didn't say anything, just sat there staring at him. Was she enjoying seeing him becoming increasingly uncomfortable with her presence?

'Where are we?' he said finally. If she wanted to play games then he would play right back.

'Does it matter?'

'You said you were from MI6, but it was the Turkish security forces who took me.' He'd recognised the uniforms, the vehicles too.

'But this isn't a jail, or a black site,' he said. 'We're still in Turkey. Just some apartment that MI6 has use of?'

He saw the flicker in her eyes. Turkey it was. That was partly a relief, though it meant they were a hell of a long way from his brothers.

'No one said you were in Turkey,' Cox said, as though she was trying to create doubt in his mind.

Aydin shook his head. 'You haven't had long enough to take me anywhere else. I've been out of it for no more than a day. I can tell that by the state of my wounds.'

He saw her face twitch again.

'Aydin, your perception is impressive, but you have to understand this is just the beginning. Yes, it's been less than a day since you were arrested, and yes, you're still in Turkey. There's no harm in me telling you that. But you're not staying here. If you don't co-operate, you're in for a hell of a downward spiral. I'm sure you're aware of what we'd do to get what we need from you.'

Aydin didn't respond. He was sure that, when necessary, the UK government still engaged in torture. He'd bet Cox herself had witnessed it, though he doubted she'd ever inflicted it herself.

During the ensuing silence, Aydin stared up at the air-conditioning unit in the wall behind Cox. There was a camera inside, there had to be. He wondered who was on the other side, watching and listening to the conversation. Was it the bad cop to Cox's good? Perhaps he was better off keeping her in this room as long as he could after all.

'I need to know your group's plans,' she said. 'Locations, dates, times. Methods.'

Aydin held his tongue.

'This isn't a game, Aydin.' Cox looked pissed off now. 'Do you really want all that blood on your hands?'

'Exactly who do you think I am?' he said, angry for the first time in the conversation. 'Don't you think perhaps I *want* blood on my hands?'

Cox was taken aback by the genuine venom in his response. And so was he. He had no choice over what he *wanted* to be, he was simply a product: of the Teacher and the Farm – of his childhood. Whatever dissatisfaction he had with his life, there was no denying that there was hatred to be found inside him.

'Actually, I don't believe that at all,' Cox said. No explanation or justification to her statement, which somehow gave it more weight in Aydin's mind. 'They killed your sister. She was asking too many questions, trying to find you. That's why you ran, isn't it? You found out what they did?'

Now Aydin couldn't find his tongue. Not only because he was unsure how to respond, but because he was intrigued to see what else this woman knew; *how* she knew.

'And then, because you ran, because you broke free, they killed your mother too. Punishment.'

Despite everything he'd been taught – all of the training, the ordeals – Aydin was shaking with anger as Cox spoke the words. It was all too raw and painful for him to be able to cast it aside.

'Don't let these people win,' Cox said. 'If not for the innocent people who will lose their lives, then do it for your mother and Nilay. Make them proud, Aydin.'

Part of him wanted to cave in. He wasn't at the Farm any more – never would be again. And he didn't want to be locked up for the rest of his life, whether in a regular jail cell or some unofficial black site. He wanted to find Wahid, to kill Wahid. He couldn't do that locked up.

'I can't help you,' he said.

'Aydin, please don't waste this opportunity.'

'You know what's most telling?' he said. 'You've already got access to everything I know.'

Cox's face changed.

'The laptop I left at my uncle's. You have that, right?' No affirmation, but of course she knew what he was talking about. 'I've already reviewed the encrypted files on there. Perhaps you'll be able to do the same in time. Yet here you are, talking to me.'

'I'm not sure I understand your point.'

'Oh, you do. You still haven't found any of my brothers, have you? You said before that you thought the timer had been set. You were right. The plan was to cut communication as far as possible in the run-up to the attacks, to avoid any heat.'

330

'Aydin, what are you saying? How long do we have?'

She was sat up straight now.

'You want to figure this out by yourself? That's fine by me. Or you can have my help.'

'I *need* your help, Aydin. That's why I'm here.'

'No. You *want* my help. Time is not on your side. Unless you take action then the blood of innocents will be on *your* hands just as much as mine. *You* have the chance to stop this.'

'How? Just tell me how.'

'You have to get me out of here. If you do that, then I'll give you everything you need.'

FIFTY-SIX

'Don't even ask me,' Flannigan said when Cox headed back into the lounge.

Cox scowled and sat down at the dining table where Flannigan had left her a cup of coffee. She took a swig. It was bitter and lukewarm. She looked over to Flannigan, who shrugged apologetically.

'We've got transport arranged in three hours,' he said. 'Two grunts are coming and you, me and Torkal are heading out to Algeria.'

'Zed site?' Cox asked.

Flannigan nodded.

Cox had been before. In truth it was an experience she'd rather forget. The off-the-map bunker complex was several metres below the desert and its cool damp air seemed to her to be perpetually filled with terror and misery. A few miles south of the country's capital, Zed site was originally built and operated by the French military, up until they lost their drawn-out fight to maintain control of the African territory in the 1960s. After that the site had passed into the control of the UK government and used for its covert operations in Africa. It had been referred to as Z site ever since. For the last ten years the place had been largely taken over by the strong-handed Americans. British wit had deemed it necessary to clarify the name of the site to Zed, to further avoid the Americanisation of the place.

'You've been given approval for . . .' Cox couldn't quite bring herself to say it.

'The Prime Minister has given the go-ahead for the use of extraordinary procedures.'

Extraordinary procedures. Aka torturing the poor sod in whatever way they saw fit. Despite everything, Cox was still hoping to avoid that. Not only because Aydin seemed to be working against the others in the Thirteen and she had to understand why, but also because the clock was ticking.

'But he's talking,' Cox said. 'I'm getting through to him.'

'No. He's playing with you. He's given you absolutely nothing other than an absurd demand.'

'Perhaps it's not so absurd,' Cox said, under her breath but just loud enough for Flannigan to hear. She wasn't quite sure she believed the words herself so couldn't find the vigour to say them any louder.

'Are you fucking with me?' Flannigan said, his hackles raised. 'You want me to let a multiple-murdering terrorist back out onto the streets? What, you think he's going to lead you to his chums and then we all shake hands and swap medals and walk off into the sunset?'

'You shouldn't get so angry,' Cox said. 'Those lines on your forehead are becoming ingrained.'

'Thanks for the advice,' Flannigan said.

Cox's phone buzzed in her handbag over on the side table by the CCTV monitor, but by the time she'd reached it the call had ended. Several missed calls from the same number; a German number. Flannigan eyed her expectantly. She quickly dialled back.

'*Ja,*' came the female voice.

333

'Polizeikommissar Rahn, it's Rachel Cox.'

'Ah, Miss Cox. You're a hard lady to get hold of.'

'Sorry. You have something for me?'

'I'm afraid so. We found the source of the cyanide.'

'So it *was* cyanide,' Cox said, looking over to Flannigan.

'We traced the metal casing to a company in Hungary who makes hydrogen cyanide pellets under license. It's taken a lot of work, but . . . it appears a company controlled by Streicher had recently purchased fifty canisters.'

'Please tell me you know where those fifty canisters are.'

A pause.

'Actually, no. I'm afraid we don't.'

Half an hour later Cox was slumped on the sofa as Flannigan made yet another call to London. The German police had finally made a breakthrough. As well as tracing the cyanide, they'd found that the dead Nazi, Streicher, had been paid two million dollars the day he'd been killed. At least the finding had kick-started the German authorities into action. A massive deployment of police and armed forces to key sites in numerous cities would surely help to quash any attack planned on German soil.

The big problem that Cox saw, though, was that they didn't even know if those canisters were still in Germany. They could be anywhere in Europe. Was fifty canisters enough for a multi-pronged attack, or would they be used for only one of many atrocities?

'Another update for you,' Flannigan said.

'Yeah?'

'I just got word from the tech at the Embassy. They've cracked the encryption on the laptop. The encryption key was on the thumb drive in Torkal's backpack.'

A murmur of anticipation fluttered in Cox's chest. 'And?'

Flannigan shook his head. 'And it's next to useless. The files aren't just encrypted, but the data inside them coded too. It's nonsense, unless we have someone explain the code.'

'Aydin can.'

'And no doubt he will once he's been put through the ringer over at Zed site. What we can see, though, are seven separate but linked datasets. It's believed each represents a target location.'

'London, Paris, Berlin, Barcelona, Rome, Bruges and Budapest.'

'That's the thinking. But we still don't know when or how, or who.'

'Sir, let me talk to him again.'

Flannigan rolled his eyes.

'We have to try. I'm not saying Torkal deserves to be a free man, but we have to find out what he knows before it's too late.'

'Absolutely. And right now I see only one solution.'

'We don't have enough time! Did you listen to anything he said? To anything I've been saying to you?'

'There's no other choice right now! And I'm getting more than a little bit pissed off with your tone. Don't forget that you're only still here, *Cox*, because of me. It would be quite easy to have you thrown into a jail cell for what you did—'

'Except Trapeze is now officially authorised. You saw to that yourself because you know it's the right thing to do. In fact it's only because of me that we've found anything so far! Just look at what's happening in Germany now. There's a real chance we could thwart whatever attack is planned there. That's because of me. And we have Aydin in custody because of a lead I followed here in Turkey. Everything we know is because of *me*.'

'Fine. You're right. You're here because you have key knowledge on this operation that nobody else does. But as long as you remain on this case, you do as I damn well tell you. Got it?'

'I don't have time for this.'

Cox got up and strode over to the door.

'Where the hell are you going?'

Cox didn't answer, just threw open the door and stormed out.

FIFTY-SEVEN

When Rachel Cox came blazing back into the room Aydin, was a little taken aback by the ferocious determination on her face. Cuffed, shackled and vulnerable, he found himself cowering slightly as she loomed over him, her chest heaving, her cheeks red with anger.

'No more bullshit, Aydin,' she said, her choice to speak rather than lash out at him seeming to calm her, just slightly. 'You've got two hours. Then you're out of here. More than likely you'll never see daylight again.'

Aydin relaxed, realising that, despite her anger and frustration, she had nothing to come at him with other than her words. She seemed to sense that too.

'Aydin,' she said, sounding more desperate. 'We're taking you to Algeria. A black site. You've heard of those?'

Aydin said nothing.

'Yeah? I'm sure you have. Well, I've seen a few. And this one is the worst of them. A bunker that's completely off the map, and like most of the scumbags we take there, I doubt you'll ever leave alive.'

Still Aydin said nothing, not reacting at all.

'It's a truly foul place. Under the desert. No light, no fresh air. And they won't take it easy on you. They're going to do

337

absolutely everything they can to get you to talk. Whatever it takes. Yes, we do still do that shit.'

'Did you know here in Turkey there's an underground city, more than a thousand years old, that in the past could house as many as twenty thousand people?'

He could see the look of confusion on her face. 'I do know it, actually,' she then said. 'Derinkuyu. I've been there. Have you?'

Aydin nodded. 'It was built as a defence for the Byzantine people during their war with the Arabs.' He shrugged. 'It's just a thought I had. You're talking about bunkers and how nasty it is to have no light and no fresh air but there's nothing unusual about bunkers. They're just extravagant caves. People have lived and taken shelter in caves for thousands of years.'

Cox shrugged. 'And people have tortured others since time began. Nothing much changes, does it? Do you really want that to be your fate, though?'

'No, I don't. But you're right, there's nothing new or unique about the position we both find ourselves in today. War is a fact of human life. In years to come no one will remember me, or you. We're just not that important.'

'Tell me about the cyanide. Where are the targets?'

Aydin was silent.

'Come on, don't give me that look. We know about the canisters. Fifty in total, purchased in Berlin by your friend, Sab'ah.'

Aydin tried his best to show no reaction to the use of his brother's name, but he saw the pleased look on Cox's face.

'I know a lot more than you think,' she said. 'Have you any idea how many people that cyanide could kill if we don't put a stop to it?'

'Do you?'

Aydin shifted. He'd seen within Itnashar's data the reference to cyanide. But that wasn't something he'd been aware of. He

338

didn't know which locations were using that as the weapon of choice, but it certainly hadn't been the plan for him.

'We broke the encryption on your laptop,' Cox said, then left the revelation dangling as though she expected her words to cause some sort of breakthrough. 'We now have access to all the information you have.'

Aydin once again held his tongue. He had no need to play along, to ask if they'd deciphered the coding that sat behind the encryption. He already knew the answer. Cox was in the room, talking to him, so of course they hadn't.

'Based on that information we've also now raided the addresses in all of the cities your *brothers* were located,' Cox said. 'So I'm sorry, Aydin.' She got up from the sofa and walked over to the door. 'But it looks like we don't really need your help now anyway. Good luck in Algeria.'

She opened the door.

'Which locations?' Aydin asked quietly.

Her little trick had worked – Aydin was intrigued. But only because he knew she was barking up the wrong tree, and because he sensed that he could still break through to her, much like she was still trying to break through to him. Of course he didn't *want* to end up in that bunker in Algeria, even though he was prepared for that to be his fate if there was no other way.

'Which locations do you think?' she said. 'Nothing you've done so far has stopped your people at all, has it? London, Paris, Bruges, Rome, all of the places you went to, the attacks are still going ahead regardless.'

'You think I went to those places to stop the attacks?'

'No, I think you went for your own selfish reasons. You *could* have stopped the attacks already, but you chose not to.'

Aydin fell silent. What she'd said was true, but it had never been his job to stop them, no matter how responsible he now felt.

339

'And we also know about Barcelona, Berlin and Budapest now. Seven locations. Seven attacks.'

Aydin shook his head. MI6 had got absolutely nowhere. The clock was ticking, his brothers had disappeared into the ether. None of the police forces or armies or security services in any of those countries would find them now. Not until it was too late.

'You're wrong.'

'About what?'

'About everything.'

'I don't think so.'

She pulled the door further open and took a step into the doorway.

'London, Paris, Bruges, Rome, Berlin, Barcelona, Budapest,' Aydin said. 'Anything strike you about those locations?'

Cox stopped. She wasn't facing him, but he could imagine the look of hesitation on her face.

'I did wonder why Bruges was among those,' she said.

'There's a good reason actually. But what else?'

'Five capital cities,' she said, turning her head to look back at him. 'Tens of millions of people between them. Maximum impact.'

'You're partly right. Five capital cities. Some of the world's most important monuments. Some of the world's most important politicians, and royal families. Celebrities. And money and power. What does every city need to look after all those . . .?'

He left it hanging. Cox got it more quickly than he'd expected. She turned round fully and shut the door again. Her brow was creased – part anger, part because she was deep in thought.

'Security,' she said, finishing the sentence.

'I imagine that each country has moved their security threat to the highest level now, expecting the worst,' Aydin said.

'Extra police on the streets, perhaps military too. Round-the-clock security for government officials and diplomats.'

The look she was giving Aydin was one of pure hate, though he didn't believe it was directed at him entirely.

'The plan isn't to attack those cities at all, is it?' she said.

'Why attack targets that are so heavily protected?' Aydin said, as though it should have been obvious all along.

'Then where?'

'No country has the resources to protect every single city and town, every home and every person. How many towns and cities across those countries have tens of thousands, hundreds of thousands of people to target?'

'Tell me, Aydin!' Cox shouted, her anger getting the better of her. 'Where will the attacks take place? You have to tell me.'

'When did you say they went dark?'

Cox's eyes narrowed. 'Midnight, Central European Time, nearly two days ago.'

'Then you still have time,' Aydin said. 'But not much.'

'*How* much, Aydin? Please!'

'The plan was always for sixty hours. Enough time to finalise equipment, get to the locations and go through final checks. But maybe it changed.'

'And then the attacks begin? All at once?'

Aydin didn't answer that. 'Worst case, you've got not much more than twelve hours to go. My original offer still stands.'

Cox was fuming. Just like when she'd first stormed in, Aydin again expected her to come for him at any second.

She didn't.

After a few seconds she simply opened the door and walked out.

FIFTY-EIGHT

'He's bluffing,' Flannigan said, though it was clear to Cox that he didn't fully believe his own words. 'There's no evidence whatsoever that the attacks will take place anywhere other than the locations we've already identified.'

'Evidence? There is no bloody evidence of what they're going to do!' Cox was standing next to him, glaring angrily at the CCTV screen. Aydin glanced up to the camera. Flannigan was still seething. 'Sorry,' Cox said.

Flannigan looked at his watch and sighed. 'By the time we land in Algeria we'll only have a few hours.'

'He's right,' Cox said. 'We can't possibly protect every-where, all at once. We *have* to know more.'

'Or is this exactly what he wants? Each country diverting its efforts *away* from the known locations.'

'I honestly believe he's telling the truth.'

'He has no reason to do so.'

'But he does. He *wants* to help. He *hates* them. I sense it. They killed his mother and sister. He wants revenge, but he wants it on his terms.'

'We've been through this before. We are *not* letting him out of our custody.'

'But that's not the same thing as keeping him locked up,

is it? There must be a way. We take him where he wants to go, under our watch. I know he'll lead us to Wahid. All we need is a failsafe that we can use should he deceive us.'

'Like a tiny explosive device that we can inject into his neck to track him and then remotely detonate the second he tries to run. Sorry, Cox, but you've been watching too many movies.'

'It was you who said all that, not me.'

'The point is, there is no magic, fool-proof failsafe. Whatever situation we try to set up in the next few hours, if Torkal is out on the streets he's nothing more than a liability.'

'No, he's an asset!' Cox shouted. 'You might not like him, but you need to start seeing him for what he is. We don't have to see eye to eye with him, but he has useful and credible knowledge, and that makes him an asset. What have we got to lose here in treating him that way?'

'Other than him turning on us and running free while his friends blow hundreds, possibly thousands of people to smithereens?'

'Yes, I agree, that's the worst case here: he double-crosses us, runs away and the attacks still happen. But right now, those attacks are going to happen anyway, so all we'd have lost from this current situation would be one man. Him. We won't break this in time any other way. There's a very real chance that he could help to stop *everything*. Could you live with knowing we didn't even try? Because I'm not sure I can.'

Flannigan seemed to me mulling it over as he looked at his watch again. Then his phone chirped with an incoming message. He pulled it out of his pocket and frowned at the screen.

'I've expedited the extraction,' he said. 'They'll be here in ten minutes.'

Cox slumped. 'Sir, have you listened to anything I've been saying?'

'Yes, Cox. I've listened to it all.'

'And?'

'And it's a no. And that's absolutely final. I don't want to hear another word of it. We go ahead as planned. We're heading to Zed site, and when we get there we're going to make this fucker wish he'd never been born.'

FIFTY-NINE

Cordoba, Southern Spain

Wahid and his brother Itnan strolled through the cool interior of the arcaded hypostyle hall of the Mezquita, passing under horseshoe arches held up by columns of jasper, onyx, marble and granite. Exiting the open doors of the centuries-old hall, they settled on a bench in the shade of the many trees in the Court of Oranges, a sweet citrus smell wafting through the hot air.

'It's beautiful, isn't it?' Wahid said to Itnan, looking back to the complex and uneven structure, put together in pieces over hundreds of years. His brother turned to him, looking a little surprised by the comment. 'Oh, come on, you have to admire great architecture, even if you don't like what it stands for.'

'I'm not so sure I agree,' Itnan said.

'I know it's hard to see it today, but this used to be one of the greatest mosques of the Moors,' Wahid said.

'I know that.'

'Of course you do.' Wahid took a deep breath, filling his lungs with the fresh, orange-scented air. 'I like to imagine what it must have been like back then, when this was a place of worship for Islam. Before the infidels came and butchered it.' He stared up at the tower of the cathedral, the traditional Renaissance-style nave erupting from the centre of the old mosque. A sight which told Wahid much about the centuries-old fight between Muslims and Christians. For hundreds of years his people had been persecuted – it was time to turn the tables for good.

'Why have you brought me here?' Itnan asked, looking uncomfortable in his surroundings.

The answer was multi-layered. For one it was a good, busy place where they could talk without fear of being overheard. The buildings and the gardens gave them cover from drones or satellites above, and they'd left the apartment without any electronic equipment on them at all should any of their devices somehow be compromised. They were entering the final few hours before the attacks began and Wahid wanted to be absolutely sure that he and the others remained undetected.

Actually, in many ways, it was liberating to ditch technology and get back to basics. But that wasn't the only reason they'd come.

'This place, for all its outer beauty, represents the whole story of our struggles,' Wahid said. 'This was a place of worship. A peaceful place where men could come and pray, and fulfil their duties to Allah. And then the Catholics rampaged through the city. Through this whole region. They butchered the Moors – our ancestors. Not satisfied with taking power, they destroyed this place too. They sat that cathedral right in the centre of our mosque, knowing the disrespect and anguish it would cause the remaining Muslims who were mercilessly persecuted.'

Wahid looked at his brother again, could see the anger in his eyes.

'More than eight hundred years have passed since then,' Wahid said. 'Despite all of the evidence that remains here, of what this place once was – the prayer hall, the *mihrab*, all of the wonderful arches and tiles and doorways and courtyards

– no Muslim has ever been allowed to pray here in all of the time since. The last two people who even attempted it, two young tourists visiting to learn about the history of this great place, were attacked by the infidel guards and thrown out, mid-prayer. Can you believe that?'

Wahid heard Itnan mutter under his breath.

'Okay,' Itnan said. 'That's enough history for today.'

'No, brother. You can never have too much history,' Wahid said. 'History is all that we are, it is what has made the world as it is today. And it will continue to define our future. We *will* get vengeance for all of the trouble our people have seen. We'll return places like this to how Allah himself intended. And if we can't, we'll raze them to the ground, burying the non-believers in the rubble.'

'We will, my brother.'

The two men sat in silence for a few moments, quietly watching the throngs of tourists happily idling by and gawking at their surroundings, smiling and posing as they clicked away on their phones and their cameras.

'Give me your update,' Wahid said.

Itnan smiled now. 'I thought you would never ask.'

'Always good to save the best until last.'

'It's all ready to go.'

'You've tested the gas?'

'Only in the lab. It's not been possible to perform a . . . live demonstration.'

Wahid had already known that, and he accepted it. The attacks in Spain, as well as using high explosives, would also include the use of phosgene – a poisonous gas they'd produced in their own lab through a chemical reaction using the more widely available chloroform. Phosgene had a rich history, being one of the first chemical weapons of modern warfare, used to great effect during World War I. Unlike other gases used in chemical weapons it was colourless and, with an odour similar to cut grass, its dispersal often went undetected until it was too late. When inhaled in high enough doses, the gas worked quickly to disrupt the blood-air barrier of the lungs, causing suffocation.

'It's going to be glorious,' Wahid said. 'And what about Phantom?'

'Phantom has been live for nearly forty-eight hours,' Itnan confirmed. 'We've already surpassed the number of intended targets.'

Phantom was malware, designed by the now deceased Roman Asrutdinov, which they were using to infect countless major corporations across the world – not to mention law enforcement agencies and security services. In just a few hours, when the clock struck zero, the malware would rear its head and every infected organisation would be dragged to its knees. Not only would the chaos that followed greatly assist the attacks and hamper the emergency services' responses, but the elders would make billions from the disruption from their short positions as share prices across the globe plummeted out of control. The financial upside would mark a colossal turning point in the wider war against the West.

'I always knew you'd succeed,' Wahid said. 'And there's no hint of any unwanted attention?'

'Of course not. Phantom will remain completely undetected until the clock has run down. The code will make sure of that. And then . . .' Itnan mimicked an explosion with his hands.

'And still no fallout from Berlin?'

'No. Everyone's looking in the wrong direction, fighting over whether it was Russia or North Korea that Asrutdinov was working with. They're blaming countless other countries for his death, too. No one will discover the truth in time. For now the trail is completely clean.'

Clean meaning that, once security forces uncovered the source of the malware, it would take them not to him or his brothers, but to Roman Asrutdinov. Wahid smiled at the thought of how that one would pan out for relations between the US, its allies and Russia.

'Are we done here?' Itnan said. 'Seeing all these gurning morons is beginning to make my blood boil.'

'Yes. We're done. It's a shame I didn't bring a camera. It would have been nice to get a picture of how this place *used* to look.'

He winked at Itnan, then got to his feet.

SIXTY

Ankara, Turkey

There was no doubt that Aydin was feeling rattled when, just a few minutes after Cox left the room, two thick-set men he'd not seen before barged in, gagged him and placed a sack over his head. They rough-handed him, giving him no chance to fight back as they quickly untied him from the radiator. The shackles between his ankles and wrists remained, the short length between the two sets of cuffs meaning he had to stoop low to walk as they shepherded – well, *dragged* – him out of there.

Soon Aydin found himself in an open-sided helicopter – the din of the rotors and the constant whoosh of air making his head sloppy and unfocused. It was impossible not to draw a parallel to what had happened to him all those years ago at the Farm – a thought that certainly didn't help.

No one had said a word to him since the men had come into the room in Ankara, though he knew Cox was on the flight too; he'd heard her voice, shouting to be understood over the noise of the helicopter, but not loud enough for Aydin to grasp anything she was saying. She and whoever else was travelling with them had earmuffs and headsets, he assumed, so they could properly communicate.

The helicopter was almost certainly military: Aydin was

sitting on a solid metal bench, there were no luxurious comforts. The chains on his ankles were tied too close around something underneath, chafing angrily at his raw skin.

For the first time, a ripple of fear expanded and began to take hold. Not just at the thought of being tortured at MI6's black site – he believed he could handle that. Instead it was, somehow, the build-up of everything bad that had ever happened to him suddenly pinging around inside his head, like a chain reaction surging out of control.

In the darkness, as the internal ripple continued to grow into a crashing wave, his mind forced him to relive his horrific treatment at the Farm, the killing of his sister and mother, the trials of the last few days as he'd scrambled across Europe a broken man. And alongside those thoughts, which were growing stronger all the time, was the knowledge that, within hours, his brothers – the cause of so much of his pain – would launch their attacks. Thousands of men, women and children would be slain.

The smiling, bloodstained faces of his brothers appeared before him, the floating grins of the elders too, knowing the long game had finally paid off, and that they'd delivered such a hammer blow to their mortal enemy. Cox was right. Aydin was the only one who could still stop them.

And there was the source of his suddenly crumbling mental state – it was the anguish of knowing that his silence, and the suffering he would endure at the black site they were heading to, wasn't to protect him, it was in order to allow the massacre of innocent civilians.

The gag in his mouth meant he was snorting heavy breaths through his partially blocked nostrils. As his mind flared, adrenaline coursed through his blood. Because of it his pulse was racing, his muscles twitching. Soon his breathing was struggling to keep up with his body's demand. He was hyperventilating, as if his lungs and heart were burning, and at the same time his mind was becoming woolly and detached.

'Aydin, what's wrong?' he heard Cox shouting. She was right next to him. Her voice gave him something to focus on, helping to take away just some of his inner turmoil . . . But he wasn't sure it was enough. Unable to feed oxygen to his brain, he drifted.

'Aydin!'

With his head lolling and his eyes rolling, the sack was pulled from his head. A flood of white light burned into his eyes, the gag was ripped from his mouth. He inhaled deeply at the sudden release, feeling the surge of blood and oxygen to his brain through the gargantuan breaths he took. With the freedom to fill his lungs once more, he couldn't stop himself taking bigger and faster breaths. Brain swimming now – no, *drowning* – it wasn't long before the blare of white he saw in front of him faded to black.

When Aydin next opened his eyes the crash of the helicopter's rotors and engine was still filling his ears, but everything somehow seemed calmer and more serene. His body was leaning to the right, suspended in mid-air by the chain connecting his wrists to his ankles, which remained secured underneath the bench. Pulling himself upright, a crick in his neck stabbed from where his head had been hanging.

The darkness was gone, and the deep blue water stretched out below, long shadows rippling on the waves as the sun set in the distance. The sky was full of orange, tinged with red. Across the open cabin were the same two men who'd dragged him out of the MI6 safe house in Turkey. They were wearing non-designated military fatigues, big black boots, utility belts crammed with equipment. Each was casually holding an M4 carbine.

Aydin looked past them, into the cockpit. He could only see the backs of the two men; one was in standard fatigues with a white crash helmet on. The pilot, Aydin guessed. The other man was more casually dressed, and while Aydin didn't know his name, he had seen him in the safe house, outside the doorway, in the moments before he'd been dragged out. Cox's boss from MI6? As if sensing Aydin was awake, the man turned and locked eyes with him. Aydin saw nothing but anger and hate as he stared.

What did the man see in him?

'Are you okay?' came Cox's voice. She was shouting as loudly as she could, her voice only just audible above the roar of the helicopter.

Aydin turned to see her looking somewhere between concerned and relieved. The microphone of her headset was pushed to the side, away from her mouth.

'Are you okay?' she asked again. 'You passed out. I think you hyperventilated. We'll leave the gag out and the hood off. For now.'

Aydin nodded. He wasn't sure why; he should have given her nothing. But there was something about Rachel Cox. She wasn't like the others. For one thing, she didn't look at him as though he was pure scum.

She pulled the microphone back into position and began a conversation that Aydin couldn't hear. The two grunts weren't speaking, and when Aydin looked over to Cox's boss he could see the muscles of his jaw tensing and relaxing as he and Cox continued their exchange. The boss caught Aydin's eye for a moment. Cox was now looking more than a little bit pissed off. It wasn't hard to figure how that conversation just went. The boss wanted Aydin to be their plaything, thinking that the worse they treated him, the more likely he was to talk. The impression he got was that Cox at least wanted to treat him like a human.

'How much longer?' Aydin yelled to her.

The darkening blue of the Med below would soon give way to the rising form of land now visible in the distance.

'Please don't tell me you need the toilet!' Cox shouted back, once again lifting her microphone out of the way. Aydin didn't respond to her quip. 'Not long,' she said, looking slightly embarrassed. 'Half an hour or so.'

Aydin noticed that the two grunts were both now glaring at him. One was giving his best evil eye, though the other looked faintly amused.

'You have to help me, Aydin,' Cox said, leaning a little closer to him. He kept his eyes on the men in front. She was still shouting, but there was no way the others could hear her. 'Please. Promise me you'll do the right thing.'

Aydin had expected to see pleading doe eyes. Instead he was faced with a look of steely determination. Even though he didn't know exactly what she'd meant, the command of her words led Aydin to nod in agreement.

She pushed the microphone back over her mouth, pointed out towards the line of land in the distance and struck up a conversation with the others. The eyes of the two commandos followed her pointing finger. Aydin had no idea what she was saying, but it was clear to him that it was a simple subterfuge, because after a couple of seconds her right hand sprang out to him and he reflexively twisted his wrist and opened his hand as she dropped an object into his palm. Her hand whipped back onto her leg as he clasped his fingers around the hairgrip she'd passed him.

Aydin's heart raced as the men turned their attention back to him and he did his best to show no reaction.

He didn't dare look at Cox, though he could hear that she was still talking away. Once again the men looked to where she was pointing. Aydin quickly worked away on the lock on his wrists. He'd practised releasing himself from cuffs hundreds of times. He'd been able to do it within seconds when he was only twelve years old. Before the men even looked back he'd already released the simple lock, though he left the cuffs in place, over his wrists. The trickiest part would be releasing his ankles. He needed a bigger distraction to achieve that and would bide his time.

The conversation around him stopped. He knew Cox had eyes on him but he resisted the temptation to look back. Instead he just waited.

Soon after, he was given the chance.

He felt the jolt as the helicopter banked left and began to descend. With the helicopter's movement, he found himself sliding across the bench. He saw the men in front tensing and pulling as they tried to keep to their rigid positions. With Aydin's backside already sliding he flung his weight further to the left and slammed into Cox, digging his elbow into her ribs. She'd given him this chance – why, he didn't know – but until he escaped she was still a threat. Cox doubled over from the blow, and Aydin sprang up as best as he was able to with his ankles secured to the bench. He couldn't move his feet forward more than a few inches, but with his hands free it was enough to reach out and grab at the M4 of the grunt directly in front of him before the guy had figured out what was going on – after all, he'd had no idea Aydin's hands were now free.

Aydin snatched the gun, turned it and fired a shot that blasted through the toes of the soldier's black boot. Blood burst up out of the hole and he screamed and writhed as he went for his sidearm. Aydin had just enough leverage to swipe the M4's butt across his head. He was out.

The second grunt was moving his heavy weapon towards Aydin, but he didn't have enough time; the momentum from

Aydin hitting the first guy was already pulling the M4 into position. Aydin held down the trigger and automatic gunfire rattled. Several bullets smacked into his opponent's Kevlar vest, his body jolting with each strike. It was possible at such close range that at least one of the bullets would pass through the supposedly bulletproof material, but the vest would still be enough to seriously slow the bullets and potentially save him from what would otherwise be certain death.

Either way, the sheer force of the rapid gunfire was enough to subdue him for as long as Aydin needed.

Just then Aydin saw a glint of black metal out of the corner of his eye. A handgun. Would Cox actually shoot him, having given him this chance? Or was it all just part of her charade?

Aydin couldn't take the chance. He launched himself at her again and this time his elbow caught her in the face. Her gun flew from her grip and out of the cabin. With all three of them temporarily subdued, Aydin fell back onto the bench and ducked down, quickly released the lock on his ankles, then pulled the chains free. When he straightened back up he saw Cox's boss glaring at him from the cockpit – armed, and twisting the gun round. Aydin reached forward for the nearest grunt, grabbed him around the neck and pulled him in close, cover from the boss's gun.

'I knew what you were,' Cox's boss spat, his disgust clear. 'Once a terrorist, always a terrorist.'

'No,' Aydin said. 'I'm your last hope.'

He shoved the grunt forward, aiming to topple him into the boss, then dived to his right, grabbing the strap of a parachute from under then bench as he went. He didn't know if Cox's boss fired at him or not as his body slammed painfully against the edge of the cabin and he tumbled out, sending him into a clumsy spin as he cascaded towards the water below.

Hurtling at frightening speed towards the sea, he grappled with the backpack, trying to release the chute. He managed to sling the straps around his shoulders but the release button was stuck. Air rushed against his face, his eyes welled up from the battering of air making it impossible to see clearly, though he was sure he was only seconds from crashing into the water.

He pushed again and again on the release button as his body twisted around and around in the air, out of control. Finally it worked, and Aydin felt the jerk as the chute launched. No time for relief. As he looked up, he saw the fabric was twisted around the lines, not even half of the chute properly unfurled. And there was nothing else Aydin could do.

He tried his best to set himself straight just a second before his body crashed into the water, the impact like his body had smacked into concrete, and he was soon floundering underneath, trying to get his battered body under control.

As his arms and legs flailed about hopelessly, he fought the urge to gasp – knowing that inhaling the water would be a fatal move. Finally he found his sense of direction, and pushed and kicked with everything he had to try to get back up to the surface. His lungs burned, his heavy body ached, but somehow he managed it. He shot up to the surface and sucked in a huge breath that made his lungs sting even more and sent his head into another spin. It took him a few seconds, and a few more shallow breaths, to regain clarity of mind.

He expected to see the helicopter circling above, the M4s trained on the water waiting to cut him into pieces. Instead he saw a line of black smoke across the now purple-pink sky. He followed the trail to the helicopter – damaged by a stray bullet perhaps? – already fading into the distance, heading towards the setting sun.

He heaved a sigh of relief, which was quickly followed by an ominous shiver. The reality was that he was far from home and dry. He had no idea where he was, or how to get where to where he needed.

But he was alive.

There wasn't much time, but he'd do whatever he could to get to Wahid before it was too late. He had to stop his brothers – for his sister, his mother. Because he was sure now that was what *they'd* want him to do.

It was time to finally prove his worth.

SIXTY-ONE

Gibraltar, Iberian Peninsula

'Cox, wake up, damn it!'

Cox bolted upright, feeling the twinge in her neck from the uncomfortable position she found herself in. Quite how she'd drifted off sitting on the hard metal chair even she didn't know, but such was her level of exhaustion.

'What time is it?' Cox asked, rubbing her neck as she squinted up at Flannigan. He too looked weary and dishevelled.

'Six a.m. Get your shit together, this is no time for catching up on sleep. We've got a call with London waiting.'

He wasn't hiding the fact that he was seriously pissed off with her. With everything really. He hadn't yet come out and directly accused her of helping Aydin escape, but she could tell he was thinking that was the case. Even though she had taken an elbow to the ribs and one to the face in the process.

'Of course, sir,' Cox said, groggily getting to her feet. 'I think it's just the concussion that pushed me over the edge.'

Flannigan just shook his head at that.

Cox followed her boss as they were escorted through the Portakabin labyrinth of the RAF base, until they came to a meeting room with a large but cheap-looking desk, set up with twelve chairs. Only Cox and Flannigan stayed inside as

Flannigan went and sat down and dialled into the conference call on the room's star phone.

'Back to basics, eh?' Cox said, taking a seat across the large desk from her boss.

'We don't have time for anything better,' Flannigan said, which Cox took to mean they were ignoring the risk that this room and the line could be in some way compromised. She could understand the urgency though. Although they were on UK soil, this wasn't an SIS site and it wasn't kitted out for their needs. But there were surely only hours left until it was game over. After that the attacks would begin. Where and how, they still had no clue, but they had to push on and do everything they could to find out the answers.

Over the last few hours there'd been several briefings given to politicians and to the security services in the various countries thought to be targets, but not a single arrest had been made, and all of the Thirteen – other than Itnashar, who was now slowly rotting in a morgue in Belgium – were still roaming the streets as free men. Aydin Torkal included. The German authorities were the most prepared for an attack, but had so far had no success either in identifying the intended target or in locating the cyanide that everyone now believed would form part of the attack there.

Cox looked over to her boss as he punched in the numbers for the call. The pissed-off look had remained on his face for hours on end now. After Aydin escaped from the helicopter, Flannigan had ranted and blasted for a good half hour at the poor helicopter pilot, whose only focus had been on getting the damaged craft to safety, and saving himself and the others onboard from crashing into the Mediterranean. Flannigan had seemed oblivious to that risk, only concerned with waiting for Aydin to surface so they could shoot him dead.

What would that have achieved, anyway?

They'd landed safely in Algeria, albeit some distance short of their destination at Zed site. Pretty soon the local police had descended and taken them into custody. It wouldn't have been long before a mini-political fallout ensued as Cox was sure the Algerians would have brought them up on espionage charges for landing in the middle of their country unannounced like that. It had taken quite a bit of work to get themselves not just released, but with onward transport out of the country. They'd had to pull in favours with the French DGSE to achieve that, who in turn had negotiated with the Algerian DRS to provide Cox and Flannigan, their pilot and the two injured contractors, safe harbour onward to British soil at Gibraltar.

In the end they'd not stepped foot anywhere near Zed site, which Cox was quite glad about. Without Aydin there was nothing at the black site that could help them, and Gibraltar was not just safe territory, but was much closer to where the imminent attacks would take place. But the timer was edging closer and closer to zero, and they still had next to nothing to work with.

'Have you got a problem, sir?' Cox said, returning her boss's glare, feeling herself becoming riled by his persistent death stare.

'I've got lots of problems, Cox. Number one being I'm still mulling over how that bastard escaped from us like that.' He spoke through gritted teeth and it wasn't hard to see who his anger was directed at. Blips were coming from the phone's speaker as the call waited to connect.

'I've been telling you all along how highly trained the Thirteen are,' Cox said. 'These aren't just brainwashed losers. You saw yourself how quick Torkal was. He's put two highly trained soldiers in hospital. It's a miracle we're both still standing.' Cox rubbed the bruise on her face for effect. 'There was nothing we could do.'

361

Flannigan opened his mouth to respond when the call connected – a hiss of static before a voice came down the line.

'Flannigan and Cox, I'm guessing?'

It was Roger Miles.

'Yes,' Flannigan said. 'We're both here.'

'Good. We've got a full room here. Charles Greenfield, Wendy Acaster, Caroline Branding, Bob Stokes and myself.'

Cox suddenly felt all the more exposed at hearing the list of names. The Home Secretary, Foreign Secretary, as well as both MI5 and MI6 chiefs.

Flannigan snorted when he saw Cox's reaction.

'Do you have an update for us?' Miles asked.

'Yes. I do. I got off the line with the director of Trapeze just a few minutes ago,' Flannigan said, which was certainly news to Cox. Was he deliberately keeping her in the dark now? But then if that was the case why bother asking her to come on his call? 'Our targets remain completely dark.'

'And Torkal?'

Flannigan sighed. 'We believe he's back on European soil.'

'Excuse me?' Miles said. 'When the hell did you find this out?'

'I just said I was on the phone with Trapeze a few minutes ago,' Flannigan responded quickly, standing his ground. 'We believe he washed up in Algeria a few miles west of Algiers. A local fisherman called in to the police that he'd spotted a man walking in from the sea. We have another local report from a few hours ago of a missing dinghy at a small private quay near to the port of Oran. It's only a short hop from around there to Southern Spain. Putting two and two together . . .'

'But the Spanish coast guard haven't alerted us to anyone attempting to smuggle themselves in?' The words of an unfamiliar female voice echoed from the speaker.

362

Cox guessed it was Caroline Branding, the MI5 chief, because she'd seen the other woman, foreign secretary Wendy Acaster, plenty of times on TV, and there wasn't a hint of her Welsh accent.

'Not yet, no,' Flannigan said. 'Torkal took a chance and got lucky, it's as simple as that. That coastline is a common landing point for drug smugglers from Africa so I agree it's a surprise he wasn't picked up. Perhaps because of the time of day or the type of craft he used he didn't hit their radars at the time, but you could just put it down to them being lazy bastards, I guess. Regardless, we should assume that unless he drowned he's back on European soil now.'

'Miss Cox, are you there?' came another male voice, softer and with a definite Midlands accent. Cox recognised it as that of the Home Secretary. A relatively young cabinet minister who'd always come across to her as being too nice and plain to successfully command such a position of authority. But she knew better than anyone not to let herself be swayed by misconceptions like that.

'Yes, sir,' she said.

'This is Charles Greenfield. I understand you know more about this . . . *group* than anyone else.'

'That's possible. I've been investigating them for over a year.'

'Which is why I find it very unusual that I'm only now hearing about them, when we're allegedly hours away from imminent terrorist attacks.'

The comment was met with absolute silence, though Cox didn't feel embarrassed or uncomfortable about his words, only disappointed. The way Flannigan was squirming suggested he realised the dig was aimed more at him than her. It wasn't as though she hadn't been trying to raise the alarm before now.

'Do you have any more details about when and where the attacks will take place?'

'No, sir.'

'Or where Torkal is going?'

'No, sir.'

Another silence followed.

'We've now got full co-operation of the security services in each of the six other countries we believe are targets,' Miles said. 'And, with their assistance, raids have been conducted on every address we can link to the Thirteen.'

'But with no additional useful intelligence found, I gather,' came a gruff voice with an upper class English drawl. Bob Stokes, the mid-sixties MI6 boss.

'Unfortunately not,' Miles continued.

'So I'd say we're into *what the hell next* mode now. It's getting to the point where we have to seriously consider making the threat public and getting the military involved.'

'I agree,' Cox said, unable to hold her tongue.

'Have you both lost your minds?' Greenfield said. 'You think putting tanks and soldiers on the streets is the answer?'

'That has to be an absolute last resort,' Acaster said.

'Last resort is exactly what we need,' Stokes countered.

'It'll cause chaos!' Greenfield said. 'And there's no way we can control that type of response over multiple countries.'

'It could be the only way,' Miles said.

'What are you suggesting exactly?' Wendy Acaster piped up. 'We don't know where the attacks will happen. To get an effective response we'd have to close all ports, airports, train stations. We'd need to get three hundred million people across Europe sold on the idea, and agreeing to lock themselves inside their homes until further notice.'

'Even if we had more time that would be next to impossible to achieve,' Branding said. 'I mean, perhaps it's *possible* that the Home Secretary and MI5 can have a curfew organised on home soil, but to co-ordinate that across most of Western Europe?'

'I think the other countries will follow our lead,' Stokes said.

'At the very least we need to inform the public of the threat level,' Miles said. 'We need to consider deploying the military to key cities and sites.'

'But which cities? Which sites?' Greenfield said.

The conversation was quickly descending into aimless back and forth, and Cox was even losing track of who was saying what and which side of the argument each of them was on. She *wanted* to offer up her thoughts, to try and give sound advice, to give focus and clarity to the situation, but in truth she was just as lost as the others. The only difference, unlike these desk jockeys, was she knew when to shut up.

She saw that Flannigan now had his head in hands, as though he too had nothing useful to add.

'Flannigan. What do you think?' Miles asked. Flannigan raised his head and glared over at Cox. 'You and Cox have been out at street level with this. What do we need to do to contain this threat? Is there *anything* we can do now?'

'Other than pray?' Flannigan said before giving a nervous laugh. His churlish comment was met with silence and Cox saw his cheeks flush a little. 'I see no choice. Torkal was our way in, and now he's on the loose I'm not sure how else we get to the others. We have to do everything we can to protect civilian life. Public announcements, transport closures, event cancellations, police and military presence on the streets. You need to put into place whatever measures you can.'

'And, Miss Cox, do you agree with that?' Greenfield said. 'Is there anything else we're missing here?'

'My fear is that if we don't find them in time, they'll attack anyway,' Cox said, 'regardless of what measures we now put in place.'

'What do you mean exactly?'

'Their plans are too well laid. They're already weaponised. You close down a site where they were planning to attack and they'll just go somewhere else. All of the training and the set-up is long over. They're ready to attack, and they'll likely have backups – or they'll simply improvise. I know this group. Maybe we're even playing into their hands right now.'

'Sorry, but you've lost me,' Greenfield said.

Cox sighed. 'Look, if some nutter with a readymade bomb wants an explosion then he's going to get a damn explosion. We're too late here. They're ready. You can put measures in place, curfews to stop them blowing up a stadium, or a crowded airport or a shopping centre, but we can't make millions of people disappear. Our targets can just as easily walk down a plain old residential street and blow up an apartment block. We can't protect everyone, everywhere, all at once.'

'Are you saying you have evidence that they're planning to attack civilian residences?'

'No. I'm saying they *will* attack, no matter what. As long as they are out there, they won't stop.'

'What should we do then?'

'Take the necessary precautions, by all means. Doing so may save *some* lives. But the only way to stop this is to find every last one of the Thirteen.'

'And how do we do that, exactly?'

But Cox didn't have a realistic answer to that.

'And what about this cyanide?' Greenfield said. 'Do we even know how they're planning to weaponise it?'

'No,' Cox said. 'And I'm no chemist, but I'd say it's most likely they would need to feed the gas into an enclosed air system for it to be effective. I've never heard of it being used any other way.'

'So, what are we talking about? Offices? Airports?'

'Given the historical comparisons, most probably.'

'That still leaves dozens of potential targets,' Acaster said.

Both Cox and Flannigan flinched at a double tap on the door. The door opened and the same female flight lieutenant who'd escorted them to the room earlier was standing there, a concerned look on her face.

'For God's sake—' Flannigan started.

'I'm so sorry for the interruption,' the woman said. 'But, Miss Cox, there's been an urgent phone call for you.'

'Who is it?' Cox said, feeling a buzz of anticipation at the flight lieutenant's unease.

'He didn't stay on the line,' she said, coming into the room and handing Cox a torn piece of paper. 'That's the number he said to call. He says he'll speak only to you, and no one else. He gave his name as Aydin Torkal.'

SIXTY-TWO

Cordoba, Spain

Aydin glanced at the Casio digital watch he'd stolen from an angry English drunk man roaming the early morning streets of Cordoba, perhaps after a good night out. Good for Aydin, that was. They'd crossed paths as the drunk wobbled along and Aydin had followed him for several minutes as he shouted obscenities at young women out on their morning commute. As well as the guy's watch, Aydin got his wallet, which contained a debit card, three credit cards and nearly two hundred euros in cash. He didn't feel bad for the man. Some people were far more deserving as victims of crime than others.

The drunk hadn't been Aydin's only victim over the last few hours. Having lost all of his possessions after escaping the clutches of MI6, he'd had to quickly re-equip himself, largely through simple pickpocketing. It was the most low-profile way of gaining quick cash.

It was nearly quarter to ten and he was sipping freshly squeezed orange juice under the awnings of a wood-panelled Spanish bar, the air filled with the smell of toasted bread, *huevos revueltos* and fresh coffee. A clutch of eager tourists were out and about but most were still in their hotels, and the bars and cafes were mostly busy with businessmen and women stopping for refreshments before heading to the office.

368

Aydin took another swig of juice then set the glass back down and saw the phone's screen flash with an incoming call.

'Are you alone?' he asked, when he answered the call.

There was a short pause before the lie. 'Yes,' Cox said. 'Where are you?'

'You'll know soon enough.' They would of course be scrabbling to triangulate the position of the burner phone he was using. That was fine. 'I'm sorry for hitting you.'

'I've got quite a shiner.'

He looked at his watch again.

'There're about two hours left now.'

'Help me, Aydin. Tell us what you can. We have to try to stop them.'

'I'll give you what I can, the locations, but I don't have full details of the targets. You'll have to do the rest yourselves.'

She sighed, as though he was still playing hardball, but he was giving her all that he had. 'Go on,' she said.

'Birmingham in England. Leipzig in Germany. Ghent in Belgium. Nantes in France. Graz in Austria. Naples in Italy, and—'

'And I'm guessing Cordoba in Spain?'

That hadn't taken long. He couldn't afford to stay on the line much longer. No doubt she'd have the local police up his arse in minutes.

'What else can you tell me, Aydin?' she said. 'Just knowing the towns and cities might not be enough. We need to know what the targets are, how the attacks will happen.'

Aydin realised then there was so much to tell and not enough time. He and his brothers had been planning the attacks for years. It was true he didn't have every last detail, but even what he knew would take hours to properly explain.

'Each attack will be different,' he said. 'Chemical weapons, incendiary devices, high explosives, drones.'

Cox seemed to be searching for a response.

'I've got to go,' he said.

'Don't screw with me now, Aydin! You may not get another chance.'

'Rachel, I can give you the means, but you have to find them all yourself. I'm not lying to you, I really don't have the full details of all the plans. Only one man does.'

'Wahid.'

'But he's mine. That's the condition. I'll tell you everything I know, but Wahid is mine.'

'What do you mean, yours?'

'Let me find him. Let me kill him.'

'I can't do that. Not only is there absolutely no legal or ethical basis for me to agree but it's simply too big a risk.'

'Then you'll never hear from me again. Bye, Rachel.'

He pulled the phone away from his ear and could hear Cox protesting. He paused.

'Aydin, are you still there?'

He pulled the phone back into place. 'That's the condition.'

'I can't agree. I'm sorry, Aydin. But . . . if you get to him first, then there's nothing we can do really, is there?'

Was she speaking hypothetically? It didn't matter – he just had to do what he could to make sure the authorities didn't beat him to Wahid.

'They're not dark,' Aydin said.

'What? How do you mean?'

'They're not dark,' he said again. 'They've been communicating for the last sixty hours.'

'That's not possible, we've—'

'The messages, just like the data on the computers, are coded. It's time consuming, but you can crack them. Every number in the messages represents a single word. Each can be found in the Quran. Passage, paragraph, word number.'

'Aydin, we've intercepted nothing. There are no messages to decode.'

'You've been looking in the wrong places. Tell your experts they're using frequency hopping, they'll understand.'

That was enough. He killed the call, left the phone on the table and walked away.

As he walked he took out the radio transceiver from his backpack and checked the traffic again. Using a simple patch to connect the handheld radio to a tablet computer, he'd effectively created a device that not only acted as a radio but that could be used to locate the origin of the radio traffic he was receiving and intercepting. He wasn't interested in the coded messages that were coming through now. He didn't have time to sit and decode them and figure out what it all meant. MI6 could handle that. He only cared about getting to Wahid. And Aydin believed Wahid was not just in Cordoba, but inside the three-storey apartment building that he was approaching.

The entrance to the small apartment block was set to the side of a working men's bar that took up the ground floor. The door had a straightforward pin tumbler lock, and judging by the state of the building, and from having seen other people come and go, he saw no extra security in place. He walked straight up to the door, and just like someone who was approaching with the key he casually inserted the torsion wrench and flicked it around to release the series of pins. It took him all of five seconds to pick the lock. Longer than if he'd had the key, but it was a quick, smooth movement and anyone watching would be none the wiser.

The door opened with a push. Inside, the building was dark and dusty, a bare wooden staircase off to his right. On the left was a series of letterboxes for the apartments; six in total. He didn't know which apartment he was looking for, but he was confident there'd be a tell soon enough.

He started up the stairs.

SIXTY-THREE

The windowless room was lit by a single fluorescent strip light. Wahid sat on a wooden desk chair, Itnan by his side in front of the radio equipment, listening to the blips coming through the speakers. With every sound, Itnan wrote the corresponding number on the piece of paper with his pencil, and Wahid flicked through the well-worn Quran to find the corresponding word. The process was so well ingrained now that for much of it Wahid could simply directly correlate the reference to the word without even looking.

'That's it,' Itnan said, dropping his pencil and clicking the radio off.

Wahid quickly finished decoding the last few numbers. He placed the written message onto the desk and leant back in his chair.

'Everyone's in place,' he said. He looked at his watch. 'It's done.'

Itnan smiled.

'And Phantom?'

Itnan spun away from the radio equipment and over to this computer terminal. He rapidly flicked through windows and folders and files, and within seconds Wahid was lost. He had a good understanding of computer programming – he and every one of his brothers had been taught extensively. Itnan, though, was something else. Computing was his expertise, his strongest field by far. Electronics too. Following Itnashar's untimely death in Bruges, the control of the radio system had naturally passed to Itnan, though Wahid had wanted to be in Spain with him throughout the countdown period. Ensuring everything was operating smoothly with Phantom was the final priority.

'It's all good,' Itnan confirmed. 'Phantom will take control of more than three hundred and fifty systems.'

That was more than seventy over even their highest original estimate. They'd had specific targets for the malware, but the beauty of its design meant that the code had been spread not by their efforts, but by individual unsuspecting users who had inadvertently transmitted the code to colleagues and acquaintances, clients and customers through their routine email communications. So far less than ten systems had managed to fully rebuff the infectious malware, and none of those were companies that mattered.

Wahid slapped Itnan's back. 'Outstanding,' he said.

Itnan looked at his watch. 'I can't wait to see the others,' he said.

'Soon, my brother. Very soon.'

They'd been dark and communicating exclusively over radio for over two days. When the lights finally came back on, it truly would be glorious.

Beyond the room, there was a knock on the front door of the apartment. Both men looked at each other. The jubilant atmosphere evaporated in an instant.

'Protect the equipment,' Wahid said. By which he meant hit the kill switch to destroy it all, if needed.

'Yes, brother. I know what to do.'

Wahid got to his feet and pulled the Beretta from his jeans. He headed for the front door.

SIXTY-FOUR

Aydin stood in the hallway and waited. There were three doors on the floor, but he was certain he had the right one. The locks looked new, and he knew from the apartment's position that it looked out over the front of the building to the street, rather than the other two apartments which looked out to the back, across an enclosed square. It was simple threat management.

As he waited he began to feel exposed. All he'd need was a gun, but there'd been no opportunity to re-arm since he'd washed up in Spain. Time was up. If the door opened and he was faced with a threat he'd have to just deal with it the old-fashioned way.

A minute passed. He could have sworn a creak came from the other side of the door, but still it didn't open. He pushed his ear closer to the scratched wood. Nothing. Then nearly jumped out of his skin when the door across the hall on his left suddenly opened. A young woman. He smiled, doing his best to appear relaxed, as if he had a right to be there.

He knocked on the door again, then stood patiently as the woman closed her apartment door and came towards him.

'*Buenos días,*' he said, with a smile.

She looked uncertain, but returned the gesture before heading off to the stairwell.

Another creak sounded from beyond the door. Still the door didn't open. When the woman down below was out on the street, he decided he'd waited long enough.

The door had both a pin tumbler lock and a more sophisticated mortice lock. Both could be picked, but he'd rather opt for sudden explosive entry on this occasion, in order to take the upper hand from those who were inside.

He stood back and brought up his knee, then lurched forward, crashing the heel of his foot into the door, aiming for the hinge side. The locks were new, but the door wasn't, and he was banking that the hinges were the same age as the door, and thus more vulnerable to breakage by extreme force. Locks were where most people paid their attention, but even if hinges were new it was common for them to be the weakest part of any standard door.

The door shifted slightly from the blow, and he quickly hammered it again, throwing as much strength as he could behind the second kick. This time the hinges failed and the screws holding them in place tore out of the wooden frame as the door crashed inward. Aydin barrelled into the apartment, expecting and ready for a counter attack.

But no attack came, and it only took him a second to realise there was no one else in the room. It was a tiny apartment: one living space with just two doors off it. He was standing in the lounge/diner/kitchen. Basic, worn furniture reminded him of the apartment back in Paris, but there were no signs whatsoever that anyone had been there recently.

He heard that noise again.

Not a creak at all, he now realised, but an electronic blip – coming from off to his left. He cautiously moved towards the two doorways that led off from the lounge. One was a bedroom with a small en suite beyond. The other was a small box room.

'Shit,' he said out loud.

In the smaller room was a desk filled with radio equipment. This was definitely where the signal he'd tracked was coming from. The problem was he'd been tracking the wrong signal. He'd expected to be barging in on Wahid and his brother Itnan. But they'd fooled him. All he was looking at was a radio repeater, equipment used to bounce the initial, weaker signal onward.

Aydin growled in anger. Too much time had been wasted on tracking this place and he still had no idea where his brothers really were.

Outside he heard commotion. Revved engines; panicked voices of pedestrians. Car doors opening and closing. Quick footsteps. He moved to the lounge window and looked down below. The Policia Local. Not coming to the apartment, but swarming on the bar across the street where he'd eaten breakfast minutes earlier, where the burner phone remained on the table untouched. So much for Cox giving him some breathing space to catch up with Wahid.

There was nothing else he could do there. It was time to go. He left the radio equipment in place and rushed for the door.

SIXTY-FIVE

The name of the man driving the black BMW was Grant Ledley. Cox had never met him before. All she knew was that he too worked for MI6, though he wasn't a field agent, just an asset of some description. The ins and outs didn't really matter. All that did was that Ledley drove the car as quickly as he could to get Cox to where she needed to be. Once again, they'd failed to bring Aydin Torkal into custody. Not that Cox was particularly angry about that. She'd pleaded with Flannigan to hold the pack off Aydin, to keep him under surveillance but to *not* bring him in. Flannigan had outranked her on that, and had the local police in Cordoba flood to the location where the signal from Aydin's phone emanated.

It really wasn't too much surprise that what the police found was Aydin's phone on a table and what looked to be the remnants of his breakfast, but no sign of the man himself. He'd not cared about allowing MI6 to track his position to Cordoba, but – perhaps rightly so – he didn't trust Cox or her colleagues fully and was still using evasive measures to stay in the game.

'What's our ETA?' Cox said.

'Sat nav says just after one p.m,' Ledley said, without taking his eyes off the road.

'Shit,' was all Cox said to that. How much time did they have left? By one p.m. the attacks could be over and hundreds, thousands perhaps, would be dead.

Her phone vibrated on her lap. Her eyes flicked to the screen, hoping that perhaps it was Aydin. Instead, she recognised the prefix as coming from MI6.

'Cox,' she answered.

'Clarissa Poulter,' came the grating voice of the Trapeze supervisor. 'And Flannigan is on the line too, as well as our radio comms expert.'

'Christian Abbot here,' the guy said on cue.

'I'm guessing you've some news?' Cox said.

'Yes, actually,' Abbot said. Somehow his croaky tone reminded Cox of an aged, white-haired wizard.

'To give you some background,' Poulter said, 'Trapeze *do* monitor radio frequencies as part of our routine operations.'

'Then why wasn't this already picked up?' Flannigan asked. He still sounded pissed off.

'Because we didn't know what we were looking for,' Poulter said. 'You have to bear in mind that there are countless ways to transmit radio data, and also countless measures that can be put into place to limit eavesdropping on whichever transmission method is being used.'

'Aydin said frequency hopping,' Cox said.

'Exactly,' Abbot said. 'Frequency hopping on its own is far from military grade security, but for everyday civilian communications it's more than enough to cover tracks, and is why Trapeze didn't pick up these messages initially. To do so we first need to understand what we're looking for. The prearranged transmission key perhaps, or some details of the content of the messages, or at least data on the start and end receivers.'

'Look, guys, enough of the arse-covering,' Flannigan said.

'We understand you've missed this, we don't need the excuses as to why. Just tell us what's going on.'

Abbot sighed. 'Basically, frequency hopping is a method of transmitting radio signals over rapidly changing frequencies, using a sequence known only to both transmitter and receiver. It means that the signal appears as little more than an increase in the background noise to a narrowband receiver, so it's protected against straightforward eavesdropping.'

'Okay, okay!' Flannigan said, sounding even more irritated. 'I really couldn't give a flying rat's arse about frequencies and transponders and gizmos and shit-sticks, just give me some fucking good news.'

Cox smiled at her boss's rather unorthodox communication skills. She had to admit, she'd been thinking the same thing.

'Essentially, we've tracked their signals,' Poulter said. 'Although we weren't given the transmission key, which tells us which frequencies the messages travel over and in which order, Abbot's team have managed to perform analysis on the noise and have worked out the key for themselves. That in turn allowed them to identify the transmitters and receivers, not to mention repeater stations set up to intercept and bounce the signals.'

'And?' Flannigan said.

'And we're still transcribing the messages. These aren't voice messages but text, basically on-off tones. Think of it almost like Morse code.'

'But I explained the code?'

'Yes, but it still takes time.'

'What about the locations the transmissions are originating from?' Cox said. 'Do you have those now?'

'Yes. We have addresses in each of the seven locations you believe are targets, so it looks like these radio signals are consistent with your other intel. Those addresses will hit your inboxes any second now.'

'Clarissa, for Cordoba, please can you repeat the address on the line now?' Cox said. 'I'm travelling there as we speak.'

'Cordoba isn't one of the locations.'

'What do you mean? We have credible intel that Cordoba is a target.'

There were muffled voices for a few seconds.

'Cordoba was the location of one of the repeaters,' Abbot said. 'Perhaps it had been used as a transmitter at some point, but not in the communications we've intercepted this morning. There's no one sending or receiving messages from that particular location now.'

'So where *is* the transmitter then?'

'Granada.'

'Shit.' Cox ended the call. 'Change of plan,' she said to Ledley. 'We need to get to Granada instead.'

'Not a problem, it's actually closer. Should be there well before half-twelve.'

'That's still too late.'

'Understood. I'll do what I can.'

A second later Cox was pressed back against the seat as she watched the needle of the speedometer blur upward.

SIXTY-SIX

Aydin cursed his stupidity. He had the transmission key for the radio messages but hadn't even thought about the possibility that Wahid and Itnan would use a repeater to bounce the signals. He'd wasted hours tracking his brothers to Cordoba and had come away with nothing. But having tracked the signal more thoroughly, he did now know where they were. And he was closing in.

He was travelling in a stolen Seat Ibiza, as fast as he could across newly laid motorway that was as smooth as silk. But no matter how fast he went, he wouldn't get to Granada before midday. On the passenger seat he had both a new burner phone and the radio transceiver. He considered calling Rachel Cox again. But what would he say to her now?

A blur of mountains and rolling hills filled with olive trees and burned grass passed by the windows. He resisted the urge to check and re-check the clock on the dashboard every five seconds. By the time he reached his destination, the attacks may well have begun, that he just had to accept. In fact, it was possible they'd have already ended.

When he next failed to keep his eyes off the clock, he saw that it was already ten to twelve. To his dismay he was still over twenty miles from Granada.

A crackling burst out of the radio transceiver, and he picked it up and cranked up the volume.

'Ten minutes to go,' came the voice.

It was Wahid. Aydin was shocked to hear him speaking. The other messages had all been coded text. The fact Wahid was now speaking showed just how close they were to fulfilling their plans. Wahid felt there was nothing to stop him now. Perhaps he was right.

Aydin felt a wave of nausea pass through him, and images of Wahid's gurning face flashed in his vision. He imagined his brother sitting calmly in expectation, the radio in his hand as he waited for the bombs to explode and the poisonous gases to disperse. He saw the satisfaction on Wahid's face as bloodied bodies lay strewn in debris all around him.

Aydin couldn't let that happen.

He picked up the phone.

SIXTY-SEVEN

Cox answered the call from the withheld number, crossing her fingers as she waited for the caller to announce themselves.

'Wahid's in Granada,' Aydin said.

Cox sighed. 'I know,' she said. 'I'm on my way there now.'

She looked over at the speedometer. They were doing nearly two hundred km/h.

'Have you found the others?' Aydin asked.

'I can't tell you that,' Cox said. She saw she had another call coming through. It was Flannigan.

'Aydin, how far from Granada are you?' No response. 'Aydin, talk to me?' The call clicked off. 'Shit.'

Cox answered the call from Flannigan.

'We've cracked all of the messages we've intercepted and we've got teams readying in every location,' Flannigan said. 'We're closing in on them all.'

'Good. But you realise we've less than six minutes to go now?'

'I know. But we're going to get them. I just had word that we found the cell in Germany.'

'Seriously?'

'The German intelligence services came up trumps. The cell were ready to release cyanide into the air system at a high-rise office complex in Leipzig. The police swarmed the building

383

just a few minutes ago and caught the wannabe terrorist bastards red-handed. Twenty-five canisters of hydrogen cyanide recovered.'

'Twenty-five, but—'

'I know. I know. But it's a start.'

'Most likely the rest has been transported nearby. What was the next closest target to Germany? Graz or Ghent?'

'Either would make sense.'

'There's something else. I just spoke to Aydin again.'

'What? Where the fuck is that sod now?'

'On his way to Granada.'

'Cox, what the hell—'

She ended the call.

'How far away are we?' she said to Ledley.

'Ten minutes,' he said.

'Is your foot to the floor?' Cox said, looking at the speedometer, which was still hovering just below two hundred km/h.

'Not quite,' Ledley said.

'Then what on earth are you waiting for!'

'Yes, ma'am,' Ledley said, thumping his foot down.

SIXTY-EIGHT

They'd left behind the windowless room and were now out in the glorious, fresh air of Granada, the sun high up in the pristine blue sky. From the enclosed walled garden high up in the Albaicín district, Wahid looked out across the city. Off to his left the glorious palace fortress of the Alhambra sat proudly behind its lush green gardens. In front of him, the winding, narrow Moorish streets of Albaicín trailed downward to the wider, traffic-heavy roads of the modern city – though it was the more historic buildings that remained dominant to the eye even down there. In particular the looming grey and brown Cathedral de Granada with its massive tower and domed roof rising into the sky.

Not for much longer, though.

'It's almost time,' Itnan said, sitting next to him on the bench.

'Yes,' Wahid responded.

He had feared the worst minutes earlier with the impromptu knock on the front door, but it had only been a courier with a parcel for the neighbour. He would be the last visitor afforded such a kindly reception. The door – the whole building, in fact – was laced with booby traps, armed and ready. Any further interruptions would simply be ignored. If someone wanted to break in that was their own fault.

Wahid picked up the tablet computer and laid it on his lap. At noon, he and his brothers would come out of the dark. He wanted to see and hear – and *feel* – what they were about to do.

The radio handset crackled and Itnan picked it up. Wahid frowned. There were still four minutes to go, what the hell was this? The message that came through was the code, rather than voice. Wahid listened to the intermittent beeps, trying to figure out the words in his head, already fearing the worst.

Itnan transcribed the short message for him.

'It's Germany,' he said, turning to Wahid, his face dropping. 'An SOS.'

'Impossible,' Wahid said, feeling rage bursting inside his chest.

Another message blipped over just seconds later.

Itnan grunted in anger. 'Nantes too.'

Wahid, his whole body shaking with rage, looked at his watch. Still more than two minutes to twelve.

'Push the button on Phantom. Do it now.'

'Of course.'

Itnan scrolled through on his laptop, typing at lightning speed. Wahid held his breath. He realised his foot was tapping furiously.

Itnan stopped typing. He turned to Wahid, a strangely nervous look on his face, as though the magnitude of the situation had finally dawned on him.

'It's done,' he said.

A wave of relief swept over Wahid, even though losing two locations already felt like a hammer blow.

'Okay. Get everyone else online.'

Wahid pushed the speaker bud into his ear and navigated into the live video app that would connect him to each of his brothers. One by one there were clicks as they all came online and the black screen on the tablet divided, then sub-divided as head-cam video from each location came through live. Only five screens.

'I'm not getting anything from Leipzig or Nantes,' Itnan said.

Wahid didn't respond. There was nothing either of them could do about that now.

Another glance at his watch.

Fifty-six, fifty-seven, fifty-eight, fifty-nine . . .

'Now.'

SIXTY-NINE

Naples, Italy

Hamsah, in the driver's seat of the silver Mercedes Sprinter, showed his paperwork to the guard then waited. After a few seconds, the guard gave him a sullen nod, and the red and white barrier lifted. Hamsah drove the van down the ramp, into the underground car park of the thirty-three-storey Telecom Italia Tower. The car park was filled with gleaming silver and black and white executive cars. Hamsah drove round them to the service area where two other emblazoned vans – one for an electricity company, the other an office supplies company – were already parked. He slotted his van alongside them, then stepped from the vehicle into the musty air. Without bothering to lock the van he moved over to the service entrance and bound up the stairs two at a time to the ground floor. He came out of the stairwell into the main foyer and, head down, walked purposefully for the exit.

'Number five in position,' Hamsah said into his phone.

'Received,' Wahid responded.

SEVENTY

Cordoba, Spain

Tis'ah, wearing his security uniform, walked through the old prayer hall of the Moorish Mezquita. Such a glorious piece of history. It was a shame to see it going to such waste with that vile infidel structure crammed inside. At least today the grand former mosque would serve a worthy purpose once more.

Striding out into the open-air courtyard he felt the blazing sun hitting his skin. The exit was just in front.

'See you tomorrow,' José called to him as he headed out.

'Of course,' Tis'ah said.

He lifted up his phone. 'Number nine in position,' he said.

'Received,' Wahid responded.

SEVENTY-ONE

Nantes, France

Sittah was on his knees in the apartment, his hands behind his head. An armed police officer stood before him, the barrel of a handgun pointed at his head while they searched the place.

'Okay. It's just him,' came a gruff male voice from behind Sittah. 'Get him out of here.'

The officer lowered his gun and came for Sittah. This was the last opportunity he'd have to make his brothers proud. He had to try. Sittah sprang into the air and caught the policeman beneath his chin with an elbow. In a flash of movement Sittah took the gun, fired three times into the officer's chest as he fell, turned, crouched and fired three more at the man behind him. Both were wearing Kevlar vests, but the power of the rounds was still enough to knock them out of action.

Sittah was up on his feet and darted across the room for his phone. The detonator. If he was going down, he'd take as many of these heathens with him as possible. He frog-hopped over the sofa, then reached out for the phone on the table.

The *rat-a-tat* of gunfire blared behind him, and he felt warm thuds as the bullets tore into his back.

Sittah collapsed to the ground.

The phone was in his hand. He gargled and his lungs hissed. He couldn't breathe, his sight was blurring. It took all his strength to tap the phone's screen, trying his best to do what he needed, but he was drifting. A recognisable blur appeared on the screen, and he tried to muster every ounce of energy remaining to push his finger down onto it . . .

SEVENTY-TWO

Ghent, Belgium

Tamaniyyah dragged the body of the security guard leaving a trail of blood on the floor, then shut the door behind him in the maintenance room. The kill had been impromptu, but necessary. Sooner or later the guard's colleagues would realise he was missing, but it would be too late to stop the poison by then. The cyanide canisters in the van in the car park just outside the room were already opened, the tubing from the van hooked up to the building's ventilation system. Soon every person inside the twenty-seven-storey Arteveldetoren office block would be dead. Apart from Tamaniyyah, that was.

Having killed or subdued each of the guards on duty in the basement, the shutters for the car park were now rolled down. No one else would be coming in that way. As for the rest of the building? Itnashar had been careful. At the push of a button the building's remaining security would be locked down, all access doors sealed shut, and booby-trapped with explosive strips should they be manually opened.

Tamaniyyah pushed the enter key on his laptop and for a second the room fell into darkness, before the emergency lighting system kicked it. He pressed the next button to open up the vent to take the cyanide gas from the van and into the building's air system. Within minutes the cyanide would be working its magic. Several hundred people inside the building would be choking and convulsing in agony, their skin welting, their eyes, ears and noses bleeding, their mouths frothing as the poison worked through their systems. Wahid had said how incredible the sight was, and Tamaniyyah couldn't wait to see for himself.

'Number eight in position,' Tamaniyyah said into his phone.

'Received,' Wahid responded.

Tamaniyyah quickly pulled the mask over his face. Then heard noises outside. He opened the door and looked out across the car park. Beyond the metal shutters he could hear banging, could see movement in the small gap between the floor and the metal.

Police.

Tamaniyyah whipped off his mask and picked up the radio.

'The police are here,' he said quickly. Just then there was a piercing siren as the building's fire alarm was triggered.

'Do what you can,' Wahid said. 'Don't let anyone leave.'

Tamaniyyah replaced the mask and darted to the van, snatching the AK-47 from the passenger seat and the utility belt crammed with grenades. He slammed shut the door and strapped the belt around his waist. Then he headed for the doors that led up to the ground floor. Standing at a safe distance he lifted the rifle and fired at the explosive strips on the door. The small explosion blasted a hole in the doorway and, while the smoke cleared, Tamaniyyah uttered a final prayer.

'*Allahu Akbar*,' he said to himself, before bursting out into the open in the building's main foyer, the AK-47 raised and ready to fire.

SEVENTY-THREE

Birmingham, England

Arab'ah crouched low as he and Hidashar made their way through the labyrinth of tunnels in the disused sewer. He didn't need to look back, he could tell his brother was right there with him because of his heavy breaths.

'We're here,' Arab'ah said. 'We go up first, then we'll hoist the equipment up after.'

'You first then.'

'Cover me, just in case.'

There was a *thunk* as Hidashar dropped the handles of the sled he'd been dragging and brought the M4 rifle on his shoulder round, pointing the barrel upward.

'Ready when you are.'

Arab'ah nodded and clambered up. Light flooded in as he pushed the manhole cover away and climbed out into the tepid English air. All was quiet, except for the nearby roar of jet engines as planes taxied around Birmingham airport.

'Come on,' he shouted down to Hidashar.

Moments later the big man emerged and straightened himself out. Arab'ah checked his watch. It was already three minutes past twelve.

'Hurry. We need to finish this quickly.'

Hidashar set to it, pulling the equipment up. It only took

him a couple of minutes and they were soon getting set to drag both the drones and the homemade bombs up the mound to the top. They'd spent many days perfecting the recipe for the plastic explosives that were made from what were essentially common household ingredients; potassium chlorate crystals from bleach, Vaseline, wax and camping gas. Hidashar was confident the blocks they'd made would be more than adequate. They would crash the first bomb into the row of parked planes, the explosives together with the jet fuel enough to start a chain reaction of explosions across the airport's gates. The second drone they'd fly straight into the terminal building where thousands of holidaymakers were crammed.

Many hundreds, if not thousands of people would die.

Just then, as they moved towards the mound, there was an almighty roar as a plane came in to land above them. They both instinctively craned their heads, their gaze following the plane as it headed for the runway. Arab'ah followed the jet until it disappeared out of sight beyond the mound.

'What the—' he said, and froze.

In front of them, at the top of the mound, a line of half a dozen armed police officers appeared.

'Drop the weapons!' came the shouts from both Arab'ah's left and right.

The two men looked around. Police were surrounding them on all sides. Over twenty armed officers, weapons drawn, closing in on them.

Arab'ah made a move for his radio, then flinched at a warning shot that smacked into the grassy ground in front of his feet.

'Drop the weapons. Now.'

Arab'ah slumped. There was no way they could complete their mission now. But they wouldn't go down without a fight. Arab'ah turned to Hidashar. Hidashar nodded back. As Arab'ah flung his hand down to his side, in a desperate attempt to reach the detonator on his rigged vest, he didn't hear the boom as the first trigger was pulled.

SEVENTY-FOUR

Graz, Austria

Asarah spied from the roof of the apartment building over to the Graz Hauptbahnhof – the city's largest train station – a hundred metres away.

'It's already filling up,' he said into his mouthpiece.

'It's chaos,' Talatah said in delight. He was sitting across from Asarah at the far end of the east side of the lead rooftop, pressed up against the short wall that wrapped around them, binoculars in hand. 'There're no trains coming or going.'

'Should we wait, or do it now?'

'We wait for five more minutes. Phantom is working. It will only get busier. The more people the better.'

'Absolutely.'

Asarah's earbud went quiet. He looked across the lead rooftop to the open crates beside them where the small drones were already set with their payloads – bombs that would explode in the air and disperse deadly phosgene gas over an area more than a hundred metres wide. Within seconds, well over a thousand people would be struck by the deadly gas. Talatah also had a wooden crate next to him that was filled with the bulbous rockets they'd created to fit the weighty Russian-made RPG-7. Each rocket was essentially a glorified Molotov cocktail, filled with a homemade incendiary mixture

397

of petrol and liquid detergent that, on explosion, would stick to anything it touched and rapidly spread fire and panic across the hundreds of people in the packed station. Asarah smiled to himself.

'Number three in position,' he heard his brother say.

'Received,' came Wahid's response.

SEVENTY-FIVE

Granada, Spain

'Still no word from Birmingham?' Itnan asked.

'No. The video link is down now too. We have to assume they're dead.'

Just then the video feed from Tamaniyyah in Ghent went down. Wahid growled in anger and ripped off his headset before flinging it across the garden.

'Don't be so disheartened, brother,' Itnan said, not looking up from his screen. 'It's not over yet.'

Just then Wahid heard a rush of static from Itnan's headset. He turned to his brother, who just shook his head.

'Nantes is offline now too.'

'He detonated the failsafe,' Wahid said, with some satisfaction. His brother was gone, and he would be sorely missed, but the blast in the apartment block would surely consume many.

'What about Ghent?'

'He must be dead. But he'd already released the gas.'

'And England?'

'The video is down. Their radio is still active, but I can't get a response.'

Wahid shook his head. 'So they're either dead too or in custody.'

Itnan didn't respond to that.

'They knew,' Wahid said, gritting his teeth. 'The police knew. We don't have time to wait now, we need all remaining locations to go ahead *immediately*. Before it's too late.'

'Agreed.'

There was a whirring tone from Itnan's laptop. A warning. Wahid again looked to his brother, who was staring at a video stream of the outside of their compound.

'Looks like we've got company,' he said.

SEVENTY-SIX

Cox, Glock in hand, held back from the black-clad men and women of the Grupos Operativos Especiales de Seguridad, or GOES, the SWAT team of the Spanish National Police. With her headset on she was receiving real-time updates from Flannigan, who was overseeing the raids in each of the locations. It had already been confirmed that the two terrorists in Birmingham were dead – a suicide blast that had also taken out an unconfirmed number of policemen. In Ghent the terrorist had been shot dead by police but not before he'd released deadly cyanide gas into an office block containing over a thousand people. AK-47 rounds had also been sprayed at the terrified members of the public trying to flee the building. And that wasn't the worst of it. In Nantes, the efforts to capture number six had just turned deadly, with the suspect successfully exploding a booby trap inside his apartment building, despite the presence of local armed police who had, moments earlier, confirmed they had him under control. The death toll of that explosion was still unclear.

'What about the other locations?' Cox asked, as she crept along.

'We've got teams on each site, finding these bastards and beginning to clear civilians. Wait . . .' Flannigan suddenly said. 'Shit. We've got confirmed explosions in Graz now too, in the central train station.'

Cox shook her head.

'Reports of gunfire in Naples too,' Flannigan said. 'Though the police were already in the process of evacuating an office block there and securing the explosives that had been set.'

Just then, the GOES team out in front stopped dead. The squad commander, fronting the tip of the diamond formation, turned and gave his team instructions and hand signals.

'We're right outside now,' Cox said. But her comment was met with silence. 'Sir, are you still there?'

Nothing.

Cox took the phone out of her pocket. No signal.

'Shit.'

Was that just because of the area they were in? No, she didn't think so. Up ahead she could see the GOES guys turning and looking at each other quizzically. Cox had no idea why, but their comms were kaput. They were running blind now.

As the whispered debate in front of her quickly became more heated, Cox heard a clattering off to her left – a small stone scuttling across the cobbled street. She turned, pointing the gun out, looking into the mouth of a narrow, high-walled alley that snaked further up the hill.

No one there.

Or was there?

She was certain a shadow had moved across the ground, just next to where the alley veered off to the left.

'Hey,' she shouted out to the GOES group in front. '*Puede uno de ustedes ayudar?*'

One of the men at the back of the group nodded and jogged over to her, both hands around his Heckler & Koch MP5 submachine gun.

'*Qué es?*'

'Follow me.'

Cox moved towards the alley, treading carefully. She glanced behind her. The GOES officer was two steps behind, crouched low, the MP5 pulled up close to his face. Cox moved to the right, trying to get a better view up the alley. When she took one more step forward the shadow on the ground flickered again.

Cox's eyes darted from the shadow and up to the figure who now lurched towards her. She pulled on her trigger . . .

Too late. The attacker dodged to the side, knowing exactly how she would react. The GOES officer shouted a warning, but he didn't pull his trigger. He couldn't – Cox was in his line of fire.

Before Cox could do anything else she'd been twisted around and pinned in position, an arm clasped tightly around her neck, choking her. Her Glock was pressed up against her temple. The man holding her pulled her back, so that just the tips of the heels of her feet were on the ground, giving her no room to counter and kick out behind her.

'Lower your weapon!' the man shouted in Spanish.

Cox gasped and choked as she tried to breathe. She recognised the voice. It was Aydin Torkal.

'It's okay, it's okay,' Cox pleaded with the GOES officer. He seemed less than sure about that. 'Aydin, please. They'll kill you.'

'Not before I kill you.'

'Please, lower your weapon,' Cox said again to the policeman.

'Tell the men not to enter that compound,' Aydin said.

'What?'

'The compound you're surrounding! They can't go in.'

'Wahid's in there!'

'It's a trap! You'll kill them all.'

'They know what they're doing.'

'No. They really don't.'

Aydin shuffled forward, pushing Cox with him. The GOES officer stepped back in time with them. Two of his colleagues appeared at the end of the alley, alerted by the shouting no doubt.

'It's okay,' Cox pleaded again. 'He won't hurt me.'

'Don't be so sure about that,' Aydin said.

'We want the same thing. We have to end this. Now. Aydin, it's already begun. The killings have already started. We have to strike now.'

'Not like this.'

They reached the end of the alley. The main group of GOES officers were still up ahead, crouched in position outside the compound. There was a loud call. A go signal.

'No!' Aydin shouted. Cox found herself echoing his calls. Perhaps it was the desperation in his voice that told her it was the right thing to do.

The GOES team took no notice. There was clattering and banging as the charges they'd laid blew the entrance open, and echoing sounds from further away as a second team stormed from the other side. Cox braced herself, held her breath, expecting a blast, a booby trap, just like Aydin had warned. It didn't come. Instead, one by one the GOES team disappeared inside.

After a few short moments, the last man stepped in, moving out of sight.

'Get down!' Aydin screamed, letting go of Cox and flinging himself away, just a split second before the huge explosion.

SEVENTY-SEVEN

Aydin was expecting the blast. That was why he'd kept his distance from the entrance of the compound, yet the force was still far greater than he'd imagined. Even though they were standing several yards away from the entrance, and already diving for cover, he was blown off his feet and dispatched onto the hard cobbles several yards down the road. The force of the blast, together with the jarring impact of the fall, was enough to send him to the brink of unconsciousness. Perhaps he *had* been unconscious for a short while, it was hard for him to know for sure.

As he started to regain his senses he realised he was on his side, lying on the ground. His bleary gaze fixed upon Rachel Cox's bloodied face less than a yard in front of him. She already had a bruise from where he'd clocked her on the helicopter, but there was now a thick line of blood that snaked down from her hairline too. She was breathing, but otherwise unmoving.

Aydin groaned as he pulled himself up into a sitting position. Out in front of him there was a huge plume of smoke rising into the sky. No sounds of armed officers shouting or shooting filled the air now, only the hiss of fire and the whine of car alarms. Everyone inside that compound was surely dead. It was just a pile of smouldering rubble.

Which did beg one very important question. Where the hell was Wahid? Because Aydin was absolutely certain his brother wouldn't martyr himself just like that. And yet this was the place that both Aydin and MI6 had traced him to.

Cox murmured. She didn't look to be seriously injured, just dazed. The GOES officers who'd been in front, trying to protect Cox . . . Aydin didn't fancy their chances. One had a two-foot shard of metal sticking out of his back; another was wedged into the shattered windscreen of a nearby parked car. The third, the one closest to them who'd had his MP5 pointed at Aydin's face just moments before, was missing a leg and writhing awkwardly. It was more luck than judgement that Aydin and Cox were comparatively unscathed. Or was it simply that those three men had inadvertently acted as a shield for them?

But there was no time to dwell. As groggy as he was, Aydin needed to move. There would be more police on hand at any second, and they wouldn't take kindly to his presence at the massacre. More importantly, he needed to find Wahid before he escaped for good.

Aydin heard gunshots in the distance, coming from further down the hill. He pulled himself to his feet, grabbed Cox's gun from the floor and darted over to the front wall of the house next to them. He clambered to the top and looked out below at the maze of winding streets that led down from Albaicín to the cathedral, crammed with white-washed townhouses topped with red tiles. He saw bobbing heads: a couple of men in front; several with black helmets further behind them.

That had to be Wahid – and Itnan? – being chased by the police. Aydin didn't know how they'd got out of the compound in time, but they had. From his prominent position, he quickly took in the network of streets below, trying to work out not just the best route down, but also where Wahid would most likely come out so that he could try and intercept.

Aydin had just about figured it out when he heard noise behind him. Shouting. Footsteps. Weapons cocking. He only managed to half-turn before the rattle of gunfire filled his ears. Someone was shooting at him. He hauled himself forward, landing with a crashing thud atop the terracotta tiles in the front yard of the house. The high wall he'd jumped from would at least protect him from whoever was shooting, and he had no wish to engage whoever it was in a tit-for-tat fight. He needed to go.

He picked himself up, checked over Cox's Glock, then headed for the front door of the house. It was unlocked, and he barged in, gun held out, and quickly made his way through the small space to the back. A middle-aged woman cowered in the kitchen behind a table, a bubbling pot on the stove behind her gave off a sweet scent of tomato sauce that filled the air. Aydin said nothing, and neither did the woman. He carried on out into the lush back garden, sprinting towards the white wall at the back that was lined with apricot trees. He swept up a white plastic garden chair as he moved and propped the chair against the wall, using it to clamber over the top.

On the other side, he dropped down onto another cobbled street. Going through the house proved a welcome shortcut. He darted off to the right, initially moving up a slight incline, but he knew there was an alley on the left soon that would take him downhill, towards the fleeing Wahid. His body ached – from old wounds not yet healed, and newer ones from the blast – but he wasn't going to stop now. Using all of his training and survival instincts to push through was vital.

The *whop-whop* of rotors blistered the air. A police helicopter, circling a couple of hundred yards in the sky. No doubt they'd got Wahid in their sights. Aydin didn't have long. The police surely couldn't let Wahid get away now. But then

Aydin knew to never underestimate his brother. They'd been planning the attacks for years. Plus, Aydin knew Phantom had fully kicked in and the authorities were operating at far from full capacity, the malware having chewed through their systems and their comms. It was going to seriously hamper both the police and MI6's efforts to keep track of each of his former brothers now.

Another explosion rose from further down the hill. Not a big one this time. Either a minor booby trap or just a simple hand grenade. Aydin saw the small wisp of smoke rising upward, helping him to keep his bearings. A left, then a quick right took him to the top of a steep street lined with shops selling North African curios; *hookahs*, incense, rugs, silks and cashmere. At the sight of him barrelling towards them, gun in hand, people shouted and scattered, but not all were quick enough and Aydin had to barge and shove several civilians out of the way. But it was slowing him down, and he took the first opportunity to move away onto a quieter alley, taking a right that snaked downward again, and hopefully would allow him to intercept Wahid.

He continued running, lungs on fire, trying to eke out every last ounce of energy he had left, pushing his tired body to breaking point. A sharp bend in the alley made him hesitate. Rather than follow the bend, he headed straight for the white wall in front of him, and used his speed and momentum to run two, three steps up it before reaching and grabbing the top, pulling himself up and scrambling over.

A thicket of bushes broke his fall, and he forced himself to ignore the stabbing and scraping of the jagged and prickly branches. He kept moving across the small space of overgrown wasteland – the garden of a derelict building as far as he could make out – as he headed to the wall at the other side. This one wasn't as high and didn't take as much effort to climb. As he got to the top he saw two figures off to his right, hurtling down the street.

His heart almost exploded in his chest. It was Itnan and Wahid.

Perched on the wall, Aydin lifted the gun and fired. His brothers both sensed him, and were forced to duck and weave out of the way. It saved Wahid's life. Itnan wasn't so lucky: one bullet to the chest, the other straight through his scapula. He skidded to the ground, face first. Aydin dove from the wall, on top of Wahid as he tried to scramble past. They rolled to the ground in a heap. Whatever Wahid was holding in his hand – a gun, a phone? – clattered away, as did Aydin's Glock. They grappled for a few seconds, both of them dazed. The longer they stayed there on the ground, though, the bigger the chance of the police arriving and taking them both out.

Wahid must have realised that too, because he fought with ferocious speed and urgency, and it was too much for Aydin. He'd never been a physical match for his brother. It was one of the many reasons why Wahid was number one and Aydin was the lowly thirteen. Aydin's many injuries only made the fight even more one-sided, and after several strikes too many to his gut and his kidneys, Wahid managed to scrabble out and away.

He dashed forward, scooping up from the ground the device that he'd dropped moments before. A phone, Aydin thought. He made a grab for Aydin's gun too, but didn't attempt to turn and shoot, just made off down the street.

Aydin somehow managed to find the strength to get to his feet. He hobbled forward, more or less dragging his right leg behind him, it seemingly having deserted him. Was it broken?

Wahid too was moving sluggishly. In front of them the narrow street opened out and they soon found themselves in the middle of a long, straight main road, four lanes wide. But it was strangely deserted.

Aydin soon saw why. Up to the left, past the soaring structure of the Renaissance cathedral, were a multitude of flashing blue lights. A police cordon. He heard the shouts as the officers spotted him and Wahid emerging.

'It's over, brother,' Aydin said.

Wahid stopped and turned to him, a strange grin on his face. He dropped the gun to the ground. There was a line of policemen rushing forward towards both of them. Wahid lifted his hands in the air, as if in surrender. But he was still clutching on to the phone . . .

'No!' Aydin shouted. He scrambled back, falling and landing on his backside. Wahid winked at him.

'*Allahu Akbar*,' he said, calm and composed.

His thumb touched the screen.

SEVENTY-EIGHT

Aydin couldn't see. He couldn't breathe. Dust and grit filled the air all around. It hadn't been just one explosion. When Wahid pressed the detonator a series of blasts had fanned out all around, bangs and rattles and booms – not just bombs exploding, but also the rumble as the buildings on all sides faltered and then collapsed. Aydin's guess was that the cathedral was the main target. That's why the police cordon was positioned where it was. He could only hope the police had enough time to move civilians away from the area, but the cordon was surely too close. He'd be surprised if any of the waiting police had survived.

Aydin coughed and spluttered, trying to find a fresh breath of air in the thick dust. But it wasn't just the dust, there was a strange odour in the air too, almost like musty hay – Aydin's lungs burned more and more with each breath.

And he knew why. Phosgene.

He had to get away, and his only hope was that he was far enough from the central blast to be inhaling non-lethal doses.

There was another distant rumble, and moments later another rush of air and grit blasted into him. Not a bomb, just another building saying goodbye to the world, more collateral damage.

'Wahid!' Aydin shouted out as loudly as he could manage with his lungs burning. His brother wouldn't escape, not this time.

Aydin somehow hauled himself up. Blood covered his ragged clothes, spilt from a large gash above his ear. Another on his shoulder. His arms were grazed, his legs were on fire – literally. He swiped at the flames that were leaping up his trousers and managed to smother them before they took hold.

Rocks and stones and chunks of concrete scraped beneath his feet, the thick dust swirling in the air around him meant he could barely see a metre in front of him. Above the din of raging fires he could hear moans and groans, coughing. People screamed in pain. Voices too – perhaps paramedics or police tending to the scene of destruction.

But he could see no one.

Wahid had been all of five yards ahead of him before the bombs went off. Aydin had moved that far already, but there was no sign of Wahid now. But then Aydin didn't even know which direction he was moving in.

'Argghhh!' Aydin shouted in frustration when he saw the head of the street he'd come down earlier. Disorientated, he'd gone in the wrong direction.

He turned and pulled his body along, back the other way. There was another rush of air, but this time rather than adding to the dust, it cleared it momentarily. Just a gust of wind? At that moment, he saw a clouded figure in front of him, scrabbling over debris. Aydin picked up the pace, stepping over stones and round boulders.

'Wahid!' he shouted again.

The figure stopped, turned. It was him.

Aydin picked a rock up from the floor, he took two more steps . . .

But then Wahid was gone, vanishing into the dust as though he and it were one and the same. Aydin carried on forward, with more trepidation, the rock held up ready to smash it down.

He sensed movement. He spun desperately to his left. He didn't see Wahid until his brother's hands were just inches away, and the big man barged into him, grabbing him around the waist and hauling him backward. Wahid carried him along, growling in anger with each step. Aydin lifted the rock and smacked it down onto the base of Wahid's neck, but he didn't even flinch.

Wahid launched Aydin, whose back smashed off something hard. A car, an industrial bin – he didn't know what, but he was soon on the ground even more dazed than before, the rock nowhere to be seen.

Wahid dived on top and began to rain punches onto Aydin's head. Among the blur of fists Aydin caught a flickering glimpse of his brother's face. He saw the pure hatred in Wahid's eyes; the anger. Out of control, he was pummelling Aydin, and the attack was simply too savage for him to offer a response.

Aydin did his best to lift his arms to block, but had too little strength left, and Wahid easily punched through the pathetic defence. Aydin began to drift. Wahid wouldn't stop, of that he was certain. Not until Aydin's head was a mush of blood and brain and skull.

Aydin's hand searched at his side, looking for anything that he could use to try and fight Wahid off. His fingertips scraped desperately across the floor, skin peeling off. He found a loose rock and grabbed at it, but he barely had the strength to hold on.

He screamed in desperation, one last final attempt to save his life. The rock was lifted up shakily, and he pulled back his arm, and drove the stone into Wahid's face. His nose crunched as blood spurted. Aydin hit him again in the face, then twice more on the side of the head. All of a sudden it was the animal in Aydin that was in control, and now Wahid's fire was going out.

After another vicious blow with the bloody rock, Aydin heaved Wahid off him, swivelled, and was the one on top.

He held the rock in both hands, above his head. One more killer blow was all that was needed. Wahid's face was a mess. His nose had all but disappeared, his left eye socket crushed, blood dribbled out from his spluttering lips.

'Why?' Aydin asked, his voice trembling. 'My sister. My mother. You didn't have to kill them.'

'Your sister was too close,' Wahid managed to say. '*You* should have done it. But I wasn't sure you could. It was a test.'

A test? They killed his sister as a test of his allegiance? And what about his mother?

'Your father . . .' Wahid said, and Aydin was sure his brother was trying to smile. 'Your father will be so disappointed.'

The was no emotion in the taunt. No anger or anything else. Just a blunt, measured statement.

Aydin froze. *Your father*. Not *my* father, or *our* father. Wahid wasn't talking about the Teacher. He was talking about Aydin's real dad. Ergun Torkal. The man who'd taken him away from his mother and sister. Who'd forced this life on him. Aydin hadn't seen his father since he was nine years old. All he knew was that his father had been dead for years . . .

So why would Wahid say that?

Aydin screamed with pure rage and his arms tensed, ready to crash the rock down.

'Aydin, no!'

A woman. It was Cox. He heard her cock the gun.

'Please,' she begged, before coughing and spluttering.

Once again, she hadn't kept to her word. She'd said if he got to Wahid first, there was nothing that could be done. That

Wahid was his to kill. Yet there she was, pointing a gun at his back just as he was about to put Wahid out of his misery.

'This isn't the way, Aydin,' she pleaded. 'We need him. We need to understand.'

'He'll never talk,' Aydin said weakly. 'And he doesn't deserve to live.'

The conversation was done. No more delays. Aydin's arms twitched, then he swung the rock down towards Wahid's face.

But he didn't see where the rock ended up. Before contact was made, Aydin heard the blast of the gun.

SEVENTY-NINE

London, England

Cox looked over the benches, beyond the altar to the large wooden cross hanging there. She had headphones in her ears as she listened to the live BBC broadcast of the funeral that was taking place outside the chapel. The newsreader talked through the devastation. Over a hundred people killed across Europe, many of them police officers who were trying to thwart the attacks. Many hundreds more injured. There'd been a great financial toll too – billions of pounds, dollars, euros had been lost on stock markets across the world as the malware the Thirteen had let loose worked through corporate systems, derailing businesses everywhere. It was still unclear just how much money the terrorist sponsors had made short-selling those companies' stocks. Then there was the money needed to account for the physical destruction, mostly notably of World Heritage buildings destroyed in Southern Spain.

And what of the Thirteen? Seven attackers were dead. Five were in custody, including Wahid.

One insurgent, Aydin Torkal, was still on the loose.

Cox squeezed her eyes tightly shut and winced in pain as she took a large inhale of breath. The after-effects of the residual phosgene she'd inhaled back in Spain.

The newsreader began to talk about the heroes of the day. Not just the police who had lost their lives, but the ones who had helped to save so many more. The security services were given praise too, as was the one outstanding operative of MI6 who'd become labelled in the tabloid media as 'Plain Jane'. There had already been calls from the public and in the media for the unnamed operative to be awarded the George Cross.

Cox cringed. She hated that she was being made out to be some sort of hero. The situation was as much down to the political machine as it was because of her actions, she knew. In desperate times, people needed a hero.

A hand on her shoulder made her jerk.

It was just Flannigan. Cox pulled the buds from her ears and the stoic voice of the BBC broadcaster faded away.

'You sure you're not going to join me?' Flannigan was dressed in a smart black suit and Cox had to admit, with his sombre face showing none of his more usual anger, he looked almost welcoming.

'I just can't,' Cox said, looking down.

'You've got to stop beating yourself up.'

'Not until we find the rest of them.'

'The rest of them? There's only one of them left. And we will find him.'

Cox cringed. Aydin had been named and shamed in the press. There was simply no way round that. He was one of *them,* and he was still on the loose. Yet Cox firmly believed Aydin's actions had helped save hundreds, if not thousands, of lives.

'I didn't mean Aydin,' Cox said. 'I mean the ones who recruited and trained him, and all the others. The people responsible for the Thirteen.'

'We will find them. And you're going to help.'

'I thought you said I needed to take time off.'

'You do. But after that you'll come back stronger. I know you will. You're *Plain Jane*,' he said with a small grin. 'You're indestructible, apparently.'

Cox smiled. 'So I keep hearing. Pretty much a real-life James Bond.'

'Jane Bond, don't you mean? I hear Hollywood are already interested.'

Cox scoffed. 'We haven't even buried our dead and producers are already seeing the dollar signs.'

Flannigan was serious again now. 'It's not your fault they died. Not any of them.'

'More than a hundred people lost their lives. We could have stopped it all. We were so close.'

'You need to think about the lives we – *you* – saved. More than three thousand, by most accounts. And we all know how horrific it would have been. Bombs, fire, chemicals. Those attacks were designed not just to kill but to cause agony and misery.'

Cox didn't respond, just felt herself flinch at the thought of how much worse events could have been.

Flannigan held out his hand. Cox hesitated for a moment, but then reached out and took it. She stood up and her eyes caught his.

'Shall we go?'

Cox nodded. They walked slowly, side by side over to the doors. Flannigan stepped in front and pushed them open and they both stepped out into the driving rain. Flannigan quickly opened up his giant golfing umbrella and huddled next to Cox. She stopped and looked over to the mass of people in the near distance, many dressed in police uniforms.

'Come on. We'll watch from a safe distance.'

'This is close enough,' Cox said.

One or two heads turned in their direction, but quickly looked away again. Further in the distance, by the large wrought iron gates to the cemetery, the officers on horseback came into view, guarded either side by a parade of police officers stretching past where the eye could see. Behind the horses trailed the long line of black hearses.

Cox felt her legs go weak.

'I need to go,' she said.

Cox turned and traipsed across the wet ground, towards the exit, not once looking back.

EIGHTY

Birmingham, England

Aydin was sitting on a bench in Canon Hill Park, not far from the centre of England's second biggest city. With a steadily thickening beard and cap on his head, no one recognised him from the grainy photos in the newspapers.

In front of him families pedalled oversized plastic swans on the small boating lake. Kids whizzed around the play area beyond. People on bikes glided by, joggers huffed and puffed. So many people out and about just getting on with their lives, even though it was just days since the attacks that nearly crippled their society. Their resilience wasn't just heads-in-the-sand, though. The attacks had brought communities together.

She approached slowly from the opposite side of the park dressed casually in jeans and trainers, a woollen jumper and a baseball cap that did the trick of covering much of her face. But Aydin knew it was her.

She sat down without saying a word.

'Why you haven't turned me in?' he asked, trying his best not to cough, knowing that it would send a wave of stabbing pain right through him.

'Because you did the right thing,' Cox said, though she didn't sound too convinced by that. They both knew he could have done more, that he could have acted sooner. 'It's not your fault, what *they* made you into. You're fighting it. That's what counts.'

Cox looked away. Aydin knew she'd crossed the line more than once to help him. She was probably the only person in the world who didn't now want him dead. What was Cox to him? He didn't know how to explain what their relationship was.

'We got most of your brothers,' she said, 'but the Teacher and the others at the Farm are still out there. They'll come for you.'

'I hope they do.'

They both fell silent for a moment.

'Is there any news?' he asked.

Now that the attacks were over, now that his *original purpose* had expired, he felt alienated and lost. He had no idea what came next for him, for his brothers in custody, or what was happening at the Farm. But Cox and MI6 surely had a plan. They'd always have their tentacles reaching out across the globe, looking for something, *anything*, to get stuck into. Aydin would leave this place today, and he was sure he'd be on their hit list too, regardless of the good Cox may or may not have seen in him.

'Wahid and the others aren't talking,' she said. 'But we'll keep on trying.'

Aydin ground his teeth. He was still angry that she hadn't let him kill Wahid. That she shot Aydin instead, in the back. Once the bullet hit, he was out of it. He couldn't remember what came next. All he knew was that when Cox came over to check him, Wahid managed to fight back. She was busy apprehending him as Aydin stumbled away and disappeared into the cloud of dust. Cox insisted she only intended to wound him. Perhaps that was the truth. After all, she was talking to him now.

421

'You should have let me kill him,' Aydin said.

'I couldn't.'

'You let him off.'

'I tried to do the right thing. Maybe I could have done more. We both could have.'

Aydin looked at her and saw the hurt in her eyes. She was feeling just as bruised about what happened as he was.

'And what about my father?'

'There's no clear evidence that he's still alive.'

'That's a strange way of putting it,' he said. 'You could have said *all the evidence we've seen suggests he's dead*. Instead you turned it round. Essentially it means the same thing, but really it's quite the opposite.'

'You think he's still alive?'

Aydin didn't answer the question, didn't even know if he wanted it to be true.

'It's possible Nilay thought the same thing,' Cox said. 'She was searching for what happened to both you *and* him.'

'And that's what got her killed.'

A longer, more awkward silence followed, and Aydin felt he was done. He really didn't know what else could be said. But Cox wasn't quite finished.

'What are you going to do?' she asked.

He considered the question for some time, his mind going back to his teachings at the Farm.

'There's a well-known fable about an archer and an eagle. Have you heard it?' he asked.

'I don't think so,' Cox said. He saw the look of both confusion and intrigue in her eyes.

'The story goes that there's a predatory eagle, swooping over fields of barley. This eagle is the king of its domain. It spies a beast bounding through the field below. A rabbit. This vicious eagle, belly grumbling in anticipation, swoops down. Now, this eagle never misses, and whatever the rabbit can offer isn't enough. The eagle crashes down on top and digs its talons into the little critter's neck. The eagle is just about to fly away with its catch when there's a whoosh, and an arrow comes flying out of nowhere, and plunges into the eagle's chest . . .'

'Kills it?'

'It's a bad wound. The eagle falls to the ground. Its talons are still wedged firmly in the rabbit, who's writhing and crying. The eagle struggles to keep hold of its prey. Even though it's dying, its instinct is that it can't let this kill get away. It can't fail this time. *It never fails*. But the rabbit somehow pulls itself free, and darts away into the barley. The eagle turns its head and looks at the arrow. And what does it see?'

Cox pursed her lips and shook her head.

'It sees that the quills of the arrow are made from its own feathers. And the eagle says, "I should have felt bad indeed, to think any other eagle had a hand in this." By the time the archer comes along, the eagle is dead.'

'So, what are you saying?' Cox asked. 'You're the eagle? The hunter is me shooting you in the back?'

Aydin laughed. It made his head pound and chest ache. 'Actually, that almost fits, doesn't it? But no, that's not it at all, because there's no moral there.'

'Then what's the moral? That we are the cause of our own doom?'

'Closer. You asked me what I'm going to do next. Well, I'm the *arrow*. I am a product of *them*. The Teacher and the others at the Farm made me what I am. They're the predator, like the eagle. They've tried to kill the innocent. They failed. And now this arrow will come back to destroy them all.'

Cox just stared at him and he'd loved to have known what she was thinking in that moment.

'Then perhaps I should be the hunter,' Cox said eventually. 'Arrows are deadly, but they're not much use on their own. They need direction, and power behind them.'

Aydin smiled. He got to his feet.

'It was good to see you under more casual circumstances,' he said.

'And I'm sure we'll see each other again,' Cox said.

Aydin turned and walked away.

Acknowledgements

A special thanks goes to Ben Willis at Orion Publishing, without whom this book wouldn't have happened. Thanks also to my agent, Camilla, and the rest of the publishing team behind the scenes who have helped make *Sleeper 13* what it is. I've enjoyed writing every one of my books in different ways, and for different reasons, but *Sleeper 13* feels particularly special to me. I'm massively grateful to all those readers, reviewers and bloggers who have been with me since I first self-published my work back in 2014, and to the many who have joined me along the way. *Sleeper 13* may well be the first of my books you've read, and if it is I hope you've enjoyed it, and that I've earned your loyalty now too.